NIGHT OF THE JABBERWOCK / THE DEEP END

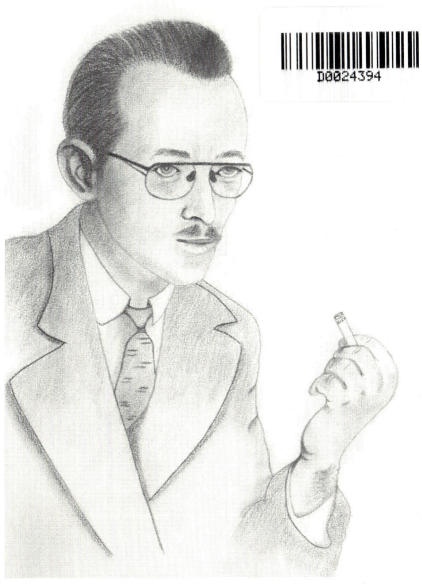

D0024394

A Fredric Brown Double-Novel

THE
DEEP
END

FREDRIC
BROWN

NIGHT
OF THE
JABBBERWOCK

FREDRIC
BROWN

Introduced by Barry N. Malzberg

Double
Novel

· · · · · · ·

Bruin
Books

Edited by Jonathan Eeds
Cover design by Michelle Policicchio

Original cover art provided by the Viet Hung Gallery,
Ho Chi Minh City, Vietnam

Special thanks to Mark Terry who provided the digital
Dust Jacket images that the new cover paintings were inspired
by. Mark's website, Facsimile Dust Jackets, can be found at
WWW.dustjackets.com

Most of all, Bruin Books is indebted to Barry N. Malzberg for his
ongoing support

This book was crafted in the USA but is printed globally

Printed in the USA
ISBN 978-0-9987065-5-9
Published December 10, 2018
Bruin Books, LLC
Eugene, Oregon, USA

For inquiries: bruinbooks@comcast.net

The Furthest Cry

Fredric Brown (1909-1972) shares one distinction with no other writer: he was equally prominent, equally appreciated in the genres of the mystery and science fiction. He is the only writer of equal stature in both (it could be argued that Edgar Allan Poe is a contender but Poe, dead in 1849, was writing about Arthur Pym's journey a hundred years before science fiction in this country became a separately defined genre and Poe regardless never published a novel.) Brown won the first MWA Best First Novel Edgar for *The Fabulous Clipjoint* (1947), his many mystery novels found a wide and distinct audience many of whom were barely aware of and not at all interested in his science fiction. His 1958 mystery, *The Screaming Mimi* was the basis of a cult film; many of his short stories were adapted for television. As a science fiction writer he published five novels and about a hundred stories and short-short stories, one of which, *Martians Go Home* (1955) was adapted for a 90's well distributed and disastrous film. Regarded in science fiction as the master of the short-short story under 500 words of which he was practically the originator, he wrote the first and best novel of science fiction fandom, *What Mad Universe* (1948), and his novelette *Arena* (1944) was one of the most reprinted and quasi-plagiarized stories of the 1940's; *Star Trek* cheerfully swiped it for an episode and finally paid something, grudgingly. Brown, as some scholars have noted, was perhaps the only prominent science fiction writer who was not shaped by John W. Campbell and his 40's *Astounding*; Brown sold to that market (*Arena* was there) but not too often and disappeared from its pages for good after the novelette version of *Martians Go Home* in 1954. He went his own way. Perhaps his most famous short story (everybody knows the payoff, very few know the author) is of the scientists who after years of labor produce the first Omni-potent Computer. Their first question, long debated and awaited: "Is there a God?" The room rumbles, all the power goes off. *"There is now"* a threatening voice booms.

Brown was a typesetter before he was a writer and the mechanics and folklore of printing appears, understandably, disproportionately in his writing. (*Etaoin Shrudlu* about a typographer and an instrument gone mad is an early story.) After a while he quit typesetting to become that anomaly, a "full-time" writer. His early sales were in bulk to the pulp mystery and detective magazines, he branched to science fiction soon and then *The Fabulous Clipjoint*. The Mystery Writers of America, founded in 1941, originated its Edgar Awards in the mid-forties. For a while the Edgar for novel for which Brown was the first winner, was only for a first novel, the determine-ation of the Secret Masters being that to give it for Best Novel was to single out one and disappoint another two hundred and this was a bad policy for a fledgling organization seeking to build a membership. That policy changed of course, although Cornell Woolrich was to win in 1948 only for "contributions to the short story".

Brown was a savage writer, bleak and despairing, not quite the gentle comic satirist for which he was often mistaken. Even the sf satires *Martians Go Home* and *What Mad Universe* were bitter and dealt with unpleasant intruders who disrupted the lives of less unpleasant characters like his hapless trapped fans in the latter novel or the failing, drunken science fiction writer of *Martians*. Brown's view of humanity was difficult to mistake as saccharine; the novels (like the two which follow) glow with a kind of turgid pain flaring into violence and he was portraying intelligent, murderous psychopaths long, long before Westlake or Thomas Harris, psychopaths like the principals of *Here Comes A Candle* or *The Far Cry* who would more often than not be unaware of their nature or, worse yet *were* aware and delighted in it as their personalities split, isolating the "bad" part so that the "good" part could claim an unfounded innocence. His novels are uneven (everybody prolific is uneven) and the shabbiness of contour and character of some of the later works are distancing but in the two accompanying novels he was still very much in control of his material and in enough control of his life to allow the characters to march unimpeded.

The Lights In The Sky Are Stars, his fifth and last science fiction novel and one which was largely ignored, is remarkably anticipatory; it is about a broken astronaut who has survived his childhood dreams of space to become what he beheld but there is a mean rehshaping of the apparent material in the last chapter and this novel, published almost two decades before my own cynical and despairing *Beyond Apollo*, is a sad and scary presentation of material with which science fiction in the main was absolutely unwilling to deal until 2001, the collapse of the Apollo program and the centering of technological adventure on the Vietnam adventure all in their way affected the equation. But by then it was too late for Brown who had died of emphysema in 1972, having been publicly silent for almost a decade. There had been a negligible collaborative story in Fantasy & Science Fiction in 1964 and a year before that the savage *Puppet Show* in *Playboy* but essentially Brown had been wiped out as a writer for at least half a decade before he stopped. He was frail, he probably smoked too much, he definitely drank too much and his last years, isolated in Arizona where he had resettled with his second wife for health reasons were difficult for him. A glance at this for me was the letter he wrote shortly before his death, responding to his agent's note that Robert Wyatt, a senior editor at Avon, was a fan and really would like to explore a new novel. "I appreciate that," Brown wrote, "but writing is just not for me anymore."

One could consider—looking at the panorama of writerly biography—whether the trade is, from the mental health standpoint, good for *anyone* but that falls outside the compass of literary exploration or redemption. Writing is for writers, that is the proper response and Brown with his rather astonishing range, his originality, his quirky, sidewise view of the human condition was certainly for writing. The last line of his 1949 fantasy, *Come And Go Mad* ("about the man who was not Napoleon") is an epitaph which might have pleased him, certainly spoke for his work: "But don't you understand? It doesn't matter. Nothing matters!"

Barry N. Malzberg
November 2018
New Jersey

NIGHT OF THE JABBERWOCK

Bruin Crimeworks

NIGHT
OF THE
JABBERWOCK

FREDRIC
BROWN

ALL VERSES

INTRODUCING CHAPTERS

ARE FROM THE WORKS OF

CHARLES LUTWIDGE DODGSON,

KNOWN IN WONDERLAND AS

LEWIS CARROL

~§~

CHAPTER ONE

'Twas brillig, and the slithy toves
Did gyre an gimble in the wabe:
All mimsy were the borogoves,
And the mome raths outgrabe.

IN MY DREAM I was standing in the middle of Oak Street and it was dark night. The street lights were off; only pale moonlight glinted on the huge sword that I swung in circles about my head as the Jabberwock crept closer. It bellied along the pavement, flexing its wings and tensing its muscles for the final rush; its claws clicked against the stones like the clicking of mats down the channels of a Linotype. Then, astonishingly, it spoke.

"Doc," it said. "Wake up, Doc."

A hand—not the hand of a Jabberwock—was shaking my shoulder.

And it was early dusk instead of black night and I was sitting in the swivel chair at my battered desk, looking over my shoulder at Pete. Pete was grinning at me.

"We're in, Doc," he said. "You'll have to cut two lines on this last take and we're in. Early, for once."

He put a galley proof down in front of me, only one stick of type long. I picked up a blue pencil and knocked off two lines and they happened to be an even sentence, so Pete wouldn't have to reset anything.

He went over to the Linotype and shut it off and it was suddenly very quiet in the place, so quiet that I could hear the drip of the faucet way in the far corner.

I stood up and stretched, feeling good, although a little groggy from having dozed off while Pete was setting that final take. For once, for one Thursday, the *Carmel City Clarion* was ready for the press early. Of course, there wasn't any real news in it, but then there never was.

And only half-past six and not yet dark outside. We were through hours earlier than usual. I decided that that called for a drink, here and now.

The bottle in my desk turned out to have enough whisky in it for one healthy drink or two short ones. I asked Pete if he wanted a snort and he said no, not yet, he'd wait till he got over to Smiley's, so I treated myself to a healthy drink, as I'd hoped to be able to do. And it had been fairly safe to ask Pete; he seldom took one before he was through for the day, and although my part of the job was done Pete still had almost an hour's work ahead of him on the mechanical end.

The drink made a warm spot under my belt as I walked over to the window by the Linotype and stood staring out into the quiet dusk. The lights of Oak Street flashed on while I stood there. I'd been dreaming—what had I been dreaming?

On the sidewalk across the street Miles Harrison hesitated in front of Smiley's Tavern as though the thought of a cool glass of beer tempted him. I could almost feel his mind working: "No, I'm a deputy sheriff of Carmel County and I have a job to do yet tonight and I don't drink while I'm on duty. The beer can wait."

Yes, his conscience must have won, because he walked on.

I wonder now—although of course I didn't wonder then—whether, if he had known that he would be dead before midnight, he wouldn't have stopped for that beer. I think he would have. I know I would have, but that doesn't prove anything because I'd have done it anyway; I've never had a conscience like Miles Harrison's.

Behind me, at the stone, Pete was putting the final stick of type into the chase of the front page. He said, "Okay, Doc, she fits. We're in."

"Let the presses roll," I told him.

Just a manner of speaking, of course. There was only one press and it didn't roll, because it was a *Miehle* vertical that shuttled up and down. And it wouldn't even do that until morning. The *Clarion* is a weekly paper that comes out on Friday; we put it to bed on Thursday evening and Pete runs it off the press Friday morning. And it's not much of a run.

Pete asked, "You going over to Smiley's?"

That was a silly question; I always go over to Smiley's on a Thursday evening and usually, when he's finished locking up the forms, Pete joins me, at least for a while. "Sure," I told him.

"I'll bring you a stone proof, then," Pete said.

Pete always does that, too, although I seldom do more than glance at it. Pete's too good a printer for me ever to catch any important errors on him and as for minor typographicals, Carmel City doesn't mind them.

I was free and Smiley's was waiting, but for some reason I wasn't in any hurry to leave. It was pleasant, after the hard work of a Thursday—and don't let that short nap fool you; I *had* been working—to stand there and watch the quiet street in the quiet twilight, and to contemplate an intensive campaign of doing nothing for the rest of the evening, with a few drinks to help me do it.

Miles Harrison, a dozen paces past Smiley's, stopped, turned, and headed back. Good, I thought, I'll have someone to drink with. I turned away from the window and put on my suit coat and hat.

I said, "Be seeing you, Pete," and I went down the stairs and out into the warm summer evening.

I'd misjudged Miles Harrison; he was coming out of Smiley's already, too soon even to have had a quick one, and he was opening a pack of cigarettes. He saw me and waved, waiting in front of Smiley's door to light a cigarette while I crossed the street.

"Have a drink with me, Miles," I suggested.

He shook his head regretfully. "Wish I could, Doc. But I got a job to do later. You know, go with Ralph Bonney over to Neilsville to get his pay roll."

Sure, I knew. In a small town everybody knows everything.

Ralph Bonney owned the Bonney Fireworks Company, just outside of Carmel City. They made fireworks, mostly big pieces for fairs and municipal displays, that were sold all over the country. And during the few months of each year up to about the first of July they worked a day and a night shift to meet the Fourth of July demand.

And Ralph Bonney had something against Clyde Andrews, president of the Carmel City Bank, and did his banking in Neilsville. He drove over to Neilsville late every Thursday night and they opened the bank there to give him the cash for his night shift pay roll. Miles Harrison, as deputy sheriff, always went along as guard.

Always seemed like a silly procedure to me, as the night side pay roll didn't amount to more than a few thousand dollars and Bonney could have got it along with the cash for his day side pay roll and held it at the office, but that was his way of doing things.

I said, "Sure, Miles, but that's not for hours yet. And one drink isn't going to hurt you."

He grinned, "I know it wouldn't, but I'd probably take another just because the first one didn't hurt me. So I stick to the rule that I don't have even one drink until I'm off duty for the day, and if I don't stick to it I'm sunk. But thanks just the same, Doc. I'll take a rain check."

He had a point, but I wish he hadn't made it. I wish he'd let me buy him that drink, or several of them, because that rain check wasn't worth the imaginary paper it was printed on to a man who was going to be murdered before midnight.

But I didn't know that, and I didn't insist. I said, "Sure, Miles," and asked him about his kids.

"Fine, both of 'em. Drop out and see us sometime."

"Sure," I said, and I went into Smiley's.

Big, bald Smiley Wheeler was alone. He smiled as I came in and said, "Hi, Doc. How's the editing business?" And then he laughed as though he'd said something excruciatingly funny. Smiley hasn't the ghost of a sense of humor and he has the mistaken idea that he disguises that fact by laughing at almost everything he says or hears said.

"Smiley, you give me a pain," I told him. It's always safe to tell Smiley a truth like that; no matter how seriously you say and mean it, he thinks you're joking. If he'd laughed I'd have told him where he gave me a pain, but for once he didn't laugh.

He said, "Glad you got here early, Doc. It's damn dull this evening."

"It's dull every evening in Carmel City," I told him. "And most of the time I like it. But Lord, if only something would happen just once on a Thursday evening, I'd love it. Just once in my long career, I'd like to have *one* hot story to break to a panting public."

"Hell, Doc, nobody looks for hot news in a country weekly."

"I know," I said. "That's why I'd like to fool them just once. I've been running the *Clarion* twenty-three years. One hot story. Is that much to ask?"

Smiley frowned. "There've been a couple of burglaries. And one murder, a few years ago."

"Sure," I said, "and so what? One of the factory hands out at Bonney's got in a drunken argument with another and hit him too hard in the fight they got into. That's not murder; that's manslaughter, and anyway it happened on a Saturday and it was old stuff—everybody in town knew about it—by the next Friday when the *Clarion* came out."

"They buy your paper anyway, Doc. They look for their

names for having attended church socials and who's got a used washing machine for sale and—want a drink?"

"It's about time one of us thought of that," I said.

He poured a shot for me and, so I wouldn't have to drink alone, a short one for himself. We drank them and I asked him, "Think Carl will be in tonight?"

I meant Carl Trenholm, the lawyer, who's about my closest friend in Carmel City, and one of the three or four in town who play chess and can be drawn into an intelligent discussion of something besides crops and politics. Carl often dropped in Smiley's on Thursday evenings, knowing that I always came in for at least a few drinks after putting the paper to bed.

"Don't think so," Smiley said. "Carl was in most of the afternoon and got himself kind of a snootful, to celebrate. He got through in court early and he won his case. Guess he went home to sleep it off."

I said, "Damn. Why couldn't he have waited till this evening? I'd have helped him—Say, Smiley, did you say Carl was celebrating because he *won* that case? Unless we're talking about two different things, he lost it. You mean the Bonney divorce?"

"Yeah."

"Then Carl was representing Ralph Bonney, and Bonney's wife won the divorce."

"You got it that way in the paper, Doc?"

"Sure," I said. "It's the nearest thing I've got to a good story this week."

Smiley shook his head. "Carl was saying to me he hoped you wouldn't put it in, or anyway that you'd hold it down to a short squib, just the fact that she got the divorce."

I said, "I don't get it, Smiley. Why? And *didn't* Carl lose the case?"

Smiley leaned forward confidentially across the bar, although he and I were the only ones in his place. He said, "It's like this, Doc. Bonney wanted the divorce. That wife of his was a bitch, see? Only he didn't have any grounds to sue on, himself—not any that he'd have been willing to bring up in court, anyway, see? So he—well, kind of bought his freedom. Gave her a settlement if she'd do the suing, and he admitted to the grounds she gave against him. Where'd you get your version of the story?"

"From the judge," I said.

"Well, he just saw the outside of it. Carl says Bonney's a good joe and those cruelty charges were a bunch of hokum. He never laid a hand on her. But the woman was such hell on wheels that Bonney'd have admitted to anything to get free of her. And give her a settlement of a hundred grand on top of it. Carl was worried about the case because the cruelty charges were so damn silly on the face of them."

"Hell," I said, "that's not the way it's going to sound in the *Clarion*."

"Carl was saying he knew you couldn't tell the truth about the story, but he hoped you'd play it down. Just saying Mrs. B. had been granted a divorce and that a settlement had been made, and not putting in anything about the charges."

I thought of my one real story of the week, and how carefully I'd enumerated all those charges Bonney's wife had made against him, and I groaned at the thought of having to rewrite or cut the story. And cut it I'd have to, now that I knew the facts.

I said, "Damn Carl, why didn't he come and tell me about it before I wrote the story and put the paper to bed?"

"He thought about doing that, Doc. And then he decided he didn't want to use his friendship with you to influence the way you reported news."

"The damn fool," I said. "And all he had to do was walk across the street."

"But Carl did say that Bonney's a swell guy and it would be a bad break for him if you listed those charges because none of them were really true and—"

"Don't rub it in," I interrupted him. "I'll change the story. If

Carl says it's that way, I'll believe him. I can't say that the charges weren't true, but at least I can leave them out."

"That'd be swell of you, Doc."

"Sure it would. All right, give me one more drink, Smiley, and I'll go over and catch it before Pete leaves."

I had the one more drink, cussing myself for being sap enough to spoil the only mentionable story I had, but knowing I had to do it. I didn't know Bonney personally, except just to say hello to on the street, but I did know Carl Trenholm well enough to be damn sure that if he said Bonney was in the right, the story wasn't fair the way I'd written it. And I knew Smiley well enough to be sure he hadn't given me a bum steer on what Carl had really said.

So I grumbled my way back across the street and upstairs to the *Clarion* office. Pete was just tightening the chase around the front page.

He loosened the quoins when I told him what we had to do, and I walked around the stone so I could read the story again, upside down, of course, as type is always read.

The first paragraph could stand as written and could constitute the entire story. I told Pete to put the rest of the type in the hell-box and I went over to the case and set a short head in tenpoint, *"Bonney Divorce Granted,"* to replace the twenty-four point head that had been on the longer story. I handed Pete the stick and watched while he switched heads.

"Leaves about a nine-inch hole in the page," he said. "What'll we stick in it?"

I sighed. "Have to use filler," I told him. "Not on the front page, but we'll have to find something on page four we can move front and then stick in nine inches of filler where it came from."

I wandered down the stone to page four and picked up a pica stick to measure things. Pete went over to the rack and got a galley of filler. About the only thing that was anywhere near the right size was the story that Clyde Andrews, Carmel City's banker and leading light of the local Baptist Church, had given me about the rummage sale the church had planned for next Tuesday evening.

It wasn't exactly a story of earth-shaking importance, but it would be about the right length if we reset it indented to go in a box. And it had a lot of names in it, and that meant it would please a lot of people, and particularly Clyde Andrews, if I moved it up to the front page.

So we moved it. Rather, Pete reset it for a frontpage box item while I plugged the gap in page four with filler items and locked up the page again. Pete had the rummage sale item reset by the time I'd finished with page four, and this time I waited for him to finish up page one, so we could go to Smiley's together.

I thought about that front page while I washed my hands. *The Front Page.* Shades of Hecht and MacArthur. Poor revolving Horace Greeley.

Now I really wanted a drink.

Pete was starting to pound out a stone proof and I told him not to bother. Maybe the customers would read page one, but I wasn't going to. And if there was an upside-down headline or a pied paragraph, it would probably be an improvement.

Pete washed up and we locked the door. It was still early for a Thursday evening, not much after seven. I should have been happy about that, and I probably would have been if we'd had a good paper. As for the one we'd just put to bed, I wondered if it would live until morning.

Smiley had a couple of other customers and was waiting on them, and I wasn't in any mood to wait for Smiley so I went around behind the bar and got the Old Henderson bottle and two glasses and took them to a table for Pete and myself. Smiley and I know one another well enough so it's always all right for me to help myself any time it's convenient and settle with him afterward.

I poured drinks for Pete and me. We drank and Pete said,

"Well, that's that for another week, Doc."

I wondered how many times he'd said that in the ten years he'd worked for me, and then I got to wondering how many times I'd thought it, which would be—

"How much is fifty-two times twenty-three, Pete?" I asked him.

"Huh? A hell of a lot. Why?"

I figured it myself. "Fifty times twenty-three is—one thousand one hundred and fifty; twice twenty-three more makes eleven ninety-six. Pete, eleven hundred and ninety-six times have I put that paper to bed on a Thursday night and never once was there a really big hot news story in it."

"This isn't Chicago, Doc. What do you expect, a murder?"

"I'd love a murder," I told him.

It would have been funny if Pete had said, "Doc, how'd you like three in one night?"

But he didn't, of course. In a way, though, he said something that was even funnier. He said, "But suppose it was a friend of yours? Your best friend, say. Carl Trenholm. Would you want him killed just to give the *Clarion* a story?"

"Of course not," I said. "Preferably somebody I don't know at all—if there *is* anybody in Carmel City I don't know at all. Let's make it Yehudi."

"Who's Yehudi?" Pete asked.

I looked at Pete to see if he was kidding me, and apparently he wasn't so I explained: "The little man. who wasn't there. Don't you remember the rhyme?

> *I saw a man upon the stair,*
> *A little man who was not there.*
> *He was not there again today;*
> *Gee, I wish he'd go away."*

Pete laughed. "Doc, you get crazier every day. Is that *Alice in Wonderland,* too, like all the other stuff you quote when you get drinking?"

"This time, no. But who says I quote Lewis Carroll only when I'm drinking? I can quote him now, and I've hardly started drinking for tonight—why, as the Red Queen said to Alice, 'One has to do *this* much drinking to stay in the same place.' But listen and I'll quote you something that's really something:

> *'Twas brillig and the slithy toves*
> *Did gyre and gimble in the wabe—"*

Pete stood up. "*Jabberwocky,* from *Alice Through the Looking-Glass*" he said. "If you've recited that to me once, Doc, it's been a hundred times. I damn near know it myself. But I got to go, Doc. Thanks for the drink."

"Okay, Pete, but don't forget one thing."

"What's that?"

I said:

> *"Beware the Jabberwock, my son!*
> *The jaws that bite, the claws that catch!*
> *Beware the Jubjub bird and shun*
> *The frumious—"*

Smiley was calling to me, "Hey, Doc!" from over beside the telephone and I remembered now that I'd heard it ring half a minute before. Smiley yelled, "Telephone for you, Doc," and laughed as though that was the funniest thing that had happened in a long time.

I stood up and started for the phone, telling Pete good night en route.

I picked up the phone and said "Hello" to it and it said "Hello" back at me. Then it said, "Doc?" and I said, "Yes."

Then it said, "Clyde Andrews speaking, Doc." His voice sounded quite calm. "This is murder."

Pete must be almost to the door by now; that was my first thought. I said, "Just a second, Clyde," and then jammed my hand over the mouthpiece while I yelled, "Hey, Pete!"

He *was* at the door, but he turned.

"Don't go," I yelled at him, the length of the bar. "There's *a murder story* breaking. We got to remake!"

I could feel the sudden silence in Smiley's Bar. The conversation between the two other customers stopped in the middle of a word and they turned to look at me. Pete, from the door, looked at me. Smiley, a bottle in his hand, turned to look at me—and he didn't even smile. In fact, just as I turned back to the phone, the bottle dropped out of his hand and hit the floor with a noise that made me jump and close my mouth quickly to keep my heart from jumping from it. That bottle crashing on the floor had sounded—for a second—just like a revolver shot.

I waited until I felt that I could talk again without stammering and then I took my hand off the mouthpiece of the phone and said calmly, or almost calmly, "Okay, Clyde, go ahead."

CHAPTER TWO

"Who are you, aged man?" I said.
"And how is it you live?"
His answer trickled through my head,
Like water through a sieve.

"YOU'VE gone to press, haven't you, Doc?" Clyde's voice said. "You must have because I tried phoning you at the office first and then somebody told me if you weren't there, you'd be at Smiley's, but that'd mean you were through for the—"

"That's all right," I said. "Get on with it."

"I know it's murder, Doc, to ask you to change a story when you've already got the paper ready to run and have left the office, but—well, that rummage sale we were going to have Tuesday; it's been called off. Can you still kill the article? Otherwise a lot of people will read about it and come around to the church Tuesday night and be disappointed."

"Sure, Clyde," I said. "I'll take care of it."

I hung up. I went over to the table and sat down. I poured myself a drink of whisky and when Pete came over I poured him one.

He asked me what the call had been and I told him.

Smiley and his two other customers were still staring at me, but I didn't say anything until Smiley called out, "What happened, Doc? Didn't you say something about a murder?"

I said, "I was just kidding, Smiley." He laughed.

I drank my drink and Pete drank his. He said, "I knew there was a catch about getting through early tonight. Now we got a nine-inch hole in the front page all over again. What are we going to put in it?"

"Damned if I know," I told him. "But the hell with it for tonight. I'll get down when you do in the morning and figure something out then."

Pete said, "That's what you say now, Doc. But if you *don't* get down at eight o'clock, what'll I do with that hole in the page?"

"Your lack of faith horrifies me, Pete. If I say I'll be down in the morning, I will be. Probably."

"But if you're not?"

I sighed. "Do anything you want." I knew Pete would fix it up somehow if I didn't get down. He'd drag something from a back page and plug the back page with filler items or a subscription ad. It was going to be lousy because we had one sub ad in already and too damn much filler; you know, those little items that tell you the number of board feet in a sequoia and the current rate of mullet manufacture in the Euphrates valley. All right in small doses, but when you run the stuff by the column—

Pete said he'd better go, and this time he did. I watched him go, envying him a little. Pete Corey is a good printer and I pay him just about what I make myself. We put in about the same number of hours, but I'm the one who has to worry whenever there's any worrying to be done, which is most of the time.

Smiley's other customers left, just after Pete, and I didn't want to sit alone at the table, so I took my bottle over to the bar.

"Smiley," I said, "do you want to buy a paper?"

"Huh?" Then he laughed. "You're kidding me, Doc. It isn't off the press till tomorrow noon, is it?"

"It isn't," I told him. "But it'll be well worth waiting for this week. Watch for it, Smiley. But that isn't what I meant."

"Huh? Oh, you mean do I want to buy the *paper*. I don't think so, Doc. I don't think I'd be very good at running a paper.

I can't spell very good, for one thing. But look, you were telling me the other night Clyde Andrews wanted to buy it from you. Whyn't you sell it to him, if you want to sell it?"

"Who the devil said I wanted to sell it?" I asked him. "I just asked if you wanted to buy it."

Smiley looked baffled.

"Doc," he said, "I never know whether you're serious or not. Seriously, do you really want to sell out?"

I'd been wondering that. I said slowly, "I don't know, Smiley. Right now, I'd be damn tempted. I think I hate to quit mostly because before I do I'd like to get out one *good* issue. Just one *good* issue out of twenty-three years."

"If you sold it, what'd you do?"

"I guess, Smiley, I'd spend the rest of my life not editing a newspaper."

Smiley decided I was being funny again, and laughed.

The door opened and Al Grainger came in. I waved the bottle at him and he came down the bar to where I was standing, and Smiley got another glass and a chaser of water; Al always needs a chaser.

Al Grainger is just a young squirt—twenty-two or -three—but he's one of the few chess players in town and one of the even fewer people who understand my enthusiasm for Lewis Carroll. Besides that, he's by way of being a Mystery Man in Carmel City. Not that you have to be very mysterious to achieve that distinction.

He said, "Hi, Doc. When are we going to have another game of chess?"

"No time like the present, Al. Here and now?"

Smiley kept chessmen on hand for screwy customers like Al Grainger and Carl Trenholm and myself. He'd bring them out, always handling them as though he expected them to explode in his hands, whenever we asked for them.

Al shook his head. "Wish I had time. Got to go home and do some work."

I poured whisky in his glass and spilled a little trying to fill it to the brim. He shook his head slowly. "The White Knight is sliding down the poker," he said. "He balances very badly."

"I'm only in the second square," I told him. "But the next move will be a good one. I go to the fourth by train, remember."

"Don't keep it waiting, Doc. The smoke alone is worth a thousand pounds a puff."

Smiley was looking from one of us to the other. "What the hell are you guys talking about?" he wanted to know.

There wasn't any use trying to explain. I leveled my finger at him. I said, "Crawling at your feet you may observe a bread-and-butter fly. Its wings are thin slices of bread-and-butter, its body a crust and its head is a lump of sugar. And it lives on weak tea with cream in it."

Al said, "Smiley, you're supposed to ask him what happens if it can't find any."

I said, "Then I say it would die of course and you say that must happen very often and I say it *always* happens."

Smiley looked at us again and shook his head slowly. He said, "You guys are *really* nuts." He walked down the bar to wash and wipe some glasses.

Al Grainger grinned at me. "What are your plans for tonight, Doc?" he asked. "I just might possibly be able to sneak in a game or two of chess later. You going to be home, and up?"

I nodded. "I was just working myself up to the idea of walking home, and when I get there I'm going to read. And have another drink or two. If you get there before midnight I'll still be sober enough to play. Sober enough to beat a young punk like you, anyway."

It was all right to say that last part because it was so obviously untrue. Al had been beating me two games out of three for the last year or so.

He chuckled, and quoted at me:

> *"'You are old, Father William" the young man said,*
> *'And your hair has become very white;*
> *And yet you incessantly stand on your head —*
> *Do you think, at your age, it is right?'"*

Well, since Carroll had the answer to that, so did I:

> *"'In my youth,' Father William replied to his son,*
> *'I feared it might injure the brain;*
> *But, now that I'm perfectly sure I have none*
> *'Why, I do it again and again.'"*

Al said, "Maybe you got something there, Doc. But let's quit alternating verses on that before you get to *'Be off, or I'll kick you downstairs!'* Because I got to be off anyway."

"One more drink?"

"I—think not, not till I'm through working. You can drink and think too. Hope I can do the same thing when I'm your age. I'll try my best to get to your place for some chess, but don't look for me unless I'm there by ten o'clock—half past at the latest. And thanks for the drink."

He went out and, through Smiley's window, I could see him getting into his shiny convertible. He blew the Klaxon and waved back at me as he pulled out from the curb.

I looked at myself in the mirror back of Smiley's bar and wondered how old Al Grainger thought I was. *"Hope I can do the same thing when I'm your age,"* indeed. Sounded as though he thought I was eighty, at least. I'll be fifty-three my next birthday.

But I had to admit that I looked that old, and that my hair was turning white. I watched myself in the mirror and that whiteness scared me just a little. No, I wasn't old yet, but I was getting that way. And, much as I crab about it, I like living. I don't want to get old and I don't want to die. Especially as I can't look forward, as a good many of my fellow townsmen do, to an eternity of harp playing and picking bird-lice out of my wings. Nor, for that matter, an eternity of shoveling coal, although that would probably be the more likely of the two in my case.

Smiley came back. He jerked his finger at the door. "I don't like that guy, Doc," he said.

"Al? He's all right. A little wet behind the ears, maybe. You're just prejudiced because you don't know where his money comes from. Maybe he's got a printing press and makes it himself. Come to think of it, *I've* got a printing press. Maybe I should try that myself."

"Hell, it ain't that, Doc. It's not my business how a guy earns his money—or where he gets it if he don't earn it. It's the way he talks. *You* talk crazy, too, but—well, you do it in a nice way. When he says something to me I don't understand he says it in a way that makes me feel like a stupid bastard. Maybe I *am* one, but—"

I felt suddenly ashamed of all the things I'd ever said to Smiley that I knew he wouldn't understand.

I said, "It's not a matter of intelligence, Smiley. It's merely a matter of literary background. Have one drink with me, and then I'd better go."

I poured him a drink and—this time—a small one for myself. I was beginning to feel the effects, and I didn't want to get too drunk to give Al Grainger a good game of chess if he dropped in.

I said, for no reason at all, "You're a good guy, Smiley, and he laughed and said, "So are you, Doc. Literary background or not, you're a little crazy, but you're a good guy."

And then, because we were both embarrassed at having caught ourselves saying things like that, I found myself staring past Smiley at the calendar over the bar. It had the usual kind of picture one sees on barroom calendars—an almost too voluptuous naked woman—and it was imprinted by Beal Brothers Store.

It was just a bit of bother to keep my eyes focused on it, I noticed, although I hadn't had enough to drink to affect my mind at all. Right then, for instance, I was thinking of two things at one and the same time. Part of my brain, to my disgust, persisted in wondering if I could get Beal Brothers to start running a quarter page ad instead of an eighth page; I tried to squelch the thought by telling myself that I didn't care, tonight, whether anybody advertised in the *Clarion* at all, and that part of my brain went on to ask me why, damn it, if I felt that way about it, I didn't get out from under while I had the chance by selling the *Clarion* to Clyde Andrews. But the other part of my mind kept getting more and more annoyed by the picture on the calendar, and I said, "Smiley, you ought to take down that calendar. It's a lie. There *aren't* any women like that."

He turned around and looked at it. "Guess you're right, Doc; there aren't any women like that. But a guy can dream, can't he?"

"Smiley," I said, "if that's not the first profound thing you've said, it's the *most* profound. You are right, moreover. You have my full permission to leave the calendar up."

He laughed and moved along the bar to finish wiping glasses, and I stood there and wondered why I didn't go on home. It was still early, a few minutes before eight o'clock. I didn't want another drink, yet. But by the time I got home, I would want one.

So I got out my wallet and called Smiley back. We estimated how many drinks I'd poured out of the bottle and I settled for them, and then I bought another bottle, a full quart, and he wrapped it for me.

I went out with it under my arm and said "So long, Smiley, and he said "So long, Doc," just as casually as though, before the gibbering night that hadn't started yet was over, he and I would not—but let's take things as they happened.

The walk home.

I had to go past the post office anyway, so I stopped in. The mail windows were closed, of course, but the outer lobby is always left open evenings so those who have post office boxes can get mail out of them.

I got my mail—there wasn't anything important in it—and then stopped, as I usually do, by the bulletin board to look over the notices and the wanted circulars that were posted there.

There were a couple of new ones and I read them and studied the pictures. I've got a good memory for faces, even ones I've just seen pictures of, and I'd always hoped that some day I'd spot a wanted criminal in Carmel City and get a story out of it, if not a reward.

A few doors farther on I passed the bank and that reminded me about its president, Clyde Andrews, and his wanting to buy the paper from me. He didn't want to run it himself, of course; he had a brother somewhere in Ohio who'd had newspaper experience and who would run the paper for Andrews if I sold it to him.

The thing I liked least about the idea, I decided, was that Andrews was in politics and, if he controlled the *Clarion*, the *Clarion* would back his party. The way I ran it, it threw mud at both factions when they deserved it, which was often, and handed either one an occasional bouquet when deserved, which was seldom. Maybe I'm crazy—other people than Smiley and Al have said so—but that's the way I think a newspaper should be run, and especially when it's the only paper in a town.

It's not, I might mention, the best way to make money. It had made me plenty of friends and subscribers, but a newspaper doesn't make money from its subscribers. It makes money from advertisers and most of the men in town big enough to be advertisers had fingers in politics and no matter which party I slammed I was likely to lose another advertising account.

I'm afraid that policy didn't help my news coverage, either. The best source of news is the sheriff's department and, at the moment, Sheriff Rance Kates was just about my worst enemy. Kates is honest, but he is also stupid, rude and full of race prejudice; and race prejudice, although it's not a burning issue in Carmel City, is one of my pet peeves. I hadn't pulled any punches in my editorials about Kates, either before or after his election. He got into office only because his opponent—who wasn't any intellectual heavyweight either—had got into a tavern brawl in Neilsville a week before election and was arrested there and charged with assault and battery. The *Clarion* had reported that, too, so the *Clarion* was probably responsible for Rance Kates' being elected sheriff. But Rance remembered only the things I'd said about *him,* and barely spoke to me on the street. Which, I might add, didn't concern me the slightest bit personally, but it forced me to get all of my police news, such as it is, the hard way.

Past the supermarket and Beal Brothers and past Deak's Music Store—where I'd once bought a violin but had forgotten to get a set of instructions with it—and the corner and across the street.

The walk home.

Maybe I weaved just a little, for at just that stage I'm never quite as sober as I am later on. But my mind—ah, it was in that delightful state of being crystal clear in the center and fuzzy around the edges, the state that every moderate drinker knows but can't explain or define, the state that makes even a Carmel City seem delightful and such things as its squalid politics amusing.

Past the corner drugstore—Pop Hinkle's place—where I used to drink sodas when I was a kid, before I went away to college and made the big mistake of studying journalism. Past Gorham's Feed Store, where I'd worked vacations while I was in high school. Past the Bijou Theater. Past Hank Greeber's Undertaking Parlors, through which both of my parents had passed, fifteen and twenty years ago.

Around the corner at the courthouse, where a light was still on in Sheriff Kates' office—and I felt so cheerful that, for a thousand dollars or so, I'd have stopped in to talk to him. But no one was around to offer me a thousand dollars.

Out of the store district now, past the house in which Elsie Minton had lived—and in which she had died while we were engaged, twenty-five years ago.

Past the house Elmer Conklin had lived in when I'd bought the *Clarion* from him. Past the church where I'd been sent to Sunday School when I was a kid, and where I'd once won a prize for memorizing verses of the Bible.

Past my past, and walking, slightly weaving, toward the house in which I'd been conceived and born.

No, I hadn't lived there fifty-three years. My parents had sold it and had moved to a bigger house when I was nine and when my sister—now married and living in Florida—had been born. I'd bought it back twelve years ago when it happened to be vacant and on the market at a good price. It's only a three-room cottage, not too big for a man to live in alone, if he likes to live alone, and I do.

Oh, I like people, too. I like someone to drop in for conversation or chess or a drink or all three. I like to spend an hour or two in Smiley's, or any other tavern, a few times a week. I like an occasional poker game.

But I'll settle, on any given evening, for my books. Two walls of my living room are lined with them and they overflow into bookcases in my bedroom and I even have a shelf of them in the bathroom. What do I mean, *even?* I think a bathroom without a bookshelf is as incomplete as would be one without a toilet.

And they're good books, too. No, I wouldn't be lonely tonight, even if Al Grainger didn't come around for that game of chess. How could I be lonesome with a bottle in my pocket and good company waiting for me? Why, reading a book is almost as good as listening to the man who wrote it talking to you. Better, in one way, because you don't have to be polite to him. You can shut him up any moment you feel so inclined and pick someone else instead. And you can take off your shoes and put your feet on the table. You can drink and read until you forget everything but what you're reading; you can forget who you are and the fact that there's a newspaper that hangs around your neck like a millstone, all day and every day, until you get home to sanctuary and forgetfulness.

The walk home.

And so to the corner of Campbell Street and my turning.

A June evening, but cool, and the night air had almost completely sobered me in the nine blocks I'd walked from Smiley's.

My turning, and I saw that the light was on in the front room of my house. I started walking a little faster, mildly puzzled. I knew I hadn't left it on when I'd left for the office that morning. And if I *had* left it on, Mrs. Carr, the cleaning woman who comes in for about two hours every afternoon to keep my place in order, would have turned it off.

Maybe, I thought, Al Grainger had finished whatever he was doing and had come early and had—but no, Al wouldn't have come without his car and there wasn't any car parked in front.

It might have been a mystery, but it wasn't.

Mrs. Carr was there, putting on her hat in front of the panel mirror in the closet door as I went in.

She said, "I'm just leaving, Mr. Stoeger. I wasn't able to get here this afternoon, so I came to clean up this evening instead; I just finished."

"Fine," I said. "By the way, there's a blizzard out."

"A—*what?*"

"Blizzard. Snowstorm." I held up the wrapped bottle. "So maybe you'd better have a little nip with me before you start home, don't you think?"

She laughed. "Thanks, Mr. Stoeger. I will. I've had a pretty rough day, and it sounds like a good idea. I'll get glasses for us."

I put my hat in the closet and followed her out into the kitchen.

"A rough day?" I asked her. "I hope nothing went wrong."

"Well—nothing too serious. My husband—he works, you know, out at Bonney's fireworks factory—got burned in a little accident they had out there this afternoon, and they brought him home. It's nothing serious, a second degree burn the doctor said, but it was pretty painful and I thought I'd better stay with him until after supper, and then he finally got to sleep so I ran over here and I'm afraid I straightened up your place pretty fast and didn't do a very good job."

"Looks spotless to me," I said. I'd been opening the bottle while she'd been getting glasses for us. "I hope he'll be all right, Mrs. Carr. But if you want to skip coming here for a while—"

Oh, no, I can still come. He'll be home only a few days, and it was just that today they brought him home at two o'clock, just when I was getting ready to come here and— That's plenty, thanks."

We touched glasses and I downed mine while she drank about half of hers. She said, "Oh, there was a phone call for you, about an hour ago. A little while after I got here."

"Find out who it was?"

"He wouldn't tell me, just said it wasn't important."

I shook my head sadly. "That, Mrs. Carr, is one of the major fallacies of the human mind. The idea, I mean, that things can be arbitrarily divided into the important and the unimportant. How can anyone decide whether a given fact is important or not unless one knows *everything* about it—and no one knows everything about anything."

She smiled, but a bit vaguely, and I decided to bring it down to earth. I said, "What would you say is important, Mrs. Carr?"

She put her head on one side and considered it seriously. "Well, *work* is important, isn't it?"

"It is not," I told her. "I'm afraid you score zero. Work is only a means to an end. We work in order to enable ourselves to do the important things, which are the things we want to do. Doing what we want to do—that's what's important, if anything is."

"That sounds like a funny way of putting it, but maybe you're right. Well, anyway, this man who called said he'd either call again or come around. I told him you probably wouldn't be home until eight or nine o'clock."

She finished her drink and declined an encore. I walked to the front door with her, saying that I'd have been glad to drive her home but that my car had two flat tires. I'd discovered them that morning when I'd started to drive to work. One I might have stopped to fix, but two discouraged me; I decided to leave the car in the garage until Saturday afternoon, when I'd have lots of time. And then, too, I know that I *should* get the exercise of walking to and from work every day, but as long as my car is in running condition, I don't. For Mrs. Carr's sake, though, I wished now that I'd fixed the tires.

She said, "It's only a few blocks, Mr. Stoeger. I wouldn't think of letting you, even if your car was working. Good night."

"Oh, just a minute, Mrs. Carr. What department at Bonney's does your husband work in?"

"The Roman candle department."

It made me forget, for the moment, what I'd been leading up to. I said, "The Roman candle department! That's a wonderful phrase; I love it. If I sell the paper, darned if I don't look up Bonney the very next day. I'd love to work in the Roman candle department. Your husband is a lucky man."

"You're joking, Mr. Stoeger. But are you really thinking of selling the paper?"

"Well—thinking of it." And that reminded me. "I didn't get any story on the accident at Bonney's, didn't even hear about it. And I'm badly in need of a story for the front page. Do you know the details of what happened? Anyone else hurt?"

She'd been part way across the front porch, but she turned and came back nearer the door. She said, "Oh, *please* don't put it in the paper. It wasn't anything important; my husband was the only one hurt and it was his own fault, he says. And Mr. Bonney wouldn't like it being in the paper; he has enough trouble now getting as many people as he needs for the rush season before the Fourth, and so many people are afraid to work around powder and explosives anyway. George will probably be tired if it gets written up in the paper and he *needs* the work."

I sighed; it had been an idea while it lasted. I assured her that I wouldn't print anything about it. And if George Carr had been the only one hurt and I didn't have any details, it wouldn't have made over a one-inch item anyway.

I would have loved, though, to get that beautiful phrase, *"the Roman candle department,"* into print.

I went back inside and closed the door. I made myself comfortable by taking off my suit coat and loosening my tie, and then I got the whisky bottle and my glass and put them on the coffee table in front of the sofa.

I didn't take the tie off yet, nor my shoes; it's nicer to do those things one at a time as you gradually get more and more comfortable.

I picked out a few books and put them within easy reach, poured myself a drink, sat down, and opened one of the books.

The doorbell rang.

Al Grainger had come early, I thought. I went to the door and opened it. There was a man standing there, just lifting his hand to ring again. But it wasn't Al; it was a man I'd never seen before.

CHAPTER THREE

How cheerfully he seems to grin,
How neatly spreads his claws,
And welcomes little fishes in
With gently smiling jaws!

H E W A S S H O R T, about my own height, perhaps, but seeming even shorter because of his greater girth. The first thing you noticed about his face was his nose; it was long, thin, pointed, grotesquely at variance with his pudgy body. The light coming past me through the doorway reflected glowing points in his eyes, giving them a cat-like gleam. Yet there was nothing sinister about him. A short pudgy man can never manage to seem sinister, no matter how the light strikes his eyes.

"You are Doctor Stoeger?" he asked.

"Doc Stoeger," I corrected him. "But not a doctor of medicine. If you're looking for a medical doctor, one lives four doors west of here."

He smiled, a nice smile. "I am aware that you are not a medico, Doctor. Ph. D., Burgoyne College—nineteen twenty-two, I believe. Author of *Lewis Carroll Through the Looking-Glass* and *Red Queen and White Queen.*"

It startled me. Not so much that he knew my college and the year of my *magna cum laude,* but the rest of it was amazing. *Lewis Carroll Through the Looking-Glass* was a monograph of a dozen pages; it had been printed eighteen years ago and only a hundred copies had been run off. If one still existed anywhere outside of my own library, I was greatly surprised. And *Red*

Queen and White Queen was a magazine article that had appeared at least twelve years ago in a magazine that had been obscure then and had long since been discontinued and forgotten.

"Yes," I said. "But how you know of them, I can't imagine, Mr.—"

"Smith," he said gravely. Then he chuckled. "And the first name is Yehudi."

"No!" I said.

"Yes. You see, Doctor Stoeger, I was named forty years ago, when the name Yehudi, although uncommon, had not yet acquired the comic connotation which it has today. My parents did not guess that the name would become a joke—and that it would be particularly ridiculous when combined with Smith. Had they guessed the difficulty I now have in convincing people that I'm not kidding them when I tell them my name—" He laughed ruefully. "I always carry cards."

He handed me one. It read:

Yehudi Smith

There was no address, no other information. Just the same, I wanted to keep that card, so I stuck it in my pocket instead of handing it back.

He said, "People *are* named Yehudi, you know. There's Yehudi Menuhin, the violinist. And there's—"

"Stop, please," I interrupted. "You're making it plausible. I liked it better the other way."

He smiled. "Then I haven't misjudged you, Doctor. Have you ever heard of the Vorpal Blades?"

"Plural? No. Of course, in Jabberwocky:

> *One, two! One, two! And through and through*
> *The vorpal blade went snicker-snack.*

But—Good God! Why are we talking about vorpal blades through a doorway? Come on in. I've got a bottle, and I hope and presume that it would be ridiculous to ask a man who talks about vorpal blades whether or not he drinks."

I stepped back and he came in. "Sit anywhere," I told him. "I'll get another glass. Want either a mix or a chaser?"

He shook his head, and I went out into the kitchen and got another glass. I came in, filled it and handed it to him. He'd already made himself comfortable in the overstuffed chair.

I sat back down on the sofa and lifted my glass toward him. I said, "No doubt about a toast for this one. To Charles Lutwidge Dodgson, known, when in Wonderland, as Lewis Carroll."

He said, quietly, "Are you sure, Doctor?"

"Sure of what?"

"Of your phraseology in that toast. I'd word it: To Lewis Carroll, who masqueraded under the alleged identity of Charles Lutwidge Dodgson, the gentle don of Oxford."

I felt vaguely disappointed. Was this going to be another, and even more ridiculous, Bacon-was-Shakespeare deal? Historically, there couldn't be any possible doubt that the Reverend Dodgson, writing under the name Lewis Carroll, had created *Alice in Wonderland* and its sequel.

But the main point, for the moment, was to get the drink drunk. So I said solemnly, "To avoid all difficulties, factual or semantic, Mr. Smith, let's drink to the author of the Alice books."

He inclined his head with solemnity equal to my own, then tilted it back and downed his drink. I was a little late in downing mine because of my surprise at, and admiration for, his manner of drinking. I'd never seen anything quite like it. The glass had stopped, quite suddenly, a good three inches from his mouth. And the whisky had kept on going and not a drop of it had been lost. I've seen people toss down a shot before, but never with such casual precision and from so great a distance.

I drank my own in a more prosaic manner, but I resolved to try his system sometime—in private and with a towel or handkerchief ready at hand.

I refilled our glasses and then said, "And now what? Do we argue the identity of Lewis Carroll?"

"Let's start back of that," he said. "In fact, let's put it aside until I can offer you definite proof of what we believe—rather, of what we are certain."

"We?"

"The Vorpal Blades. An organization. A very small organization, I should add."

"Of admirers of Lewis Carroll?"

He leaned forward. "Yes, of course. Any man who is both literate and imaginative is an admirer of Lewis Carroll. But— much more than that. We have a secret. A quite esoteric one."

"Concerning the identity of Lewis Carroll? You mean that you believe—the way some people believe, or used to believe, that the plays of Shakespeare were written by Francis Bacon— that someone other than Charles Lutwidge Dodgson wrote the Alice books?"

I hope he'd say no.

He said, "No. We believe that Dodgson himself— How much do you know of him, Doctor?"

"He was born in eighteen thirty-two," I said, "and died just before the turn of the century—in either ninety-eight or nine. He was an Oxford don, a mathematician. He wrote several treatises on mathematics. He liked—and created—acrostics and other puzzles and problems. He never married but he was very fond of children, and his best writing was done for them. At least he *thought* he was writing only for children; actually, *Alice in Wonderland* and *Alice Through the Looking-Glass,* while having plenty of appeal for children, are adult literature, and great literature. Shall I go on?"

"By all means."

"He was also capable of—and perpetrated—some almost

incredibly bad writing. There ought to be a law against the printing of volumes of *The Complete Works of Lewis Carroll*. He should be remembered for the great things he wrote, and the bad ones interred with his bones. Although I'll admit that even the bad things have occasional touches of brilliance. There are moments in *Sylvie and Bruno* that are almost worth reading through the thousands of dull words to reach. And there are occasional good lines or stanzas in even the worst poems. Take the first three lines of *The Palace of Humbug:*

> *I dreamt I dwelt in marble halls,*
> *And each damp thing that creeps and crawls*
> *Went wobble-wobble on the walls.*

"Of course should have stopped there instead of adding fifteen or twenty bad triads. But *'Went wobble-wobble on the walls'* is marvelous."

He nodded. "Let's drink to it."

We drank to it.

He said, "Go on."

"No," I said. "I'm just realizing that I could easily go on for hours. I can quote every line of verse in the Alice books and most of *The Hunting of the Snark*. But, I both hope and presume, you didn't come here to listen to me lecture on Lewis Carroll. My information about him is fairly thorough, but quite orthodox. I judge that yours isn't, and I want to hear it."

I refilled our glasses.

He nodded slowly. "Quite right, Doctor. My—I should say *our*—information is extremely unorthodox. I think you have the background and the type of mind to understand it, and to believe it when you have seen proof. To a more ordinary mind, it would seem sheer fantasy."

It was getting better by the minute. I said, "Don't stop now."

"Very well. But before I go any farther, I must warn you of

something, Doctor. It is also very dangerous information to have. I do not speak lightly or metaphorically.
I mean that there is serious danger, deadly danger."

"That," I said, "is wonderful."

He sat there and toyed with his glass—still with the third drink in it—and didn't look at me. I studied his face. It was an interesting face. That long, thin, pointed nose, so incongruous to his build that it might have been false—a veritable Cyrano de Bergerac of a nose. And now that he was in the light, I could see that there were deep laughter-lines around his generous mouth. At first I would have guessed his age at thirty instead of the forty he claimed to be; now, studying his face closely, I could see that he had not exaggerated his age. One would have to laugh a long time to etch lines like those.

But he wasn't laughing now. He looked deadly serious, and he didn't look crazy. But he said something that sounded crazy.

He said, "Doctor, has it ever occurred to you that—that the fantasies of Lewis Carroll are not fantasies at all?"

"Do you mean," I asked, "in the sense that fantasy is often nearer to fundamental truth than is would-be realistic fiction?"

"No. I mean that they are literally, actually true. That they are not fiction at all, that they are reporting."

I stared at him. "If you think that, then who—or *what*—do you think Lewis Carroll was?"

He smiled faintly, but it wasn't a smile of amusement.

He said, "If you really want to know, and aren't afraid, you can find out tonight. There is a meeting, near here. Will you come?"

"May I be frank?"

"Certainly."

I said, "I think it's crazy, but try to keep me away."

"In spite of the fact that there is danger?"

Sure, I was going, danger or no. But maybe I could use his insistence on warning me to pry something more out of him. So I said, "May I ask what *kind* of danger?"

He seemed to hesitate a moment and then he took out his wallet and from an inner compartment took a newspaper clipping, a short one of about three paragraphs. He handed it to me.

I read it, and I recognized the type and the setup; it was a clipping from the *Bridgeport Argus*. And I remembered now having read it, a couple of weeks ago. I'd considered clipping it as an exchange item, and then had decided not to, despite the fact that the heading had caught my interest. It read:

MAN SLAIN BY UNKNOWN BEAST

The facts were few and simple. A man named Colin Hawks, living outside Bridgeport, a recluse, had been found dead along a path through the woods. The man's throat had been torn, and police opinion was that a large and vicious dog had attacked him. But the reporter who wrote the article suggested the possibility that a wolf—or even a panther or a leopard—escaped from a circus or zoo might have caused the wounds.

I folded the clipping again and handed it back to Smith. It didn't mean anything, of course. It's easy to find stories like that if one looks for them. A man named Charles Fort found thousands of them and put them into four books he had written, books which were on my shelves.

This particular one was less mysterious than most. In fact, there wasn't any real mystery at all; undoubtedly some vicious dog had done the killing.

Just the same something prickled at the back of my neck.

It was the headline, really, not the article. It's funny what the word "unknown" and the thought back of it can do to you. If that story had been headed "Man Killed by Vicious Dog"—or by a lion or a crocodile or any other specified creature, however fierce and dangerous, there'd have been nothing frightening about it.

But an *"unknown beast"*—well, if you've got the same kind of imagination I have, you see what I mean. And if you haven't,

I can't explain.

I looked at Yehudi Smith, just in time to see him toss down his whisky—again like a conjuring trick. I handed him back the clipping and then refilled our glasses."

I said, "Interesting story. But where's the connection?"

"Our last meeting was in Bridgeport. That's all I can tell you. About that, I mean. You asked the nature of the danger; that's why I showed you that. And it's not too late for you to say no. It won't be, for that matter, until we get there."

"Get where?"

"Only a few miles from here. I have directions to guide me to a house on a road called the Dartown Pike. I have a car."

I said, irrelevantly, "So have I, but the tires are flat. Two of them."

I thought about the Dartown Pike. I said, "You wouldn't, by any chance, be heading for the house known as the Wentworth place?"

"That's the name, yes. You know of it?"

Right then and there, if I'd been completely sober, I'd have seen that the whole thing was too good to be true. I'd have smelled fish. Or blood.

I said, "We'll have to take candles or flashlights. That house has been empty since I was a kid. We used to call it a haunted house. Would that be why you chose it?" "Yes, of course."

"And your group is meeting there tonight?"

He nodded. "At one o'clock in the morning, to be exact. You're sure you're not afraid?"

God, yes, I was afraid. Who wouldn't be, after the build-up he'd just handed me?

So I grinned at him and said, "Sure, I'm afraid. But just try to keep me away."

Then I had an idea. If I was going to a haunted house at one o'clock in the morning to hunt jabberwocks or try to invoke the ghost of Lewis Carroll or some equally sensible thing, it wouldn't hurt to have someone along whom I already knew.

And if Al Grainger dropped in—I tried to figure out whether or not Al would be interested. He was a Carroll fan, all right, but—for the rest of it, I didn't know.

I said, "One question, Mr. Smith. A young friend of mine might drop in soon for a game of chess. How exclusive is this deal? I mean, would it be all right if he came along, if he wants to?"

"Do you think he's qualified?"

"Depends on what the qualifications are," I said. "Off-hand, I'd say you have to be a Lewis Carroll fan and a little crazy. Or, come to think of it, are those one and the same qualification?"

He laughed. "They're not too far apart. But tell me something about your friend. You said young friend; how young?"

"About twenty-three. Not long out of college. Good literary taste and background, which means he knows and likes Carroll. He can quote almost as much of it as I can. Plays chess, if that's a qualification—and I'd guess it is. Dodgson not only played chess but based *Through the Looking-Glass* on a chess game. His name, if that matters, is Al Grainger."

"Would he *want* to come?"

"Frankly," I admitted, "I haven't an idea on that angle."

Smith said, "I hope he comes; if he's a Carroll enthusiast, I'd like to meet him. But, if he comes, will you do me the favor of saying nothing about—what I've told you, at least until I've had a chance to judge him a bit? Frankly, it would be almost unprecedented if I took the liberty of inviting someone to an important meeting like tonight's on my own. You're being invited because we know quite a bit about you. You were voted on—and I might say that the vote to invite you was unanimous."

I remembered his familiarity with the two obscure things about Lewis Carroll that I'd written, and I didn't doubt that he—or they, if he really represented a group—did know something about me.

He said, "But—well, if I get a chance to meet him and think

he'd really fit in, I might take a chance and ask him. Can you tell me anything more about him? What does he do—for a living, I mean?"

That was harder to answer. I said, "Well, he's writing plays. But I don't think he makes a living at it; in fact, I don't know that he's ever sold any. He's a bit of a mystery to Carmel City. He's lived here all his life—except while he was away at college —and nobody knows where his money comes from. Has a swanky car and a place of his own—he lived there with his mother until she died a few years ago—and seems to have plenty of spending money, but nobody knows where it comes from." I grinned. "And it annoys the hell out of Carmel City not to know. You know how small towns are."

He nodded. "Wouldn't it be a logical assumption that he inherited the money?"

"From one point of view, yes. But it doesn't seem too likely. His mother worked all her life as a milliner, and without owning her own shop. The town, I remember, used to wonder how she managed to own her own house and send her son to college on what she earned. But she couldn't possibly have earned enough to have done both of those things and still have left him enough money to have supported him in idleness— Well, maybe writing plays isn't idleness, but it isn't remunerative unless you sell them—for several years."

I shrugged. "But there's probably no mystery to it. She must have had an income from investments her husband had made, and Al either inherited the income or got the capital from which it came. He probably doesn't talk about his business because he enjoys being mysterious."

"Was his father wealthy?"

"His father died before he was born, and before Mrs. Grainger moved to Carmel City. So nobody here knew his father. And I guess that's all I can tell you about Al, except that he can beat me at chess most of the time, and that I hope you'll have a chance to meet him."

Smith nodded. "If he comes, we'll see."

He glanced at his empty glass and I took the hint and filled it and my own. Again I watched the incredible manner of his drinking it, fascinated. I'd swear that, this time, the glass came no closer than six inches from his lips. Definitely it was a trick I'd have to learn myself. If for no other reason than that I don't really like the taste of whisky, much as I enjoy the effects of it. With his way of drinking, it didn't seem that he had the slightest chance of tasting the stuff. It was there, in the glass, and then it was gone. His Adam's apple didn't seem to work and if he was talking at the time he drank there was scarcely an interruption in what he was saying.

The phone rang. I excused myself and answered it.

"Doc," said Clyde Andrews' voice, "this is Clyde Andrews."

"Fine," I said, "I suppose you realize that you sabotaged my this week's issue by canceling a story on my front page. What's called off this time?"

"I'm sorry about that, Doc, if it really inconvenienced you, but with the sale called off, I thought you wouldn't want to run the story and have people coming around to—"

"Of course," I interrupted him. I was impatient to get back to my conversation with Yehudi Smith. "That's all right, Clyde. But what do you want now?"

"I want to know if you've decided whether or not you want to sell the *Clarion.*"

For a second I was unreasonably angry. I said, "God damn it, Clyde, you interrupt the only really interesting conversation I've had in years to ask me that, when we've been talking about it for months, off and on? *I* don't know. I do and I don't want to sell it."

"Sorry for heckling you, Doc, but I just got a special delivery letter from my brother in Ohio. He's got an offer out West. Says he'd rather come to Carmel City on the proposition I'd made to him—contingent on your deciding to sell me the *Clarion,* of course. But he's got to accept the other offer right away—within a day or so, that is—if he's going to accept it at all.

"So you see that makes it different, Doc. I've got to know right away. Not tonight, necessarily; it isn't in that much of a rush. But I've got to know by tomorrow sometime, so I thought I'd call you right away so you could start coming to a decision."

I nodded and then realized that he couldn't see me nod so I said, "Sure, Clyde, I get it. I'm sorry for popping off. All right, I'll make up my mind by tomorrow morning. I'll let you know one way or the other by then. Okay?"

"Fine," he said. "That'll be plenty of time. Oh, by the way, there's an item of news for you if it's not too late to put it in. Or have you already got it?"

"Got what?"

"About the escaped maniac. I don't know the details, but a friend of mine just drove over from Neilsville and he says they're stopping cars and watching the roads both sides of the county asylum. Guess you can get the details if you call the asylum."

"Thanks, Clyde," I said.

I put the phone back down in its cradle and looked at Yehudi Smith. I wondered why, with all the fantastic things he'd said, I hadn't already guessed.

CHAPTER FOUR

"But wait a bit," the Oyster cried,
"Before we have our chat;
For some of us are out of breath,
And all of us are fat!"

I FELT a hell of a letdown. Oh, not that I'd really quite believed in the Vorpal Blades or that we were going to a haunted house to conjure up a Jabberwock or whatever we'd have done there.

But it had been exciting even to think about it, just as one can get excited over a chess game even though he knows that the kings and queens on the board aren't real entities and that when a bishop slays a knight no real blood is shed. I guess it had been that kind of excitement, the vicarious kind, that I'd felt about the things Yehudi Smith had promised. Or maybe a better comparison would be that it had been like reading an exciting fiction story that one knows isn't true but which one can believe in for as long as the story lasts.

Now there wasn't even that. Across from me, I realized with keen disappointment, was only a man who'd escaped from an insane asylum. Yehudi, the little man who wasn't there—mentally.

The funny part of it was that I still liked him. He was a nice little guy and he'd given me a fascinating half hour, up to now. I hated the fact that I'd have to turn him over to the asylum guards and have him put back where he came from.

Well, I thought, at least it would give me a news story to fill that nine-inch hole in the front page of the *Clarion*.

He said, "I hope the call wasn't anything that will spoil our plans, Doctor."

It had spoiled more than that, but of course I couldn't tell him so, any more than I could have told Clyde Andrews over the phone, in Smith's presence, to call the asylum and tell them to drop around to my house if they wanted to collect their bolted nut.

So I shook my head while I figured out an angle to get out of the house and to put in the phone call from next door.

I stood up. Perhaps I was a bit more drunk than I'd thought, for I had to catch my balance. I remember how crystal clear my mind seemed to be—but of course nothing seems more crystal clear than a prism that makes you see around corners.

I said, "No, the call won't interrupt our plans except for a few minutes. I've got to give a message to the man next door. Excuse me—and help yourself to the whisky."

I went through the kitchen and outside into the black night. There were lights in the houses on either side of me, and I wondered which of my neighbors to bother. And then I wondered why I was in such a hurry to bother either of them.

Surely, I thought, the man who called himself Yehudi Smith wasn't dangerous. And, crazy or not, he was the most interesting man I'd met in years. He *did* seem to know something about Lewis Carroll. And I remembered again that he'd known about *my* obscure brochure and equally obscure magazine article. How?

So, come to think of it, why shouldn't I stall making that phone call for another hour or so, and relax and enjoy myself? Now that I was over the first disappointment of learning that he was insane, why wouldn't I find talk about that delusion of his almost as interesting as though it was factual.

Interesting in a different way, of course. Often I had thought I'd like the chance to talk to a paranoiac about his delusions—neither arguing with him nor agreeing with him, just trying to find out what made him tick.

And the evening was still a pup; it couldn't be later than about half past eight so my neighbors would be up at least another hour or two.

So why was I in a hurry to make that call? I wasn't.

Of course I had to kill enough time outside to make it reasonable to believe that I'd actually gone next door and delivered a message, so I stood there at the bottom of my back steps, looking up at the black velvet sky, star-studded but moonless, and wondering what was behind it and why madmen were mad. And how strange it would be if one of them was right and all the rest of us were crazy instead.

Then I went back inside and I was cowardly enough to do a ridiculous thing. From the kitchen I went into my bedroom and to my closet. In a shoebox on the top shelf was a short-barreled thirty-eight caliber revolver, one of the compact, lightweight models they call a Banker's Special. I'd never shot at anything with it and hoped that I never would—and I wasn't sure I could hit anything smaller than an elephant or farther away than a couple of yards. I don't even like guns. I hadn't bought this one; an acquaintance had once borrowed twenty bucks from me and had insisted on my taking the pistol for security. And later he'd wanted another five and said if I gave it to him I could keep the gun. I hadn't wanted it, but he'd needed the five pretty badly and I'd given it to him.

It was still loaded with bullets that were in it when we'd made the deal four or five years ago, and I didn't know whether they'd still shoot or not, but I put it in my trouser pocket. I wouldn't use it, of course, except in dire extremity—and I'd miss anything I shot at even then, but I thought that just carrying the gun would make my coming conversation seem dangerous and exciting, more than it would be otherwise.

I went into the living room and he was still there. He hadn't poured himself a drink, so I poured one for each of us and then sat down on the sofa again.

I lifted my drink and over the rim of it watched him do that marvelous trick again—just a toss of the glass toward his lips. I drank my own less spectacularly and said, "I wish I had a movie camera. I'd like to film the way you do that and then study it in slow motion."

He laughed. "Afraid it's my one way of showing off. I used to be a juggler once."

"And now? If you don't mind my asking."

"A student," he said. "A student of Lewis Carroll—and mathematics."

"Is there a living in it?" I asked him.

He hesitated just a second. "Do you mind if I defer answering that until you've learned—what you'll learn at tonight's meeting?"

Of course there wasn't going to be any meeting tonight; I knew that now. But I said, "Not at all. But I hope you don't mean that we can't talk about Carroll, in general, until after the meeting."

I hoped he'd give the right answer to that; it would mean that I could get him going on the subject of his mania.

He said, "Of course not. In fact, I *want* to talk about him. There are facts I want to give you that will enable you to understand things better. Some of the facts you already know, but I'll refresh you on them anyway. For instance, dates. You had his birth and death dates correct, or nearly enough so. But do you know the dates of the Alice books or any other of his works? The sequence is important."

"Not exactly," I told him. "I think that he wrote the first Alice book when he was comparatively young, about thirty."

"Close. He was thirty-two. *Alice in Wonderland* was published in eighteen sixty-three, but even before then he was on the trail of something. Do you know what he had published before that?"

I shook my head.

"Two books. He wrote and published *A Syllabus of Plane Geometry* in eighteen sixty and in the year after that his *Formulae of Plane Trigonometry.* Have you read either of them?"

I had to shake my head again. I said, "Mathematics isn't my forte. I've read only his non-technical books."

He smiled. "There aren't any. You simply failed to recognize the mathematics embodied in the Alice books and in his poetry. You do know, I'm sure, that many of his poems are acrostics."

"Of course."

"All of them are acrostics, but in a much more subtle manner. However, I can see why you failed to find the clues if you haven't read his treatises on mathematics.

You wouldn't have read his *Elementary Treatise on Determinants,* I suppose. But how about his *Curiosa Mathematica?*"

I hated to disappoint him again, but I had to.

He frowned at me. "That at least you should have read. It's not technical at all, and most of the clues to the fantasies are contained in it. There are further—and final—references to them in his *Symbolic Logic,* published in eighteen ninety-six, just two years before his death, but they are less direct."

I said, "Now, wait a minute. If I understand you correctly your thesis is that Lewis Carroll—leaving aside any question of who or what he really was—worked out through mathematics and expressed in fantasy the fact that—what?"

"That there is another plane of existence besides the one we are now living in. That we can have—and do sometimes have—access to it."

"But what kind of a plane? A through-the-looking-glass plane of fantasy, a dream plane?"

"Exactly, Doctor. A dream plane. That isn't strictly accurate, but it's about as nearly as I can explain it to you just yet." He leaned forward. "Consider dreams. Aren't they the almost perfect parallel of the Alice adventures? The wool-and-water sequence, for instance, where everything Alice looks at changes into something else. Remember in the shop, with the old sheep knitting, how Alice looked hard to see what was on the shelves, but the shelf she looked at was always empty although the others about it were always full—of something, and she never found out what?"

I nodded slowly. I said, "Her comment was, 'Things flow about so here.' And then the sheep asked if Alice could row and handed her a pair of knitting needles and the needles turned into oars in her hands and she was in a boat, with the sheep still knitting."

"Exactly, Doctor. A perfect dream sequence. And consider that *Jabberwocky*—which is probably the best thing in the second Alice book—is in the very *language* of dreams. It's full of words like *frumious, manxome, tulgey,* words that give you a perfect picture in context—but you can't put your finger on what the context is. In a dream you fully understand such meanings, but you forget them when you awaken."

Between *"manxome"* and *"tulgey"* he'd downed his latest drink. I didn't pour another this time; I was beginning to wonder how long the bottle—or we—would last. But he showed no effect whatsoever from the drinks he'd been downing. I can't quite say the same for myself. I knew my voice was getting a bit thick.

I said, "But why postulate the *reality* of such a world? I can see your point otherwise. The Jabberwock itself is the epitome of nightmare creatures—with eyes of flame and jaws that bite and claws that catch, and it whiffles and burbles—why, Freud and James Joyce in tandem couldn't have done any better. But why not take it that Lewis Carroll was trying, and damned successfully, to write as in a dream? Why make the assumption that that world is real? Why talk of getting through to it—except, of course, in the sense that we invade it nightly in our dreams?"

He smiled. "Because that world *is* real, Doctor. You'll hear evidence of that tonight, mathematical evidence. And, I hope, actual proof. I've had such proof myself, and I hope you'll have. But you'll see the calculations, at least, and it will be explained to you how they were derived from *Curiosa Mathematica,* and then corroborated by evidence found in the other books.

"Carroll was more than a century ahead of his time, Doctor. Have you read of the recent experiments with the subconscious made by Liebnitz and Winton—the feelers they're putting forth in the right direction, which is the mathematical approach?"

I admitted I hadn't heard of Liebnitz or Winton.

"They aren't well known," he conceded. "You see, only recently, except for Carroll, has anyone even considered the possibility of our reaching—let's call it the dream plane until I've shown you what it really is—physically as well as mentally."

"As Lewis Carroll reached it?"

"As he must have, to have known the things he knew. Things so revolutionary and dangerous that he did not dare reveal them openly."

For a fleeting moment it sounded so reasonable that I wondered if it *could* be true. Why not? Why couldn't there be other dimensions beside our own? Why couldn't a brilliant mathematician with a fantastic mind have found a way through to one of them?

In my mind, I cussed out Clyde Andrews for having told me about the asylum break. If only I hadn't learned about that, what a wonderful evening this one would be. Even knowing Smith was insane, I found myself—possibly with the whisky's help—wondering if he could be right. How marvelous it would have been without the knowledge of his insanity to temper the wonder and the wondering. It would have been an evening in Wonderland.

And, sane or crazy, I liked him. Sane or crazy, he belonged figuratively in the department in which Mrs. Carr's husband worked literally. I laughed and then, of course, I had to explain what I'd been laughing about.

His eyes lighted. "The Roman candle department. That's marvelous. The Roman candle department."

You see what I mean.

We had a drink to the Roman candle department, and then it happened that neither of us said anything right away and it was so quiet that I jumped when the phone rang.

I picked it up and said into it, "This is the Roman candle department."

"Doc?" It was the voice of Pete Corey, my printer. It sounded tense. "I've got bad news."

Pete doesn't get excited easily. I sobered up a little and asked, "What, Pete?"

"Listen, Doc. Remember just a couple of hours ago you were saying you wished a murder or something would happen so you'd have a story for the paper—and remember how I asked you if you'd like one even if it happened to a friend of yours?"

Of course I remembered; he'd mentioned my best friend, Carl Trenholm. I took a tighter grip on the phone. I said, "Cut out breaking it gently, Pete. Has something happened to Carl?"

"Yes, Doc."

"For God's sake, what? Cut the build-up. Is he dead?"

"That's what I heard. He was found out on the pike; I don't know if he was hit by a car or what."

"Where is he now?"

"Being brought in, I guess. All I know is that Hank called me—" Hank is Pete's brother-in-law and a deputy sheriff. "—and said they got a call from someone who found him alongside the road out there. Even Hank had it third-hand— Rance Kates phoned him and said to come down and take care of the office while he went out there. And Hank knows Kates doesn't like you and wouldn't give you the tip, so Hank called me. But don't get Hank in trouble with his boss by telling anybody where the tip came from."

"Did you call the hospital?" I asked. "If Carl's just hurt—"

"Wouldn't be time for them to get him there yet—or to wherever they do take him. Hank just phoned me from his own place before he started for the sheriff's office, and Kates had just called him from the office and was just leaving there."

"Okay, Pete," I said. "Thanks. I'm going back downtown; I'll call the hospital from the *Clarion* office. You call me there if you hear anything more."

"Hell, Doc, I'm coming down too."

I told him he didn't have to, but he said the hell with having to; he wanted to. I didn't argue with him.

I cradled the phone and found that I was already standing up. I said, "Sony, but something important's come up—an accident to a friend of mine." I headed for the closet to get my coat. "Do you want to wait here—or—"

"If you don't mind," he said. "That is, if you think you won't be gone very long."

"I don't know that, but I'll phone here and let you know as soon as I can. If the phone rings answer it; it'll be me. And help yourself to whisky and books."

He nodded. "I'll get along fine. Hope your friend isn't seriously hurt."

That was all I was worrying about myself. I put on my hat and hurried out, again, and this time seriously, cussing those two flat tires on my car and the fact that I hadn't taken time to fix them that morning. Nine blocks isn't far to walk when you're not in any hurry, but it's a hell of a distance when you're anxious to get there quickly.

I walked fast, so fast, in fact, that I winded myself in the first two blocks and had to slow down.

I kept thinking the same thing Pete had obviously thought —what a hell of a coincidence it was that we'd mentioned the possibility of Carl's being—

But we'd been talking about murder. Had Carl been murdered? Of course not; things like that didn't happen in Carmel City. It must have been an accident, a hit-run driver. No one would have the slightest reason for killing, of all people, Carl Trenholm. No one but a—

Finishing that thought made me stop walking suddenly. *No one but a maniac* would have the slightest reason for killing Carl Trenholm. But there was an escaped maniac at large tonight and—unless he'd left instead of waiting for me—he was sitting right in my living room. I'd thought he was harmless— even though I'd taken the precaution of putting that gun in my pocket—but how could I be sure? I'm no psychiatrist; where did I get the bright idea that I could tell the difference between a harmless nut and a homicidal maniac?

I started to turn back and then realized that going back was useless and foolish. He would either have left as soon as I was out of sight around the corner, or he hadn't guessed that I suspected him and would wait as I'd told him to, until he heard from me. So all I had to do was to phone the asylum as soon as I could and they'd send guards to close in on my house and take him if he was still there.

I started walking again. Yes, it would be ridiculous for me to go back alone, even though I still had that gun in my pocket. He might resist, and I wouldn't want to have to use the gun, especially as I hadn't any real reason to believe he'd killed Carl. It could have been an auto accident just as easily; I couldn't even form an intelligent opinion on that until I learned what Carl's injuries were.

I kept walking, as fast as I could without winding myself again.

Suddenly I thought of that newspaper clipping—"MAN SLAIN BY UNKNOWN BEAST." A prickle went down my spine—*what if Carl's body showed*—

And then the horrible thought pyramided. What if the *unknown beast* who had killed the man near Bridgeport and the escaped maniac were one and the same. What if he had escaped before at the time of the killing at Bridgeport—or, for that matter, hadn't been committed to the asylum until after that killing, whether or not he was suspected of it.

I thought of lycanthropy, and shivered. *What* might I have been talking about Jabberwocks and unknown beasts with?

Suddenly the gun I'd put in my pocket felt comforting there. I looked around over my shoulder to be sure that nothing was coming after me. The street behind was empty, but I started walking a little faster just the same.

Suddenly the street lights weren't bright enough and the night, which had been a pleasant June evening, was a frightful, menacing thing. I was really scared. Maybe it's as well that I didn't guess that things hadn't even started to happen.

I felt glad that I was passing the courthouse—with a light on in the window of the sheriff's office. I even considered going in. Probably Hank would be there by now and Rance Kates would still be gone. But no, I was this far now and I'd carry on to the *Clarion* office and start my phoning from there. Besides, if Kates found out I'd been in his office talking to Hank, Hank would be in trouble.

So I kept on going. The corner of Oak Street, and I turned, now only a block and a half from the *Clarion*. But it was going to take me quite a while to make that block and a half.

A big, dark blue Buick sedan suddenly pulled near the curb and slowed down alongside me. There were two men in the front seat and the one who was driving stuck his head out of the window and said, "Hey, Buster, what town is this?"

CHAPTER FIVE

When the sands are all dry, he is gay as a lark,
And will talk in contemptuous tones of the Shark:
But, when the tide rises and sharks are around,
His voice has a timid and tremulous sound.

IT HAD BEEN a long time since anyone had called me "Buster," and I didn't particularly like it. I didn't like the looks of the men, either, or the tone of voice the question had been asked in. A minute ago, I'd thought I'd be glad of any company short of that of the escaped maniac; now I decided differently.

I'm not often rude, but I can be when someone else starts it. I said, "Sony, pal, I'm a stranger here myself." And I kept on walking.

I heard the man behind the wheel of the Buick say something to the other, and then they passed me and swung in to the curb just ahead. The driver got out and walked toward me.

I stopped short and tried not to do a double-take when I recognized him. My attention to the wanted circulars on the post office bulletin board was about to pay off—although from the expression on his face, the payoff wasn't going to be the kind I'd want.

The man coming toward me and only two steps away when I stopped was Bat Masters, whose picture had been posted only last week and was still there on the board. I couldn't be wrong about his face, and I remembered the name clearly because of its similarity to the name of Bat Masterson, the famous gunman

of the old West. I'd thought of it as a coincidence at first and
then I realized that the similarity of Masters to Masterson had
made the nickname "Bat" a natural.

He was a big man with a long, horse-like face, eyes wide
apart and a mouth that was a narrow straight line separating a
lantern jaw from a wide upper lip; on the latter there was a two-
day stubble of hair that indicated he was starting a mustache.
But it would have taken plastic surgery and a full beard to
disguise that face from anyone who had recently, however
casually, studied a picture of it. Bat Masters, bank robber and
killer.

I had a gun in my pocket, but I didn't remember it at the
time. It's probably just as well; if I'd remembered, I might have
been frightened into reaching for it. And that probably would
not have been a healthful thing to do. He was coming at me
with his fists balled but no gun in either of them. He didn't
intend to kill me—although one of those fists might do it quite
easily and unintentionally. I weigh a hundred and forty wring-
ing wet, and he weighed almost twice that and had shoulders
that bulged out his suit coat.

There wasn't even time to turn and run. His left hand came
out and caught the front of my coat and pulled me toward him,
almost lifting me off the sidewalk.

He said, "Listen, Pop, I don't want any lip. I asked you a
question."

"Carmel City," I said. "Carmel City, Illinois."

The voice of the other man, still in the car, came back to us.
"Hey, Bill, don't hurt the guy. We don't want to—" He didn't
finish the sentence, of course; to say you don't want to attract
attention is the best way of drawing it.

Masters looked past me—right over my head—to see if
anybody or anything was coming that way and then, still
keeping his grip on the front of my coat, turned and looked the
other way. He wasn't afraid of my swinging at him enough to
bother keeping his eyes on me, and I didn't blame him for

feeling that way about it.

A car was coming now, about a block away. And two men came out of the drugstore on the opposite side of the street, only a few buildings down. Then behind me I could hear the sound of another car turning into Oak Street.

Masters turned back to me and let go, so we were just two men standing there face to face if anyone noticed us. He said, "Okay, Pop. Next time somebody asks you a question, don't be so God damn fresh."

He still glared at me as though he hadn't yet completely given up the idea of giving me something to remember him by —maybe just a light open-handed slap that wouldn't do anything worse than crack my jawbone and drive my dentures down my throat.

I said, "Sure, sorry," and let my voice sound afraid, but tried not to sound quite as afraid as I really was—because if he even remotely suspected that I might have recognized him, I wasn't going to get out of it at all.

He swung around and walked back to the car, got in and drove off. I suppose I should have got the license number, but it would have been a stolen car anyway—and besides I didn't think of it. I didn't even watch the car as it drove away; if either of them looked back I didn't want them to think I was giving them what criminals call the big-eye. I didn't want to give them any possible reason to change their minds about going on.

I started walking again, keeping to the middle of the sidewalk and trying to look like a man minding his own business. Also trying to keep my knees from shaking so hard that I couldn't walk at all. It had been a narrow squeak all right. If the street had been completely empty—

I could have notified the sheriff's office about a minute quicker by turning around and going back that way, but I didn't take the chance. If someone was watching me out of the back window of the car, a change in direction wouldn't be a good idea. There was a difference of only a block anyway; I was half a block past the courthouse and a block and a half from Smiley's and the *Clarion* office across the street from it. From either one I could phone in the big news that Bat Masters and a companion had just driven through Carmel City heading north, probably toward Chicago. And Hank Ganzer, in the sheriff's office, would relay the story to the state police and there was probably better than an even chance that they'd be caught within an hour or two.

And if they were, I might even get a slice of the reward for giving the tip—but I didn't care as much about that as about the story I was going to have. Why, it was a story, even if they weren't caught, and if they were, it would be a really big one. And a local story—if the tip came from Carmel City—even if they were actually caught several counties north. Maybe there'd even be a gun battle—from my all too close look at Masters I had a hunch that there would be.

Perfect timing, too, I thought. For once something was happening on a Thursday night. For once I'd beat the Chicago papers. They'd have the story, too, of course, and a lot of Carmel City people take Chicago dailies, but they don't come in until the late afternoon train and the *Clarion* would be out hours before that.

Yes, for once I was going to have a newspaper with *news* in it. Even if Masters and his pal weren't caught, the fact that they'd passed through town made a story. And besides that, there was the escaped maniac, and Carl Trenholm

Thinking about Carl again made me walk faster. It was safe by now; I'd gone a quarter of a block since the Buick had driven off. It wasn't anywhere in sight and again the street was quiet; thank God it hadn't been this quiet while Masters had been making up his mind whether or not to slug me.

I was past Deak's Music Store, dark. Past the supermarket, ditto. The bank—

I had passed the bank, too, when I stopped as suddenly as though I'd run into a wall. The bank had been dark too. And it shouldn't have been; there's a small night light that always burns over the safe. I'd passed the bank thousands of times after dark and never before had that light been off.

For a moment the wild thought went through my head that Bat and his companion must have just burglarized the bank—although robbery, not burglary, was Masters' trade—and then I saw how ridiculous that thought had been. They'd been driving toward the bank and a quarter of a block away from it when they'd stopped to ask me what town they were in. True, they could have burglarized the bank and then circled the block in their car, but if they had they'd have been intent on their getaway. Criminals do pretty silly things sometimes but not quite so silly as to stop a getaway car within spitting distance of the scene of the crime to ask what town they're in, and then to top it by getting out of the car to slug a random pedestrian because they don't like his answer to their question.

No, Masters and company couldn't have robbed the bank. And they couldn't be burglarizing it now, either. Their car had gone on past; I hadn't watched it, but my ears had told me that it had kept on going. And even if it hadn't, I had. My encounter with them had been only seconds ago; there wasn't possibly time for them to have broken in there, even if they'd stopped.

I went back a few steps and looked into the window of the bank.

At first I saw nothing except the vague silhouette of a window at the back—the top half of the window, that is, which was visible above the counter. Then the silhouette became less vague and I could see that the window had been opened; the top bar of the lower sash showed, clearly, only a few inches from the top of the frame.

That was the means of entry all right—but was the burglar still in there, or had he left, and left the window open behind him?

I strained my eyes against the blackness to the left of the window, where the safe was. And suddenly a dim light flickered briefly, as though a match had been struck but had gone out before the phosphorus had ignited the wood. I could see only the brief light of it, as it was below the level of the counter; I couldn't see whoever had lighted it.

The burglar was still there.

And suddenly I was running on tiptoe back through the areaway between the bank and the post office.

Good God, don't ask me *why*. Sure, I had money in the bank, but the bank had insurance against burglary and it wasn't any skin off my backside if the bank was robbed. I wasn't even thinking that it would be a better story for the *Clarion* if I got the burglar—or if he got me. I just wasn't thinking at all. I was running back alongside the bank toward that window that he'd left open for his getaway.

I think it must have been reaction from the cowardice I'd shown and felt only a minute before. I must have been a bit punch drunk from Jabberwocks and Vorpal Blades and homicidal maniacs with lycanthropy and bank bandits and a bank burglar—or maybe I thought I'd suddenly been promoted to the Roman candle department.

Maybe I was drunk, maybe I was a little mentally unbalanced—use any maybe you want, but there I was running tiptoe through the areaway. Running, that is, as far as the light from the street would let me; then I groped along the side of the building until I came to the alley. There was dim light there, enough for me to be able to see the window.

It was still open.

I stood there looking at it and vaguely beginning to realize how crazy I'd been. Why hadn't I run to the sheriff's office for Hank? The burglar—or, for all I knew, burglars—might be just starting his work on the safe in there. He might be in a long time, long enough for Hank to get here and collar him. If he came out now, what was I going to do about it? Shoot him? That was ridiculous; I'd rather let him get away with robbing the bank than do that.

And then it was too late because suddenly there was a soft shuffling sound from the window and a hand appeared on the sill. He was coming out, and there wasn't a chance that I could get away without his hearing me. What would happen then, I didn't know. I would just as soon not find out.

A moment before, just as I'd reached the place beside the window where I now stood, I'd stepped on a piece of wood, a one-by-two stick of it about a foot long. That was a weapon I could understand. I reached down and grabbed it and swung, just in time, as a head came through the window.

Thank God I didn't swing too hard. At the last second, even in that faint light, I'd thought—

The head and the hand weren't in the window anymore and there was the soft thud of a body falling inside. There wasn't any sound or movement for seconds. Long seconds, and then there was the sound of my stick of wood hitting the dirt of the alley and I knew I'd dropped it.

If it hadn't been for what I'd thought I'd seen in that last fraction of a second before it was too late to stop the blow, I could have run now for the sheriff's office. But—

Maybe here went *my* head, but I had to chance it. The sill of the window wasn't much over waist high. I leaned across it and struck a match, and I'd been right.

I climbed in the window and felt for his heart and it was beating all right. He seemed to be breathing normally. I ran my hands very gently over his head and then held them in the open window to look at them; there wasn't any blood. There could be, then, nothing worse than a concussion.

I lowered the window so nobody would notice that it was open and then I felt my way carefully toward the nearest desk— I'd been in the bank thousands of times; I knew its layout—and groped for a telephone until I found one.

The operator's voice said, "Number, please?" and I started to give it and then remembered; she'd know where the call came from and that the bank was closed. Naturally, she'd listen in.

Maybe she'd even call the sheriff s office to tell them someone was using the telephone in the bank.

Had I recognized her voice? I'd thought I had. I said, "Is this Milly?"

"Yes. Is this—Mr. Stoeger?"

"Right," I said. I was glad she'd known *my* voice. "Listen, Milly, I'm calling from the bank, but it's all right. You don't need to worry about it. And—do me a favor, will you? Please don't listen in."

"All right, Mr. Stoeger. Sure. What number do you want?"

I gave it; the number of Clyde Andrews, president of the bank. As I heard the ringing of the phone at the other end, I thought how lucky it was that I'd known Milly all her life and that we liked one another. I knew that she'd be burning with curiosity but that she wouldn't listen in.

Clyde Andrews' voice answered. I was still careful about what I said because I didn't know offhand whether he was on a party line.

I said, "This is Doc Stoeger, Clyde. I'm down at the bank. Get down here right away. Hurry."

"Huh? Doc, are you drunk or something? What would you be doing at the bank. It's closed."

I said, "Somebody was inside here. I hit him over the head with a piece of wood when he started back out of the window, and he's unconscious but not hurt bad. But just to be sure, pick up Doc Minton on your way here. And hurry."

"Sure," he said. "Are you phoning the sheriff or shall I?"

"Neither of us. Don't phone anybody. Just get Minton and get here quick."

"But—I don't get it. Why not phone the sheriff? Is this a gag?"

I said, "No, Clyde. Listen—you'll want to see the burglar first. He isn't badly hurt, but for God's sake quit arguing and get down here with Dr. Minton. Do you understand?"

His tone of voice was different when he said, "I'll be there. Five minutes."

I put the receiver back on the phone and then lifted it again. The "Number, please" was Milly's voice again and I asked her if she knew anything about Carl Trenholm.

She didn't; she hadn't known anything had happened at all. When I told her what little I knew she said yes, that she'd routed a call from a farmhouse out on the pike to the sheriff's office about half an hour before, but she'd had several other calls around the same time and hadn't listened in on it.

I decided that I'd better wait until I was somewhere else before I called to report either Bat Masters' passing through or about the escaped maniac at my own house. It wouldn't be safe to risk making the call from here, and a few more minutes wouldn't matter a lot.

I went back, groping my way through the dark toward the dim square of the window, and bent down again by the boy, Clyde Andrews' son. His breathing and his heart were still okay and he moved a little and muttered something as though he was coming out of it. I don't know anything about concussion, but I thought that was a good sign and felt better. It would have been terrible if I'd swung a little harder and had killed him or injured him seriously.

I sat down on the floor so my head would be out of the line of sight if anyone looked in the front window, as I had a few minutes before, and waited.

So much had been happening that I felt a little numb. There was so much to think about that I guess I didn't think about any of it. I just sat there in the dark.

When the phone rang I jumped about two feet.

I groped to it and answered it. Milly's voice said, "Mr. Stoeger, I thought I'd better tell you if you're still there. Somebody from the drugstore across the street just phoned the sheriff's office and said the night light in the bank is out, and whoever answered at the sheriff's office—it sounded like one of the deputies, not Mr. Kates—said they'd come right around."

I said, "Thanks, Milly. Thanks a lot."

A car was pulling up at the curb outside; I could see it through the window. I breathed a sigh of relief when I recognized the men getting out of it as Clyde Andrews and the doctor.

I switched on the lights inside while Clyde was unlocking the front door. I told him quickly about the call that had been made to the sheriff's office while I was leading them back to where Harvey Andrews was lying. We moved him slightly to a point where neither he nor Dr. Minton, bending over him, could be seen from the front of the bank, and we did it just in time. Hank was rapping on the door.

I stayed out of sight, too, to avoid having to explain what I was doing there. I heard Clyde Andrews open the door for Hank and explain that everything was all right, that someone had phoned him, too, that the night light was out and that he'd just got here to check up and that the bulb had merely burned out.

When Hank left, Clyde came back, his face a bit white. Dr. Minton said, "He's going to be all right, Clyde. Starting to come out of it. Soon as he can walk between us, we'll get him to the hospital for a checkup and be sure."

I said, "Clyde, I've got to run. There's a lot popping tonight. But as soon as you're sure the boy's all right will you let me know? I'll probably be at the *Clarion,* but I might be at Smiley's—or if it's a long time from now, I might be home."

"Sure, Doc." He put his hand on my shoulder. "And thanks a lot for—calling me instead of the sheriff's office."

"That's all right," I told him. "And, Clyde, I didn't know who it was before I hit. He was coming out of the back window and I thought—"

Clyde said, "I looked in his room after you phoned. He'd packed. I—I can't understand it, Doc. He's only fifteen. Why he'd do a thing like—" He shook his head. "He's always been headstrong and he's got into little troubles a few times, but—I don't understand this." He looked at me very earnestly. "Do you?"

I thought maybe I did understand a little of it, but I was remembering about Bat Masters and the fact that he was getting farther away every minute and that *I'd* better get the state police notified pretty quickly.

So I said, "Can I talk to you about it tomorrow, Clyde? Get the boy's side of it when he can talk—and just try to keep your mind open until then. I think—it may not be as bad as you think right now."

I left him still looking like a man who's just taken an almost mortal blow, and went out.

I headed down the street thinking what a damn fool I'd been to do what I'd done. But then, where had I missed a chance to do something wrong anywhere down the line tonight? And then, on second thought, this one thing might not have been wrong. If I'd called Hank, the boy just might have been shot instead of knocked out. And in any case he'd have been arrested.

That would have been bad. This way, there was a chance he could be straightened out before it was too late. Maybe a psychiatrist could help him. The only thing was, Clyde Andrews would have to realize that he, too, would have to take advice from the psychiatrist. He was a good man, but a hard father. You can't expect the things of a fifteen-year-old boy that Clyde expected of Harvey, and not have something go wrong somewhere down the line. But burglarizing a bank, even his own father's bank—I couldn't make up my mind whether that made it better or worse—was certainly something I hadn't looked for. It appalled me, a bit. Harvey's running away from home wouldn't have surprised me at all; I don't know that I'd even have blamed him.

A man can be too good a man and too conscientious and strict a father for his son ever to be able to love him. If Clyde Andrews would only get drunk—good and stinking drunk—just once in his life, he might get an entirely different perspective on things, even if he never again took another drink. But he'd never taken a drink yet, not one in his whole life. I don't think he'd ever smoked a cigarette or said a naughty word.

I liked him anyway; I'm pretty tolerant, I guess. But I'm glad I hadn't had a father like him. In my books, the man in town who was the best father was Carl Trenholm. Trenholm— and I hadn't found out yet whether he was dead or only injured!

I was only half a block, now, from Smiley's and the *Clarion*. I broke into a trot. Even at my age, it wouldn't wind me to trot that far. It had probably been less than half an hour since I'd left home, but with the things that had happened en route, it seemed like days. Well, anyway, nothing could happen to me between here and Smiley's. And nothing did.

I could see through the glass that there weren't any customers at the bar and that Smiley was alone behind it. Polishing glasses, as always; I think he must polish the same glasses a dozen times over when there's nothing else for him to do.

I burst in and headed for the telephone. I said, "Smiley, hell's popping tonight. There's an escaped lunatic, and something's happened to Carl Trenholm, and a couple of wanted bank robbers drove through here fifteen or twenty minutes ago and I got to—"

I was back by the telephone by the time I'd said all that and I was reaching up for the receiver. But I never quite touched it.

A voice behind me said, "Take it easy, Buster."

CHAPTER SIX

"What matters it how far we go?" his scaly friend replied.
"The further off from England the nearer is to France.
There is another shore, you know, upon the other side.
Then turn not pale, beloved snail, but come and join the
dance ."

I TURNED around slowly. They'd been sitting at the table around the el of the tavern, the one table that can't be seen through the glass of the door or the windows. They'd probably picked it for that reason. The beer glasses in front of them were empty. But I didn't think the guns in their hands would be.

One of the guns—the one in the hand of Bat Masters' companion—was aimed at Smiley. And Smiley, not smiling, was keeping his hands very still, not moving a muscle.

The gun in Masters' hand was aimed at me.

He said, "So you knew us, huh, Buster?"

There wasn't any use denying it; I'd said too much already. I said, "You're Bat Masters." I looked at the other man, whom I hadn't seen clearly before, when he'd been in the car. He was squat and stocky, with a bullet head and little pig eyes. He looked like a caricature of a German army officer. I said, "I'm sorry; I don't know your friend."

Masters laughed. He said, "See, George, I'm famous and you're not. How'd you like that?"

George kept his eyes on Smiley. He said, "I think you better come around this side of the bar. You just might have a gun back there and take a notion to dive for it."

"Come on over and sit with us," Masters said. "Both of you. Let's make it a party, huh, George?"

George said, "Shut up," which changed my opinion of George quite a bit. I personally wouldn't have cared to tell Bat Masters to shut up, and in that tone of voice. True, I *had* been fresh with him about twenty minutes before, but I hadn't known who he was. I hadn't even seen how big he was.

Smiley was coming around the end of the bar. I caught his eye, and gave him what was probably a pretty sickly grin. I said, "I'm sorry, Smiley. Looks like I put our foot in it this time."

His face was completely impassive. He said, "Not your fault, Doc."

I wasn't too sure of that myself. I was just remembering that I'd vaguely noticed a car parked in front of Smiley's place. If my brains had been in the proper end of my anatomy I'd have had the sense to take at least a quick look at that car. And if I'd had that much sense, I'd have had the further sense to go across to the *Clarion* office instead of barging nitwittedly into Smiley's and into the arms of Bat Masters and George.

And if the state police had come before they'd left Smiley's, the *Clarion* would have had a really good story. This way, it might be a good story too, but who would write it?

Smiley and I were standing close together now, and Masters must have figured that one gun was enough for both of us. He stuck his into a shoulder holster and looked at George. "Well?" he said.

That proved again that George was the boss, or at least was on equal status with Masters. And as I studied George's face, I could see why. Masters was big and probably had plenty of brass and courage, but George was the one of the two who had the more brains.

George said, "Guess we'll have to take 'em along, Bat."

I knew what that meant. I said, "Listen, there's a back room. Can't you just tie us up? If we're found a few hours from now, what does it matter? You'll be clear."

"And you might be found in a few minutes. And you probably noticed what kind of a car we got, and you know which way we're heading." He shook his head, and it was definite.

He said, "We're not sticking around, either, till somebody comes in. Bat, go look outside."

Masters got up and started toward the front; then he hesitated and went back of the bar instead. He took two pint bottles of whisky and put one in either coat pocket. And he punched "No Sale" on the register and took out the bills; he didn't bother with the change. He folded the bills and stuck them in his trouser pocket. Then he came back around the bar and started for the door.

Sometimes I think people are crazy. Smiley stuck out his hand. He said, "Five bucks. Two-fifty apiece for those pints."

He could have got shot for it, then and there, but for some reason Masters liked it. He grinned and took the wadded paper money out of his pocket, peeled a five loose and put it in Smiley's hand.

George said, "Bat, cut the horseplay. Look outside." I noticed that he watched very carefully and kept the gun trained smack in the middle of Smiley's chest while Smiley stuck the five dollar bill into his pocket.

Masters opened the door and stepped outside, looked around casually and beckoned to us. Meanwhile George had stood up and walked around behind us, sliding his gun into a coat pocket out of sight but keeping his hand on it.

He said, "All right, boys, get going."

It was all very friendly. In a way.

We went out the door into the cool pleasant evening that wasn't going to last much longer, the way things looked now. Yes, the Buick was parked right in front of Smiley's. If I'd only glanced at it before I went in, the whole mess wouldn't have happened.

The Buick was a four-door sedan. George said, "Get in back," and we got in back. George got in front but sat sidewise, turned around facing us over the seat.

Masters got in behind the wheel and started the engine. He said over his shoulder, "Well, Buster, where to?"

I said, "About five miles out there are woods. If you take us back in them and tie us up, there isn't a chance on earth we'd be found before tomorrow."

I didn't want to die, and I didn't want Smiley to die, and that idea was such a good one that for a moment I hoped. Then Masters said, "What town is this, Buster?" and I knew there wasn't any chance. Just because I'd given him a fresh answer to a fresh question half an hour ago, there wasn't any chance.

The car pulled out from the curb and headed north.

I was scared, and sober. There didn't seem to be any reason why I had to be both. I said, "How about a drink?"

George reached into Masters' coat pocket and handed one of the pint bottles over the back of the seat. My hands shook a little while I got the cellophane off with my thumb nail and unscrewed the cap. I handed it to Smiley first and he took a short drink and passed it back. I took a long one and it put a warm spot where a very cold one had been. I don't mean to say it made me happy, but I felt a little better. I wondered what Smiley was thinking about and I remembered that he had a wife and three kids and I wished I hadn't remembered that.

I handed him back the bottle and he took another quick nip. I said, "I'm sorry, Smiley," and he said, "That's all right, Doc." And he laughed. "One bad thing, Doc. There'll be a swell story for your *Clarion,* but can Pete write it?"

I found myself wondering that, quite seriously. Pete's one of the best all-around printers in Illinois, but what kind of a job would he make of things tonight and tomorrow morning? He'd get the paper out all right, but he'd never done any news writing—at least as long as he'd worked for me—and handling all the news he was going to have tomorrow would be plenty tough. An escaped maniac, whatever had happened to Carl, and whatever—as if I really wondered—was going to happen to

Smiley and me. I wondered if our bodies would be found in time to make the paper, or if it would be merely a double disappearance. We'd both be missed fairly soon. Smiley because his tavern was still open but no one behind the bar. I because I was due to meet Pete at the *Clarion* and about an hour from now, when I hadn't shown up yet, he'd start checking.

We were just leaving town by then, and I noticed that we'd got off the main street which was part of the main highway. Burgoyne Street, which we were on, was turning into a road.

Masters stopped the car as we came to a fork and turned around. "Where do these roads go?" he asked.

"They both go to Watertown," I told him. "The one to the left goes along the river and the other one cuts through the hills; it's shorter, but it's trickier driving."

Apparently Masters didn't mind tricky driving. He swung right and we started up into the hills. I wouldn't have done it myself, if I'd been driving. The hills are pretty hilly and the road through them is narrow and does plenty of winding, with a drop-off on one side or the other most of the time. Not the long precipitous drop-off you find on real mountain roads, but enough to wreck a car that goes over the edge, and enough to bother my touch of acrophobia.

Phobias are ridiculous things, past reasoning. I felt mine coming back the moment there was that slight drop-off at the side of the road as we started up the first hill. Actually, I was for the moment more afraid of that than of George's gun. Yes, phobias are funny things. Mine, fear of heights, is one of the commonest. Carl is afraid of cats. Al Grainger is a pyrophobiac, morbidly afraid of fire.

Smiley said, "You know, Doc?"

"What?" I asked him.

"I was thinking of Pete having to write that newspaper. Whyn't you come back and help him. Ain't there such things as ghost writers?"

I groaned. After all these years, Smiley had picked a time

like this to come up with the only funny thing I'd ever heard him say.

We were up high now, about as high as the road went; ahead was a hairpin turn as it started downhill again. Masters stopped the car. "Okay, you mugs," he said. "Get out and start walking back."

Start, he'd said; he hadn't made any mention of finishing. The tail lights of the car would give them enough illumination to shoot us down by. And he'd probably picked this spot because it would be easy to roll our bodies off the edge of the road, down the slope, so they wouldn't be found right away. Both of them were already getting out of the car.

Smiley's big hand gave my arm a quick squeeze; I didn't know whether it was a farewell gesture or a signal. He said, "Go ahead, Doc," as calmly as chough he was collecting for drinks back of his bar.

I opened the door on my side, but I was afraid to step out. Not because I knew I was going to be shot—that would happen anyway, even if I didn't get out. They'd either drag me out or else shoot me where I sat and bloody up the back seat of their car. No, I was afraid to get out because the car was on the outside edge of the road and the slope started only a yard from the open door of the car. My damned acrophobia. It was dark out there and I could see the edge of the road and no farther and I pictured a precipice beyond. I hesitated, half in the door and half out of it.

Smiley said again, "Go ahead, Doc," and I heard him moving behind me.

Then suddenly there was a click—and complete and utter darkness. Smiley had reached a long arm across the back of the seat to the dashboard and had turned the light switch off. All the car lights went out.

There was a shove in the middle of my back that sent me out of that car door like a cork popping out of a champagne bottle; I don't think my feet touched that yard-wide strip of

road at all. As I went over the edge into darkness and the unknown I heard swearing and a shot behind me. I was so scared
of falling that I'd gladly have been back up on the road trying to
outrun a bullet back toward town. At least I'd have been dead
before they rolled me over the edge.

I hit and fell and rolled. It wasn't really steep, after all; it
was about a forty-five degree slope, and it was grassy. I flat-
tened a couple of bushes before one stopped me. I could hear
Smiley coming after me, sliding, and I scrambled on as fast as I
could. All of my arms and legs seemed to be working, so I
couldn't be seriously hurt.

And I could see a little now that my eyes were getting used
to the darkness. I could see trees ahead, and I scrambled toward
them down the slope, sometimes running, sometimes sliding
and sometimes simply falling, which is the simplest if not the
most comfortable way to go down a hill.

I made the trees, and heard Smiley make them, just as the
lights of the car flashed on, on the road above us. Some shots
snapped our way and then I heard George say, "Don't waste it.
Let's get going," and Bat's, "You mean we're gonna—"

George growled, "Hell, yes. That's woods down there. We
could waste an hour playing hide and seek. Let's get going."

They were the sweetest words I'd heard in a long time. I
heard car doors slam, and the car started.

Smiley's voice, about two yards to my left, said, "Doc? You
okay?"

"I think so," I said. "Smart work, Smiley. Thanks."

He came around a tree toward me and I could see him now.
He said, "Save it, Doc. Come on, quick. We got a chance—a little
chance, anyway—of stopping them."

"*Stopping them?* I said. My voice went shrill and sounded
strange to me. I wondered if Smiley had gone crazy. I couldn't
think of anything in the whole wide world that I wanted to do
less than stop Bat Masters and George.

But he had hold of my arm and was starting downhill,

through the dimly seen trees and away from the road, taking me with him.

He said, "Listen, Doc, I know this country like the palm of my foot. I've hunted here, often."

"For bank robbers?" I asked him.

"Listen, that road makes a hairpin and goes by right below us, not forty yards from here. If we can get just above the road before they get there and if I can find a big boulder to roll down as the car goes by—"

I wasn't crazy about it, but he was pulling me along and we were through the trees already. My eyes were used to the darkness by now and I could see the road dimly, a dozen yards ahead and a dozen yards below. In the distance, around a curve, I could hear the sound of the car; I couldn't see it yet. It was a long way off, but coming fast.

Smiley said, "Look for a boulder, Doc. If you can't find one big enough to roll, then something we can throw. If we can hit their windshield or something—"

He was bending over, groping around. I did the same, but the bank was smooth and grassy. If there were stones, I couldn't find any.

Apparently Smiley wasn't having any luck either. He swore. He said, "If I only had a gun—"

I remembered something. "I've got one," I said.

He straightened up and looked at me—and I'm glad it was dark enough that he couldn't see my face and that I couldn't see his.

I handed him the gun. The headlights of the car were coming in sight now around the curve. Smiley pushed me back into the trees and stood behind one himself, leaning out to expose only his head and his gun hand.

The car came like a bat out of hell, but Smiley took aim calmly. He fired his first shot when the car was about forty yards away, the second when it was only twenty. The first shot went into the radiator—I don't mean we could tell that then, but that's where it was found afterwards. The second went through the windshield, almost dead center but, of course, at an angle. It plowed a furrow along the side of Masters' neck. The car careened and then went off the road on the downhill side, away from us. It turned over once, end for end, the headlight beams stabbing the night with drunken arcs, and then it banged into a tree with a noise like the end of the world and stopped.

For just a second after all that noise there was a silence that was almost deafening. And then the gas tank exploded.

The car caught fire and there was plenty of light. We saw, as we ran toward it, that one of the men had been thrown clear; when we got close enough we could see that it was Masters. George was still in the car, but we couldn't do a thing for him. And in that roaring inferno there wasn't a chance on earth that he could have lived even the minute it took us to get to the scene of the wreck.

We dragged Masters farther away from the fire before we checked to see whether or not he was alive. Amazingly, he was. His face looked as though he'd held it in a meat grinder and both of his arms were broken. Whether there was anything wrong with him beyond that we couldn't tell, but he was still breathing and his heart was still beating.

Smiley was staring at the flaming wreck. He said, "A perfectly good Buick shot to hell. A fifty model at that. He shook his head sadly and then jumped back, as I did, when there was another explosion in the car; it must have been the cartridges in George's pistol going off all at once.

I told Smiley, "One of us will have to walk back. One had better stay here, on account of Masters' still being alive."

"I guess so," he said. "Don't know what either of us can do for him, but we can't both just walk off and leave him. Say, look, that's a car coming."

I looked where he was pointing, toward the upper stretch of road where we'd got out of the car before it made the hairpin turn, and there were the headlights of a coming car all right.

We got out on the road ready to hail it, but it would have stopped anyway. It was a state police car with two coppers in it. Luckily, I knew one of them—Willie Peeble—and Smiley knew the other one, so they took our word for what had happened. Especially as Peeble knew about Masters and was able to identify him in spite of the way his face was cut up.

Masters was still alive and his heartbeat and breathing were as good as they'd been when we'd got to him. Peeble decided he'd better not try to move him. He went back to the police car and used the two-way radio to get an ambulance started our way and to report in to headquarters what had happened.

Peeble came back and said, "We'll give you and your friend a lift into town as soon as the ambulance gets here. You'll have to make and sign statements and stuff, but the chief says you can do that tomorrow; he knows both of you and says it's all right that way."

"That's swell," I said. "I've got to get back to the office as soon as I can. And as for Smiley here, his place is open and nobody there." I had a sudden thought and said, "Say, Smiley, you don't by any chance still have that pint we had a nip out of in the car, do you?"

He shook his head. "What with turning off the lights and pushing you out and getting out myself—"

I sighed at the waste of good liquor. The other pint bottle, the one that had been in Bat Masters' left coat pocket, hadn't survived the crash. Still, Smiley *had* saved our lives, so I had to forgive him for abandoning the bottle he'd been holding.

The fire was dying down now, and I was getting a little sick at the barbecue odor and wished the ambulance would come so we could get away from there.

I suddenly remembered Carl and asked Peeble if there'd been any report on the police radio about a Carl Trenholm. He shook his head. He said, "There was a looney loose, though. Escaped from the county asylum. Must've been caught, though;

we had a cancellation on it later."

That was good news, in a way. It meant that Yehudi hadn't waited at my place after all. And somehow I'd hated the thought of having to sick the guards on him while he was there. Insane or not, it didn't seem like real hospitality to a guest.

And the fact that nothing had been on the police radio about Carl at least wasn't discouraging.

A car came along from the opposite direction and stopped when its driver saw the smoldering wreckage and the state police car. It turned out to be a break for Smiley and me. The driver was a Watertown man whom Willie Peeble knew and who was on his way to Carmel City. When Peeble introduced us and vouched for us, he said he'd be glad to take Smiley and me into Carmel City with him.

I didn't believe it at first when I saw by the clock dial on the instrument panel of the car that it was only a few minutes after ten o'clock as we entered Carmel City; it seemed incredible that so much had happened in the few hours—less than four—since I'd left the *Clarion*. But we passed a lighted clock in a store window and I saw that the clock in the car was right after all, within a few minutes, anyway. It was only a quarter after ten.

We were let off in front of Smiley's. Across the street I could see lights were on at the *Clarion,* so Pete would be there. I thought I'd take a quick drink with Smiley, though, before I went to the office, so I went in with him.

The place was as we'd left it. If any customer had come in, he'd got tired of waiting and had left.

Smiley went around back of the bar and poured us drinks while I went to the phone. I was going to call the hospital to find out about Carl Trenholm; then I decided to call Pete instead. He'd surely have called the hospital already. So I gave the *Clarion* number.

When Pete recognized my voice, he said, "Doc, where the hell have you been?"

"Tell you in a minute, Pete. First, have you got anything

about Carl?"

"He's all right. I don't know yet what happened, but he's okay. I called the hospital and they said he'd been treated and released. I tried to find out what the injuries had been and how they'd happened, but they said they couldn't give out that information. I tried his home, but I guess he hadn't got there yet; nobody answered."

"Thanks, Pete," I said. "That's swell. Listen, there's going to be plenty to write up. Carl's accident, when we get in touch with him, and the escape and capture of the lunatic, and—something even bigger than either of those. So I guess we might as well do it tonight, if that's okay by you."

"Sure, Doc. I'd rather get it over with tonight. Where are you?"

"Over at Smiley's. Come on over for a quick one—to celebrate Carl's being okay. He can't even be badly hurt if they released him that quickly."

"Okay, Doc, I'll have one. But where were you? And Smiley, too, for that matter? I looked in there on my way to the office—saw the lights weren't on here, so I knew you weren't here yet—and you and Smiley were both gone. I waited five or ten minutes and then I decided I'd better come across here in case of any phone calls and to start melting metal in the Linotype."

I said, "Smiley and I had a little ride. I'll tell you about it."

"Okay, Doc. See you in a couple of minutes."

I went back to the bar and when I reached for the shot Smiley had poured for me, my hand was shaking.

Smiley grinned and said, "Me too, Doc." He held out his hand and I saw it wasn't much steadier than mine.

"Well," he said, "you got your story, Doc. What you were squawking about. Say, here's your gun back." He took out the short-barreled thirty-eight and put it on the bar. "Good as new, except two bullets gone out of it. How'd you happen to have it with you, Doc?"

For some reason I didn't want to tell him, or anyone, that

the escaped lunatic had made such a sap out of me and had been a guest at my house. So I said, "I had to walk down here, and Pete had just phoned me there was a lunatic loose, so I stuck that in my pocket. Jittery, I guess."

He looked at me and shook his head slowly. I know he was thinking about my having had that gun in my pocket all along, during what we thought was our last ride, and never having even tried to use it. I'd been so scared that I'd completely forgotten about it until Smiley had said he wished he had a gun.

I grinned and said, "Smiley, you're right in what you're thinking. I've got no more business with a gun than a snake has with roller skates. Keep it."

"Huh? You mean it, Doc? I've been thinking about getting one to keep under the bar."

"Sure, I mean it," I told him. "I'm afraid of the damn things and I'm safer without one."

He hefted it appraisingly. "Nice gun. It's worth something."

I said, "So's my life, Smiley. To me, anyway. And you saved it when you pushed me out of that car and over the edge tonight."

"Forget it, Doc. I couldn't have got out that door myself with you asleep in it. And getting out of the other side of the car wouldn't have been such a hot idea. Well, if you really mean it, thanks for the gun."

He put it out of sight under the bar and then poured us each a second drink. "Make it short," I told him. "I've got a lot of work to do."

He glanced at his clock and it was only ten thirty. He said, "Hell, Doc, the evening's only a pup."

I thought, but didn't say, *what a pup!*

I wonder what I'd have thought if I'd even guessed that the pup hadn't even been weaned yet.

Pete came in.

CHAPTER SEVEN

"It seems a shame," the Walrus said
"To play them such a trick.
After we've brought them out so far,
And made them trot so quick!"

NEITHER SMILEY nor I had touched, as yet, the second drink he'd poured us, so there was time for Pete Corey to get in on the round; Smiley poured a drink for him.

He said, "Okay, Doc, now what's this gag about Smiley and you going for a ride? You told me your car was laid up and Smiley doesn't drive one."

"Pete," I said, "Smiley doesn't *have* to be able to drive a car. He's a gentleman of genius. He kills or captures killers. That's what we were doing. Anyway, that's what Smiley was doing. I went along, just for the ride."

"Doc, you're kidding me."

I said, "If you don't believe me, read tomorrow's *Clarion.* Ever hear of Bat Masters?"

Pete shook his head. He reached for his drink.

"You will," I told him. "In tomorrow's *Clarion.* Ever hear of George?"

"George Who?"

I opened my mouth to say I didn't know, but Smiley beat me to the punch by saying, "George Kramer."

I stared at Smiley. "How'd you know his last name?"

"Saw it in a fact detective magazine. And his picture, too, and Bat Masters. They're members of the Gene Kelley mob."

I stared harder at Smiley. "You recognized them? I mean, before I even came in here?"

"Sure," Smiley said. "But it wouldn't have been a good idea to phone the cops while they were here, so I was going to wait till they left, and then phone the state cops to pick 'em up between here and Chicago. That's where they were heading. I listened to what they said, and it wasn't much, but I did get that much out of it. Chicago. They had a date there tomorrow afternoon."

"You're not kidding, Smiley?" I asked him. "You really had them spotted before I came in here?"

"I'll show you the magazine, Doc, with their pictures in it. Pictures of all the Gene Kelley mob."

"Why didn't you tell me?"

Smiley shrugged his big shoulders. "You didn't ask. Why didn't you tell *me* you had a gun in your pocket? If you coulda slipped it to me in the car, we'd have polished 'em off sooner. It would have been a cinch; it was so dark in that back seat after we got out of town, George Kramer wouldn't of seen you pass it."

He laughed as though he'd said something funny. Maybe he had.

Pete was looking from one to the other of us. He said, "Listen, if this is a gag, you guys are going a long way for it. What the hell happened?"

Neither of us paid any attention to Pete. I said, "Smiley, where is that fact detective magazine? Can you get it?"

"Sure, it's upstairs. Why? Don't you believe me?"

"Smiley," I said, "I'd believe you if you told me you were lying. No, what I had in mind is that that magazine will save me a lot of grief. It'll have background stuff on the boys we were playing cops and robbers with tonight. I thought I'd have to phone to Chicago and get it from the cops there. But if there's a whole article on the Gene Kelley mob in that mag, I'll have enough without that."

"Get it right away, Doc." Smiley went through the door that led upstairs.

I took pity on Pete and gave him a quick sketch of our experience with the gangsters. It was fun to watch his mouth drop open and to think that a lot of other mouths in Carmel City would do that same thing tomorrow when the *Clarion* was distributed.

Smiley came back down with the magazine and I put it in my pocket and went to the phone again. I still had to have the details about what had happened to Carl, for the paper. I still wanted it for my own information too, but that wasn't so important as long as he wasn't seriously hurt.

I tried the hospital first but they gave me the same run-around they'd given Pete; sorry, but since Mr. Trenholm had been discharged, they could give out no information. I thanked them. I tried Carl's own phone and got no answer, so I went back to Pete and Smiley.

Smiley happened to be staring out the window. He said, "Somebody just went in your office, Doc. Looked like Clyde Andrews."

Pete turned to look, too, but was too late. He said, "Guess that's who it must've been. Forgot to tell you, Doc; he phoned about twenty minutes ago while I was waiting for you over at the office. I told him I expected you any minute."

"You didn't lock the door, did you, Pete?" I asked. He shook his head.

I waited a minute to give the banker time to get up the stairs and into the office and then I went back to the phone and called the *Clarion* number. It rang several times while Clyde, apparently, was making up his mind whether to answer it or not. Finally he did.

"This is Doc, Clyde," I said. "How's the boy?"

"He's all right, Doc. He's fine. And I want to thank you

again for what you did and—I want to talk to you about something. Are you on your way here?"

"I'm across the street at Smiley's. How about dropping over here if you want to talk?"

He hesitated. "Can't you come here?" he asked.

I grinned to myself. Clyde Andrews is not only a strict temperance advocate; he's head of a local chapter (a small one, thank God) of the Anti-Saloon League. He'd probably never been in a tavern in his life.

I said, "I'm afraid I can't, Clyde." I made my voice very grave. "I'm afraid if you want to talk to me, it will have to be here at Smiley's."

He got me, all right. He said stiffly, "I'll be there."

I sauntered back to the bar. I said, "Clyde Andrews is coming here, Smiley. Chalk up a first."

Smiley stared at me. "I don't believe it," he said. He laughed.

"Watch," I told him.

Solemnly I went around behind the bar and got a bottle and two glasses and took them to a table—the one in the far corner farthest from the bar. I liked the way Pete and Smiley stared at me.

I filled both the glasses and sat down. Pete and Smiley stared some more. Then they turned and stared the other way as Clyde came in, walking stiffly. He said, "Good evening, Mr. Gorey," to Pete and "Good evening, Mr. Wheeler," to Smiley, and then came back to where I was sitting.

I said, "Sit down, Clyde," and he sat down.

I looked at him. I said sternly, "Clyde, I don't like—in advance—what you're going to ask me."

"But, Doc," he said earnestly, almost pleadingly, "*must* you print what happened? Harvey didn't mean to—"

"That's what I meant," I said. "What makes you think I'd even think of printing a word about it?"

He looked at me and his face changed. "Doc! You're not

going to?"

"Of course not." I leaned forward. "Listen, Clyde, I'll make you a bet—or I would if you were a betting man. I'll bet I know exactly the amount of money the kid had in his pocket when he was leaving—and, no, I didn't look in his pockets. I'll bet he had a savings account—he's been working summers several years now, hasn't he?—and he was running away. And he knew damn well you wouldn't let him draw his own money and that he couldn't draw it without your knowing it. Whether he had twenty dollars or a thousand, I'll bet you it was the exact amount of his own account."

He took a deep breath. "You're right. Exactly right. And— thanks for thinking that, before you knew it. I was going to tell you."

"For a fifteen-year-old, Harvey's a good kid, Clyde. Now listen, you'll admit I did the right thing tonight calling you instead of calling the sheriff? And in keeping the story out of the paper?"

"Yes."

"You're in a saloon, Clyde. A den of iniquity. You should have said 'Hell, yes.' But I don't suppose it would sound natural if you did, so I won't insist on it. But, Clyde, how much thinking have you been doing about *why* the boy was running away? Has he told you that yet?"

He shook his head slowly. "He's all right now, in bed, asleep. Dr. Minton gave him a sedative, but told me Harvey had better not do any talking till tomorrow."

"I'll tell you right now," I said, "that he won't have any very coherent story about it. Maybe he'll say he was running away to join the army or to go on the stage or—or almost anything. But it won't be the truth, even if he thinks it is. Clyde, whether he knows it or not, he was running *away*. Not toward."

"Away from what?"

"From you," I said.

For a second I thought he was going to get angry and I'm

glad he didn't, because then I might have got angry too and that would have spoiled the whole thing.

Instead, he slumped a little. He said, "Go on, Doc."

I hated to, then, but I had to strike while the striking was good. I said, "Listen, Clyde, get up and walk out any time you want to; I'm going to give it to you straight. You've been a lousy father." At any other time he'd have walked out on me on that one. I could tell by his face that, even now, he didn't like it. But at any other time he wouldn't have been sitting at a back table in Smiley's tavern, either.

I said, "You're a good man, Clyde, but you work at it too hard. You're rigid, unyielding, righteous. Nobody can love a ramrod. There's nothing wrong with your being religious, if you want to. Some good men *are* religious. But you've got to realize that everybody who doesn't think as you do isn't necessarily wrong."

I said, "Take alcohol—literally, if you wish; there's a glass of whisky in front of you. But take it figuratively, anyway. It's been a solace to the human race, one of the things that can make life tolerable, since—damn it, since before the human race was even human. True, there are a few people who can't handle it—but that's no reason to try to legislate it away from the people who *can* handle it, and whose enjoyment of life is increased by its moderate use—or even by its occasional immoderate use, providing it doesn't make them pugnacious or otherwise objectionable.

"But—let's skip alcohol. My point is that a man can be a good man without trying to interfere with his neighbor's life too much. Or with his son's. Boys are human, Clyde. People in general are human; people are more human than anybody."

He didn't say anything, and that was a hopeful sign. Maybe a tenth of it was sinking in.

I said, "Tomorrow, when you can talk with the kid, Clyde, what are you going to say?"

"I—I don't know, Doc,"

I said, "Don't say anything. Above all, don't ask him any questions. Not a damn question. And let him keep that money, in cash, so he can run away any time he decides to. Then maybe he won't. If you change your attitude toward him.

"But, damn it, Clyde, you *can't* change your attitude toward him, and unbend, without unbending in general toward the human race. The kid's a human being, too. And you could be, if you wanted to. Maybe you think it will cost you your immortal soul to be one—I don't think so, myself, and I think there are a great many truly religious people who don't think so either—but if you persist in not being one, then you're going to lose your son."

I decided that that was it. There wasn't anything more that I could say that couldn't weaken my case. I decided I'd better shut up. I did shut up.

It seemed like a long, long time before he said anything. He was staring at the wall over my head. When he answered what I'd said, he still didn't say anything. He did better, a lot better.

He picked up the whisky in front of him. I got mine picked up in time to down it as he took a sip of his. He made a face.

"Tastes horrible," he said. "Doc, do you really *like* this stuff?"

"No," I told him. "I hate the taste of it. You're right, Clyde, it *is* horrible."

He looked at the glass in his hand and shuddered a little. I said, "Don't drink it. That sip you took proved your point. And don't try to toss it off; you'll probably choke."

He said, "I suppose you have to learn to like it. Doc, I've drunk a little wine a few times, not recently, but I didn't dislike it too much. Does Mr. Wheeler have any wine?"

"The name is Smiley," I said, "and he does." I stood up. I clapped him on the back, and it was the first time in my life I'd ever done so. I said, "Come on, Clyde, let's see what the boys in the back room will have."

I took him over to the bar, to Pete and Smiley. I told Smiley,

"We want a round, and it's on Clyde. Wine for him, and I'll take a short beer this time; I've got to rewrite a paper tonight."

I frowned at Smiley because of the utterly amazed look on his face, and he got the hint and straightened it out. He said, "Sure, Mr. Andrews. What kind of wine?"

"Do you have sherry, Mr. Wheeler?"

I said, "Clyde, meet Smiley. Smiley, Clyde."

Smiley laughed, and Clyde smiled. The smile was a bit stiff, and would take practice, but I knew and knew damned well that Harvey Andrews wasn't going to run away from home again.

He was going, henceforth, to have a father who was human. Oh, I don't mean that I expected Clyde suddenly to turn into Smiley's best customer. Maybe he'd never come back to Smiley's again. But by ordering one drink—even of wine—across a bar, he'd crossed a Rubicon. He wasn't perfect any more.

I was beginning to feel my own drinks again and I didn't really want the one Clyde bought for me, but it was an Occasion, so I took it. But I was getting in a hurry to get back across the street to the *Clarion* and get to work on all the stories I had to write, so I downed it fairly quickly and Pete and I left. Clyde left when we did, because he wanted to get back to his son; I didn't blame him for that.

At the *Clarion,* Pete checked the pot on the Linotype—and found it hot enough—while I pulled up the typewriter stand beside my desk and started abusing the ancient Underwood. I figured that, with the dope in the fact detective magazine Smiley had given me for background, I could run it to three or four columns, so I had a lot of work ahead of me. The escaped looney and Carl could wait—now that the former was captured and now that I knew Carl was safe—until I got the main story done.

I told Pete, while he was waiting for the first take, to hand set a banner head, "Tavernkeeper Captures Wanted Killers," to see if it would fit. Oh, sure, I was going to put myself in the story, too, but I was going to make Smiley the hero of it, for one simple reason: he had been.

Pete had the head set up—and it fitted—by the time I had a take for him to start setting on the machine.

In the middle of the second take I realized that I didn't know for sure that Bat Masters was still alive, although I'd put it that way in the lead. I might as well find out for sure that he really was, and what condition he was in.

I knew better than to call the hospital for anything more detailed than whether he was dead or not, so I picked up the phone and called the state police office at Watertown. Willie Peeble answered.

He said, "Sure, Doc, he's alive. He's even been conscious and talked some. Thinks he's dying, so he really opened up."

"Is he dying?"

"Sure, but not the way he thinks. It'll cost the state some kilowatts. And he can't beat the rap; they've got the whole gang cold, once they catch them. There were six people—two of 'em women—killed in that bank job they pulled at Colby."

"Was George in on that?"

"Sure. He was the one that shot the women. One was a teller and the other one was a customer who was too scared to move when they told her to lie flat."

That made me feel a little better about what had happened to George. Not that it had worried me too much.

I said, "Then I can put in the story that Bat Masters confesses?"

"I dunno about that, Doc. Captain Evans is at the hospital talking to him now, and we had one report here that Masters is talking, but not the details. I don't think the cap would even bother asking him about that stuff."

"What would he ask him, then?"

"The rest of the mob, where they are. There are two others besides Gene Kelley, and it'd be a real break if the cap can get out of Masters something that would help us find the others. Especially Kelley. The two we got tonight are peanuts compared to Kelley."

I said, "Thanks a lot, Willie. Listen, if anything more breaks on the story, will you give me a ring? I'll be here at the *Clarion* for a while yet."

"Sure," he said. "So long."

I hung up and went back to the story. It went sweetly. I was on the fourth take when the phone rang and it was Captain Evans of the state police, calling from the hospital where they'd taken Masters. He'd just phoned Watertown and knew about my call there.

He said, "Mr. Stoeger? You going to be there another fifteen or twenty minutes?"

I was probably going to be working another several hours, I told him.

"Fine," he said, "I'll drive right around."

That was duck soup; I'd have my story about his questioning Masters right from the horse's mouth. So I didn't bother asking him any questions over the phone.

And I found myself, when I'd finished that take, up to the point in the story where the questioning of Masters should come, so I decided I might as well wait until I'd talked to Evans, since he was going to be here so soon.

Meanwhile I might as well start checking on the other two stories again. I called Carl Trenholm, still got no answer. I called the county asylum.

Dr. Buchan, the superintendent, wasn't there, the girl at the switchboard told me; she asked if I wanted to talk to his assistant and I said yes.

She put him on and before I'd finished explaining who I was and what I wanted, he'd interrupted me. "He's on his way over to see you now, Mr. Stoeger. You're at the *Clarion* office?"

"Yes" I said, "I'm here now. And you say Dr. Buchan's on his way? That's fine."

My stories were coming to me, I thought happily, as I put the phone back. Both Captain Evans and Dr. Buchan. Now if only Carl would drop in too and explain what had happened to him.

He did. Not that exact second, but only about two minutes later. I'd wandered over to the stone and was looking gloatingly at the horrible front page with no news on it and thinking how lovely it was going to look a couple of hours from now and listening with pleasure to the click of the mats down the channels of the Linotype, when the door opened and Carl walked in.

His clothes were a little dusty and disheveled; he had a big patch of adhesive tape on his forehead and his eyes looked a little bleary. He had a sheepish grin.

He said, "Hi, Doc. How's everything?"

"Wonderful," I told him. "What happened to you, Carl?"

"That's what I dropped in to tell you, Doc. Thought you might get a garbled version of it and be worried about me."

"I couldn't even get a garbled version. No version at all; the hospital wouldn't give. What happened?"

"Got drunk. Went for a walk out the pike to sober up and got so woozy I had to lie down a minute, so I headed for the grassy strip the other side of the ditch alongside the road and— well, my foot slipped as I was stepping across the ditch and the ground, with a chunk of rock in its hand, reached up and slapped me in the face."

"Who found you, Carl?" I asked him.

He chuckled. "I don't even know. I woke up—or came to— in the sheriff's car on the way to the hospital. Tried to talk him out of taking me there, but he insisted. They checked me for a concussion and let me go."

"How do you feel now?"

"Do you really want to know?"

"Well," I said, "maybe not. Want a drink?"

He shuddered. I didn't insist. Instead, I asked him where he'd been since he'd left the hospital.

"Drinking black coffee at the Greasy Spoon. Think I'm able to make it home by now. In fact, I'm on my way. But I knew you'd have heard about it and thought you might as well have the—uh—facts straight in case—uh—"

"Don't be an ass, Carl," I told him. "You don't rate a stick of type, even if you wanted it. And, by the way, Smiley gave me the inside dope on Bonney's divorce, so I cut down the story to essentials and cut out the charges against Bonney."

"That's swell of you, Doc."

"Why didn't you tell me the truth about it yourself?" I asked him. "Afraid of interfering with the freedom of the press? Or of taking advantage of a friendship?"

"Well—somewhere in between, I guess. Anyway, thanks. Well, maybe I'll see you tomorrow. If I live that long."

He left and I wandered back to my desk. The Linotype was caught up to the typewriter by now, and I hoped Evans would show up soon—or Dr. Buchan from the asylum so I could get ahead with at least one of the stories and not keep Pete working any later than necessary. For myself, I didn't give a damn. I was too keyed up to have been able to sleep anyway.

Well, there was one thing we could be doing to save time later. We went over to the stone and started pulling all the filler items out of the back pages so we could move back the least important stories on page one to make room for the two big stories we still had coming. We'd need at least two full page one columns—and more if we could manage it—for the capture of the bank robbers and the escape of the maniac.

We were just getting the pages unlocked, though, when Dr. Buchan came in. An elderly lady—she looked vaguely familiar to me but I couldn't place her—was with him.

She smiled at me and said, "Do you remember me, Mr. Stoeger?" And the smile did it; I did remember her. She'd lived next door to me when I was a kid, forty-some years ago, and she'd given me cookies. And I remembered now that, while I was away at college, I'd heard that she had gone mildly, not dangerously, insane and had been taken to the asylum. That must have been—Good Lord—thirty-some years ago. She must be well over seventy by now. And her name was—

"Certainly, Mrs. Griswald," I told her. "I even remember the cookies and candy you used to give me."

And I smiled back at her. She looked so happy that one couldn't help smiling back at her.

She said, "I'm so glad you remember, Mr. Stoeger. I want you to do me a big favor—and I'm so glad you remember those days, because maybe you'll do it for me. Dr. Buchan—he's so wonderful—offered to bring me here so I could ask you. I—I really wasn't running away this evening. I was just confused. The door was open and I forgot. I was thinking that it was forty years ago and I wondered what I was doing there and why I wasn't home with Otto, and so I just started home, that's all. And by the time I remembered that Otto was dead for so long and that I was—" The smile was tremulous now, and there were tears in her eyes. "Well, by that time I was lost and couldn't find my way back, until they found me. I even—*tried* to find my way back, once I remembered and knew where I was supposed to be."

I glanced over her head at tall Dr. Buchan, and he nodded to me. But I still didn't know what it was all about. I didn't see, so I said, "I see, Mrs. Griswald."

Her smile was back. She nodded brightly. "Then you *won't* put it in the paper? About my wandering away, I mean? Because I didn't really mean to do it. And Clara, my daughter, lives in Springfield now, but she still subscribes to your paper for news from home, and if she reads in the *Clarion* that I—escaped—she'll think I'm not happy there and it'll worry her. And I *am* happy, Mr. Stoeger—Dr. Buchan is wonderful to me—and I don't want to make Clara unhappy or have her worry about me, and—you won't write it up, will you?"

I patted her shoulder gently. I said, "Of course not, Mrs. Griswald."

And then suddenly she was against my chest, crying, and I was embarrassed as hell. Until Dr. Buchan pulled her gently away and started her toward the door. He stepped back a second and said to me so quietly that she couldn't hear, "It's straight, Stoeger. I mean, it probably would worry her daughter a lot and she really wasn't escaping—she just wandered off. And her daughter really does read your paper."

"Don't worry," I said. "I won't mention it."

Past him, I could see the door open and Captain Evans of the state police was coming in. He left the door open and Mrs. Griswald was wandering through it.

Dr. Buchan shook hands quickly. He said, "Thanks a lot, then. And on my behalf as well as Mrs. Griswald's. It doesn't do an institution like ours any good to have publicity on escapes, of course. Not that I'd have asked you, myself, to suppress the story on that account. But since our patient had a really good, and legitimate, reason to ask you not to—"

He happened to turn and see that his patient was already heading down the stairs. He hurried after her before she could again become confused and wander into limbo.

Another story gone, I thought, as I shook hands with Evans. Those cookies had been expensive—if worth it. I thought, suddenly, of all the stories I'd had to kill tonight. The bank burglary—for good and obvious reasons. Carl's accident—because it had been trivial after all, and writing it up would have hurt his reputation as a lawyer. The accident in the Roman candle department, because it might have lost Mrs. Carr's husband a needed job. Ralph Bonney's divorce—well, not killed, exactly, but played down from a long, important story to a short news item. Mrs. Griswald's escape from the asylum—because she'd given me cookies once and because it would have worried her daughter. Even the auction sale at the Baptist Church—for the most obvious reason of all, that it had been called off.

But what the hell did any of that matter as long as I had one really big story left, the biggest of them all? And there wasn't any conceivable reason why I couldn't print that one.

Captain Evans took the seat I pulled up for him by my desk and I sank back into the swivel chair and got a pencil ready for what he was going to tell me.

"Thanks a hell of a lot for coming here, Cap. Now what's the score about what you got out of Masters?"

He pushed his hat back on his head and frowned. He said, "I'm sorry, Doc. I'm going to have to ask you—on orders from the top—not to run the story at all."

CHAPTER EIGHT

He took his vorpal sword in hand:
Long time the manxome foe he sought —
So rested he by the Tumtum tree.
And stood a while in thought,

I DON'T KNOW what my face looked like. I know I dropped the pencil and that I had to clear my throat when what I started to say wouldn't come out the first time.

The second time, it came out, if a bit querulously. "Cap, you're kidding me. You can't really mean it. The one big thing that's ever happened here—is this a gag?"

He shook his head. "Nope, Doc. It's the McCoy. It comes right from the chief himself. I can't *make* you hold back the story, naturally. But I want to tell you the facts and I hope you'll decide to."

I breathed a little more freely when he said he couldn't make me hold it back. It wouldn't hurt me to listen, politely.

"Go ahead," I told him. "It had better be good."

He leaned forward. "It's this way, Doc. This Gene Kelley mob is nasty stuff. Real killers. I guess you found that out tonight about two of them. And, by the way, you did a damn good job."

"Smiley Wheeler did. I just went along for the ride."

It was a weak joke, but he laughed at it. Probably just to please me. He said, "If we can keep it quiet for about forty more hours—till Saturday afternoon—we can break up the gang completely. Including the big shot himself, Gene Kelley."

"Why Saturday afternoon?"

"Masters and Kramer had a date for Saturday afternoon with Kelley and the rest of the mob. At a hotel in Gary, Indiana. They've been separated since their last job, and they'd arranged that date to get together for the next one, see? When Kelley and the others show up for that date, well, we've got 'em.

"That is, unless the news gets out that Masters and Kramer are already in the bag. Then Kelley and company won't show up."

"Why can't we twist one little thing in the story," I suggested. "Just say Masters and Kramer were both dead?"

He shook his head. "The other boys wouldn't take any chances. Nope, if they know our two boys were either caught or killed, they'll stay away from Gary in droves."

I sighed. I knew it wouldn't work, but I said hopefully, "Maybe none of the gang members reads the *Carmel City Clarion*."

"You know better than that, Doc. Other papers all over the country would pick it up. The Saturday morning papers would have it, even if the Friday evening editions didn't get it." He had a sudden thought and looked startled. "Say, Doc, who represents the news services here? Have they got the story yet?"

"I represent them," I said sadly. "But I hadn't wired either of them on this yet. I was going to wait till my own paper was out. They'd have fired me, sure, and it would have cost me a few bucks a year, but for once I was going to have a big story break in my own paper before I threw it to the wolves."

He said, "I'm sorry, Doc. I guess this is a big thing for you. But now, at least, you won't lose out with the news services. You can say you held the story at the request of the police—until, say, mid-afternoon Saturday. Then send it in to them and get credit for it."

"Cash, you mean. I want the credit of breaking it in the *Clarion*, damn it."

"But will you hold it up, Doc? Listen, those boys are *killers*.

You'll be saving lives if you let us get them. Do you know anything about Gene Kelley?"

I nodded; I'd been reading about him in the magazine Smiley had lent me. He wasn't a very nice man. Evans was right in saying it would cost human lives to print that story if the story kept Kelley out of the trap he'd otherwise walk into.

I looked up and Pete was standing there listening. I tried to judge from his face what he thought about it, but he was keeping it carefully blank.

I scowled at him and said, "Shut off that God damn Linotype. I can't hear myself think."

He went and shut it off.

Evans looked relieved. He said, "Thanks, Doc." For no reason at all—the evening was moderately cool—he pulled out a handkerchief and wiped his forehead. "What a break it was that Masters hated the rest of the mob enough to turn them in for us when he figured he was done himself. And that you're willing to hold the story till we get 'em. Well, you can use it next week."

There wasn't any use telling him that I could also print a chapter or two of Caesar's *Gallic Wars* next week; it was ancient history too.

So I didn't say anything and after a few more seconds he got up and left.

It seemed awfully quiet without the Linotype running. Pete came over. He said, "Well, Doc, we still got that nine-inch hole in the front page that you said you'd find some way of filling in the morning. Maybe while we're here anyway—"

I ran my fingers through what is left of my hair. "Run it as is, Pete," I told him, "except with a black border around it."

"Look, Doc, I can pull forward that story on the Ladies' Aid election and if I reset it narrow measure to fit a box, it'll maybe run long enough."

I couldn't think of anything better. I said, "Sure, Pete," but when he started toward the Linotype to turn it back on, I said, "But not tonight, Pete. In the morning. It's half past eleven. Get home to the wife and kiddies."

"But I'd just as soon—"

"Get the hell out of here," I said, "before I bust out blubbering. I don't want anybody to see me do it."

He grinned to show he knew I didn't really mean it and said, "Sure, Doc. I'll get down a little early, then. Seven-thirty. You going to stick around a while now?"

"A few minutes," I said. "'Night, Pete. Thanks for coming down, and everything."

I kept sitting at my desk for a minute after he'd left, and I didn't blubber, but I wanted to all right. It didn't seem possible that so much had happened and that I couldn't get even a stick of type out of any of it. For a few minutes I wished that I was a son-of-a-bitch instead of a sucker so I could go ahead and print it all. Even if it let the Kelley mob get away to do more killing, lost my housekeeper's husband her job, made a fool out of Carl Trenholm, worried Mrs. Griswald's daughter and ruined Harvey Andrews' reputation by telling how he'd been caught robbing his father's bank while running away from home. And while I was at it, I might as well smear Ralph Bonney by listing the untrue charges brought against him in the divorce case and write a humorous little item about the leader of the local anti-saloon faction setting up a round for the boys at Smiley's. And even run the rummage sale story on the ground that the cancellation had been too late and let a few dozen citizens make a trip in vain. It would be wonderful to be a son-of-a-bitch instead of a sucker so I could do all that. Sons-of-bitches must have more fun than people. And definitely they get out bigger and better newspapers.

I wandered over and looked at the front page lying there on the stone, and for something to do I dropped the filler items back in page four. The ones we'd taken out to let us move back the present junk from page one to make room for all the big stories we were going to break. I locked up the page again.

It was quiet as hell.

I wondered why I didn't get out of there and have another drink—or a hell of a lot of drinks—at Smiley's. I wondered why I didn't want to get stinking drunk. But I didn't.

I wandered over to the window and stood staring down at the quiet street. They hadn't rolled the sidewalks in yet—closing time for taverns is midnight in Carmel City—but nobody was walking on them.

A car went by and I recognized it as Ralph Bonney's car, heading probably, to pick up Miles Harrison and take him over to Neilsville to pick up the night side pay roll for the fireworks plant, including the Roman candle department. To which I had briefly—

I decided I'd smoke one more cigarette and then go home. I reached into my pocket and pulled out the cigarette package and something fluttered to the floor—a card.

I picked it up and stared at it. It read.

Yehudi Smith

Suddenly the dead night was alive again. I'd written off Yehudi Smith when I'd heard that the escaped lunatic had been captured. I'd written him off so completely that I'd forgotten to write him on again when Dr. Buchan had brought in Mrs. Griswald to talk to me.

Yehudi Smith *wasn't* the escaped lunatic.

Suddenly I wanted to jump up into the air and click my heels together, I wanted to run, I wanted to yell.

Then I remembered how long I'd been gone and I almost ran to the telephone on my desk. I gave my own number and my heart sank as it rang once, twice, thrice—and then after the fourth ring Smith's voice answered with a sleepy-sounding hello.

I said, "This is Doc Stoeger, Mr. Smith. I'm starting home now. Want to apologize for having kept you waiting so long. Some things happened."

"Good. I mean, good that you're coming now. What time is it?"

"About half past eleven. I'll be there in fifteen minutes. And thanks for waiting."

I hurried into my coat and grabbed my hat. I almost forgot to turn out the lights and lock the door.

Smiley's first, but not for a drink; I picked up a bottle to take along. The one at my house had been getting low when I left; only God knew what had happened to it since.

Leaving Smiley's with the bottle, I swore again at the fact that my car was laid up with those flat tires. Not that it's a long walk or that I mind walking in the slightest when I'm not in a hurry, but again I was in a hurry. Last time it had been because I thought Carl Trenholm was dead or seriously injured—and to get away from Yehudi Smith. This time it was to get back to him.

Past the post office, now dark. The bank, this time with the night light on and no evidence of crime in sight. Past the spot where the Buick had pulled up and a voice had asked someone named Buster what town this was. There wasn't a car in sight now, friend or foe. Past everything that I'd passed so many thousand times, and off the main street into the friendly, pleasant side streets no longer infested with homicidal maniacs or other horrors. I didn't look behind me once, all the way home.

I felt so good I felt silly. Best of all I was cold-sobered by everything that had been happening, and I was ready and in the mood for a few more drinks and some more screwy conversation.

I still didn't completely believe he'd be there, but he was.

And he looked so familiar sitting there that I wondered why I'd doubted. I said "Hi," and shied my hat at the hat-rack and it hit a peg and stayed there. That was the first time that had happened in months so I knew from that that I was lucky tonight. As if I needed that to prove it.

I took the seat across from him, just as we'd been sitting before, and I poured us each a drink—still from the first bottle; apparently he hadn't drunk much while I'd been gone—and started to renew the apologies I'd made over the phone for having been away so long.

He waved the apologies away with a casual gesture. "It doesn't matter at all, as long as you got back." He smiled. "I had a nice nap."

We touched glasses and drank. He said, "Let's see; just where were we when you got that phone call—oh, which reminds me; you said it was about an accident to a friend. May I ask—?

He's all right," I told him. "Nothing serious. It was—well, other things kept coming up that kept me away so long."

"Good. Then—oh, yes, I remember. When the phone rang we were talking about the Roman candle department. We'd just drunk to it."

I remembered and nodded. "That's where I've been, ever since I left here."

"Seriously?"

"Quite," I said. "They fired me half an hour ago, but it was fun while it lasted. Wait; no, it wasn't. I won't lie to you. At the time it was happening, it was pretty horrible."

His eyebrows went up a little. "Then you're serious. Something did happen. You know, Doctor—"

"Doc," I said.

"You know, Doc, you're different. Changed, somehow."

I refilled our glasses, still from the first bottle, although that round killed it.

"It's temporary, I think. Yes, Mr. Smith, I had—"

"Smitty," he said.

"Yes, Smitty, I had a rather bad experience, while it lasted, and I'm still in reaction from it, but the reaction won't last. I'm still jittery from it and I may be even more jittery tomorrow when I realize what a narrow squeak I had, but I'm still the same guy. Doc Stoeger, fifty-three, genial failure both as a hero and as an editor."

Silence for a few seconds and then he said, "Doc, I like you. I think you're a swell guy. I don't know what happened, and I don't suppose you want to tell me, but I'll bet you one thing."

"Thanks, Smitty," I said. "And it's not that I don't want to tell you what happened this evening; it's just that I don't want to talk about it at all, right now. Some other time I'll be glad to tell you, but right now I want to stop thinking about it—and start thinking about Lewis Carroll again. What's the one thing you want to bet me, though?"

"That you're not a failure as an editor. As a hero, maybe—damned few of us are heroes. But I'll bet you said you were a failure as an editor because you killed a story—for some good reason. And not a selfish one. Would I win that bet?"

"You would," I said. I didn't tell him he'd have won it five times over. "But I'm not proud of myself—the only thing is that *I'd* have been ashamed of myself otherwise. This way, I'm going to be ashamed of my paper. All newspapermen, Smitty, should be sons-of-bitches."

"Why?" And before I could answer he tossed off the drink I'd just poured him—tossed it off as before with that fascinating trick of the glass never really nearing his lips—and answered it himself with a more unanswerable question. "So that newspapers will be more entertaining?—at the expense of human lives they might wreck or even destroy?"

The mood was gone, or the mood was wrong. I shook myself a little. I said, "Let's get back to Jabberwocks. And—My God, every time I get to talking seriously it sobers me up. I had such a nice edge early in the evening. Let's have another—and to Lewis Carroll again. And then go back to that gobbledegook you were giving me, the stuff that sounded like Einstein on a binge."

He grinned. "Wonderful word, gobbledegook. Carroll might have originated it, except that there was less of it in his time. All right, Doc, to Carroll."

And again his glass was empty. It was a trick I'd *have* to learn, no matter how much time it took or how much whisky it wasted. But, the first time, in private.

I drank mine and it was the third since I'd come home, fifteen minutes ago; I was beginning to feel them. Not that I feel three drinks, starting from scratch, but these didn't start from scratch. I'd had quite a few early in the evening, before the fresh air of my little ride with Bat and George had cleared my head, and several at Smiley's thereafter.

They were hitting me now. Not hard, but definitely.

There was a mistiness about the room. We were talking about Carroll and mathematics again, or Yehudi Smith was talking, anyway, and I was trying to concentrate on what he was saying. He seemed, for a moment, to blur a little and to advance and recede as I looked at him. And his voice was a blur, too, a blur of sines and cosines. I shook my head to clear it a bit and decided I'd better lay off the bottle for a while.

Then I realized that what he'd just said was a question and I begged his pardon.

"The clock on your mantel," he repeated, "is it correct?"

I managed to focus my eyes on it. Ten minutes to twelve. I said, "Yes, it's right. It's still early. You're not thinking of going, surely. I'm a little woozy at the moment, but—"

"How long will it take us to get there from here? I have directions how to reach it, of course, but you could probably estimate the time it will take us better than I can."

For a second I stared at him blankly, wondering what he was talking about.

Then I remembered.

We were going to a haunted house to hunt a Jabberwock— or something.

CHAPTER NINE

"First, the fish must be caught."
That is easy: a baby, I think, could have caught it.
"Next, the fish must be bought."
That is easy: a penny, I think, would have bought it.

MAYBE you won't believe that I could have forgotten that, but I had. So much had happened between the time I'd left my house and the time I returned that it's a wonder, I suppose, that I still remembered my own name, and Yehudi's.

Ten minutes before twelve and we were due there, he'd said, at one o'clock.

"You have a car?" I asked him.

He nodded. "A few doors down. I got out at the wrong place to look for street numbers, but I was close enough that I didn't bother moving the car."

"Then somewhere between twenty and thirty minutes will get us there," I told him.

"Fine, Doctor. Then we've got forty minutes yet if we allow half an hour."

The woozy spell was passing fast, but I refilled his glass this time without refilling my own. I wanted to sober up a bit—not completely, because if I were sober I might get sensible and decide not to go, and I didn't want to decide not to go.

Smith had settled back in his chair, not looking at me, so I looked at him, and wondered what I was doing even to listen to the absurd story he'd told me about Vorpal Blades and the old Wentworth house.

He wasn't the escaped lunatic, but that didn't mean he wasn't a screwball, and that I wasn't a worse one. What the hell *were* we going to do out there? Try to fish a Bandersnatch out of limbo? Or break through a looking-glass or dive down a rabbit hole to go hunting one in its native element?

Well, as long as I didn't get sober enough to spoil things, it was wonderful. Crazy or not, I was having a marvelous time. The best time I'd had since the Halloween almost forty years ago when we—But never mind that; it's a sign of old age to reminisce about the things you did when you were young, and I'm not old yet. Not very, anyway.

Yes, my eyes were focusing all right again now, but the mistiness in the room was still there, and I realized that it wasn't mistiness but smoke. I looked across at the window and wondered if I wanted it open badly enough to get up and open it.

The window. A black square framing the night.

The midnight. *Where were you at midnight?* With Yehudi. *Who's Yehudi?* A little man who wasn't there. But I have the card. *Let's see it, Doc. Hmmm. What's your bug number?* My bug number?

And the black rook takes the white knight.

The smoke was definitely too thick, and so was I. I walked to the window and threw up the bottom sash. The lights behind me made it a mirror. There was my reflection. An insignificant little man with graying hair, and glasses, and a necktie badly askew.

He grinned at me and straightened his necktie. I remembered the verse from Carroll that Al Grainger had quoted at me early in the evening:

"You are old, Father William," the young man said.
"And your hair has become very white.
And yet you incessantly stand on your head.
Do you think, at your age, it is right?"

And that made me think of Al Grainger. I wondered if there was still any chance of his showing up. I'd told him to come around any time up to midnight and it was that now. I wished now that he would come. Not for chess, as we'd planned, but so he could go along on our expedition. Not that I was exactly afraid, but—well, I wished that Al Grainger would show up.

It occurred to me that he might have come or phoned and that Yehudi had failed to mention it. I asked him.

He shook his head, "No, Doc. Nobody came and the only phone call was the one you yourself made just before you came home."

So that was that, unless Al showed up in the next half hour or unless I phoned him. And I didn't want to do that. I'd been enough of a coward earlier in the evening.

Just the same I felt a little hollow—

My God, I *was* hollow. I'd had a sandwich late in the afternoon, but that had been eight hours ago and I hadn't eaten anything since. No wonder the last couple of drinks had hit me.

I suggested to Yehudi that we raid the icebox and he said it sounded like a wonderful idea to him. And it must have been, for it turned out that he was as hungry as I. Between us we killed a pound of boiled ham, most of a loaf of rye and a medium-sized jar of pickles.

It was almost half past twelve when we finished. There was just time for a stirrup cup, and we had one. With food in my stomach, it tasted much better and went down much more smoothly than the last one had. It tasted so good, in fact, that I decided to take the bottle—we'd started the second one by then —along with us. We might, after all, run into a blizzard.

"Ready to go?" Smith asked.

I decided I'd better put the window down. In its reflecting pane, over my shoulder I could see Yehudi Smith standing by the door waiting for me. The reflection was clear and sharp; it brought out the bland roundness of his face, the laughter-tracks around his mouth and eyes, the rotund absurdity of his body.

And an impulse made me walk over and hold out my hand to him and shake his hand when he put it into mine rather wonderingly. We hadn't shaken hands when we'd introduced ourselves on the porch and something made me want to do it now. I don't mean that I'm clairvoyant. I'm not, or I'd never have gone. No, I don't know why I shook hands with him.

Just an impulse, but one I'm very glad I followed. Just as I'm glad I'd given him food and drink instead of letting him go to his strange death sober or on an empty stomach.

And I'm even gladder that I said, "Smitty, I like you."

He looked pleased, but somehow embarrassed. He said, "Thanks, Doc," but for the first time his eyes didn't quite meet mine.

We went out and walked up the quiet street to where he'd left his car, and got in.

It's odd how clearly you remember some things and how vague others are. I recall that there was a push button radio on the dashboard and that the button for *WBBM* was pushed in, and I recall that the gear shift knob was brightly polished onyx. But I don't recall whether the car was a coupe or a sedan, and haven't the vaguest idea what make or color it was. I recall that the engine was quite noisy—my only clue as to whether it was an old car or a new one, that and the fact that the gear shift was on the floor and not on the steering wheel post.

I remember that he drove well and carefully and talked little, probably because of the noisiness of the motor.

I directed him, but I don't recall now, not that it matters, what route we took. I remember, though, that I didn't recognize the driveway of the old Wentworth place—the house itself was set quite far back from the road and you couldn't see it through the trees even in daylight—but a little farther on I recognized the farm that an aunt and uncle of mine had lived in many years ago and knew we'd passed our objective.

He turned back, then, and this time I spotted the driveway

and we turned in and followed the drive back among the trees to the house itself. We parked alongside it.

"First ones here," Smith said in the sudden silence as he turned off the engine.

I got out of the car and—I don't know why; or do I?—I took the bottle with me. It was so dark outside that I couldn't see the bottle in front of my eyes as I tilted it upward.

Smith had turned out the headlights and was getting out of his side of the car. He had a flashlight in his hand and I could see again as he came around to my side of the car. I held out the bottle to him and said, "Want one?" and he said, "You read my mind, Doc," and took one. My eyes were getting a little used to the dark now and I could see the outlines of the house, and I thought about it.

God, but the place must be old, I realized. I knew it well from the weeks in summer when, as a kid, I'd visited my aunt and uncle just down the road for a taste of farm life—as against the big city of Carmel City, Illinois.

That had been over forty years ago and it had been old then, and untenanted. It had been lived in since, but for brief intervals. Why the few people who had tried to live there had left, I didn't know. They'd never complained—publicly, at least of its being haunted. But none had ever stayed there for long. Perhaps it was merely the house itself; it really was a depressing place. A year or more ago the *Clarion* had carried an ad for the rental of it—and at a very reasonable price—but no one had taken it.

I thought of Johnny Haskins, who lived on the farm between my uncle's place and this one. He and I had explored the place several times together, in daylight. Johnny was dead now. He'd been killed in France in 1918, near the end of the first world war. In daytime, I hope, for Johnny had always been afraid of the dark—just as I was afraid of heights and as Al Grainger was afraid of fire and as everyone is afraid of something or other.

Johnny had been afraid of the old Wentworth place, too—even more afraid than I was, although he was several years older than I. He'd believed in ghosts, a little; at least he'd been afraid of them, although not as afraid as he was of the dark. And I'd picked up a little of that fear from him and I'd kept it for quite a few years after I grew up.

But not anymore. The older you get the less afraid of ghosts you are—whether you believe in them or not.

By the time you pass the fifty mark you've known so many people who are now dead that ghosts, if there are any such, aren't all strangers. Some of your best friends are ghosts; why should you be afraid of them? And it's not too many years before you'll be on the other side of the fence yourself.

No, I wasn't afraid of ghosts or the dark or of the haunted house, but I was afraid of something. I wasn't afraid of Yehudi Smith, I liked him too well to be afraid of him. Undoubtedly I was a fool to come here with him, knowing nothing at all about him. Yet I would have bet money at long odds that he wasn't dangerous. A crackpot, maybe, but not a dangerous one.

Smith opened the car door again and said, "I just remembered I brought candles; they told me the electricity wouldn't be on. And there's another flashlight in here, if you want one, Doc."

Sure I wanted one. I felt a little better, a little less afraid of whatever I was afraid of once I had a flashlight of my own and was in no sudden danger of being alone in darkness.

I ran the beam of the flashlight up on the porch, and the house was just as I remembered it. It had been lived in just often enough for it to have been kept in repair, or at least in fairly good shape.

Yehudi Smith said, "Come on, Doc. We might as well wait inside," and led the way up the porch steps. They creaked as we walked up them but they were solid.

The front door wasn't locked. Smith must have known that it wouldn't be, from the confident way he opened it.

We went in and he closed the door behind us. The beams of our flashlights danced ahead of us down the long dimness of the hallway. I noticed with surprise that the place was carpeted and furnished; it had been empty and bare at the time I'd explored it as a kid. The most recent tenant or owner who had lived here, for whatever reason he had moved away, had left the place furnished, possibly hoping to rent or sell it that way.

We turned into a huge living room on the left of the hallway. There was furniture there, too, white-sheeted. Covered fairly recently, from the fact that the sheets were not too dirty nor was there a great amount of dust anywhere.

Something made the back of my neck prickle. Maybe the ghostly appearance of that sheeted furniture.

"Shall we wait here or go up in the attic?" Smith asked me.

"The attic? Why the attic?"

"Where the meeting is to be held."

I was getting to like this less and less. *Was* there going to be a meeting? Were others really coming here tonight? It was five minutes of one o'clock already.

I looked around and wondered whether I'd rather stay here or go on up into the attic. Either alternative seemed crazy. Why didn't I go home? Why hadn't I stayed there?

I didn't like that spectral white-covered furniture. I said, "Let's go on up into the attic. Might as well, I guess."

Yes, I'd come this far. I might as well see it through the rest of the way. If there was a looking-glass up there in the attic and he wanted us to walk through it, I'd do that, too. Provided only that he went first.

But I wanted another short nip out of that bottle I was carrying. I offered it to Smith and he shook his head so I went ahead and took the nip and it slightly warmed the coldness that was beginning to develop in my stomach.

We went up the stairs to the second floor and we didn't meet any ghosts or any snarks. We opened the door that led to the steps to the attic.

We walked up them, Smith in the lead and I following, his plump posterior just ahead of me.

My mind kept reminding me how ridiculous this was. How utterly insane it was for me to have come here at all.

Where were you at one o'clock? In a haunted house. *Doing what?* Waiting for the Vorpal Blades to come. *What are these Vorpal Blades?* I don't know. *What were they going to do?* I don't know, I tell you. Maybe anything. Get with child a mandrake root. Hold court to see who stole the tarts or put the white knight back on his horse. Or maybe only read the minutes of the last meeting and the treasurer's report, by Benchley. *Who's Benchley?* WHO'S YEHUDI?

Who's your little whoozis?

Doc, I hate to say this, but—

I'm afraid that—

Very pitying, and oh, so sensibly true. *You were drunk, weren't you, Doc?* Well, not exactly, but—

Yehudi Smith's plump posterior ascending the attic stairs. A horse's posterior ascending after him.

We reached the top and Smith asked me to hold my flashlight aimed at the post of the stair railing until he got a candle lighted there. He took a short, thick candle from his pocket—one that would balance easily by itself without a holder—and got it lighted.

There were trunks and a few pieces of broken or worn-out furniture scattered about the sides of the attic; the middle of it was clear. The only window was at the back and it was boarded up from the inside.

I looked around and, although the furniture here wasn't sheeted, I didn't like the place any better than I'd liked the big room downstairs. The light of one candle was far too dim to dispel the darkness, for one thing, in so large a space. And I didn't like the flickering shadows it cast. They might have been Jabberwocks or anything your imagination wanted to name them. There ought to be Rorschach tests with flickering shadows; what the mind would make out of them ought to be a lot more revealing than what the mind makes out of ink blots.

Yes, I could have used more light, a lot more light. But Smith had put his flashlight in his pocket and I did the same with the other one; it was his, too, and I didn't have any excuse to wear out the battery keeping it on. And besides it didn't do much good in so large a room.

"What do we do now?" I asked.

"Wait for the others. What time is it, Doc?"

I managed to read my watch by the light of the candle and told him that it was seven minutes after one.

He nodded. "We'll give them until a quarter after. There's something that I must do then, at that exact time, whether they're here or not. Listen, isn't that a car?"

I listened and I thought it was. Way up here in the attic, it wasn't clearly audible, but I thought I heard a car that could have been coming back from the main road to the house. I was pretty sure of it.

I uncorked the bottle again and offered it. This time Smith took a drink, too. Mine was a fairly long pull. I was getting sober, I thought, and this was no time or place to get sober. It was silly enough to be here, drunk.

I couldn't hear the car any more, and then suddenly—as though it had stopped and then started again—I could hear it, and louder than before. But the sound seemed to diminish, as though the car had driven back from the road, stopped a minute, and then headed for the main road again. The sound died out.

The shadows flickered. There was no sound from downstairs. I shivered a little.

Smith said, "Help me look for something, Doc. It's supposed to be here somewhere, ready. A small table."

"A table?"

"Yes, but don't touch it if you find it."

He had his flashlight out again and was working his way

along one wall of the attic, and I went the other way, glad of a chance to use my flashlight on those damned shadows. I wondered what the hell kind of a table I was looking for. Thou preparest a table before me in the presence of mine enemies, I thought. But there weren't any of my enemies here, I hoped.

I found it first. It was in the back corner of the attic.

It was a small, three-legged, glass-topped table, and there were two small objects lying on it.

I started laughing. Ghosts and shadows or not, I laughed out loud. One of the objects on the table was a small key and the other was a small vial with a tag tied to it.

The glass-topped table Alice had found in the hall at the bottom of the rabbit hole—the table on which had been the key that opened the little door to the garden and the bottle with the paper label that said " DRINK ME" tied around its neck.

I'd seen that table often—in the John Tenniel illustration of it in *Alice in Wonderland.*

Smith's footsteps coming up behind me made me stop laughing. After all, this ridiculous flummery might be something of a ritual to him. It was funny to me, but I liked him and I didn't want to hurt his feelings.

He wasn't even smiling. He said, "Yes, that's it. Is it one fifteen yet?"

"Almost on the head."

"Good." He picked up the key with one hand and the bottle with the other. "The others must be delayed, but we shall take the first step. This, keep." He dropped the key into my pocket. "And this, I drink." He took the cork out of the bottle. "I apologize for not being able to share it with you—as you have so generously shared your drinks with me—but you understand, until you have been fully initiated—"

He seemed genuinely embarrassed, so I nodded understanding and forgiveness.

I wasn't afraid anymore, now. It had become too ridiculous for fear. What was that "DRINK ME" bottle supposed to do?

Oh, yes, he'd shrink in size until he was only a few inches high—and then he'd have to find and use a little box labeled "EAT ME" and eat the cake inside and he'd suddenly grow so big that—

He lifted the bottle and said, "To Lewis Carroll."

Since that was the toast, I said, "Wait!" and got the cork quickly out of the bottle of whiskey I was still carrying, and raised it, too. There wasn't any reason why I couldn't and shouldn't get in on that toast as long as my lips, as a neophyte's, didn't defile whatever sacred elixir the "DRINK ME" bottle held.

He clinked the little bottle lightly against the big one I held, and tossed it off—I could see from the corner of my eye as I tilted my bottle—in that strange conjuring trick again, the bottle stopping inches away from his lips and the drink keeping on going without the loss of a drop.

I was putting: the cork into the whisky bottle when Yehudi Smith died.

He dropped the bottle labeled "DRINK ME" and started to clutch at his throat, but he died, I think, even before the bottle hit the floor. His face was hideously contorted with pain, but the pain couldn't have lasted over a fraction of a second. His eyes, still open, went suddenly blank, utterly blank. And the thud of his fall shook the floor under my feet, seemed to shake the whole house.

CHAPTER TEN

And, as in uffish thought be stood,
The Jabberwocky with eyes of flame.
Came whiffling through the tulgey wood,
And burbled as it came!

I THINK I must have done nothing but stand there and jitter for seconds. Finally I was able to move.

I'd seen his face and I'd seen and heard him fall; I didn't have the slightest doubt that he was dead. But I had to be sure. I got down on my knees and groped my hand inside his coat and shirt, hunting for a heartbeat. There wasn't any.

I made even surer. The flashlight he'd given me had a round flat lens; I held it over his mouth and in front of his nostrils for a while and there was no slightest trace of moisture.

The small empty bottle from which he'd drunk was of fairly heavy glass. It hadn't broken when he'd dropped it, and the tag tied around its neck had kept it from rolling far. I didn't touch it, but I got on my hands and knees and sniffed at the open end. The smell was the smell of good whisky, nothing else that I could detect. No odor of bitter almonds, but if what had been in that whisky hadn't been prussic acid, it had been some corrosive poison just about as strong. Or could it have been prussic, and would the smell of whisky have blanketed the bitter almond smell? I didn't know.

I stood up again and found that my knees were shaking. This was the second man I'd seen die tonight. But I hadn't so much minded about George. He'd had it coming, for one thing, and for another his body had been inside the crumpled-up car; I'd not actually seen him die. Nor had I been alone then; Smiley had been with me. I'd have given my whole bank account, all three hundred and twelve dollars of it, to have had Smiley with me there in the attic.

I wanted to get out of there, fast, and I was too scared to move. I thought I'd be less scared if I could figure out what it was all about, but it was sheerly mad. It didn't make sense that even a madman would have brought me out here under so weird a pretext so that I could be an audience of one to his suicide.

In fact, if I was sure of anything, I was sure that Smith hadn't killed himself. But who had, and why? The Vorpal Blades? *Was* there such a group?

Where were they? Why hadn't they come?

A sudden thought put shivers down my spine. *Maybe they had.* I'd thought I heard a car come and go, while we'd waited. Why couldn't it have dropped off passengers? Waiting for me downstairs—or even now creeping up the attic steps toward me.

I looked that way. The candle flickered and the shadows danced. I strained my ears, but there wasn't any sound. No sound anywhere.

I was afraid to move, and then gradually I found that I was afraid not to move. I had to get *out* of here before I went crazy. If anything was downstairs I'd rather go down and meet it than wait till it decided to come up here after me.

I wished to hell and back that I hadn't given Smiley that revolver, but wishing didn't get me the revolver back.

Well, the whisky bottle was a weapon of sorts. I shifted the flashlight to my left hand and picked up the whisky-bottle, by its neck, in my right. It was still more than half full and heavy enough for a bludgeon.

I tiptoed to the head of the steps. I don't know why I tiptoed unless it was to avoid scaring myself worse by making

noise; we hadn't been quiet up here before and Smith's fall had
shaken the whole house. If anyone was downstairs, he knew he
wasn't alone in the building.

I looked at the square post at the top of the railing and the
short, thick candle still burning on top of it. I didn't want to
touch it; I wanted to be able to say that I hadn't touched anything at all, except to feel for a heartbeat that wasn't there. Yet I
couldn't leave the candle burning, either; it might set the house
afire if it fell over, as Smith hadn't anchored it down with
molten wax but had merely stood it on its base.

I compromised by blowing it out but not touching it otherwise.

My flashlight showed me there was nothing or no one on
the stairs leading down to the second floor and that the door at
the bottom of them was still closed, as we had left it. Before I
started down them I took one last look around the attic with my
flash. The shadows jumped as the beam swept around the walls,
and then, for some reason, I brought the circle of light to rest on
Yehudi Smith's body lying sprawled there on the floor, eyes
wide open and still staring unseeingly at the rafters overhead,
his face still frozen in the grimace of that horrible, if brief, pain
in which he'd died.

I hated to leave him alone there in the dark. Silly and
sentimental as the thought was, I couldn't help feeling that way.
He'd been such a nice little guy. Who the hell had killed him,
and why, and why in such a bizarre manner, and what was it all
about? And he'd said it was dangerous to come here tonight,
and he was dead right, as far as he himself was concerned. And
I—?

With that thought, I was afraid again. I wasn't out of here
yet. Was someone or something waiting downstairs?

The attic stairs were uncarpeted and they squeaked so
loudly that I gave up trying to walk quietly and hurried. The
attic door creaked, too, but nothing was waiting for me on the
other side of it. Or downstairs. I flashed my light into the big

living room as I passed the doorway and got a momentary fright as I thought something white was coming toward me—but it was only the sheeted table and it had only seemed to move.

The porch and down the porch steps.

The car was still there on the driveway beside the house. It was a coupe, I noticed now, and the same make and model as mine. My feet crunched gravel as I walked to it; I was still scared but I didn't dare let myself run. I wondered if Smith had left the key in the car, and hoped frantically that he had. I should have thought of it while

I was still in the attic and could have felt in his pockets. I wouldn't go back up there now, I realized, for anything in the world. I'd walk back to town first.

At least the car door wasn't locked. I slid in under the wheel, and flashed my light on the dashboard. Yes, the ignition key was in the lock. I slammed the door behind me and felt a little more secure inside the closed car.

I turned the key and stepped on the starter and the engine started the first *try*. I shifted into low gear and then, before I let out the clutch, I carefully shifted back into neutral again and sat there with the motor idling.

This wasn't the car in which Yehudi Smith had driven me here. The gear shift knob was hard rubber with a ridge around it, not the smooth onyx ball I'd noticed on the gear shift lever of his car. It was like the one on my car, which was back home in the garage with two flat tires that I hadn't got around to fixing.

I turned on the dome light, although by then I didn't really have to. I knew already from the feel of the controls in starting and in shifting, from the sound of the engine, from a dozen little things.

This was *my car*.

It was so impossible that I forgot to be afraid, that I was in such a hurry to get away from the house. Oh, there was a little logic in my lack of fear, too; if anybody had been laying for me, the house would have been the place. He wouldn't have let me get this far and he wouldn't have left the ignition key in the car so I could get away in it.

I got out of the car and looked, with the flashlight, at the two tires which had been flat this morning. They weren't flat now. Either someone had fixed them, or someone had simply let the air out of them last night and had subsequently pumped them up again with the hand pump I keep in my luggage compartment. The second idea seemed more likely; now that I thought of it, it was strange that two tires—both in good shape and with good tubes in them—should have gone flat, completely flat, at the same time and while the car was standing in my garage.

I walked all the way around the car, looking at it, and there wasn't anything wrong with it that I could see. I got back in under the wheel and sat there a minute with the engine running, wondering if it was even remotely possible that Yehudi Smith had driven me here in my own car.

No, I decided, not remotely. I hadn't noticed his car at all except for three things, but those three things were plenty to make me sure. Besides the gear shift knob, I remembered that push button radio with the button for *WBBM* pushed in—and my car has no radio at all—and there was the fact that his engine was noisy and mine is quiet. Right then, with it idling, I could barely hear it.

Unless I was crazy—

Could I have imagined that other car? For that matter, could I have imagined Yehudi Smith? Could I have driven out here by myself in my own car, gone up to the attic alone—?

It's a horrible thing to suspect yourself suddenly of complete insanity, equipped with hallucinations.

I realized I'd better quit thinking along those lines, here alone in a car, alone in the night, parked beside a haunted house. I might drive myself nutty, if I wasn't already.

I took a long drink out of the bottle that was now on the seat beside me, and then drove out to the highway and back to town. I didn't drive fast, partly because I was a little drunk—physically anyway. The horrible thing that had happened up in the attic, the fantastic, incredible death of Yehudi Smith, had shocked me sober, mentally.

I *couldn't* have imagined—

But at the edge of town the doubts came back, then the answer to them. I pulled to the side of the road and turned on the dome light. I had the card and the key and the flashlight, those three souvenirs of my experience. I took the flashlight out of my coat pocket and looked at it. Just a dime store flashlight; it meant nothing except that it wasn't mine. The card was the thing. I hunted in several pockets, getting worried as hell, before I found it in the pocket of my shirt. Yes, I had it, and it still read *Yehudi Smith*. I felt a little better as I put it back in my pocket. While I was at it, I looked at the key, too. The key that had been with the "DRINK ME" bottle on the glass-topped table.

It was still there in the pocket Smith had dropped it into; I'd not touched it or looked at it closely. It was, of course, the wrong kind of key, but I'd noticed that at first glance when I'd seen it on the table in the attic; that had been part of my source of amusement when I'd laughed. It was a Yale key, and it should have been a small gold key, the one Alice used to open the fifteen-inch-high door into the lovely garden.

Come to think of it, all three of those props in the attic had been wrong, one way or another. The table had been a glass-topped one, but it should have been an all-glass table; the wooden legs were wrong. The key shouldn't have been a nickel-plated Yale, and the "DRINK ME" should not have contained poison. *(It had, in fact, a sort of mixed flavour of cherry-tart, custard, pineapple, roast turkey, toffy, and hot buttered toast.)* —according to Alice. It couldn't have tasted anything like that to Smith.

I started driving again, slowly. Now that I was back in town I had to make up my mind whether I was going to the sheriff's office or going to call the state police. Reluctantly I decided I'd better go right to the sheriff. Definitely this case was in his department, unless he called on the state police for help. They'd dump it in his lap anyway, even if I called them. And he hated my guts enough as it was, without my making it any worse by bypassing him in reporting a major crime. Not that I didn't hate his guts just as much, but tonight he was in a better position to make trouble for me than I for him.

So I parked my coupe across the street from the courthouse and took one more swig from the bottle to give me courage to tell Kates the story I was going to have to tell him. Then I marched myself across the street and up the courthouse stairs to the sheriff's office on the second floor.

If I was lucky, I thought, Kates might be out and his deputy, Hank Ganzer, might be there.

I wasn't lucky. Hank wasn't there at all, and Kates was talking on the phone. He glared at me when I came in and then went back to his call.

"Hell, I could have done it on the phone from here. Go see the guy. Wake him up and be sure he's awake enough to remember any little thing that might have been said. Yeah, then call me again before you start back."

He put the receiver down and his swivel chair squeaked shrilly as he swung about to face me. He yelled, "There isn't any story on it yet." Rance Kates always yells; I've never heard him say anything in a quiet tone, or even a normal one. His voice matches his red face, which, always looks angry. I've often wondered if he looks like that even when he's in bed. Wondered, but had no inclination to find out.

What he'd just yelled at me, though, made so little sense that I just looked at him.

I said, "I've come to report a murder, Kates."

"Huh?" He looked interested. "You mean you found either Miles or Bonney?"

For a minute neither name registered at all. I said, "The

man's name is Smith." I thought I'd better sneak up on the Yehudi part gradually, maybe let Kates read it himself off the card. "The body is in the attic of the old Wentworth place out on the pike."

"Stoeger, are you drunk?"

"I've been drinking," I told him. "I'm not drunk." At least I hoped I wasn't. Maybe that last one I'd taken in the car just before I'd left it had been one too many. My voice sounded thick, even to me, and I had a hunch my eyes were looking a trifle bleary from the outside; they were beginning to feel that way from my side of them.

"What were you doing in the attic of the Wentworth place? You mean you were there tonight?"

I wished again that Hank Ganzer had been there instead of Kates. Hank would have taken my word for it and gone out for the body; then my story wouldn't have sounded so incredible when I'd have got around to telling it.

I said, "Yes, I just came from there. I went there with Smith, at his request."

"Who is this Smith? You know him?"

"I met him tonight for the first time. He came to see me."

"What for? What were you doing out there? A haunted house!"

I sighed. There wasn't anything I could do but answer his damn questions and they were getting tougher all the time. Let's see, how could I put it so it wouldn't sound *too* crazy?

I said, "We went there because it *is* supposed to be a haunted house, Kates. This Smith was interested in the occult—in psyhic phenomena. He asked me to go out there with him to perform an experiment. I gathered that some other people were coming, but they didn't."

"What kind of an experiment?"

"I don't know. He was killed before we got around to it."

"You and him were there alone?"

"Yes," I said, but I saw where that was leading so I added,

"But I didn't kill him. And I don't know who did. He was poisoned."

"Poisoned how?"

Part of my brain wanted to tell him, "Out of a little bottle labeled 'DRINK ME' on a glass table, as in *Alice in Wonderland.*" The sensible part of my brain told me to let him find that out for himself. I said, "Out of a bottle that was planted there for him to drink. By whom, I don't know. But you sound like you don't believe me. Why don't you go out and see for yourself, Kates? Damn it, man, I'm reporting a *murder.*" And then it occurred to me there wasn't really any proof of that, so I amended it a little: "Or at least a death by violence."

He stared at me and I think he was becoming convinced, a little. His phone rang and his swivel chair screamed again as he swung around. He barked "Hello. Sheriff Kates," into it.

Then his voice tamed down a little. He said, "No, Mrs. Harrison, haven't heard a thing. Hank's over at Neillsville, checking up at that end, and he's going to watch the road again on his way back. I'll call you the minute I learn anything at all. But don't worry; it can't be anything serious."

He turned back. "Stoeger, if this is a *gag,* I'm going to take you apart." He meant it, and he could do it, too. Kates is only a medium-sized man, not too much bigger than I, but he's tough and hard as a rock physically. He can handle men weighing half again as much as he does. And he's got enough of a sadistic streak to enjoy doing it whenever he has a good excuse for it.

"It's no gag," I said. "What's this about Miles Harrison and Ralph Bonney?"

"Missing. They left Neilsville with the Bonney pay roll a little after half past eleven and should have been back here around midnight. It's almost two o'clock and nobody knows where they are. Look, if I thought you were sober and there *was* a stiff out on the pike, "I'd call the state cops. I *got* to stay here till we find what happened to Miles and Bonney."

The state cops were fine, as far as I was concerned. I'd reported it where it should have been reported, and Kates would have no kickback if he himself called the state police. I was just opening my mouth to say that might be a good idea when the phone rang again.

Kates yelled into it, and then, "As far as the teller knew, they were heading right back, Hank? Nothing unusual happened at that end, huh? Okay, come back, and watch both sides of the road all the way in case they ran off it or something . . . Yeah, the pike. That's the only way they could've come. Oh, and listen, stop at the Wentworth place on your way and take a look in the attic . . . Yeah, I said the attic. Doc Stoeger's here, drunk as a coot, and he says there's a stiff in the attic there. If there *is* one, I'll worry about it."

He slammed the receiver down and started shuffling papers on his desk, trying to look busy. Finally he thought of something to do and phoned the Bonney Fireworks Company to see if Bonney had showed up there yet, or called them. Apparently, from what I could hear of the conversation, he hadn't done either.

I realized that I was still standing up and that now, since Kates had given that order to his deputy, nothing was going to happen until Hank got back—at least half an hour if he drove slowly to watch both sides of the road. So I found myself a chair and sat down. Kates shuffled papers again and paid no attention to me.

I got to wondering about Bonney and Miles, and hoped they hadn't had an accident. If they had had one, and were two hours overdue, it must have been a bad one. Unless both were seriously hurt, one of them would have reached a phone long before this. Of course they could have stopped somewhere for a drink, but it didn't seem likely, not for two hours at least. And, come to think of it, they couldn't have; the closing hour for taverns applied to the whole county, not just to Carmel City. Twelve o'clock had been almost two hours ago.

I wished that it wasn't. Not that I either needed or wanted a drink particularly at that moment, but it would have been much more pleasant to do my waiting at Smiley's instead of here in the sheriff's office.

Kates suddenly swiveled his chair at me. "*You* don't know anything about Bonney and Harrison, do you?"

"Not a thing," I told him.

"Where were you at midnight?"

With Yehudi. Who's Yehudi? The little man who wasn't there.

I said, "Home, talking to Smith. We stayed there until half past twelve."

"Anybody else there?"

I shook my head. Come to think of it, nobody but myself had, as far as I knew, even seen Yehudi Smith. If his body *wasn't* in the attic at the Wentworth place, I was going to have a hell of a time proving he'd ever existed. A card and a key and a flashlight.

"Where'd this Smith guy come from?"

"I don't know. He didn't say."

"What was his first name?"

I stalled on that one. I said, "I don't remember. I've got his card somewhere. He gave me one." Let him think the card was probably out at the house. I wasn't ready to show it to him yet.

"How'd he happen to come to *you* to go to a haunted house with him if he didn't even know you?"

I said, "He knew *of* me, as a Lewis Carroll fan."

"A what?"

"Lewis Carroll. *Alice in Wonderland, Alice Through the Looking-Glass.*" And a "DRINK ME" bottle on a glass table, and a key, and Bandersnatches and Jabberwocks. But let Kates find that out for himself, after he'd found a body and knew that I wasn't either drunk or crazy.

He said, *"Alice in Wonder land,"* and sniffed. He glared at me a full ten seconds and then decided, apparently, that he was wasting his time on me and swiveled back to his paper shuffling.

I felt in my pockets to make sure that the card and the key were still there. They were. The flashlight was still in the car, but the flashlight didn't mean anything anyway. Maybe the key didn't, either. But that card was my contact with reality, in a sense. As long as it still said *Yehudi Smith,* I knew I wasn't stark raving mad. I knew that there'd really been such a person and that he wasn't a figment of my imagination.

I slipped it out of my pocket to look at it again. Yes, it still said *"Yehudi Smith,"* although my eyes had a bit of trouble focusing on it clearly. The printing looked fuzzy, which meant I needed either one more drink or several less.

Yehudi Smith, in fuzzy-edged type. Yehudi, the little man who wasn't there.

And suddenly—don't ask me how I knew, but I knew.

I didn't see the pattern, but I saw that much of it. The little man who wasn't there.

Wouldn't be there.

Hank was going to come in and say, "What's this about a stiff in the Wentworth attic? *I* couldn't find one."

Yehudi. The little man who wasn't there. *I saw a man upon the stair, A little man who wasn't there. He wasn't there again today; Gee, I wish he'd go away.*

It was preordained; it *had* to be. That much of the pattern I saw. The name Yehudi hadn't been an accident. I think that *almost,* just then, I had a flash of insight that would have shown me most of the pattern, if not all of it. You know how it is sometimes when you're drunk, but not too drunk, you think you're trembling on the verge of understanding something important and cosmic that has eluded you all your life? And— just barely possibly—you really are. I think I was, at that moment.

Then I looked up from the card and the thread of my thought was lost because Kates was staring at me. He'd turned just his head this time instead of the squeaking swivel chair he was sitting on. He was looking at me speculatively, suspiciously.

I tried to ignore it; I was trying to recapture my thoughts and let them lead me. I was close to something. *I saw a man upon the stair.* Yehudi Smith's plump posterior ascending the attic stairs, just ahead of me.

No, the dead body with the contorted face—the poor piece of cold clay that had been a nice little guy with laughter lines around his eyes and the corners of his mouth—wouldn't be there in the attic when Hank Ganzer looked for it. It couldn't be there; its presence there wouldn't fit the pattern that I still couldn't see or understand.

Squeal of the swivel chair as Rance Kates turned his body to match the position of his head. "Is that the card that guy gave you?"

I nodded.

"What's his full name?"

The hell with Kates. "Yehudi," I said. "Yehudi Smith."

Of course it wasn't really; I knew at least that much now. I got up and walked to Kates, desk. Unfortunately for my dignity, I weaved a little. But I made it without falling. I put the card down in front of him and went back and sat down again, managing to walk straight this time.

He looked at the card and then at me and then at the card and then at me.

And then I knew I *must* be crazy.

"Doc," he asked—and his voice was quieter than I'd ever heard it before—*"What's your bug number?"*

CHAPTER ELEVEN

"O Oysters, said the Carpenter,
"You've had a pleasant run!
Shall we be trotting home again?"
But answer came there none—

I JUST STARED at him. Either he was crazy or I was—and several times in the last hour I'd been wondering about myself. *What's your bug number?* What a question to ask a man in the spot I was in. What's yours?

Finally I managed to answer. "Huh?" I said.

"Your bug number. Your label number."

I got it then. I wasn't crazy after all. I knew what he meant.

I run a union shop, which means that I've signed a contract with the International Typographical Union and pay Pete, my only employee, union wages. In a town as small as Carmel City, you can get by with a non-union shop, but I happen to believe in unions and to think the typographical union is a good one. Being a union shop, we put the union label on everything we print. It's a little oval-shaped dingus, so small you can barely read the type if you've got good eyesight. And alongside it is an equally tiny number which is the number of my particular shop among the other union shops in my area. By the combination of the place name which is part of the label itself and the number of the shop beside it, you can tell where any given piece of union printing has been done.

But that little oval logotype is known to non-union printers as "the bug." It does, I'll admit, look rather like a tiny bug crawling across the bottom corner of whatever it's put on. And non-union printers call the shop number alongside the "bug" the "bug number." Kates wasn't a printer, union or otherwise, but I remember now that two of his brothers, both living in Neilsville, were non-union printers, and naturally he'd have picked up the language—and the implied prejudice back of it—from them.

I said, "My label number is seven."

He slapped the calling card down on the desk in front of him. He snorted—quite literally; you often read about people snorting but seldom hear them do it. He said, "Stoeger, you printed this damn thing yourself. The whole thing is a gag. Damn you—"

He started to get up and then sat down again and looked at the papers in front of him. He looked back at me and I think he was going to tell me to get the hell out, and then apparently he decided he might as well wait till Hank got back.

He shuffled papers.

I sat there and tried to absorb the fact that—apparently, at any rate—that *Yehudi Smith* calling card had been printed in my own shop. I didn't get up to look at it. Somehow, I was perfectly willing to take Kates's word for it.

Why not? It was part of the pattern. I should have guessed it myself. Not from the typeface; almost every shop has eight-point Garamond. But from the fact that the "DRINK ME" bottle had contained poison and Yehudi wasn't going to be there when Hank looked for him. It followed the pattern, and I knew now what the pattern was. It was the pattern of madness.

Mine—or whose? I was getting scared. I'd been scared several times already that night, but this was a different variety of scaredness. I was getting scared of the night itself, of the *pattern* of the night.

I needed a drink, and I needed it bad. I stood up and started for the door. The swivel chair screamed and Kates said, "Where the hell you think you're going?"

"Down to my car. Going to get something. I'll be back." I didn't want to get into an argument with him.

"Sit down. You're not going out of here."

I did want to get into an argument with him. "Am I under arrest? And on what charge?"

"Material witness in a murder case, Stoeger. *If* there's a corpse where you say there's one. If there isn't, we can switch it to drunk and disorderly. Take your choice."

I took my choice. I sat down again.

He had me over a barrel and I could see that he loved it. I wished that I'd gone to my office and phoned the state police, regardless of repercussions.

I waited. That "bug number" angle of Kates' had thrown me off thinking about how it could be and why it would be that Yehudi Smith's calling card had been printed in my own print shop. Not that, come to think of it, the "how" had been difficult. I lock the door when I leave, but I lock it with a dime-store skeleton key. They come two on a card for a dime. Yes, Anybody could have got in. And Anybody, whoever he was, could have printed that card without knowing a damn thing about printing. You have to know the printer's case to set type in quantity, but anybody could pick out a dozen letters, more or less, to spell out Yehudi Smith simply by trial and error. The little hand press I print cards on is so simple that a child—well, anyway, a high school kid—could figure out how to operate it. True, he'd get lousy impressions and waste a lot of cards trying to get one good one. But Anybody, if he'd tried long enough, could have printed one good card that said Yehudi Smith and carried my union label in the bottom corner.

But why would Anybody have done something like that?

The more I thought about it the less sense it made, although one thing did emerge that made even less sense than the rest of it. It would have been easier to print that card without the union label than with it, so Anybody had gone to a little additional trouble to bring out the fact that the card had been printed at the *Clarion*. Except for the death of Yehudi Smith the whole thing might have been the pattern of a monstrous practical joke. But practical jokes don't include sudden death. Not even such a fantastic death as Yehudi Smith had met.

Why had Yehudi Smith died?

Somewhere there had to be a key.

And that reminded me of the key in my pocket and I took it out and stared at it, wondering what I could open with it. Somewhere there was a lock that it fitted.

It didn't look either familiar or unfamiliar. Yale keys don't. Could it be mine? I thought about all the keys I owned. The key to the front door of my house was a Yale type key, but not actually a Yale. Besides—

I took the keytainer from my pocket and opened it. My front door key is on the left and I compared it with the key I'd brought away from the attic. The notches didn't match; it wasn't a duplicate of that one. And it was still more different from my back door key, the one on the other side of the row. In between were two other keys but both were quite different types. One was the key to the door at the *Clarion* office and the other was for the garage behind my house. I never use the garage key; I keep nothing of value in the garage except the car itself and I always leave it locked.

It seemed to me that I'd had five keys instead of four, there on the keytainer, but I couldn't remember for sure and I couldn't figure out what the missing one was, if one really was missing.

Not the key to my car; I didn't keep that on the keytainer (I hate a keytainer dangling and swinging from my ignition lock, so I carry the car key loose in my vest pocket).

I put the keytainer back in my pocket and stared at the single key again. I wondered suddenly if it could be a duplicate of my car key. But I couldn't compare it to see because, this time, I'd left the key in the lock when I'd got out of the car, thinking I was going to be up here in the sheriff's office only a minute or two and chat then he'd be heading out to the Wentworth place with me.

Kates must have turned his head—not his swivel chair, for it didn't squeak—and seen me staring at the key. He asked, "What's that?"

"A key," I said. "A key to unlock a riddle. A key to murder."

The chair did squeak then. "Stoeger, what the hell? Are you just drunk, or are you crazy?"

"I don't know," I said. "Which do you think?"

He snorted. "Let's see that key." I handed it to him.

"What's it open?"

"I don't know." I was getting mad again—not particularly at Kates this time; at everything. "I know what it's supposed to open."

"What?"

"A little door fifteen inches high off a room at the bottom of a rabbit hole. It leads to a beautiful garden."

He looked at me a long time. I looked back. I didn't give a damn.

I heard a car outside. That would be Hank Ganzer, probably. He wouldn't have found the body of Yehudi Smith in the attic out on the pike. I knew that, somehow.

And how Kates was going to react to that, I could guess. Even though, obviously, he didn't believe a damn word of it to begin with. I'd have given a lot, just then, to be inside Rance Kates' mind, or what he uses for one, to see just what he *was* thinking. I'd have given a lot more, though, to be inside the mind of Anybody, the person who'd printed Yehudi Smith's card on my hand press and who'd put the poison in the "DRINK ME" bottle.

Hank's steps coming up the stairs.

He came in the door and his eyes happened to be looking in my direction first. He said, "Hi, Doc," casually and then turned to Kates. "No sign of an accident, Rance. I drove slow, watched both sides of the road. No sign of a car going off. But look, maybe we should both do it. If one of us could keep moving the spotlight back and forth while the other drove, we could see back farther." He looked at his wrist watch. "It's only two-thirty. Won't get light until six, and in that long a time—"

Kates nodded. "Okay, Hank. But listen, I'm going to get the state boys in on this in case—well, in case Bonney's car turns up somewhere else. We know when they left Neilsville, but we can't be positive they started for Carmel City."

"Why wouldn't they?"

"How would I know?" Kates said. "But if they did start here, they didn't get here."

I might as well not have been there at all.

I cut in. "Hank, did you go to the Wentworth place?"

He looked at me. "Sure, Doc. Listen, what kind of a gag was that?"

"Did you look in the attic?"

"Sure. Looked all around it with my flashlight."

I'd known it, but I closed my eyes.

Kates surprised me, after all. His voice was almost gentle. "Stoeger, get the hell out of here. Go home and sleep it off."

I opened my eyes again and looked at Hank. "All right," I said, "I'm drunk or crazy. But listen, Hank, was there a candle stub standing on top of the post at the top of the attic steps?"

He shook his head slowly.

"A glass-topped table, standing in one corner—it'd be the northwest corner of the attic?"

"I didn't see it, Doc. I wasn't looking for tables. But I'd have noticed a candle stub, if it had been on the stair post. I remember putting my hand on it when I started down."

"And you don't recall seeing a dead body on the floor?"

Hank didn't even answer me. He looked back at Kates. "Rance, maybe I'd better drive Doc home while you're making those calls. Where's your car, Doc?"

"Across the street."

"Okay, we won't give you a parking ticket. I'll drive you home in mine." He looked at Kates for corroboration.

Kates gave it. I hated Kates for it. He was grinning at me. He had me in such a nasty spot that, damn him, he could afford to be generous. If he threw me in the can overnight, I could fight back. If he sent me home to sleep it off—and even gave me a chauffeur to take me there—

Hank Ganzer said, "Come on, Doc." He was going through the door.

I got to my feet. I didn't *want* to go home. If I went home now, the murderer of Yehudi Smith would have the rest of the night to finish—to finish what? And what was it to me, except that I'd liked Yehudi Smith? And who the hell was Yehudi Smith?

I said, "Listen, Kates—"

Kates looked past me at the doorway. He said, "Go on, Hank. See if his car is parked straight or out in the middle of the street. I want to tell him something and then I'll send him down. I think he can make it."

He probably hoped I'd break my neck going down the steps.

"Sure, Rance." Hank's footsteps going down the stairs. Diminuendo.

Kates looked up at me. I was standing in front of his desk, trying not to look like a boy caught cheating in an examination standing in front of his teacher's desk.

I caught his eyes, and almost took a step backward. I hated Kates and knew that he hated me, but I hated him as one hates a man in office whom one knows to be a stupid oaf and a crook. He hated me, I thought, as someone who, as an editor, had power—and used it—against men like him.

But the look in his eyes wasn't that. It was sheer *personal* hatred and malevolence. It was something I hadn't suspected, and it shocked me. I don't, after fifty-three years, shock easily.

And then that look was gone, as suddenly as when you turn out a light. He was looking at me impersonally. His voice was impersonal, almost flat, not nearly as loud as usual. He said, "Stoeger, you know what I could do to you on something like this, don't you?"

I didn't answer; he didn't expect me to. Yes, I knew some of the things. The can overnight on a drunk and disorderly charge was a starting point. And if, in the morning, I persisted in my illusions, he could call in Dr. Buchan for a psychiatric once-over.

He said, "I'm not doing it. But I want you out of my hair from now on. Understand?"

I didn't answer that, either. If he wanted to think silence was consent, all right. Apparently he did. He said, "Now get the hell out of here."

I got the hell out of there. I'd got off easy. Except for that look he'd given me.

No, I didn't feel like a conquering hero about it. I should have faced up to it, and I should have insisted that there *had* been a murder in that attic, whether there was a *corpus delicti* there now or not. But I was too mixed up myself. I wanted time to think things out, to figure what the hell had really happened.

I went down the stairs and out into the night again.

Hank Ganzer's car was parked right in front, but he was just getting out of my car, across the street. I walked over toward him.

He said, "You *were* a little far out from the curb, Doc. I moved it in for you. Here's your key."

He handed me the key and I stuck it in my pocket and then reopened the door he'd just closed to get the bottle of whisky that was lying on the seat. No use leaving that, even if I had to leave the car here.

I stepped back, then, to the back of the car to take another look at those back tires. I still couldn't believe them; this morning they'd been completely flat. That was part of the puzzle, too.

Hank came back and stood by me. "What's the matter, Doc?" he asked. "If you're looking at your tires, they're okay." He kicked the one nearest to him and then walked around and kicked the other. He started back, and stopped.

He said, "Say, Doc, something you got in your luggage compartment must've spilled over. Did you have a can of paint or something in there?"

I shook my head and came around to see what he was looking at. It did look as though something had run out from under the bottom edge of the luggage compartment door. Something thick and blackish.

Hank turned the handle and tried to lift.

"It's not locked," I said. "I never bother to lock it. Nothing in there but a worn-out tire without a tube in it."

He tried again. "The hell it's not locked. Where's the key?"

Another piece of the pattern fell into place. I knew now what the fifth key, the middle one, on my keytainer should have been. I never lock the luggage compartment of my car except on the rare occasions when I take a trip and really have luggage in it. But I carry the key on my keytainer. And it was a Yale key and it hadn't been there when I'd looked a few minutes ago.

I said, "Kates has got it." It had to be. One Yale key looks like another, but the card, Yehudi Smith's card, had been printed in my own shop. The key would be mine, too.

Hank said, "Huh?"

I said again, "Kates has got it."

Hank looked at me strangely. He said, "Wait just a minute, Doc," and walked across to his own car. Twice, on the way, he looked back as though to be sure I wasn't going to get in and drive away.

He got a flashlight out of his glove compartment and came back. He bent down with it and took a close look at those streaks.

I stepped closer to look, too. Hank stepped back, as though he was suddenly afraid to have me behind him and peering over his shoulder.

So I didn't have to look. I knew what those streaks were, or what Hank thought they were.

He said, "Seriously, Doc, where's the key?"

"I'm serious," I told him. "I gave it to Rance Kates. I didn't know what key it was then. I'm pretty sure I do, now."

I thought I knew what was in that luggage compartment now, too.

He looked at me uncertainly and then walked part way across the street, angling so he could watch me. He cupped his hands around his lips and called out, "Rance! Hey, Rance!" And then looked quickly back to see that I was neither sneaking up on him nor trying to get into the car to drive away.

Nothing happened and he did it again.

A window opened and Kates was silhouetted against the light back of it. He called back, "What the hell, Hank, if you want me come up here. Don't wake up the whole God damned town."

Hank looked back over his shoulder at me again. Then he called, "Did Doc give you a key?"

"Yes. Why? What kind of a yam is he feeding you?"

"Bring down the key, Rance. Quick."

He looked back over his shoulder again, started toward me, and then hesitated. He compromised by staying where he was, but watching me.

The window slammed down.

I walked back around the car and I almost decided to light a match and look at those stains myself. And then I decided, what the hell.

Hank came a few steps closer. He said, "Where you going, Doc?"

I was at the curb by then. I said, "Nowhere," and sat down.

To wait.

CHAPTER TWELVE

Then fill up the glasses as quick as you can,
And sprinkle the table with buttons and bran:
Put cats in the coffee, and mice in the tea—
And welcome Queen Alice with thirty-times three!

THE COURTHOUSE DOOR opened and closed. Kates crossed the street. He looked at me and asked Hank, "What's wrong?"

"Don't know, Rance. Looks like blood has dripped from the luggage compartment of Doc's car. It's locked. He says he gave you the key. I didn't want to—uh—leave him to come up and get it. So I yelled for you."

Kates nodded. His face was toward me and Hank Ganzer couldn't see it. I could. It looked happy, very happy.

His hand went inside his coat and came out with a pistol. He asked, "Did you frisk him, Hank?"

"No."

"Go ahead."

Hank came around Kates and came up to me from the side. I stood up and held out my hands to make it easy for him. The bottle of whisky was in one of them. He found nothing more deadly than that.

"Clean," Hank said.

Kates didn't put his pistol away. He reached into a pocket with his free hand and took out the key I'd given him. He tossed it to Hank. "Open the compartment, he said.

The key fitted. The handle turned. Hank lifted the door.

I heard the sudden intake of his breath and I turned and looked. Two bodies; I could see that much. I couldn't tell who they were from where I stood. Hank leaned farther in, using his flashlight.

He said, "Miles Harrison, Rance. And Ralph Bonney. Both dead."

"How'd he kill, em?"

"Hit over the head with something. Hard. Must've been several blows apiece. There's lots of blood."

"Weapon there?"

"What looks like it. There's a revolver—an old one—with blood on the butt. Nickel-plated Iver-Johnson, rusty where the plating's off. Thirty-eight, I think."

"The money there? The pay roll?"

"There's what looks like a brief case under Miles." Hank turned around. His face was as pale as the starlight. "Do I got to—uh—move him, Rance?"

Kates thought a minute. "Maybe we better not. Maybe we better take a photo first. Listen, Hank, you go upstairs and get that camera and flash-gun. And while you're there, phone Dr. Heil to get here right away. Uh—you're sure they've both dead?"

"Christ yes, Rance. Their heads are beaten in. Shall I call Dorberg, too?" Dorberg is the local mortician who gets whatever business the sheriff's office can throw his way; he's Kates' brother-in-law, which may have a bearing on the fact.

Kates said, "Sure, tell him to bring the wagon. But tell him no hurry; we want the coroner to have a look before we move 'em. And we want the pix even before that."

Hank started for the courthouse door and then turned again. "Uh—Rance, how about calling Miles' wife and Bonney's factory?"

I sat down on the curb again. I wanted a drink more badly than before, and the bottle was in my hand. But it didn't seem right, just at that moment, to take one. Miles, wife, I thought, and Bonney's factory. What a hell of a difference that was. But

Bonney had been divorced that very day; he had no children, no relatives at all—at least in Carmel City—that I knew of. But then I didn't have either. If I was murdered, who'd be notified? The Carmel City *Clarion*, and maybe Carl Trenholm, if whoever did the notifying knew that Trenholm was my closest friend. Yes, maybe on the whole it was better that I'd never married. I thought of Bonney's divorce and the facts behind it that Carl— through Smiley—had told me. And I thought of how Miles Harrison's wife would be feeling tonight as soon as she got the news. But that was different; I didn't know whether it was good or bad that nobody would feel that way about me if I died suddenly.

Just the same I felt lonely as hell. Well, they'd arrest me now and that would mean I could call Carl as my attorney. I was going to be in a hell of a spot, but Carl would believe me—and believe that I was sane—if anybody would.

Kates had been thinking. He said, "Not yet—either of them, Hank. Milly especially; she might rush down here and get here before we got the bodies to Dorberg's. And we might as well be able to tell the factory whether the pay roll's there when we phone them. Maybe Stoeger hid it somewhere else and we won't get it back tonight."

Hank said, "That's right, about Milly. We wouldn't want her to see Miles—that way. Okay, so I'll call Heil and Dorberg and then come back with the camera."

"Quit talking. Get going."

Hank went on into the courthouse.

It wasn't any use, but I had to say it. I said, "Listen, Kates, I didn't do that. I didn't kill them."

Kates said, "You son of a bitch. Miles was a good guy."

"He was. I didn't kill him." I thought, I wish Miles had let me buy him that drink early in the evening. I wish I'd known I'd have insisted and talked him into it. But that was silly, of course; you can't know things in advance. If you could, you could stop them from happening. Except of course in the Looking-Glass country where people sometimes lived backwards, where the White Queen had screamed first and then later had stuck the needle into her finger. But even then—except, of course, that the Alice books were merely delightful nonsense—why hadn't she simply not picked up the needle she knew she was going to stick herself with?

Delightful nonsense, that is, until tonight. Tonight somebody was making gibbering horror out of Lewis Carroll's most amusing episodes. "DRINK ME"—and die suddenly and horribly. That key—it had been supposed to open a fifteen-inch-high door into a beautiful garden. What it had opened the door to— well, I didn't care to look.

I sighed and thought, what the hell, it's over with now. I'm going to be arrested and Kates thinks I killed Miles and Bonney, but I can't blame him for thinking it. I've got to wait till Carl can get me out of this.

Kates said, "Stand up, Stoeger."

I didn't. Why should I? I'd just thought, who would Miles or Ralph mind if I took a drink out of this bottle in my hand? I started to unscrew the top.

"Stand up, Stoeger. Or I'll shoot you right there."

He meant it. I stood up. His face, as he stood then, was in the shadow, but I remembered that look of malevolence he'd given me in his office, the look that said, "I'd like to kill you."

He was going to shoot me. Here and now.

It was safe as houses for him to do so. He could claim—if I turned and ran and he shot me in the back—that he'd shot because I was trying to escape. And if from the front that I—a homicidal maniac who had already killed Miles and Bonney— was coming toward him to attack him.

That was why he'd sent Hank away and given him two phone calls to make so he wouldn't be back for minutes.

I said, "Kates, you're not serious. You wouldn't shoot a man down in cold blood."

"A man who'd killed a deputy of mine, yes. If I don't, Stoeger, you might beat the rap. You might get certified as a looney and get away with it. I'll make sure." That wasn't all of it, of course, but it gave him an excuse to help his own conscience. I'd killed a deputy of his, he'd thought. But he'd hated me enough to want to kill me even before he'd thought that. Hatred and sadism—given a perfect excuse.

What could I do? Yell? It wouldn't help. Probably nobody awake—it was well after three o'clock by now—would hear me in time to see what happened. Hank would be phoning in the back office; he wouldn't get to the window in time.

And Kates would claim that I yelled as I jumped him; yelling would just trigger the gun.

He stepped closer; if he shot me in the front there'd have to be powder marks to show that he'd shot while I was coming at him. The gun muzzle centered on my chest, barely a foot away. I could live seconds longer if I turned and ran; he'd probably wait until I was a dozen steps away in that case.

His face was still in the shadow, but I could see that he was grinning. I couldn't see his eyes or most of the rest of his face, just that grin. A disembodied grin, like that of the Cheshire cat in Alice. But unlike the Cheshire cat, he wasn't going to fade away.

I was. Unless something unexpected happened. Like maybe a witness coming along, over there on the opposite sidewalk. He wouldn't shoot me in cold blood before a witness. Carl Trenholm, Al Grainger, anybody.

I looked over Kates' shoulder and called out, "Hi, Al!"

Kates turned. He had to; he couldn't take a chance on the possibility that there was really someone coming.

He turned his head just for a quick glance, to be sure. I swung the whisky bottle. Maybe I should say my hand swung it; I hadn't even remembered that I still held it. It hit Kates alongside the head and like as not the brim of his hat saved his life. I think I swung hard enough to have killed him if he'd been bare headed.

Kates and the revolver he'd been holding hit the street, separately. The whisky bottle slid out of my hand and hit the paving; it broke. The paving must have been harder than Kates' head—or maybe it would have broken on Kates' head if it hadn't been for the brim of his hat.

I didn't even stop to find out if he was dead. I ran like hell.

Afoot, of course. The ignition key of my car was still in my pocket, but driving off with two corpses was just about the last thing in the world I wanted to do.

I ran a block and winded myself before I realized I hadn't the faintest idea where I was going. I slowed down and got off Oak Street. I cut back into the first alley. I fell over a garbage can and then sat down on it to get my wind back and to think out what I was going to do. But I had to move on because a dog started barking.

I found myself behind the courthouse.

I wanted, of course, to know who had killed Ralph Bonney and Miles Harrison and put their bodies in my car, but there was something that seemed of even more immediate interest; I wanted to know if I'd killed Rance Kates or seriously injured him. If I had, I was in a hell of a jam because—in addition to everything else against me—it would be my word against his that I'd done it in self-defense, to save my own life. My word against his, that is, if he were only injured. My word against nothing at all if I'd killed him.

And my word wouldn't mean a damn thing to anybody until and unless I could account for two corpses in my car.

The first window I tried was unlocked. I guess they've careless about locking windows of the courthouse because, for one reason, there's nothing kept there that any ordinary burglar would want to steal, and for another reason because the sheriff's office is in the building, and somebody's on duty there all night long.

I slid the window up very slowly and it didn't make much noise, not enough, anyway, to have been heard in the sheriff's office, which is on the second floor and near the front. I put it down again, just as quietly, so it wouldn't be an open give-away if the search for me went through the alley.

I groped in the dark till I found a chair and sat down to collect what wits I had left and figure what to do next. I was fairly safe for the moment. The room I'd entered was one of the small anterooms off the court room; nobody would look for me here, as long as I kept quiet.

They'd found the sheriff, all right, or the sheriff had come around and found himself. There were footsteps on the front stairs, footsteps of more than one person. But back here I was too far away to hear what was being said, if any talking was going on.

But that could wait for a minute or two.

I wished to hell that I had a drink; I'd never wanted one worse in my life. I cussed myself for having dropped and broken that bottle—and after it had saved my life, at that. If I hadn't happened to have it in my hand, I'd have been dead.

I don't know how long I sat there, but it probably wasn't over a few minutes because I was still breathing a little hard when I decided I'd better move. If I'd had a bottle to keep me company, I'd have gladly sat there the rest of the night, I think.

But I had to find out what happened to Kates. If I'd killed him—or if he'd been taken to the hospital and was out of the picture—then I'd better give myself up and get it over with. If he was all right, and was still running things, that wouldn't be a very smart thing to do. If he'd wanted to kill me before I'd knocked him out with that bottle, he'd want to do it so badly now that he would do it, maybe without even bothering to find an excuse, right in front of Hank or any of the other deputies who were undoubtedly being waked up to join the manhunt, in front of the coroner or anybody else who happened to be around.

I bent down and took my shoes off before I got up. I put one in each of the side pockets of my coat and then tiptoed out through the court room to the back stairs. I'd been in the building so many thousand times that I knew the layout almost as well as that of my own home or the *Clarion* office, and I didn't run into anything or fall over anything.

I guided myself up the dark back staircase with a hand on the banister and avoiding the middle of the steps, where they'd be most likely to creak.

Luckily there is an el in the upstairs hallway that runs from the front stairs to the back ones so there wasn't any danger of my being seen, when I'd reached the top of the stairs, by anyone entering or leaving the sheriff's office. And I had dim light now, from the light in the front hallway near the sheriff's office door.

I tiptoed along almost to the turn of the hall and then tried the door of the county surveyor's office, which is next to the sheriff's office and with only an ordinary door with a ground glass pane between them. The door was unlocked.

I got it open very quietly. It slipped out of my hand when I started to close it from the inside and almost slammed, but I caught it in time and eased it shut. I would have liked to lock it, but I didn't know whether the lock would click or not, so I didn't take a chance on that.

I had plenty of light, comparatively, in the surveyor's office; the ground glass pane of the door to the sheriff's office was a bright yellow rectangle through which came enough light to let me see the office furniture clearly. I avoided it carefully and tiptoed my way toward that yellow rectangle.

I could hear voices now and as I neared the door I could hear them even better, but I couldn't quite make out whose they were or what they were saying until I put my ear against the glass. I could hear perfectly well, then.

Hank Ganzer was saying, "It still throws me, Rance. A gentle little old guy like Doc. Two murders and—"

"Gentle, hell!" It was Kates' voice. "Maybe when he was sane he was, but he's crazier than a bedbug now. Ow! Go easy with that tape, will you?"

Dr. Heil's voice was soft, harder to understand. He seemed to be urging that Kates should let himself be taken to the hospital to be sure there wasn't any concussion.

"The hell with that" Kates said. "Not till we get Stoeger before he kills anybody else. Like he killed Miles and Bonney and damn near killed me. Hank, what's about the bodies?"

"I made a quick preliminary examination." Heil's voice was clearer now. "Cause of death is pretty obviously repeated blows on their heads with what seems to have been that rusty pistol on your desk. And with the stains on the pistol butt, I don't think there's any reason to doubt it."

"They still out front?"

Hank said, "No, they're at Dorberg's—or on their way there now. He and one of his boys came around with his meat wagon."

"Doc." It was Kates' voice and it made me jump a little until I realized that he was talking to Dr. Heil and not to me. "You about through? With that God damn bandage, I mean. I got to get going on this. Hank, how many of the boys did you get on the phone? How many are coming down?"

"Three, Rance. I got Watkins, Ehlers and Bill Dean. They're all on their way down. Be here in a few minutes. That'll make five of us."

"Guess that fixes up things as well as I can here, Rance," Dr. Heil's voice said. "I still suggest you go around to the hospital for an X-ray and a check-up as soon as you can."

"Sure, Doc. Soon as I catch Stoeger. And he can't get out of town with the state police watching the roads for us, even if he steals a car. You go on around to Dorberg's and take care of things there, huh?"

Heil's voice, soft again, said something I couldn't hear, and there were footsteps toward the outer hall. I could hear other footsteps coming up the stairs. One or more of the day-shift deputies were arriving.

Kates said, "Hi, Bill, Walt. Ehlers with you?"

"Didn't see him. Probably be here in a minute." It sounded like Bill Dean's voice.

"That's all right. We'll leave him here, anyway. You both got your guns? Good. Listen, you two are going together and Hank and I are going together. We'll work in pairs. Don't worry about the roads leading out; the state boys are watching them for us. And there's no train or bus out till late tomorrow morning. We just comb the town."

"Divide it between us, Rance?"

"No. You, Walt, and Bill cover the whole town. Drive through every street and alley. Hank and I will take places he might have holed in to hide. We'll search his house and the *Clarion* office, whether there are lights on or not, and we'll try any place else that's indoors where he might've holed in. He might pick an empty house, for instance. Anybody got any other suggestions where he might think of holing in?"

Bill Dean's voice said, "He's pretty thick with Carl Trenholm. He might go to Carl."

"Good idea, Bill. Anybody else?"

Hank said, "He looked pretty drunk to me. And he broke that bottle he had. Might get into his head he wants another drink and break into a tavern. Probably Smiley's; that's where he hangs out, mostly."

"Okay, Hank. Well check— That must be Dick coming. Any more ideas, anybody, before we split up?

Ehlers was coming in now. Hank said, "Sometimes a guy doubles back where he figures nobody'll figure where he is. I mean, Rance, maybe he doubled back here and got in the back way or something, thinking the safest place to hide's right under our noses. Right here in the building."

Kates said, "You heard that, Dick. And you're staying here to watch the office, so that's your job. Search the building here first before you settle down."

"Right, Rance."

Kates said, "One more thing. He's dangerous. He's probably armed by now. So don't take any chances. When you see him, start shooting."

"At Doc Stoeger?" Someone's voice sounded surprised and a little shocked. I couldn't tell which of the deputies it was.

"At Doc Stoeger," Kates said. "Maybe you think of him as a harmless little guy—but that's the kind that generally makes homicidal maniacs. He's killed two men tonight and tried to kill me, probably thought he did kill me, or he'd stayed and finished the job. And don't forget who one of the men he did kill was. Miles."

Somebody muttered something.

Bill Dean—I think it was Bill Dean—said, "I don't get it, though. A guy like Doc. He isn't broke; he's got a paper that makes money and he's not a crook. Why'd he suddenly want to kill two men for a couple of thousand lousy bucks?

Kates swore. He said, "He's nuts, went off the beam. The money probably didn't have much to do with it, although he took it all right. It was in that brief case under Miles, body. Now listen, this is the last time I tell you; he's a homicidal maniac and you better remember Miles the minute you spot him and shoot quick. He's crazy as a bedbug. Came in here with a cock and bull story about a guy being croaked out at the Wentworth place—a guy named Yehudi Smith, of all names. And Doc had a card to prove it, only he printed the card himself. Crazy enough to put his own bug number—union label number—on it. Gives me a key that he says opens a fifteen-inch-high door to a beautiful garden. Well, that was the key to the luggage compartment of his own car, see? With Miles' and Bonney's bodies, and the pay roll money, in it. Parked right in front. He'd driven it here. Comes up and gives me the key. And tries to get me to go to a haunted house with him."

"Did anybody look there?" Dean asked.

Hank said, "Sure, Bill. On my way back from Neilsville. Went through the whole dump. Nothing. And listen, Rance is right about him being crazy. I heard some of the stuff he said, myself. And if you don't think he's dangerous, look at Rance. I'm sorry about it, I liked Doc. But damn it, I'm with Rance on shooting first and catching him afterwards."

Somebody: "God damn it, if he killed Miles—"

"If he's *that* crazy—" I think it was Dick Ehlers. "—we'd be doing him a favor, the way I figure it. If I ever go that far off the beam, homicidal, damn if I wouldn't rather be shot than spend the rest of my life in a padded cell. But what *made* him go off that way? All of a sudden, I mean?"

"Alcohol. Softens the brain, and then all of a sudden, whang."

"Doc didn't drink that much. He'd get drunk, a little, a night or two a week, but he wasn't an alcoholic. And he was such a nice—"

A fist hit a desk. It would have been Kates' fist and Kates' desk. It was Kates' swivel chair that squealed and his voice that said, "What the hell are we having a sewing circle for. Come on, let's go out and get him. And about shooting first, that's orders. I've lost one deputy tonight already. Come on."

Footsteps, lots of them, toward the door.

Kates' voice calling back from it. "And don't forget to search this building, Dick. Cellar to roof, before you settle down here."

"Right, Rance."

Footsteps, lots of heavy footsteps, going down the steps. And one set of them turning back along the hallway.

Toward the County Surveyor's office.

Toward me.

CHAPTER THIRTEEN

And he was very proud and stiff;
He said "I'd go and wake them, if—
I took a corkscrew from the shelf;
I went to wake them up myself.

I HOPED he'd take Rance Kates' orders literally and search the place from cellar to attic, in that order. If he did, I could get out either the front or back way while he was in the basement. But he might start on this floor, with this room.

So I tiptoed to the door, pulling one of my shoes out of my pocket as I went. I stood flat against the wall by the door, gripping the shoe, ready to swing the heel of it if Ehlers' head came in.

It didn't. The footsteps went on past and started down the back staircase. I breathed again.

I opened the door and stepped out into the hall as soon as the footsteps were at the bottom of the back steps. Out there in the hall, in the quiet of the night, I could hear him moving about down there. He didn't go to the basement; he was taking the main floor first. That wasn't good. With him on the first floor I couldn't risk either the front or the back stairs; I was stuck up here.

Outside I heard first one car start and then another. At least the front entrance was clear if I had to try to leave that way, if Ehlers started upstairs by the back staircase.

I took a spot in the middle of the hallway, equidistant from both flights of steps. I could still hear him walking around down on the floor below, but it was difficult to tell just where he was. I had to be ready to make a break in either direction.

I swore to myself at the thoroughness of Kates' plans for finding me. My house, my office, Carl's place, Smiley's or another tavern—every place I'd actually be likely to go. Even here, the courthouse, where I really was. But luckily, instead of all of them pitching in for a quick once-over here, he'd left only one man to do the job, and as long as I could hear him and he couldn't hear me—and probably didn't believe I was really here at all—I had an edge.

Only, damn it, why didn't Ehlers hurry? I wanted a drink, and if I could get out of here, I could get one somewhere, somehow. I was shaking like a leaf, and my thoughts were, too. Even one drink would steady me enough to think straight.

Maybe Kates kept a bottle in the bottom drawer of his desk.

The way I felt just then, it was worth trying. I listened hard to the sounds below me and decided Ehlers was probably at the back of the building and I tiptoed to the front and into Kates' office.

I went back to his desk and pulled the drawer open very quietly and slowly. There was a whisky bottle there. It was empty.

I cussed Kates under my breath. It wasn't bad enough that he'd tried to kill me; on top of that, he'd had to finish off that bottle without leaving a single drink in it. And it had been a good brand, too.

I closed the drawer again as carefully as I'd opened it, so there'd be no sign of my having been there.

Lying on the blotter on Kates' desk was a revolver. I looked at it, wondering whether I should take it along with me. For a second the fact that it was rusty didn't register and then I remembered Hank's description of the gun that had been used as a bludgeon to kill Miles and Bonney, and I bent closer. Yes, it was an Iver-Johnson, nickel-plated where the plating wasn't worn or knocked off. This was the death weapon, then.

Exhibit A.

I reached out to pick it up, and then jerked my hand back. Hadn't I been framed well enough without helping the framer by putting my fingerprints on that gun? That was all I needed, to have my fingerprints on the weapon that had done the killing. Or were they there already? Considering everything else, I wouldn't have been too surprised if they were.

Then I almost went through the ceiling. The phone rang.

I could hear, in the silence between the first ring and the second, Ehlers' footsteps starting upstairs. But back here in the office, I couldn't tell whether he was coming up the front way or the back, and I might not have time to make it anyway, even if I knew.

I looked around frantically and saw a closet, the door ajar. I grabbed up the Iver-Johnson and ducked into the closet, behind the door. And I stood there, trying not to breathe, while Ehlers came in and picked up the phone.

He said, "Sheriff's office," and then, "Oh, you, Rance," and then he listened a while.

"You're phoning from the *Clarion*? Not at Smiley's or there, huh? . . . No, no calls have come in . . . Yeah, I'm almost through looking around here. Searched the first floor and the basement. Just got to go over this floor yet."

I swore at myself. He'd been down in the basement, then, and I could have got away. But the building had been so quiet chat his walking around down there had sounded to me as though it had been on the main floor.

"Don't worry, I'm not taking any chances, Rance. Gun in one hand and a flashlight in the other."

There was a gun in my hand, too, and suddenly I realized

what a damned foolish thing I'd done to pick it up off Kates, desk. Ehlers must have known it was there. If he missed it, if he happened to glance down at the desk while he was talking on the phone—

God must have loved me. He didn't. He said, "Okay, Rance," and then he put the phone down and walked out.

I heard him go back along the hallway and around the el and start opening doors back there. I had to get out quick, down the front steps, before he worked his way back here. As a matter of routine, he'd probably open this closet door too when he'd searched his way back to the office he'd started from.

I let myself out and tiptoed down the steps. Out into the night again, onto Oak Street. And I had to get off it quick, because either of the two cars looking for me might cruise by at any moment. Carmel City isn't large; a car can cruise all of its streets and alleys in pretty short order. Besides I still had my shoes in my pockets and—I realized now—I still had a gun in my hand.

Hoping Ehlers wouldn't happen to be looking out of any of the windows, I ran around the corner and into the month of the alley behind the courthouse. As soon as I was comparatively safe in the friendly darkness, I sat down on the alley curbstone and put my shoes back on, and put the gun into my pocket. I hadn't meant to bring it along at all, but as long as I had I couldn't throw it away now.

Anyway, it was going to get Dick Ehlers in trouble with Kates. When Kates looked for that gun and found it was missing, he'd know that I'd been in the courthouse and that Ehlers had missed me. He'd know that I'd been right in his own office while he'd been out searching for me.

And so there I was in the dark, in safety for a few minutes until a car full of deputies decided to cruise down that particular alley looking for me. And I had a gun in my pocket that might or might not shoot—I hadn't checked that—and I had my shoes on and my hands were shaking again.

I didn't even have to ask myself, Little man, what now. The little man not only wanted a drink; he really needed one.

And Kates had already been to Smiley's looking for me and had found that I wasn't there.

So I started down the alley toward Smiley's.

Funny, but I was getting over being scared. A little, anyway. You can get only just so scared, and then something happens to your adrenal glands or something. I can't remember offhand whether your adrenals make you frightened or whether they get going and operate against it, but mine were getting either into or out of action, as the case might be. I'd been scared so much that night that I—or my glands—was getting tired of it.

I was getting brave, almost. And it wasn't Dutch courage, either; it had been so long since I'd had a drink that I'd forgotten what one tasted like. I was cold damn sober. About three times during the course of the long evening and the long night I'd been on the borderline of intoxication, but always something had happened to keep me from drinking for a while and then something had sobered me up. Some foolish little thing like being taken for a ride by gangsters or watching a man die suddenly or horribly by quaffing a bottle labeled "DRINK ME" or finding murdered men in the back of my own car or discovering that a sheriff intended to shoot me down in cold grue. Little things like that.

So I kept going down the alley toward Smiley's. The dog that had barked at me before barked again. But I didn't waste time barking back. I kept on going down the alley toward Smiley's.

There was the street to cross. I took a quick look both ways but didn't worry about it beyond that. If the sheriff's car or the deputies' car suddenly turned the corner and started spraying me with headlights and then bullets, well, then that was that. You can only get so worried; then you quit worrying. When things can't get any worse, outside of your getting killed, then either you get killed or things start getting better.

Things started to get better; the window into the back room of Smiley's was open. I didn't bother taking off my shoes this time. Smiley would be asleep upstairs, but alone, and Smiley's so sound a sleeper that a bazooka shell exploding in the next room wouldn't wake him. I remember times I'd dropped into the tavern on a dull afternoon and found him asleep it was almost hopeless to try to wake him, and I'd generally help myself and leave the money on the ledge of the register. And he dropped asleep so quickly and easily that even if Kates and Hank had wakened him when they'd looked for me here, he'd be asleep again by now.

In fact—yes, I could hear a faint rumbling sound overhead, like very distant thunder. Smiley snoring.

I groped my way through the dark back room and opened the door to the tavern. There was a dim light in there that burned all night long, and the shades were left up. But Kates had already been here and the chances of anyone else happening to pass and look in at half past three of a Friday morning were negligible.

I took a bottle of the best bonded Bourbon Smiley had from the back bar and because it looked as though there were still at least a fair chance that this might be the last drink I ever had, I took a bottle of seltzer from the case under the bar. I took them to the table around the el, the one that's out of sight of the windows, the table at which Bat and George had sat early this evening.

Bat and George seemed, now, to have sat there a long time ago, years maybe, and seemed not a tenth as frightening as they'd been at the time. Almost, they seemed a little funny, somehow.

I left the two bottles on the table and went back for a glass, a swizzle stick, and some ice cubes from the refrigerator. This drink I'd waited a long time for, and it was going to be a good one.

I'd even pay a good price for it, I decided, especially after I looked in my wallet and found I had several tens but nothing smaller. I put a ten-dollar bill on the ledge of the register, and I wondered if I'd ever get my change out of it.

I went back to the table and made myself a drink, a good one.

I lighted up a cigar, too. That was a bit risky because if Kates came by here again for another check, he might see cigar smoke in the dim light, even though I was out of his range of vision. But I decided the risk was worth it. You can, I was finding, get into such a Godawful jam that a little more risk doesn't seem to matter at all.

I took a good long swig of the drink and then a deep drag from the cigar, and I felt pretty good. I held out my hands and they weren't shaking. Very silly of them not to be, but they weren't.

Now, I thought, is my first chance to think for a long time. My first real chance since Yehudi Smith had died.

Little man, what now?

The pattern. Could I make any sense out of the pattern?

Yehudi Smith—only that undoubtedly wasn't his real name, else the card he gave me wouldn't have been printed in my own shop—had called to see me and had told me—

Skip what he told you, I told myself. That was gobble-degook, just the kind of gobbledegook that would entice you to go to such a crazy place at such a crazy time. He knew you—that is, I corrected myself—he knew a lot about you. Your hobby and your weakness and what you were and what would interest you.

His coming there was planned. Planned well in advance; the card proved that.

According to a plan, then, he called on you at a time when no one else would be there. Probably, sitting in his car, he'd watched you come home, knowing Mrs. Carr was there—in all probability he or someone had been watching the house all evening—and waiting until she'd left to present himself.

No one had seen him, no one besides yourself.

He led you on a wild-goose chase. There weren't any Vorpal Blades; that was gobbledegook, too.

Connect that with the fact that Miles Harrison and Ralph Bonney had been killed while Yehudi Smith was keeping you entertained and busy, and that their bodies had been put in the back compartment of your car.

Easy. Smith was an accomplice of the murderer, hired to keep you away from anybody else who might alibi you while the crime was going on. Also to give you such an incredible story to account for where you really were that your own mother, if she were still alive, would have a hard time believing it.

But connect that with the fact that Smith had been killed, too. And with the fact that the pay roll money had been left in your car along with the bodies.

It added up to gibberish.

I took another sip of my drink and it tasted weak. I looked at it and saw I'd been sitting there so long between sips that most of the ice had melted. I put more of the bonded Bourbon in it and it tasted all right again.

I remembered about the gun I'd grabbed up from Kates' desk, the rusty one with which the two murders had been committed. I took it out of my pocket and looked at it. I handled it so I wouldn't have to touch those dried stains on the butt.

I broke it to see if any shots had been fired from it and found there weren't any cartridges in it, empty or otherwise. I clicked it back into position and tried the trigger. It was rusted shut. It hadn't, then, been used as a gun at all. Just as a hammer to bash out the brains of two men.

And I'd certainly made a fool of myself by bringing it along. I'd played right into the killer's hands by doing that. I put it back into my pocket.

I wished that I had someone to talk to. I felt that I might figure out things aloud better than I could this way. I wished that Smiley was awake, and for a moment I was tempted to go upstairs to get him. No, I decided, once already tonight I'd put

Smiley into danger—danger out of which he'd got both of us and without any help from me whatsoever.

And this was *my* problem. It wouldn't be fair to Smiley to tangle him in it.

Besides, this wasn't a matter for Smiley's brawn and guts. This was like playing chess, and Smiley didn't play chess. Carl might possibly be able to help me figure it out, but Smiley— never. And I didn't want to tangle Carl in this either.

But I wanted to *talk* to somebody.

All right, maybe I was a little crazy—not drunk, definitely not drunk—but a little crazy. I wanted to talk to somebody, so I did.

~§~

The little man who wasn't there.

I imagined him sitting across the table from me, sitting there with an imaginary drink in his hand. Gladly, right gladly, would I have poured him a real one if he'd been really there. He was looking at me strangely.

"Smitty," I said.

"Yes, Doc?"

"What's your real name, Smitty? I know it isn't Yehudi Smith. That was part of the gag. The card you gave me proves that."

It wasn't the right question to ask. He wavered a little, as though he was going to disappear on me. I shouldn't have asked him a question that I myself couldn't answer, because he was there only because my mind was putting him there. He couldn't tell me anything I didn't know myself or couldn't figure out.

He wavered a little, but he rallied. He said, "Doc, I can't tell you that. Any more than I can tell you whom I was working for. You know that."

Get it; he said "whom I was working for" not "who I was working for." I felt proud of him and of myself.

I said, "Sure, Smitty. I shouldn't have asked. And listen, I'm sorry—I'm sorry as hell that you died."

"That's all right, Doc. We all die sometime. And—well, it was a nice evening up to then."

"I'm glad I fed you," I said. "I'm glad I gave you all you wanted to drink. And listen, Smitty, I'm sorry I laughed out loud when I saw that bottle and key on the glass-topped table. I just couldn't help it. It *was* funny."

"Sure, Doc. But I had to play it straight. It was part of the act. But it was corny; I don't blame you for acting amused. And Doc, I'm sorry I did it. I didn't know the whole score—you've got proof of that. If I had, I wouldn't have drunk what was in that bottle. I didn't look like a man who wanted to die, did I, Doc?"

I shook my head slowly, looking at the laughter-lines around his eyes and his mouth. He didn't look like a man who wanted to die.

But he had died, suddenly and horribly.

"I'm sorry, Smitty, "I told him. "I'm sorry as hell. I'd give a hell of a lot to bring you back, to have you really sitting there."

He chuckled. "Don't get maudlin, Doc. It'll spoil your thinking. You're trying to think, you know."

"I know," I said. "But I had to get it out of my system. All right, Smitty. You're dead and I can't do anything about it. You're the little man who isn't there. And I can't ask you any questions I can't answer myself, so really you can't help me."

"Are you sure, Doc? Even if you ask the right questions?"

"What do you mean? That my subconscious mind might know the answers even if I don't?"

He laughed. "Let's not get Freudian. Let's stick to Lewis Carroll. I really *was* a Carroll enthusiast, you know. I was a fast study, but not that fast. I couldn't have memorized all that about him just for one occasion."

The phrase struck me, "a fast study." I repeated it and went on where it led me, "You were an actor, Smitty? Hell, don't answer it. You must have been. I should have guessed that. An actor hired to play a part."

He grinned a bit wryly. "Not too good an actor, then, or you wouldn't have guessed it. And pretty much of a sucker, Doc, to have accepted the role. I should have guessed that there was more in it than what he told me." He shrugged. "Well, I played you a dirty trick, but I played a worse one on myself. Didn't I?"

"I'm sorry you're dead, Smitty. God damn it, I liked you."

"I'm glad, Doc. I haven't liked myself too well these last few years. You've figured it out by now so I can tell you—I was pretty down and out to take a booking like that, and at the price he offered me for it. And damn him, he didn't pay me in advance except my expenses, so what did I gain by it? I got killed. Wait, don't get maudlin about that again. Let's drink to it."

We drank to it. There are worse things than getting killed. And there are worse ways of dying than suddenly when you aren't expecting it, when you're slightly tight and—

But that subject wasn't getting us anywhere. "You were a character actor," I said.

"Doc, you disappoint me by belaboring the obvious. And that doesn't help you to figure out who Anybody is."

"Anybody?"

"That's what you were calling him to yourself when you were thinking things out, in a half-witted sort of way, not so long ago. Remember thinking that Anybody could have got into your printing shop and Anybody could have set up one line of type and figured out how to print one good card on that little hand press, but why would Anybody."

"Unfair," I said. "You can get inside my mind, because—because, hell, that's where you are. But I can't get into yours. You know who Anybody is. But I don't."

"Even I, Doc, might not know his real name. In case something went wrong, he wouldn't have told me that. Something like—well, suppose you'd grabbed that 'DRINK ME' bottle when you first found the table and tossed it off before I could tell you that it was my prerogative to do so. Yes, there were a lot of things that could have gone wrong in so complicated a deal as that one was."

I nodded. "Yes, suppose Al Grainger had come around for that game of chess and we'd taken him along. Suppose—suppose I hadn't lived to get home at all. I had a narrow squeak earlier in the evening, you know."

"In that case, Doc, it never would have happened. You ought to be able to figure that out without my telling you. If you'd been killed, you and Smiley, earlier in the evening, then— at least if Anybody had learned about it, as he probably would have—Ralph Bonney and Miles Harrison wouldn't have been killed later. At least not tonight. A wheel would have come off the plans and I'd have gone back to—wherever I came from. And everything would have been off."

I said, "But suppose I'd stayed at the office far into the night working on one of those big stories I thought I had—and was so happy about. How would Anybody have known?"

"Can't tell you that, Doc. But you might guess. Suppose I had orders to keep Anybody posted on your movements, if they went off schedule. When you left the house, saying you'd be back shortly, I'd have used your phone and told him that. And when you phoned that you were on your way back I'd have let him know, while you were walking home, wouldn't I?"

"But that was pretty late."

"Not too late for him to have intercepted Miles Harrison and Ralph Bonney on their way back from Neilsville—under certain circumstances—if his plans had been held in abeyance until he was sure you'd be home and out of circulation before midnight."

I said, "Under certain circumstances," and wondered just what I meant by it.

Yehudi Smith smiled. He lifted his glass and looked at me mockingly over the rim of it before he drank. He said, "Go on, Doc. You're only in the second square, but your next move will be a good one. You go to the fourth square by train, you know."

"And the smoke alone is worth a thousand pounds a puff."

"And that's the answer, Doc," he said, quietly.

I stared at him. A prickle went down my back.

Outside, in the night, a clock struck four times.

"What do you mean, Smitty?" I asked him, slowly.

The little man who wasn't there poured more whisky from an imaginary bottle into his imaginary glass. He said, "Doc, you've been letting the glass-topped table and the bottle and the key fool you. They're from *Alice in Wonderland*. Originally, of course, called *Alice's Adventures Underground*. Wonderful book. But you're in the second."

"The second square? You just said that."

"The second book. *Through the Looking-Glass, and What Alice Found There*. And, Doc, you know as well as I what Alice found there."

I poured myself another drink, a short one this time, to match his. I didn't bother with ice or seltzer.

He raised his glass. "You've got it now, Doc," he said. "Not all of it, but enough to start on. You might still see the dawn come up."

"Don't be so God damn dramatic," I said; "certainly I'm going to see the dawn come up."

"Even if Kates comes here again looking for you? Don't forget when he misses that rusty gun in your pocket, he'll know you were at the courthouse when he was looking for you here. He might recheck all his previous stops. And you're awfully damned careless in filling the place with cigar smoke, you know."

"You mean it's worth a thousand pounds a puff?"

He put back his head and laughed and then he quit laughing and he wasn't there any more, even in my imagination, because a sudden slight sound made me look toward the door that led upstairs, to Smiley's rooms. The door opened and Smiley was standing there.

In a nightshirt. I hadn't known anybody wore night-shirts any more, but Smiley wore one. His eyes looked sleepy and his hair—what was left of it—was tousled and he was barefoot. He had a gun in his hand, the little short-barreled thirty-eight Banker's Special I'd given him some hours ago. In his huge hand it looked tiny, a toy. It didn't look like something that had knocked a Buick off the road, killing one man and badly injuring another, that very evening.

There wasn't any expression on his face, none at all.

I wonder what mine looked like. But through a looking-glass or not, I didn't have one to look into.

Had I been talking to myself aloud? Or had my conversation with Yehudi Smith been imaginary, within my own mind? I honestly didn't know.

If I'd really been talking to myself, it was going to be a hell of a thing to have to explain. Especially if Kates had, on his stop here, awakened Smiley and told him that I was crazy.

In any case, what the hell could I possibly say right now but "Hello, Smiley"?

I opened my mouth to say "Hello, Smiley," but I didn't.

Someone was pounding on the glass of the front door. Someone who yelled, "Hey, open up here!" in the voice of Sheriff Rance Kates.

I did the only reasonable thing to do. I poured myself another drink.

CHAPTER FOURTEEN

"You are old," said the youth, "one would hardly suppose
That your eye was as steady as ever;
Yet you balanced an eel on the end of your nose—
What made you so awfully clever?"

KATES hammered again and tried the knob.

Smiley stared at me and I stared back at him. I couldn't say anything—even if I could have thought of anything to say—to him at that distance without the probability of Kates hearing my voice.

Kates hammered again. I heard him say something to Hank about breaking in the glass. Smiley bent down and placed the gun on the step behind him and then came out of the door into the tavern. Without looking at me he walked toward the front door and, at sight of him, Kates stopped the racket there.

Smiley didn't walk quite straight toward the door; he made a slight curve that took him past my table. As he passed, he reached out and jerked the cigar out of my hand. He stuck it in his mouth and then went to the door and opened it.

I couldn't see in that direction, of course, and I didn't stick my head around the corner of the el. I sat there and sweated.

"What you want? Why such a hell of a racket?" I heard Smiley demand.

Kates' voice: "Thought Stoeger was here. That smoke—"

"Left my cigar down here," Smiley said. "Remembered it when I got back up and came down to get it. Why all the racket?"

"It was damn near half an hour ago when I was here," Kates said belligerently. "Cigar doesn't burn that long."

Smiley said patiently, "I couldn't sleep after you were here. I came down and got myself a drink five minutes ago. I left my cigar down here." His voice got soft, very soft. "Now get the hell out of here. You've spoiled my night already. Didn't get to sleep till two and you wake me at half past three and come around again at four. What's the big idea, Kates?"

"You're sure Stoeger isn't—"

"I told you I'd call you if I saw him. Now, you bastard, get out of here."

I could imagine Kates turning purple. I could imagine him looking at Smiley and realizing that Smiley was half again as strong as he was.

The door slammed so hard it must have come very near to breaking the glass.

Smiley came back. Without looking back at me he said quietly, "Don't move, Doc. He might look back in a minute or two." He went on around behind the bar, got himself a glass and poured a drink. He sat down on the stool he keeps for himself back there, facing slightly to the back so his lip movement wouldn't show to anyone looking in the front window. He took a sip of the drink and a puff of my cigar.

I kept my voice as low as he'd kept his. I said, "Smiley, you ought to have your mouth washed out with soap. You told a lie."

He grinned. "Not that I know of, Doc. I told him I'd call him if I saw you. I did call him. Didn't you hear what I called him?"

"Smiley," I said, "this is the screwiest night I've ever been through but the screwiest thing about it is that you're developing a sense of humor. I didn't think you had it in you."

"How bad trouble are you in, Doc? What can I do?"

I said, "Nothing. Except what you just did do, and thanks to hell and back for that. It's something I've got to think out, and work out for myself, Smiley. Nobody can help me."

"Kates said, when he was here the first time, you were a ho— homi— What the hell was it?"

"Homicidal maniac," I said. "He thinks I killed two men tonight. Miles Harrison and Ralph Bonney."

"Yeah. Don't bother telling me you didn't."

I said, "Thanks, Smiley." And then it occurred to me that "Don't bother telling me you didn't" could be taken either one of two ways. And I wondered again if I *had* been talking to myself aloud or only in my imagination while Smiley had been walking down those stairs and opening the door. I asked him, "Smiley, do you think I'm crazy?"

"I've always thought you were crazy, Doc. But crazy in a nice way."

I thought how wonderful it is to have friends. Even if I *was* crazy, there were two people in Carmel City that I could count on to go to bat for me. There was Smiley and there was Carl.

But, damn it, friendship should work both ways. This was my danger and my problem and I had no business dragging Smiley into it any farther than he'd already stuck his neck. If I told Smiley that Kates had tried to kill me and still intended to, then Smiley—who hates Kates' guts already—would go out looking for Kates and like as not kill him with his bare hands, or get shot trying it. I couldn't do that to Smiley.

I said, "Smiley, finish your drink and go up to bed again. I've got to think."

"Sure there's no way I can help you, Doc?"

"Positive."

He tossed off the rest of his drink and tamped out the cigar in an ash tray. He said, "Okay, Doc, I know you're smarter than I am, and if it's brains you need for help, I'm just in the way. Good luck to you."

He walked back to the door of the staircase. He looked carefully at the front windows to be sure nobody was looking in and then he reached inside and picked up the revolver from the step on which he'd placed it.

He came walking over to my table. He said, "Doc, if you *are* a ho—homi—what you said, you might want to kill somebody else tonight. That's loaded. I even replaced the two bullets I shot out of it, earlier."

He put it down on the table in front of me, turned his back to me and went back to the stairs. I watched him go, marveling. I'd never yet seen a man in a nightshirt who hadn't looked ridiculous. Until then. What more can a man do to prove he doesn't think you're insane than give you a loaded gun and then turn his back and walk away. And when I thought of all the times I'd razzed Smiley and ridden him, all the cracks I'd made at him, I wanted—

Well, I couldn't answer when he said "Goodnight, Doc," just before he closed the door behind him. Something felt a little wrong with my throat, and if I'd tried to say anything, I might have bawled.

My hand shook a little as I poured myself another drink, a short one. I was beginning to feel them and this had better be my last one, I knew.

I had to think more clearly than I'd ever thought before. I couldn't get drunk, I didn't dare.

I tried to get my mind back to what I'd been thinking about—what I'd been talking about to the little man who wasn't there—before Smiley's coming downstairs and Kates' knocking had interrupted me.

I looked across the table where Yehudi Smith, in my mind, had been sitting. But he wasn't there. I couldn't bring him back. He was dead, and he wouldn't come back.

The quiet room in the quiet night. The dim light of the single twenty-watt bulb over the cash register. The creaking of my thoughts as I tried to turn them back into the groove. Connect facts.

Lewis Carroll and bloody murder.

Through the Looking-Glass and What Alice Found There.

What *had* Alice found there?

Chessmen, and a game of chess. And Alice herself had been a pawn. That was why, of course, she'd crossed the third square by railroad. With the smoke alone worth a thousand pounds a puff—almost as expensive as the smoke from my cigar might have been had not Smiley taken it out of my hand and claimed it as his own.

Chessmen, and a game of chess.

But who was the *player*.

And suddenly I knew. Illogically, because he didn't have a shadow of a motive. The Why I did not see, but Yehudi Smith had told me the How, and now I saw the Who.

The pattern. Whoever had arranged tonight's little chess problem played chess all right, and played it well. Looking-glass chess and real chess, both. And he knew me well—which meant I knew him, too. He knew my weaknesses, the things I'd fall for. He knew I'd go with Yehudi Smith on the strength of that mad, weird story Smith had told me.

But *why?* What had he to gain? He'd killed Miles Harrison, Ralph Bonney and Yehudi Smith. And he'd left the money Miles and Ralph had been carrying in that brief case and put it in the back of my car, with the two bodies.

Then money hadn't been the motive. Either that, or the motive had been money in such large quantity that the couple of thousand dollars Bonney had been carrying didn't matter.

But wasn't a man concerned who was one of the richest men in Carmel City? Ralph Bonney. His fireworks factory, his other investments, his real estate must have added up to—well, maybe half a million dollars. A man shooting for half a million dollars can well abandon the proceeds of a two-thousand dollar holdup and leave them with the bodies of the men he has killed, to help pin the crime on the pawn he has selected, to divert suspicion from himself.

Connect facts.

Ralph Bonney was divorced today. He was murdered tonight.

Then Miles Harrison's death was incidental. Yehudi Smith had been another pawn.

A warped mind, but a brilliant mind. A cold, cruel mind. And yet, paradoxically, a mind that loved fantasy, as I did, that loved Lewis Carroll, as I did.

I started to pour myself another drink and then remembered that I still had only part of the answer, and that even if I had it all, I hadn't the slightest idea what I could do with it, without a shred of evidence, or an iota of proof.

Without even an idea, in my own mind, of the reason, the motive. But there must be one; the rest of it was too well planned, too logical.

There was one possibility that I could see.

I sat there listening a while to be sure there was no car approaching; the night was so quiet that I could have heard one at least a block away.

I looked at the gun Smiley had given me back, hesitated, and finally put it in my pocket. Then I went into the back room and let myself out of the window into the dark alley.

Carl Trenholm's house was three blocks away. Luckily, it was on the street next to Oak Street and parallel to it. I could make all of the distance through the alley except for the streets I'd have to cross.

I heard a car coming as I approached the second street and I ducked down and hid behind a garbage can until it had gone by. It was going slowly and it was probably either Hank and the sheriff or the two deputies. I didn't look out to see for fear they might flash a spotlight down the alley.

I waited until the sound of it died away completely before I crossed the street.

I let myself in the back gate of Carl's place. With his wife away, I wasn't positive which bedroom he'd be sleeping in, but I found pebbles and tossed them at the most likely window and it was the right one.

It went up and Carl's head came out. I stepped close to the

house so I wouldn't have to yell. I said, "It's Doc, Carl. Don't light a light anywhere in the house. But come down to the back door."

"Coming, Doc." He closed the window. I went up on the back porch and waited until the door opened and I went in. I closed the door behind me and the kitchen was as black as the inside of a tomb.

Carl said, "Damned if I know where a flashlight is, Doc. Can't we put on a light? I feel like hell."

"No, leave it off," I told him. I struck a match, though, to find my way to a chair and it showed me Carl in rumpled pajamas, his hair mussed and looking like he was in for the grandfather of all hangovers.

He sat down, too, while the match flared. "What's it about, Doc? Kates and Ganzer were here looking for you. Waked me up a while ago, but they didn't tell me much. Are you in a jam, Doc? *Did* you kill somebody?"

"No," I said. "Listen, you're Ralph Bonney's lawyer, aren't you? I mean on everything, not just the divorce today."

"Yes."

"Who's his heir, now that he's divorced?"

"Doc, I'm afraid I can't tell you that. A lawyer isn't supposed to tell his clients' business. You know that as well as I do."

"Didn't Kates tell you Ralph Bonney is dead, Carl? And Miles Harrison? They were murdered on their way back from Neilsville with the payroll, somewhere around midnight."

"My God," Carl said. "No, Kates didn't tell me."

I said, "I know you're still not supposed to tell his business until a will is probated, if there is one. But listen, let me make a guess and you can tell me if I'm wrong. If I guess right, you won't have to confirm it; just keep your mouth shut."

"Go ahead, Doc."

"Bonney had an illegitimate son about twenty-three years ago. But he supported the boy's mother all her life until she died recently; she worked, too, as a milliner but he gave her enough extra so that she lived better than she would have otherwise, and she sent the boy to college and gave him every break."

I stopped there and waited and Carl didn't say anything.

I went on. "Bonney still gave the boy an allowance. That's how he—hell, let's call him by name—that's how Al Grainger has been living without working. And unless he knows he's in Bonney's will, he's got proof of his parentage and can claim the bulk of the estate anyway. And it must be half a million."

Carl said, "I'll talk. It'll run about three hundred thousand. And you guessed right on Al Grainger, but how you guessed it, I don't know. Bonney's relations to Mrs. Grainger and to Al have been the best-kept secret I've ever known of. In fact, outside of the parties concerned, I was the only person who ever knew—or even suspected. How did you guess?"

"By what happened to me tonight—and that's too complicated to explain right now. But Al plays chess and has the type of mind to do things the complicated way, and that's the way they happened. And he knows Lewis Carroll and—" I stopped because I was still after facts and didn't want to start explaining.

The night was almost over. I saw a greenish gleam in the darkness that reminded me Carl wore a wrist watch with a luminous dial. "What time is it?" I asked him.

The gleam vanished as he turned the dial toward himself. "Almost five o'clock. About ten minutes of. Listen, Doc, you've got so much you might as well have the rest. Yes, Al has proof of his parentage. And, as an only child, illegitimate or not, he can claim the entire estate now that Bonney isn't married. He could have cut in for a fraction of it, of course, even before the divorce."

"Didn't he leave a will?"

"Ralph didn't ever make a will. Superstitious about it. I've often tried to talk him into making one, but he never would."

"And Al Grainger knew that?"

Carl said, "I imagine he would have."

"Is there any reason why Al would have been in such a

hurry?" I asked. "I mean, would there have been any change in status if he'd waited a while instead of killing Bonney the night after the divorce?"

Carl thought a minute. "Bonney was planning to leave tomorrow for a long vacation. Al would have had to wait several months, and maybe he figured Bonney might remarry—meet someone on the cruise he was going to take. It happens that way, sometimes, on the rebound after a divorce. And Bonney is—was only fifty-two."

I nodded—to myself, since Carl couldn't see me in the darkness. That last bit of information covered everything on the motive end.

I knew everything now, except the details and they didn't matter much. I knew why Al had done everything that he had done; he had to make an airtight frame on someone because once he claimed Bonney's estate, his own motive would be obvious. I could even guess some of the reasons why he'd picked me for the scapegoat.

He must have hated me, and kept it carefully under cover. I could see a reason for it, now that I knew more about him. I've got a loose tongue and often swear at people affectionately, if you know what I mean. How often, when Al had beaten me in a game of chess had I grinned at him and said, "All right, you bastard. But try to do it again."

Never dreaming, of course, that he was one, and knew it.

He must have hated me like hell. In some ways he could have picked an easier victim, someone more likely than I to have committed murder and robbery for money. Choosing me, his plan took more gobbledegook; he had to give me such a mad story to tell that nobody would believe a word of it and would think, instead, that I'd gone insane. Of course, too, he knew how much Kates hated me; he counted on that.

A sudden thought shook me; could Kates have been in on the deal with Al? That would account for his trying to kill me rather than lock me up. Maybe that was the deal—for a twenty or fifty thousand dollar cut of the estate, Kates had agreed to shoot me down under the pretense that I had attacked him or had tried to escape.

No, I decided on second thought, it hadn't been that way. I'd been alone with Kates in his office for almost half an hour while Hank Ganzer had been on his way back from Neilsville. It would have been too easy for Kates to have killed me then, planted a weapon on me and claimed that I'd come in and attacked him. And when the two bodies had been found in my car, the story would have been perfectly credible. It would even have pointed up the indication that I'd gone homicidally insane.

No, Kates' motive for wanting to kill me had been personal, sheer malice because of the things I'd written about him in editorials and the way I'd fought him in elections. He'd wanted to kill me and had seen a sudden opportunity when the bodies had been found in my car. He'd passed up a much better chance because, when I was alone with him for so long in his office, he hadn't known the bodies were there.

No, definitely this was a one-man job, except for Yehudi Smith. Al had hired Smith to keep me diverted, but when Smith's job was done, he was eliminated. Another pawn. Chess isn't a team game.

Carl said, "How are you mixed in this, Doc? What can I do?"

"Nothing," I said. It was my problem, not Carl's. I'd kept Smiley out of it; I'd keep Carl out of it, too. Except for the information and help he'd already given me. "Go up to bed, Carl. I've got a little more thinking to do."

"Hell with that. I can't sleep with you sitting down here thinking. But I'll sit here and shut up unless you talk to me. You can't tell whether I'm here or not anyway, if I shut up."

I said, "Shut up, then."

Proof, I thought. But what proof? Somewhere, but God knew where, was the dead body of the actor Al had hired to play the role of Yehudi. But this had been planned, and well planned.

Suitable disposal of that body had been arranged for long before Al had taken it away from the Wentworth place. It wasn't going to turn up at random and one guess was as good as another as to where he'd hidden or buried it. He'd had hours to do it in and he'd known in advance every step he was going to take.

The car in which Yehudi Smith had driven me to the Wentworth house and which he'd switched for my own car after he'd used mine for the supposed holdup. No, I couldn't find that car as proof and it wouldn't mean anything if I did. It could have been—probably was—a stolen car, and now returned to wherever he'd stolen it from, never missed by its owner. And I didn't even remember what make or model it was. All I remembered was that it had an onyx gear shift knob and a push button radio. I didn't even know whether it was a Cadillac convertible or a Ford business coupe.

Had Al arranged any kind of an alibi for himself?

Maybe, maybe not, but what did it matter unless I could find something against him besides motive? That, and my own certainty that he'd done it. I hadn't any alibi, none at all. I had an incredible story and two bodies and the stolen money in my car. And a sheriff and three deputies looking for me and ready to shoot on sight.

I had the murder weapon in my pocket. And another gun, too, a loaded one.

Could I go to Al Grainger and scare him into writing out and signing a confession?

He'd laugh at me. I'd laugh at myself for trying. A man with the warped brain that would work out something like Al's plan tonight wasn't going to tell me what time it was just because I pointed a gun at him.

A faint touch of light was showing at the windows. I could even make out Carl sitting there across the table from me.

"Carl," I said.

"Yes, Doc? Say, I was letting you think but I'm glad you spoke. Just had an idea."

"An idea's what I need," I told him. "What is it?"

"Want a drink?"

I asked, "Is that the idea?"

"That's the idea. Look, I'm hung over to hell and back and I can't have one with you, but I just realized what a lousy host I was. Do you want one?"

"Thanks," I said, "but I had a drink. Listen, Carl, talk to me about Al Grainger. Don't ask me what to say. Just talk."

"Anything, at random?"

"Anything, at random."

"Well, he's always impressed me as being a little off the beam. Brilliant, but—well, twisted, somehow. Maybe his knowledge of who and what he was contributed to that. Smiley always felt that, too; he's mentioned it to me. Not that Smiley knows who or what Al is, but he just felt something was wrong."

I said, "My opinion of Smiley has changed a lot tonight. He's smarter, and a better guy, than both of us put together, Carl. But go on about Al—"

"Touch of Oedipus, complicated by bastardry. Probably, in some obscure way, managed to blame Bonney for his mother's death. Not a real paranoiac, but near enough to do something like that. Sadism—most of us have a touch of it, but Al a little more than most."

I said, "Most of us have a touch of everything. Go on."

"Pyrophobia. But you know about that. Not that we haven't all got phobias. Your acrophobia and my being afraid of cats. But Al's is pretty bad. So afraid of fire that he doesn't smoke and I've noticed him wince when I've lighted a cig—"

"Shut up, Carl," I said.

I should have thought of it myself, sooner. A lot sooner.

I said, "I'll have that drink, Carl. Just one, but a good one."

I didn't need it physically, but I needed it mentally this time. I was scared stiff at the very thought of what I was going to do.

CHAPTER FIFTEEN

One, two! One, two! And through and through
The vorpal blade went snicker-snack!
He left it dead, and with its head
He went galumphing back.

THE WINDOWS were faint gray rectangles; now, with my eyes accustomed to the decreasing darkness, I could see Carl almost clearly as he went to the cupboard and groped until he had the bottle he was looking for.

He said, "Doc, you sound happy enough that I'll have one with you. Hair of the dog, for me. Kill or cure."

He got two glasses, too, from over the sink, breaking only one glass by knocking it into the sink in the process. He said a nasty word and then brought the glasses to the table. I struck a match and held it while he poured whisky into them.

He said, "Damn you, Doc, if you're going to do this often, I'm going to get some luminous paint. I could paint bands around the glasses and the bottles. And say, know what else I could do? I could paint a chessboard and a set of chessmen with luminous paint, too. Then we could sit here and play chess in the dark."

"I'm playing, Carl, right now. I just reached the seventh square. Maybe somebody'll crown me on the next move, when I reach the king-row. Have you got any cleaning fluid?"

He'd started to reach for his glass, but he pulled his hand back and looked at me instead.

"Cleaning fluid? Isn't whisky good enough for you?"

"I don't want it to drink," I explained. "I want it not to burn."

He shook his head a trifle. "Again and slowly."

"I want some of the kind that isn't inflammable. You know what I mean."

"Wife's got some kind of cleaning fluid around. Whether it's that kind or not, I don't know. I'll look."

He looked, using my matches and examining the labels of a row of bottles in the compartment under the sink. He came up with one and looked at it closely. "Nope. This is marked 'Danger' in big letters and 'Keep away from fire.' Guess we haven't got the non-inflammable kind."

I sighed. It would have been simple if Carl had had the right brand. I had some myself, at home, but I didn't want to go there. It meant a trip to the supermarket.

And I didn't ask Carl for a candle. I could get that at the supermarket, too, and I neither wanted Carl to think I was crazy or to have to explain to him what I was going to do.

We had our drink. Carl shuddered at his, but got it down. He said, "Doc, listen, isn't there anything I can do?"

I turned back at the door. "You've done plenty," I told him. "But if you want to do more, you might get dressed and ready. I might be phoning you soon if everything goes all right. I might need you then."

"Doc, wait. I'll get dressed now, and—"

"You'd be in the way, Carl," I told him.

And got out quickly before he could press me any farther. If he'd even guessed how bad a jam I was in or what a damn fool thing I was going to do, he'd have knocked me down and tied me up before he'd have let me out of there.

Dim gray light of early morning now, and I no longer had to grope my way. I'd forgotten to ask Carl the time again but it must be about a quarter after five.

I was under greater risk, now, of being seen if Kates and

the deputies were still cruising around looking for me, but I had a hunch that they'd have given up by now, convinced that I'd holed in somewhere. Probably now they were concentrating on the roads so I couldn't get out of town. And getting out of town was the farthest thing from my mind.

I stayed in the alleys, just the same. Back the way I'd come and ready to dive between garages or behind a garbage can at the first sound of a car. But there weren't any cars; five-fifteen is early even in Carmel City.

The supermarket wasn't open yet. I wrapped my handkerchief around the butt of one of my two revolvers—Two-Gun Stoeger, they call me—and broke a pane in one of the back windows. It made a hell of a racket, but there aren't any residences in that block and nobody heard me, or at least nobody did anything about it.

I let myself in and started my shopping.

Cleaning fluid. Two kinds; I needed some of the non-inflamemable kind and, now that I thought of it, a bottle of the kind that was marked "Danger. Keep away from fire."

I opened both of them and they smelled about alike. I poured the inflammable kind down the drain of the sink at the back and replaced it with the kind that doesn't burn.

I even made sure that it wouldn't burn; I poured some on a rag and tried to light the rag. Maybe it would have been in keeping with everything else that had been happening if that rag *had* burned and I hadn't been able to put it out, if I'd burned the supermarket down and added arson to my other accomplishments of the night. But the rag wouldn't burn any more than if I'd soaked it with water instead of the gasoline-smelling cleaning fluid.

I thought out carefully what other items I'd need, and shopped for them; some rolls of one-inch adhesive tape, a candle, and a cake of soap. I'd heard that a cake of soap, inside a sock, made a good blackjack; the soap is just soft enough to stun without killing. I took off one of my socks and made myself a blackjack.

My pockets were pretty well laden by the time I left the supermarket—by the same window through which I'd entered. I was pretty far gone in crime by then; it never occurred to me to leave money for my purchases.

It was almost daylight. A clear gray dawn that looked like the herald of a good day—for someone; whether for me or not I'd know soon.

I stuck to the alleys, back the way I'd come and three blocks on past Carl's house.

Al Grainger's. A one-story, three-room house, about the size of mine.

It was almost six o'clock by then. He was asleep by now, if he was ever going to sleep. And somehow I thought he *would* be asleep by now. He'd have been through with everything he had to do by two o'clock, four hours ago. What he'd done might have kept him awake for a while, but not into the next day.

I cased the joint, and sighed with relief at one problem solved when I saw that the bedroom window wasn't closed. It opened onto the back porch and I could step into it easily.

I bent and stepped through it. I didn't make much noise and Al Grainger, sleeping soundly in the bed, didn't awaken. I had my gun—the loaded one—in my right hand and ready to use in case he did.

But I kept my right hand and the loaded gun out of sight. I got the rusty, unloaded Iver-Johnson, the gun that had been used as a bludgeon to kill Miles and Bonney, into my left hand. I had a test in mind which, if it worked, would be absolute proof to me that Al was guilty. If it didn't work, it wouldn't disprove it and I'd go ahead just the same, but it didn't cost anything to try.

It was still dim in the room and I reached out with my left hand and turned on the lamp that stood beside the bed. I wanted him to see that gun. He moved restlessly as the light went on, but he didn't awaken.

"Al," I said

He wakened then, all right. He sat up in bed and stared at me. I said, "Put up your hands, Al," and held the gun in my left hand pointed at him, standing far enough back that he couldn't grab at me but near enough that he could see the gun clearly in the pale glow of the lamp I'd lighted.

He looked from my face to the gun and back again. He threw back the sheet to get out of bed. He said, "Don't be a fool, Doc. That gun isn't loaded and it wouldn't shoot if it was."

If I'd needed any more proof, I had it.

He was starting to move his feet toward the edge of the bed when I brought my right hand, holding the other gun, around into sight. I said, "This one is loaded, and works."

He stopped moving his feet. I dropped the rusty gun into my coat pocket. I said, "Turn around, Al."

He hesitated and I cocked the revolver. It was aimed at him from about five feet, too close to miss him if I pulled the trigger and just too far for him to risk grabbing at, especially from an awkward sitting-up-in-bed position. I could see him considering the odds, coldly, impartially.

He decided they weren't good. And he decided, probably, that if he let me take him, it wouldn't matter to his plans anyway. If I turned him over to the police along with my story, it wouldn't strengthen my story in the least.

"Turn around, Al," I repeated.

He still stared at me calculatingly. I could see what he was thinking; if he turned, I was probably going to slug him with the butt of the revolver and whatever my intentions, I might hit too hard. And if I killed him, even accidentally, it wouldn't help him any to know that they'd get me for one extra murder. I repeated, "Turn around, and put your hands out in back of you."

I could see some of the tenseness go out of him at that. If I was only going to tie him up—

He turned around. I quickly switched the revolver to my left hand and pulled out the improvised blackjack I'd made of a sock and a cake of soap. I made a silent prayer that I'd guess right on the swing and not hit too hard or not hard enough, and I swung.

The thud scared me. I thought I'd killed him, and I knew that he wasn't shamming when he dropped back flat on the bed because his head hit the head of the bed with a second thud that was almost as loud as the first.

And if he had been shamming he could have taken me easily, because I was so scared that I put the revolver down. I couldn't even put it in my pocket because it was cocked and I didn't know how to uncock it without shooting it off. So I put it on the night stand beside the bed and bent over him to feel his heart. It was still beating.

I got the rolls of adhesive tape out of my pocket and started to work. I taped around his mouth so he couldn't yell, and I taped his legs together at the ankles and at the knees. I taped his left wrist to his left thigh, and I used a whole roll of adhesive to tape his right arm against his side above the elbow. His right hand had to be free.

I found some clothesline in the kitchen and tied him to the bed, managing as I did so to pull him up into an almost sitting position against the head of the bed.

I got a pad of paper, foolscap, from his desk and I put it and my ballpoint pen within reach of his right hand.

There wasn't anything I could do but sit down and wait, then.

Ten minutes, maybe fifteen, and it was getting pretty light outside. I began to get impatient. Probably there wasn't any hurry; Al Grainger always slept late so no one would miss him for a long time yet but the waiting was horrible.

I decided that I could take a drink again and that I needed one. I went out into his kitchen and hunted till I found a bottle. It was gin instead of whisky, but it would serve the purpose. It tasted horrible.

When I got back to the bedroom he was awake. So wide awake that I felt pretty sure that he'd been playing possum for a while, stalling for time. He was trying desperately with his free right hand to peel off the tape that held his left wrist to his thigh.

But with his right arm held tight against his side at the elbow he wasn't making much headway. When I picked up the gun off the nightstand he stopped trying. He glared at me.

I said, "Hi, Al. We're in the seventh square."

I wasn't in any hurry now, none at all. I sat down comfortably before I went on.

"Listen, Al," I told him, "I left your right hand free so you can use that paper and the pen. I want you to do a little writing for me. I'll hold the pad for you so you can see what you're writing. Or don't you feel in the mood to write, Al?"

He merely lay back quietly and closed his eyes.

I said, "All I want you to write is that you killed Ralph Bonney and Miles Harrison last night. That you took my car out and intercepted them on the way back from Neilsville, probably on foot with my car out of sight. They knew you and would stop for you and let you in the car. So you got in the back seat and before Miles, who'd be driving, could start the car again you slugged him over the head and then slugged Bonney. Then you put their bodies in my car and left theirs somewhere off the road. And then you drove to the Wentworth place and left my car instead of whatever car I'd been driven there in. Or am I wrong on any little details, Al?"

He didn't answer, not that I'd expected him to.

I said, "There'll be quite a bit of writing, because I want you also to explain how you hired an actor to use the name Yehudi Smith and give me such an incredible story to tell that no one would ever believe me. I want you to tell how you had him entice me to the Wentworth place—and about that bottle you left there and what was in it. And that you'd instructed him that he was to drink it. And what his right name was and what you did with his body."

I said, "I guess that'll be enough for you to write, Al. You needn't write what the motive was; that'll be obvious after your relationship to Ralph Bonney comes to light, as it will. And you needn't write all the little details about how or when you let the air out of my tires so I wouldn't be using my car nor how or when you used my shop to print that card with the name Yehudi Smith and my union label number. And you needn't write why yon picked me to take the blame for the murders. In fact, I'm not proud of that part of it at all. It makes me a little ashamed of the thing I'm going to have to do in order to persuade you to do the writing I've been talking about."

I *was* a little ashamed, but not enough so to keep me from doing it.

I took the bottle of non-inflammable cleaning fluid that smelled like gasoline and opened it.

Al Grainger's eyes opened, too, as I began to sprinkle it over the sheets and his pajamas. I managed to hold the bottle so he could read the "Danger" warning and, if his eyes were good enough for the smaller type, the "Keep away from fire" part.

I emptied the whole bottle, ending up with quite a big wet spot of it at a point at one side of his knees where he could see it clearly. The room reeked with the gasoline-like odor.

I got out the candle and my knife and cut a piece an inch long off the top of the candle. I smoothed out the wet spot on the sheet and put the candle top down carefully.

"I'm going to light this, Al, and you'd better not move much or you'll knock it over. And I'm sure a pyrophobiac wouldn't like what would happen to him then. And you're a pyrophobiac, Al."

His eyes were wide with horror as I lighted the match. If his mouth hadn't been taped, he'd have screamed in terror. Every muscle of his body was rigid.

He tried to play possum on me again, probably figuring I wouldn't go through with it if he was unconscious, if I thought he'd fainted. He could do it with his eyes, but the muscles of the rest of his body gave him away. He couldn't relax them if it would have saved his life.

I lighted the candle, and sat down again.

"An inch of candle, Al," I said. "Maybe ten minutes if you stay as still as that. Sooner if you get reckless and wriggle a toe or finger. That candle isn't too stable standing there on a soft mattress."

His eyes were open again, staring at that candle burning down toward the soaked sheet, staring in utter horror. I hated myself for what I was doing to him, but I kept on doing it just the same. I thought of three men murdered tonight and steeled myself. And after all, Al's only danger was in his mind. That wet spot on the sheet was stuff that would keep the sheet itself from burning.

"Ready to write, Al?"

His horror-filled eyes shifted from the candle to my face, but he didn't nod. I thought for a moment that he was calling my bluff, and then I realized that the reason he didn't nod was because he was afraid to make even that slight a muscular movement for fear of knocking over the short candle.

I said, "All right, Al, I'll see if you're ready. If you aren't, I'll put the candle back where it was, and I'll let it keep burning meanwhile so you won't have gained any time." I picked up the candle gently and put it down on the night stand.

I held the pad. He started to write and then stopped, and I reached for the candle. The pen started moving again.

After a while I said, "That's enough. Just sign it."

I sighed with relief and went to the telephone. Carl Trenholm must have been sitting beside his own phone; he answered almost before it had finished ringing the first time.

"Dressed and ready?" I asked him.

"Rights Doc. What do I do?"

"I've got Al Grainger's confession. I want it turned over to the law to clear me, but it's not safe for me to do it direct. Kates would shoot before he'd read and some of the deputies might. You'll have to do it for me, Carl."

"Where are you? At Al's?"

"Yes."

"I'll be around. And I'll bring Ganzer to get Al. It's all right; Hank won't shoot. I've been talking reason to him and he admits somebody else could have put those bodies in your car. And when I tell him there's a confession from Grainger, he'll listen."

"How about Kates, though? And how come you were talking to Hank Ganzer?"

"He called up here, looking for Kates. Kates left him to go back to the office an hour or two ago and never got to the office and they don't know where he is. But don't worry, Kates won't take any shots at you if you're with Ganzer and me both. I'll be right around."

I phoned Pete and told him that all hell had been popping and that now we had a story we could use, one even bigger than the ones that had got away. He said he'd get right down to the shop and get the fire going under the Linotyped metal pot. "I was just leaving anyway, Doc," he said. "It's half past seven."

It was. I looked out the window and saw that it was broad daylight. I sat down and jittered until Carl and Hank got there.

It was eight o'clock exactly when I got to the office. Once Hank had seen that confession he'd let Carl and me talk him into letting Grainger do any explaining that remained so I could get the paper out in time. It was going to take me a good two hours to get that story written and we'd probably go to press a little later than usual anyway.

Pete got to work dismantling page one to make room for it—and plenty of room. I phoned the restaurant and talked them into sending up a big thermos jug of hot black coffee and started pounding my typewriter.

The phone rang and I picked it up. "Doc Stoeger?" it said. "This is Dr. Buchan at the asylum. You were so kind last night about not running the story about Mrs. Griswald's escape and recapture that I decided it was only fair to tell you that you can run it after all, if there's still time."

"There's still time," I said. "We're going to be late going to press anyway. And thanks. But what came up? I thought Mrs. G. didn't want to worry her daughter in Springfield."

"Her daughter knows anyway. A friend of hers here—one whom we went to see while we were hunting our patient—phoned her to tell her about it. And she telephoned the asylum to be sure her mother was all right. So she already knows and you might as well have the story after all."

I said, "Fine, Dr. Buchan. Thanks a lot for calling." Back to the typewriter. The black coffee came and I drank almost a full cup of it the first gulp and damn near scalded myself.

The asylum story was quick and easy to get out of the way so I wrote it up first. I'd just finished when the phone rang again.

"Mr. Stoeger?" it asked me. "This is Ward Howard, super-intendent of the fireworks factory. We had a slight accident in the plant yesterday that I'd like you to run a short story on, if it's not too late."

"It's not too late," I said, "provided the accident was in the Roman candle department. Was it?"

"Oh, so you already knew. Do you have the details or shall I give them to you?"

I let him give them and took notes and then I asked him how come they wanted the story printed.

"Change of policy, Mr. Stoeger. You see there have been rumors going around town about accidents here that don't happen—but are supposed to have happened and to have been kept out of the paper. I'm afraid my grammar's a bit involved there. I mean that we've decided that if the truth is printed about accidents that really do happen, it will help prevent false rumors and wild stories."

I told him I understood and thanked him.

I drank more black coffee and worked a while on the Bonney-Harrison-Smith murder story and then sandwiched in the Roman candle department story and then went back to the big story.

All I needed now was—

Captain Evans of the state police came in. I glared up at him and he grinned down at me.

I said, "Don't tell me. You've come to tell me that I can, after all, run the story of Smiley's and my little ride with the two gangsters and how Smiley captured one and killed one. It's just what I need. I can spare a stick of type back in the want ads."

He grinned again and pulled up a chair. He sat down in it, but I paid no further attention; I went on typing.

Then he pushed his hat back on his head and said quietly, "That's right, Doc."

I made four typing errors in a three-letter word and then turned around and looked at him. "Huh?" I said. "I was kidding. Wasn't I?"

"Maybe you were, but I'm not. You can run the story, Doc. They got Gene Kelley in Chicago two hours ago."

I groaned happily. Then I glared at him again. I said, "Then get the hell out of here. I've got to work."

"Don't you want the rest of the story?"

"What rest of it? I don't need details of how they got Kelley, just so they got him. That's, from my point of view, a footnote of the local angle, and the local angle is what happened here in the county to George and Bat—and to Smiley and me. Now scram."

I typed another sentence. He said, "Doc," and the way he said it made me take my hands away from the typewriter and look at him.

He said, "Doc, relax. It is local. There was one thing I didn't tell you last night because it was too local and too hot. One other thing we got out of Bat Masters. They weren't heading for Chicago or Gary right away. They were going to hole up overnight at a hideout for crooks—it's a farm run by a man named George Dixon, up in the hills. An isolated place. We knew Dixon as an ex-crook but never guessed he was running a rest home for boys who were hiding out from the law. We raided it last night. We got four criminals wanted in Chicago who were staying there. And we found, among other things, some letters and papers that told us where Gene Kelley was staying. We phoned Chicago quick and they got him, so you can run the whole story—the other members of the gang won't keep that hotel date anyway. But we'll settle for having Kelley in the bag—and the rest of our haul at the Dixon farm. And that's local, Doc. Want names and such?"

I wanted names and such. I grabbed a pencil. Where I was going to put the story, I didn't know. Evans talked a while and I took notes until I had all I wanted and then

I said again, "Now please don't give me any more. I'm going nuts already."

He laughed and got up. He said, "Okay, Doc." He strolled to the door and then turned around after he was halfway through it. "Then you don't want to know about Sheriff Kates' being under arrest."

He went on through and was halfway down the stairs before I caught him and dragged him back.

Dixon, who ran the crook-hideout, had been paying protection to Kates and had proof of it. When he'd been raided he'd thought Kates had double-crossed him, and he'd talked. The state police had headed for Kates' office and had picked him up as he was entering the courthouse at six o'clock.

I sent out for more black coffee.

There was only one more interruption and it came just before we were finally closing the forms at half past eleven.

Clyde Andrews. He said, "Doc, I want to thank you again for what you did last night. And to tell you that the boy and I have had a long talk and everything is going to be all right."

"That's wonderful, Clyde."

"Another thing, Doc, and I hope this isn't bad news for you. I mean, I hope you were deciding not to sell the paper, because I got a telegram from my brother in Ohio; he's definitely taking that offer from out West, so the deal on the paper is off. I'm sorry if you were going to decide to sell."

I said, "That's wonderful, Clyde. But hold the line a second. I'm going to put an ad in the paper to sell it instead."

I yelled across the room to Pete, "Hey, Pete, kill something somewhere and set up an ad in sixty-point type. 'FOR SALE, THE CARMEL CITY CLARION. PRICE, ONE MILLION DOLLARS.' "

Back into the phone, "Hear that, Clyde?"

He chuckled. "I'm glad you feel that way about it, Doc. Listen, there's one more thing. Mr. Rogers just called me. He says that we've discovered that the Scouts are going to use the church gym next Tuesday instead of this Tuesday. So we're going to have the rummage sale after all. If you haven't gone to press and if you haven't got enough news to fill out —"

I nearly choked, but I managed to tell him we'd run the story.

I got to Smiley's at half past twelve with the first paper off the press in my hands. Held carefully.

I put it proudly on the bar. "Read," I told Smiley. "But first the bottle and a glass. I'm half dead and I haven't had a drink for almost six hours. I'm too keyed up to sleep. And I need three quick ones."

I had three quick ones while Smiley read the headlines.

The room began to waver a little and I realized I'd better get to bed and quickly. I said, "Good night, Smiley. 'Sbeen wonnerful knowing you. I gotta—"

I started for the door.

Smiley said, "Doc. Let me drive you home." His voice came from miles and miles away. I saw him start around the end of the bar.

"Doc," he was saying, "sit down and hang on till I get there before you fall down flat on your face."

But the nearest stool was miles away through the brillig, and slithy toves were gimbling at me from the wabe. Smiley's warning had been at least half a second too late.

THE
DEEP
END

FREDRIC BROWN

Comet

Bruin Crimeworks

THE
DEEP
END

SATURDAY

SUNDAY

MONDAY

TUESDAY

WEDNESDAY

THURSDAY

FRIDAY

SATURDAY

SUNDAY

MONDAY

SATURDAY

1

THE *Herald* city room was hot enough to bake a cake, although it was only half past ten by the big electric clock on the wall. Half past ten of a Saturday morning in July, the last day before a week's vacation for me.

Up near the ceiling somewhere a fly was making a hell of a commotion. Its buzz sounded louder to me than the sporadic hammer of typewriters. I looked up and located it, a big horsefly going nowhere fast, in circles.

Looking up made my collar tight and I loosened it. You damn fool horsefly, I thought, don't you know there aren't any horses in a newspaper office?

I found myself wondering whether a horsefly starved to death if it didn't find a horse, like the bread-and-butterfly in *Through the Looking-Glass* that starved to death unless it could find weak tea with cream in it.

Someone standing by my desk said, "What the hell are you doing?"

It was Harry Rowland. I grinned at him. I said, "I was communing with a horsefly. Any objections?"

"Thank God," he said. "I thought you were praying. Ed wants to see you, Sam. Right away." He moved on toward the door. He wore a light tan Palm Beach suit and the back of the coat was soaked through with sweat over the shoulder blades.

I sat there a few more seconds getting up the courage to stand and walk. I'd been getting by without doing anything for almost half an hour and I'd begun to hope that Ed had forgotten me.

Ed is the *Herald's* city editor. A lot of editors are named Ed. It doesn't mean anything. I've known reporters named Frank and Ernest and once I knew a girl named Virginia.

I pushed my way through the stifling air into Ed's office. I sat down in the chair in front of his desk and waited for him to look up, hoping that he wouldn't. But he did.

He said, "Kid just killed on the roller coaster at White-water Beach. I want a human interest story, what a swell kid he was, bereaved parents, that kind of stuff. Lay it on thick. You know what I mean."

I knew what he meant. "I'm sobbing already," I told him. "Has the kid got a name?"

"Probably. Get the dope from Rowland."

"He just left."

"On his way out there. He'll write the news story, Sam. And Burgoyne will write an editorial. You—"

"I know," I said. "The sob story. But I've got to have *something* to work on, Ed, unless you want me to wait till Rowland gets back."

"He'll phone you the minute he gets the kid's name and a fact or two to start from. Stick by your phone till he calls. Don't start on anything else. When you hear from him get going and stay with it, clear till deadline if you can get enough dope. Use all the space you can fill. A pic if you can dig one. Hit it hard."

"And make 'em cry," I said.

He shook with silent laughter.

I went back to my desk and sat there waiting for the phone to ring.

Ed hadn't needed to draw me a diagram. I'd worked for the *Herald* eight years, so I knew the score. This was strictly a must job for dear old Yale. I'd known that the minute he mentioned Whitewater Beach, which is the amusement resort just outside of town. The *Herald* didn't carry Whitewater Beach advertising and the *Herald* never mentioned Whitewater Beach unless someone was injured or robbed there, and then we really went to town. This was the first time anyone had ever been *killed* there and the sky was going to be the limit.

You see, Whitewater Beach was owned by a man named Walter A. Campbell who topped our s.o.b. list. Colonel Ackerman, owner of the *Herald*, hated Campbell's guts with an abiding hatred. The feud between them went back over a dozen years. The most common version of how it had started was that Campbell had called the Colonel a crooked politician because Ackerman, then heading the city council, had blocked a paving project that would have improved the main route to Whitewater Beach; Campbell accused Ackerman of doing it for purposes of extortion, to force the amusement park to advertise more heavily in the *Herald*.

So now, because Colonel Ackerman never forgot or forgave an insult, I sat waiting for my phone to ring, like a runner waiting for the starter's gun. But waiting was all right with me; I didn't want to work anyway. I hoped the phone would never ring. So, of course, it rang.

But when I said, "Sam Evans," into it, it wasn't Rowland's voice that answered; it was Millie's.

"I thought I'd better call to say goodbye, Sam," she said. "I'm going to take an earlier train than the one I figured on. I found out there was one at four o'clock this afternoon and that'll be better than the eight-thirty-tonight one because it will get me there late this evening instead of the middle of the night."

I said, "That's fine, Millie, but I'm sorry I won't get a chance to see you again. I thought—well, I hoped we'd have a chance for one more talk before you left. Listen, would you have time to come downtown and have lunch with me?"

"Thanks, but I'd better not. On account of leaving sooner than I'd planned to I've got an awful lot of things to do. I've hardly started my packing. Goodbye, Sam."

"Wait," I said. "You won't have to leave more than half an hour before train time. I'll see if, I can get off at two o'clock as soon as the final goes in. Then I can get home in time to help you with a few things and we can talk a little, and then I can drive you to the station so you won't have to take a taxi."

"Thanks, Sam, but—please don't. I don't think we *should* talk any more, not until we've each been away for a week and have had time to think things over by ourselves. We've each said everything there is to say until then."

"Maybe, but—"

"Have a good time on your hunting trip, Sam. Goodbye."

"Goodbye, Millie," I said.

And the phone clicked in my ear before I could put it down. The click seemed to have an oddly final sound.

I put down the phone and sat staring at it, feeling a little empty inside, wondering how final that click had been. Was it going to be the end of things between us? Oh, we'd see one another again after our respective trips. But would we ever be *together* again, or would it be just to compare notes and agree to disagree on a permanent basis? Would it be to discuss at last the ugly seven-letter word neither of us had actually mentioned yet, the seven-letter word which would mean the end of almost five years of marriage?

It was to think that over, each of us apart from the other, that we'd arranged separate vacations. I was going hunting and fishing with two friends of mine, one of whom owned a little summer cabin on a lake fifty miles north of the city; Millie was going to spend the week with her sister and brother-in-law in

Rockford. She might stay longer than the week if she decided to, but one week was all the vacation I still had coming; I'd taken a week in advance early in the spring when my brother in Cincinnati had undergone a dangerous operation and I'd wanted to be with him.

That week had come out all right; he'd pulled through nicely. But how would this coming week turn out? Would our marriage pull through?

I didn't want to think about it just then. And suddenly I wanted something to do besides just sit and wait for the phone to ring.

It occurred to me that maybe I could get myself something to start on before Rowland's call came. I picked up my phone and asked the switchboard girl for the South Side Police Station. A moment later I recognized Louie Brandon's voice answering. I asked him if he had anything yet on a kid killed at Whitewater.

"Just a quick report. Kid's name was—just a minute—Henry O. Westphal, six-oh-three Irving Street, age seventeen. Father is Armin Westphal, owns a hosiery and lingerie store downtown."

I had that on copy paper by the time he finished. I asked, "Where's the body? Still there?"

"They're taking it to Haley's. That's the undertaking parlor nearest to Whitewater Beach. The address is nineteen hundred South—"

"I know where it is," I said. "Who made identification?"

"Wallet in his pocket. We're trying to get in touch with his parents. They're out of town for the day and we haven't reached them yet."

"Heard he was killed on the Blue Streak. Fall out of a car?"

"No. Got run over by one, climbing across the tracks."

"Okay, Louie. Thanks."

I had something to start on now. Since the father, Armin Westphal, was a businessman there'd probably be a clipping or

two on him in our morgue that would give me some background.

I called the morgue. "Got anything on an Armin Westphal?"

"Just a minute."

I sat and waited, staring up at the ceiling again. The horsefly was still flying around up there looking for a horse.

2

The telephone said, "There's an envelope, yes."

"Good. There isn't by any chance anything on a Henry
Westphal, is there? Henry O. Westphal?

"Why didn't you ask for both at once and save me a trip?
Wait a minute."

I waited a minute.

"Yes, there's an envelope on him too."

"I'll be damned," I said. "I'll send down for both envelopes."

I caught a copy boy and sent him. He was back in a few
minutes and put two nine-by-twelve manila envelopes on my
desk. I picked up Armin Westphal's first to get it out of the way.

There were four clippings in it. One of them was a real
break, a biographical sketch with a picture. A few years before
we'd run a series of brief biographies of local merchants—
chosen, needless to say, by the advertising department and run
on the business page. Armin. Westphal had made the grade and
I had more dope on him than I could possibly use. The picture,
just a half-column head, looked familiar; I'd seen him somewhere. A dour-looking man whom you'd never guess to be a
purveyor of hosiery and lingerie. The cut for that picture would
still be in the cut racks up in the composing room and it was
one we could use effectively. The dour expression made it fit;
you don't like to run a cheerful or smiling picture of a man
whom you're describing as a grief-stricken father. The other

three clippings were short ones and more recent. They concerned Chamber of Commerce activities and gave me the clue as to where I'd seen him; several years ago I'd covered a couple of Chamber of Commerce banquets and he'd spoken at one of them, very boringly.

I opened the Henry O. Westphal envelope. There were two pictures in it, both glossy prints taken by *Herald* staff photographers.

One was a football shot, the kid in uniform and helmet, poised for a drop-kick. Except that he looked big and husky for seventeen—or more likely sixteen since the shot Had been taken last fall and it was now July—you couldn't tell much about him. Not even his build, for sure; he might have been tall and thin and the rest of it padding.

The other shot was much better; it was waist-up and was a picture of a grinning, good-looking kid in a white sweatshirt holding a tennis racket. The date stamped on the back showed it had been taken only six weeks ago. It had been blocked down in crayon for a halftone but apparently the cut hadn't been made or the glossy wouldn't be in the file envelope. A cut would be made of it now, all right, probably a two-column one.

There were five or six clippings. The most recent one, the top one, was only five weeks old. It was about Westphal's performance in the state high school tennis tournament. He'd gone there representing South Side High—my own alma mater, as it happened—and, after being seeded eighteenth, had placed fourth in the tournament. Each of the other high schools in town had sent a player but none of the others had placed near the top. This was the story the picture had been taken for—before he'd left for the capital to play—but the picture hadn't been used.

The other stories were all about football. He'd been pretty good at it. The oldest clipping was three years old and got him off to a flying start; as quarterback of the freshman, team he'd led them into a 7-7 tie with the regular team in that year's intramural game. According to the other clippings he'd come right along, although he'd done nothing very spectacular in his sophomore year except to end that year as first-string halfback—having switched or having been switched by the coach to that position. But last fall, as a junior, he'd been South Side's best player—at least he'd gained more yardage than any other player. Good as a broken field runner and pass receiver in particular.

Plenty of material, at least as far as his sports activities went. Good stuff, too. I could bill him as a would-have-been star in two sports.

I could wax lyrical about what he would have become if only he'd stayed away from that place of danger, Whitewater Beach. I'd damn well *better* wax lyrical if I wanted to turn out the story that was expected of me. This made it easy, although probably one of the boys from the sports department could do a better job of it. Personally I've never seen why people get interested in, let alone excited about, spectator sports. Golf, yes. A bit of hunting or fishing a few times a year. And I play poker as often as I possibly can without getting Millie too annoyed at me.

But maybe I wouldn't have that to worry about any longer. Maybe I'd be able to play poker as often as I liked—or be driven by loneliness into playing it even oftener than I liked. Unless, of course, someday—

I pulled my mind away from my personal problems and back to the story by looking at the picture of the Westphal kid again. Maybe, if I concentrated on the cheerful grin he was wearing in that picture, I could work myself into the proper state of mind to write a really good tear-jerker.

He *was* a good-looking kid. And the shoulders in that football picture hadn't been all padding, either. Even in a sweatshirt he looked plenty husky.

I decided to keep studying the clippings until I got my call from Rowland and picked them up to read them more thoroughly; I'd just skimmed the first time.

I picked up a few things I'd missed. The kid had a nickname, Obie. Probably from his middle name, since the initial was an O. Obadiah, possibly. Somehow, Obie Westphal sounded better than Henry Westphal. Maybe I'd use it that way after the lead; it would give the story an informal touch.

3

The phone rang. It was Rowland. He said, "Got paper and pencil ready?"

"Sure. But I've got some of it already, Harry. Called the South Side Police Station and Louie was on the desk and gave me what he had. And I found morgue envelopes on the kid and his father. Here's what I've got so far." And I told him.

"Good," he said. "I can't add much. Get one thing first; we can imply Whitewater was somehow to blame but we can't say so. They weren't. The kid was where he had no business being and he was crossing the tracks right past a danger sign. At the bottom of the first dip; the tracks come down to within a foot of the ground there. Maybe there should have been a railing— that's our only angle—but then again it's around behind concession booths in territory where the public isn't allowed. He had to climb a fence to get back there."

"Anybody see it happen?"

"No. And the car that ran over him was empty—which was damn lucky. It was derailed and if there'd been any passengers they'd have been injured pretty badly at least. But it was a test run."

"That something unusual?"

"Hell, no. They do it every day before they open up for business. I guess all roller coasters do. The Blue Streak has two cars and they give each one of them a dry run around the tracks every day before they open. Usually that's early afternoon, but on Saturdays and Sundays in good weather they open in the morning. This happened at a quarter after ten as near as I can get the time."

"Was the kid pretty mangled?"

"From the chest down, yes. But his head and arms were across the track. They won't have to use a closed coffin."

"Anything new on the parents being located?"

"No, I guess there's no way they can be reached until they get back, and that won't be until after deadline so we won't have any statement from them for today's paper. Hey, wait a minute —Haley's trying to tell me something."

I waited a minute and he came back on the wire. "Haley tells me the parents *have* been reached. They were at Williamsburg, at Mr. Westphal's sister's. They're starring back right away—but it's about a four, maybe five hour drive from there so you still won't have a statement in time."

"They didn't say anything over the phone, either of them?"

"Not except that they were starting back right away and would come direct to the funeral parlor here. Anything else I can give you, Sam?"

I said, "I've got plenty on the kid's athletic record, but not much about him outside of that. Have you got a lead on anybody who knew him personally that I could get in touch with?"

"Yes, there is. Right here. Haley's got a high school girl helping out in the office this summer, a vacation job. She knew Westphal, was in some of the same classes with him. I've already talked to her but maybe you'd better get it direct. I can put her on for you."

"Swell, but first what's her name? And can she hear you now?"

"Grace Smith. No, she's in another office; she can't hear me. But listen, be careful what you say to her, will you? This hit her pretty hard; she's been crying and she's still pale around the gills. Try not to set her off again."

"Okay. Was she the kid's sweetheart?"

"I don't think so, but I'd guess she had a crush on him.

Bobby-soxer stuff. Well, I guess it's more healthy for 'em to swoon over a high school hero their own age than over some crooner old enough to be their father."

"All right," I said. "Put her on."

About a minute later a girl's voice said, "Hello. This is Grace Smith." She'd been crying hard, all right; I could tell from her voice. It sounded as though it was walking a tightrope and trying not to fall off.

I said, "This is Evans of the *Herald*, Miss Smith. I'm writing an article on Obie Westphal. Not about the accident, just about Obie himself. I'll appreciate anything you can tell me about him."

"He was—he was tops. The best football player in the school, and good at tennis too, really good."

"I've got plenty on his athletic record—but not much else. Can you tell me what kind of student he was? How he did in his classes?"

"Oh, he was smart. He got good grades in everything.

"Was he popular with his classmates? Outside of athletics, I mean?"

"Oh, yes. Everybody was just crazy about him. It's just— just awful that—"

Her voice was wavering on the tightrope and I cut in quickly with a question to distract her. "What course was he taking, Miss Smith? And do you know what he intended to be?"

"The science course. He wasn't sure, but he thought he might decide to be a d-doctor. I was in his English class last year, English Three, and in his Latin class the year before. I think he wanted to be a—you know, a laboratory doctor. The kind that does experiments and learns new things."

"I see. Do you happen to know how he got the nickname Obie?"

"From his middle name. It's Obadiah. Henry Obadiah Westphal. But nobody ever called him Henry, even the teachers. He even signed his papers Obie."

"Do you happen to know his family, Miss Smith?"

"I met his father and mother once, at a school party. But I just met them; I don't really know them. His father owns a store, I think; I don't know what kind of store."

"Any brothers or sisters?"

"N-no. Not that I know of. I'm pretty sure he hasn't— hadn't."

"Did you know him pretty well personally? Did you have dates with him?"

"N-not exactly. But I've danced with him at dances at the school. S-six times."

The poor kid, I thought. She had it bad, to have counted those dances like pearls, to have known that it wasn't five times or seven that she'd been that near him. Under other circumstances it could have been funny. It didn't strike me as funny now.

I thought of an angle. If he'd had a regular sweetheart, a steady girl, and if I could reach her by phone I might get some good sob stuff for the story. Maybe he'd even been engaged; there are plenty of puppy-love engagements in the last year or two of high school. I'd been engaged myself in my senior year— to a girl I hadn't seen in six years now, Nina Carberry. I'd heard, though, that she was working in the office at South Side High.

"Did Obie have a steady girlfriend, Miss Smith?" I asked.

"No, he didn't. He—he didn't date girls very much. He mostly came stag to school parties and dances, not always but mostly."

I said, "Thanks a lot, Miss Smith. Will you put Rowland back on? If he's still there, that is."

"Yes, he's still here. Just a sec."

When Rowland came back on I said, "Guess I got enough to do it, Harry. But keep me posted if you get anything new. Particularly if you get names of any close friends of the kid, anybody else I can call. Say, he wouldn't have any relatives living in town outside of his parents, would he?"

"Nope. Anyway none of Westphal's employees at his store know of any relatives here. And they probably would. That's how the cops found out the Westphals were visiting Mr. Westphal's aster in Williamsburg. Say, you could get a statement from her by calling long distance, if you got to have a statement from somebody."

"I'll try," I said. "Thanks for the suggestion. Hey, do you know her name?"

"Just a minute; I can get it."

He came back to the phone in a minute and gave me a name and a Williamsburg address; the name was Hattie Westphal, which would make her a maiden aunt of Obie's. And a statement from her would be the next best thing to a statement from one of the parents, and that wouldn't be available, at least not in time for the city edition.

I put in the long-distance call and while I was waiting for the connection I cradled the phone between my shoulder and my ear and ran paper into the machine. But before I figured out my lead sentence the operator said, "That number does not answer, sir. Shall I keep trying?"

I told her to keep trying.

But it probably would be useless; if the aunt wasn't home now it was more than likely that she was returning with the parents in their car.

But damn it, I ought to have a statement from somebody about how wonderful a boy Obie had been, somebody closer to him than Grace Smith had been, somebody whose name— The principal of the high school, of course. It took me a few seconds to remember his name and then I had it. Emerson, Paul E. Emerson. And I was fairly sure he was still principal there. I looked up his home phone number—even if there were summer classes at the school, he wouldn't be there on Saturday—and dialed it. The phone rang but nobody answered it.

I thought again of Nina Carberry. Working in the office of South Side High it was just possible that she could tell me where Emerson could be reached. If not, she could at least give me a fact or two about Obie, maybe the names of some of his teachers who could be reached. I looked Nina Carberry's number and called it. Again no answer. Some days are like that, nobody home anywhere you call.

I'd have to write the first story without statements, but maybe that was all to the good; some suitable quotes would add up to a good peg on which to hang a follow-up story. And the *Herald* would follow this one up as far as it could be followed. Anyway, I had plenty of material, even without quotes.

Sob story or no, the lead would have to bring in White-water Beach. I started typing. I wrote. *Today under the wheels of a Whitewater Beach roller coaster.*

It went easy from there and I wrote almost as fast as I could type, but I wrote well. While you're writing a story, you can tell, maybe by the feel of the typewriter keys, whether it's good or not. This one was good. It had what a story took. I forgot while I was writing it that a man named Campbell who owned an amusement park was on the *Herald's* s.o.b. list. I thought about a kid named Obie and I wrote it straight and the tears were there. Maybe I wasn't crying, but my tongue wasn't in my cheek either.

I finished it, six pages triple-spaced, with time to spare, so I decided it might as well be accurate too. I'd carried the dates and the home and store addresses in my head and I might as well check them against the file clips. I'd almost finished doing that when the phone rang.

It was Ed. He said, "Kill that story."

By the time it had registered the phone was dead. I put it down and stared at it a few seconds and then I got up and went into Ed's office.

When he looked up I asked him, "What the hell?"

His voice was as sour as the expression on his face. "Rowland just phoned. It wasn't the Westphal kid. It was a light-fingered juvenile delinquent from the Third Ward, with a detention home record a yard long. He'd pinched the other kid's leather; that's how the identification, was wrong."

"Swell," I said. "I'd just finished the story. Now do I start one about the poor little pickpocket?"

He glared at me. "Hell no. We can't run a sob on him; we'll have to stick to the news story and an editorial and the less said about the kid himself the better."

"*Nil nisi bonum,*" I said. "Speak only good of the dead. If no bonum, skipum."

He looked even more pained. I didn't blame him. He said, "This is your last day before vacation, isn't it?"

"Uh-huh."

"Go out for lunch now and make it short, half an hour, and then get the hell out of here as soon as the home edition's in at two."

I said, "Thanks," and meant it. The last few hours before a vacation go slowly.

He handed me some sheets of paper. "Here's upstate stuff that came in late; the desk won't have time to handle it. Put it in English as soon as you're back from lunch. Now scram."

I scrammed. I got my suit coat off the back of the chair of my desk and I picked up the Obie Westphal story and made a pass at the wastebasket with it. But I didn't let go. It had been a good story; I wanted to read it over once sometime before I threw it away. I dropped it into a drawer of my desk and closed the drawer so a copyboy wouldn't get hold of it by mistake and take it to the composing room.

Then I went down for a beer and a sandwich at Murphy's, the bar across the street from the *Herald*, and I forgot all about Obie. I thought about the trip I was going to take with Bill and Harvey Whelan and the good time I ought to have if I could forget about the trouble with Millie. And then I found myself thinking again about Nina Carberry, whom I hadn't thought about for years until this morning. Wondering whether, if Millie and I did split up, it might not be interesting to look up Nina sometime and see what six years had done to her, what she was like now. Nina and I had had a very important first experience together when we were in our last year of high school at South Side. But that had been a long time ago and we'd drifted apart during the first year or two after we were out of school. There'd been an argument over something that seemed ridiculous now but we'd each been too proud to give in, and then we'd each found other interests elsewhere. At least I had.

I went back to the *Herald* and to my desk. I started putting the upstate copy into English and sending it, a sheet or two at a time, to the composing room.

Harry Rowland came in and I waved him over to my desk. He sat down on a corner of it.

"Wha' hoppen?" I asked him. "Ed told me it was a different kid, but I didn't ask him how they corrected the identification. Somebody who knew the Westphal kid take a look or what?"

"Fingerprints. They'd taken them for routine, like they do on all D.O.A. cases, and they put 'em through the routine way in spite of the wallet. And the Bureau of Identification digested them and came up with the fact that the prints were on record and they belonged to a Polack kid named Chojnacki. Who's spent most of the last couple of years, since he was fifteen, in reform school and the detention home. Which shows there's maybe something in this routine business. It's tough, though, that they'd already phoned the Westphals that their son was dead."

"They don't know otherwise yet?"

"No way they can be reached. They won't know until they get back, and that won't be before late afternoon. You know, I think Ed's missing a bet."

"What?"

"He's running the wrong story. The big human interest angle is the Westphals driving back from Williamsburg thinking their son is dead and how they're going to feel when they find out he isn't. I asked him if I should write that up as a separate story, at least a box item in the main story, and he said no."

"Why not?"

Rowland grimaced. "Couldn't write it without explaining why the first identification was wrong, why the cops thought it was the Westphal kid. That'd have to bring out the pickpocket angle and he doesn't want that used. Nothing that will detract from the slaps we're taking at Whitewater. And *dear reader* would feel less sympathy for Jimmy Chojnacki if they knew why he was back there behind the concession booths."

For a minute I didn't get it. I asked, "Why was he?"

"Either one of two reasons, or both of them. To take the money out of the wallet and get rid of it. Or to keep on going over the outside fence of the park, to get out without having to go along the midway. Otherwise he might run into the Westphal boy again and maybe by then the wallet would have been missed, and if Obie knew Jimmy Chojnacki's record—"

"Did they know one another?"

"Probably. Anyway, they could have; Chojnacki had been in Westphal's class at South Side High. Expelled in the middle of his sophomore year, but that'd still give them a year and a half in the same class. They'd hardly have been friends but they must have known one another by sight."

"It's a pretty big school, but I guess they would. One of them famous in athletics and the other notorious for having been expelled; that's fame, too, isn't it? Did anyone see them together this morning at Whitewater?"

"How the hell would I know? We've leaving the Westphal kid out of the story so what does it matter?"

He went on over to his own desk and put paper in the typewriter.

I turned in the last of the upstate copy a few minutes after one o'clock. I could have made it last until two but Ed was giving me a break so I didn't try to stall. I stuck my head in his office and told him I was caught up.

"Good timing, Sam. Just got the word on a fire. Corner of Greenfield and Lassiter, on the south side. Get over there and phone in before deadline; you can knock off as soon as you've phoned."

I drove over in the ancient Buick—ten miles to the gallon and a quart of oil every time I get gas, but it gets me around—and got there just as the firemen were cleaning up. It hadn't been much of a fire. I found out who owned the building, the probable extent of the damage, how the fire had started and the fact that it was covered by insurance, and I went to the nearest tavern and phoned in.

It was only a quarter of two and I was free; my vacation had started. I could have gone home except for that phone call from Millie; she'd made it plain enough that she didn't want me to come home and drive her to the station. I had to kill an hour or two somehow.

I went to the bar and killed a few minutes of it by drinking a beer. It tasted good and cooled me off a little but I didn't want a second one.

It came to me that I was only a few blocks from White-water Beach. I hadn't been there in years and there wasn't any reason why I shouldn't take a look at it again.

4

It was hot on the midway at Whitewater, but there were plenty of people there. No matter how hot it gets, an amuse-ment park draws a crowd on Saturday afternoon. The Cater-pillar, the Tilt-a-Whirl, the Comet and the Loop-the-Loop were all doing big business.

The Blue Streak was closed. A cop was standing in the space between it and the next concession where, by walking back a few yards and climbing a four-foot fence, you could enter the no-man's land between the concessions and the boundary fence, where the rides run. From one point on the midway you could see back, diagonally through the opening and over the fence, where some men were working at the bottom of the first dip of the roller coaster. There was a tight little knot of people standing at that spot peering back.

I showed my press pass to the cop and went on back, over the four-foot fence, to within a few yards of where the men were working.

It was muddy back there. Someone had played a hose over that part of the structure and tracks before the workmen had started; it wasn't hard to guess why.

The tracks, I saw, had already been straightened if anything had happened to them from the derailment. The men working now were two carpenters and one painter, the latter white-painting the boards almost before the former finished nailing them down. They were almost through. The wrecked car was gone, out of sight somewhere.

From where I stood I could see up the high steep hill down which the car had come. I could picture it coming down there like a bat out of hell, like a juggernaut, like death, and the boy turning his head, seeing it coming . . .

I didn't like it. I had a hunch I might dream about it, only it would be me there on the tracks.

The carpenters were moving away now, carrying their tools and the painter took a final white swipe and then he too, brush in one hand and can of paint in the other, followed the carpenters. I stood a minute longer and then I went back over the fence and back to the cop.

I asked him, "They going to run the ride again now?"

"Sure, soon as they get it fixed. Why not?"

"They've got it fixed now."

He looked back over his shoulder. "Yeah, guess they have. Well, that lets me off."

He walked out onto the midway. The little knot of people

who'd been watching back over the fence was dispersing now that there wasn't anything to watch back there.

I wandered over to the front of the Blue Streak. There was something I wanted to know, but I didn't know what it was. Something, some question, at the back of my mind that I couldn't get hold of and bring to the front.

A big, beefy man in a sailor straw hat was engaged in tapping and studying the wheels of one of the two cars upon the loading platform behind the vacant ticket booth.

I stepped over a low gate and walked up beside him. "Going to run today?" I asked him.

He put down the hammer in his hand and stood up. He pushed the straw hat back on his forehead and looked at me. "Yeah. Why?"

I gave him a quick flash of my press pass, just enough so he could read the PRESS in big red letters but not enough to let him catch the name of the newspaper. If he knew about the enmity between the *Herald* and the park, he wouldn't feel like talking to a *Herald* man. "Associated Press," I told him. "Came around to cover the accident you had this morning."

"Wasn't our fault. Damn fool kid back where he had no business being. Going across the tracks, crazy like."

I nodded. "When did it happen?"

"'Round ten, just getting ready to open up. Sent the first car around for the test run—we run each of 'em empty once every day before we start operating. And it happened. Car went up, started down the first hill and when it got to the bottom I heard it go off the track. First accident we ever had."

"Much damage? To the tracks and the car, I mean."

"Not too much. This is the car and we got it fixed up okay and they just finished the tracks a minute ago."

"Insured?"

"Yeah, sure, but it's going to hurt business. People hear there was an accident on the ride, they get afraid and don't ride it, don't stop to think it wasn't our fault and that the guy that got killed wasn't riding."

"You can't blame them," I said. "If there had been passengers in the derailed car they'd have been hurt."

"Yeah, there's that." He mopped his forehead with a handkerchief. "Guess you can't blame them. Besides, I'm losing four-five hours business on a Saturday."

"Were you the first one there after you heard the crash?"

"Yeah. Plenty of them there a few seconds after me, but I got there first. Look, mister, I got to keep working. My ticket seller and ride boy will be here in half an hour and by then I want to have run this car around a dozen times or so to be sure it's okay and the track's okay at the dip."

"Thanks," I said. "Guess I've got enough."

He was bent down tapping wheels again. He looked up. "Just remember it was the kid's own damn foolishness, not our fault."

"I'll remember," I told him.

I went back to the midway, wondering why I'd wasted time, wondering why I'd come here. Anyway, I'd killed enough time; it was three o'clock and I was on the opposite side of town from home. By the time I got there, unless I drove too fast, Millie would be gone. But why did I want to go home?

I walked out through the main gate and got into my car in the parking lot. It had been standing in full sunshine and it was baking hot even with all the windows run down.

I started driving and decided I was ready for another cold beer; I remembered that there was a tavern diagonally across from Haley's Funeral Parlor and that I'd be driving past there anyway. So I didn't drive past. I parked in front of the tavern and went in.

There wasn't any reason why I should be interested in Haley's or anything that went on there, but I found myself sipping my beer at the end of the bar next to the window where I had a good view of Haley's entrance.

I wondered if the Westphal family had been there yet to

learn the good news they were going to learn, or already had learned, on their arrival. It was just about time for them to come. I ordered another beer and drank it slowly. I was just deciding whether to order a third when a big blue Chrysler sedan swung in to a jerky stop in front of Haley's. I recognized the man driving it from the picture of Armin Westphal I'd seen in the morgue file at the *Herald*. He was a big man, well dressed, with graying hair. His face looked frozen and expressionless.

There were two women in the car with him, all three of them in the front seat. I couldn't see them clearly until Westphal got out of the car on his side, went around and opened the door on their side. They got out and followed him toward Haley's entrance. The two women were about the same age; I judged that the one crying was Mrs. Westphal and the other, who held her arm and was talking to her, was the sister, Obie's aunt.

"Another beer, mister?" the bartender asked.

I told him, "Yeah, I guess so."

They were through the door and out of sight when I looked back. In about five minutes I saw them come out.

Westphal was walking stiffly, strangely, and his face hadn't changed at all; it still might have been carved out of ice. But the faces of the two women were radiant. Both of them seemed to be talking at once, excitedly. They were ahead; about halfway to the car one of them turned and said something to Westphal. He answered and smiled, but to me it looked as though the smile hurt him. And his face froze again as soon as the woman turned away.

They got into the car and drove off.

After a minute or two I went out and crossed the street to Haley's. I found Haley in his office but not, apparently, very busy. I looked around and asked, "Where's the girl? Grace Smith."

He smiled. "I sent her home. She threw a wingding when

she learned the kid we got back there wasn't her crush after all. So happy she cried all over the place and then started a laughing jag. My God!"

"I happened to be having a beer across the street," I said. "I just saw the Westphals drive away."

He nodded. "Swell people and it was a break for me to be able to give somebody good news for once. *Real* people. Say, you know what Westphal's going to do?"

"What?"

"Pay for the other kid's funeral. Got me off on one side and wanted to know whether arrangements had been made. And when I told him what the circumstances were, he said to go ahead and he'd pay for it."

"What are the circumstances?"

"The Chojnackis? The kid's mother's a widow, works in a laundry. No money, and she didn't carry any insurance on the boy. She came here after the police had notified her. And after I'd talked with her I advised her to make arrangements with one of the cheaper morticians who could do the job so she wouldn't be mortgaging herself for the next five years paying it off. We're just not set up to provide inexpensive services." He frowned. "That reminds me. I'd better go around and see her right away—she hasn't got a phone—before she does make other arrangements."

"She's probably out doing that now."

"I don't think so. She was in pretty bad shape. I sent her home in a cab, and paid for the cab, and made her promise she'd stay home this afternoon. I told her there wasn't any hurry in making the transfer and that I wasn't charging her anything. Say, I forgot you were a reporter; I should have kept my mouth shut. Westphal asked me not to let anybody know he was paying for the funeral. You won't print it, will you?"

I shook my head. "I'm not even working. On vacation, starting an hour ago."

"Then what are you asking questions for?"

"Just curiosity. Happened to be in the neighborhood and, like I told you, I was having a beer across the street when I saw the Westphals leave here. But I'd got kind of interested in the case when I worked on it this morning so I thought I'd drop in a minute."

"Sure. Any time."

"Has the Westphal boy turned up yet?"

"About an hour ago. Missed his wallet and went to the lost-and-found at Whitewater. They figured he would and were waiting for him there. He went on home to wait for his parents."

"Why not here? They were coming here first."

He looked at me strangely. "Are you crazy? Think of the shock if they walked in here and saw him alive, thinking him dead. People keel over for less than that. Better to let me break it to them first before they see him."

"I'm stupid," I said.

"In my business you think of things like that, that's all. You get used to seeing people in shock and knowing how they act and how to handle them." He stood up. "Well, I don't want to push you out, but I've got to go see Mrs. Chojnacki. Got a car or can I drop you off anywhere?"

"Thanks," I said. "I've got a car."

I went out and got into it and drove home.

Home was an empty house. There was a note on the kitchen table in Millie's scrawly handwriting.

Sam: Unless you want to open cans you'll have to eat out tonight. I gave away the bread and other things that were left that wouldn't keep. Don't change the setting on the refrigerator. Be sure all the doors and windows are locked when you leave and you'd better go to bed early tonight because don't forget Bill and Harvey are picking you up at five and you'll have to get up at four unless you do all your packing and everything tonight. Have a good time.

The chime clock on the mantel in the living room struck four times while I was reading. Millie would be on the train now and the train would be starting or about to start.

I decided I might as well get my packing over with right away. There wasn't much to do, just to throw some clothes into a suitcase and put it beside the front door. My fishing paraphernalia and my gun were ready, all cleaned and oiled and ready to use, and I put them by the suitcase. I even chose and laid out the clothes I was going to wear in the morning. Now I could sleep until a quarter of five and still be ready when they came. We'd stop for breakfast somewhere, we'd decided, after we were on the way.

I puttered around a while and then went out and drove to the nearest restaurant and had myself a dinner. It was not quite six when I'd finished and I sat there over coffee wondering if I should do something this evening. Even if I shorted myself a bit on sleep it seemed wasteful to spend the first evening of my vacation reading at home and early to bed.

Maybe I should call Nina Carberry. No, this wasn't the time to start anything like that. Or was it? Neither Millie nor I had done any playing around; however else either of us had failed it hadn't been that. But even if our being on the outs was temporary—in fact even more particularly if it turned out to be temporary—tonight would be my best and possibly only chance to stray a bit off the reservation at a time when it wouldn't put too much of a strain on my conscience. But no, I decided, it wouldn't be fair to Nina to pull a trick like that on her, strictly a one night stand at that. If Millie and I had already definitely broken up, things would be different; not that I'd have any intention of getting married again right away, but at least I'd be free. Besides I had no reason to believe that Nina would be even friendly if I called her or looked her up.

No, I might as well behave myself, go home and go to bed early, start my vacation trip with a full quota of sleep under my belt.

I went home, read a while, then went to bed and to sleep. I'd forgotten all about Jimmy Chojnacki and the roller coaster, and about Obie Westphal.

SUNDAY

1

PART of my mind knew that I was dreaming. It was one of those borderline things between sleep and waking when you can think "This is only a dream" and still see and hear and feel vividly the things you know are not really happening.

I was lying face down across the tracks of a roller coaster, at ground level at the bottom of the first dip. I was able to move no part of me except my head; I could turn that to see the car that was rushing down the long steep incline toward me. There were three people in the front seat of the car; they were leaning over the railing watching me. They were the three I'd seen entering and leaving the funeral parlor, Mr. and Mrs. Westphal and the aunt. The two women were crying and laughing at the same time; the man's face was rigid and emotionless, a mask. The car passed over me and I felt nothing, I wasn't hurt. But one does not wonder in a dream, so I didn't wonder why I wasn't harmed and I didn't wonder how I knew that the next car would kill me. I lay there waiting for it, watching for it up that long slope of track, waiting to die. And fear grew into utter terror as I tried to move and couldn't, not even the muscles of my throat to scream.

I heard the sound of the car that had passed over me dying away in the distance, into silence. And then I heard a new sound.

I woke up fully. The new sound was the ticking of the alarm clock beside my bed, but it hadn't been that sound in my dream; it had been the clicking of a great ratchet. The sound you hear when a roller coaster car is being pulled up the first hill of its course; an endless chain pulls it up while a loudly clicking ratchet keeps it from sliding backward in case the chain should break. If you've ever ridden, or even watched, a roller coaster you've heard that sound.

I turned my head—as I had turned it in the dream, for I was lying face down in bed as I had lain face down across the track in my dream—and looked at the luminous hands and numbers of the clock on the night stand. It was five minutes after four o'clock; the alarm was set to go off in another twenty-five minutes, at four-thirty.

I burrowed my head back into the pillow and tried to sleep again, but I couldn't. I was wide and completely awake, although I usually waken slowly and groggily. I got up and shut off the alarm, knowing I might as well get up then as later.

I took a shower and dressed and then, because there was time to kill, I went down to the kitchen and made myself coffee. I had to drink it black because there wasn't any cream, but it tasted good.

I drank two cups of it, hot, black and sweet, and still had time to make a final round of the house, checking all the doors and windows, before the doorbell rang.

2

We got to Lake Laflamme a little before seven, with the day bright and clear and the sun just rising over the hills. It looked like a good day and a good time of day for fishing so we dumped our stuff in the Whelans' cottage, got the boat our of the boat house and went our on the lake right away without taking time to unpack anything but our fishing tackle.

By noon we had a nice string of perch and walleyes. It was hot as hell by then, out in the sun, and we figured that was our day's work, so we stayed on the screened-in porch all afternoon. We played two-bit limit stud and we drank cool Tom Collinses, lots of them.

When six o'clock came around none of us was in mood or shape to cook so we made some sandwiches and kept on playing poker while we ate them. We played another half hour or so until Harv—who was a bit out of practice at drinking—showed too strong a tendency to go to sleep among his chips. Bill and I shooed him to bed and made ourselves another drink.

Then, glasses in hand, we went down to the shore to watch the sun set across the lake. It was quite a sunset, like something out of Dante.

We sat there watching until the colors faded. My body was a bit drunk but my mind felt clear. Too clear.

I said, "Bill, maybe I should go back. I shouldn't have come."

He turned to look at me. "I know you've got something on your mind, Sam. You've been like a cat on a hot stove all day. If you really want to go back to town, Harv and I'll get along all right except that we'll have to play gin rummy instead of stud."

"I'd hate to spoil the week for you and Harv."

"You won't. But listen, Sam. Are you in trouble? Anything we can do?"

I shook my head.

"This is none of my business, but is it a woman?"

"No. Bill, it's something too screwy to explain. I'd sound crazy, even to myself, if I tried."

"Is it something you can maybe do quickly and get back while we're still here?"

I said, "It could be. It's something I've got to learn, to satisfy myself about. I might be able to do it in a day or it might take God knows how long. There's a bus runs near here, isn't there, Bill?"

"Sure. Stops at Holton, three miles from here. I think there's a night bus, I mean a southbound one. Want me to telephone and find out what time it leaves?

We went back in and Bill Whelan called the bus station.

He said, "Leaves at ten. That's—let's see—about an hour and a half from now. Want me to drive you in?"

"Thanks, no. A three-mile walk is just what I need to sober up and do some thinking, and an hour and a half is plenty of time for me to make it."

"Okay, Sam. Listen, is there anything Harv or I can do? If there is—"

"No, Bill, not a thing. Except—well, I don't want to carry a suitcase three miles. Just keep all my stuff for me and bring it back to town unless I do get back here before the week is up. There's nothing in it I'll need except my razor and toothbrush and I can carry them in my pocket.

And if I find I'm coming back I'll phone you and let you meet me in Holton. Otherwise don't look for me."

I walked to Holton through bright moonlight and I was sober when I got there, sober enough to wonder just how big a fool I was making of myself.

But I took the bus.

MONDAY

1

IT was the damnedest thing, waking up that morning. I was in my own bed in my own house but everything was wrong. I wasn't supposed to be there. For awful seconds of disorienttation I couldn't remember where I *was* supposed to be or why or what everything was all about.

Then it came back to me, and I didn't like it. I remembered the long walk, the bus ride, the taxi home from the bus station, unlocking the house and crawling into bed. But it seemed as ridiculous, as unmotivated, as though I'd dreamed it. Why in God's name had I spoiled a perfectly good vacation?

The clock told me that it was eight. That meant I'd had less than six hours' sleep—I hadn't got home until after two in the morning—but I was feeling so disgusted with myself that I knew I wouldn't be able to go back to sleep. I got up and dressed, and I made coffee and drank it.

When I felt whole and human again I telephoned the bus terminal and learned that there was only one bus a day to Holton; it left at four-fifteen and got there at eight-thirty. No use, I decided, phoning the Whelans now to ask them to meet it;

they'd be out on the lake catching walleyes. I could phone them just before I left, or even from Holton after the bus got there. I might even decide to drive up in the Buick, although I knew I shouldn't; it had two tires ready to go at any moment and needed a general overhaul that I'd postponed until after vacation. In its present shape it was all right to drive around town where, at the worst, I might have to walk a few blocks to phone a garage, but it would be tempting fate to use it for a trip.

I decided I'd better wait till bus time. That gave me time to kill, about seven hours of it. Might as well start by going out for a breakfast since there wasn't anything in the house to eat. I got the Buick out of the garage and drove to a restaurant, picking up a paper—the *Journal*, the morning paper, not the *Herald*. I looked through it while I ate.

There wasn't any mention of Jimmy Chojnacki's accident in the *Journal*, but that wasn't surprising if nothing new had come up on it since Saturday; their Sunday paper would have covered the story and, since they had no grudge against Whitewater Beach, there was no reason for them to keep it alive unless there were further developments.

I wondered, though, how their yesterday's paper had handled it and whether they'd dug any facts that we'd missed, so I asked the waitress if there still happened to be a Sunday *Journal* around. She looked in a pile of papers under the counter and found one for me. The story, when I found it, was only six column inches on page two. It didn't have anything I didn't already know except the Chojnacki boy's address. It was 2908 Radnik Street, which would be within a block or two of the back entrance of Whitewater Beach, which he'd probably hung around there a lot.

Back in the Buick I looked at my watch and decided what the hell; now that I had been silly enough to come back to town I might as well do at least a few of the things I'd wanted to do, as many of them as I could before bus time. Maybe I could convince myself finally and completely that there wasn't anything back of my wild hunch.

I drove south to Radnik Street. Back of Whitewater it runs through the area known as Southtown, a tough, shabby district. It had been a red-light district a good many years ago. The city had cleaned that up, but it was still a rough place, centering around one block, the 3100 block of Radnik Street, that was a Bowery or South State Street in miniature, with taverns, bums, drunks and all the trimmings.

I found 2908 and it was a three-story tenement with sixteen mailboxes in the narrow dark hallway. I found the name Chojnacki on a rusty box numbered 306 so I went up the stairs to the third floor, found the right door and knocked.

The door opened quickly. For what must have been at least two seconds the woman who opened it and I stared at one another and my expression must have been even more surprised than hers. Then I said, "*Nina*, what on earth—?"

She put a finger to her lips. "Shh. Just wait a minute right here. I'll be out and explain." She closed the door quietly.

I knew there must be some explanation but I couldn't think of a logical one. And explanation or no it was the damnedest thing. I'd been thinking about Nina Carberry, had almost called her evening before last—and now I'd knocked on Mrs. Chojnacki's door and Nina had opened it.

And now she opened it again; this time she came out and closed it behind her. Then she turned to me. "You wanted to see Mrs. Chojnacki, Sam?"

"Yes." What are you doing—?"

"Social service work. Sam, you can't see her right now. I just got her to sleep—she's slept hardly at all since it happened and she needs sleep. Do you have paper and pencil?"

"Sure. Why?"

"Print. 'Do Not Disturb' on a piece of paper and I'll pin it on the door. I've got a pin. Then if anyone else comes around they won't wake her up."

I did the printing on a leaf of a notebook and handed it to

her as I tore it out. She had a pin, from somewhere, in her hand by then, and put the paper on the door with it.

She turned back to me. "You're still working for the *Herald*, Sam? I suppose you wanted to interview her. But maybe I can tell you whatever you want to know. I know Mrs. Chojnacki pretty well, and I knew Jimmy, ever since he started high school."

"Fine," I said. "And we've got more to talk about than that. After all these years. Where can we go to talk? And is it too early in the morning to suggest a drink?"

She looked at her wrist watch. "Well—half past ten is a little early, but I wouldn't mind having one. I've a few more calls to make today but I guess I can make them this afternoon just as well."

"Hmmm," I said. "Inviting yourself to lunch too. Okay, it's a deal. But before we take off wait a minute. Let me look at you."

I stepped back and looked. Six years had done a lot for Nina. She'd been a pretty girl; now she was a beautiful woman. Almost beautiful, at least. The dark horn-rimmed glasses gave her just a touch of primness, a schoolteacherish look. But her body didn't look schoolteacherish, not by miles. It had filled out, and in the right places and to the right degree, since I'd last seen her.

I said, "How do you dare come in a neighborhood like this one wearing a sweater like that?"

She smiled, or maybe I should say she grinned, a gamin grin. "The glasses protect me."

"Take them off."

"Not on your life, Sam. I'd say I need protection right now, the way you're looking at me."

"Maybe you do at that," I said. "All right, I've looked my fill, for the moment. Where would you like to go for that drink?"

2

We settled on the cocktail lounge at the Statler. We went there in Nina's coupe instead of my car because she'd left hers in a limited-parking zone and would have had to move it anyway.

Over Manhattans, I said, "You can take off the glasses now. We're in a public place and the bartender is watching."

She smiled and took them off.

"You *are* beautiful," I said. "Nina, how come you've never married? Or *have* you?"

She shook her head. "No, I haven't. But as to why, it's a long and dull story. Let's skip it—for now, anyway. You're still a reporter for the *Herald*?"

"Yes, but I don't do much leg work anymore. Mostly rewrite, on the city desk. And an occasional sob story."

"Is that why you were looking up Mrs. Chojnacki?"

I hesitated, and then decided to cell her the truth, or at least a little of it.

"No, I'm on vacation this week. It's just—well, I helped cover the story Saturday when it broke and I got interested, curious about a point or two. I'm afraid I'd have told Mrs. Chojnacki I was interviewing her for the paper, but I wouldn't have been."

"Don't go back there today, please, Sam. She's pretty upset and, outside of her own friends of course, the fewer people she has to talk to the better. Or tomorrow either; the funeral's tomorrow, at two o'clock. Let me answer any questions that I can answer, about her or Jimmy, meanwhile. What do you want to know?"

I said, "I'm not sure just what I do want to know. Just tell me things."

"Well—I started doing social service work three years ago; that was about the time Jimmy was just entering high school, South Side High."

"Wait," I said. "I don't want to interrupt you about the Chojnackis, but are you still working in the office at the high school or are you doing social service work full time?"

"I still work at the high school. But that's not too much of a job it's only six hours a day, five days a week."

"And nine months out of the year. Or do you work there summers, too?"

"Oh yes, summers too. They have a summer term—for students who want to make up subjects they've flunked in. Or sometimes to skip a grade or to take vocational subjects they can't work into their regular schedules. And of course they have to keep the office running too. I'm not working there today because it's a school holiday. Dr. Bradshaw is in town."

"Who the hell is Dr. Bradshaw?"

"Just about the top authority in secondary education in the country; he travels for the National Board of Education to keep teachers all over the country abreast of the trends in educational methods. He's holding a forum here today and every teacher who's in town is supposed to attend."

I said, "Good for Dr. Bradshaw then. Otherwise you'd be working at the school right now and I wouldn't have run into you. Which, in itself, is an amazing coincidence."

"Why a coincidence? I mean, it's almost strange that we've lived in the same city for the last five years—or is it six?—and *haven't* happened to meet somewhere or other."

I said, "I guess so," and let it go at that because I didn't want to tell her, not yet anyway, that I'd been thinking about her and had almost telephoned her just night before last. "But go on, tell me about the social service work—since you've started—before we get back to the Chojnacki business."

"There isn't much to tell, about that. I've always done some kind of part-time work along with my thirty hours a week at the school; that's not really a full-time job. Three years ago I learned that the Social Service Agency here took on part-time workers and I thought I'd like it so I took a job with them."

"Do you still like it?"

"Yes. You see a lot of the seamy side, of course, unpleasant things, but it gives you a good feeling to be helping people who need help. The pay is pretty nominal but with my school job it lets me make out. And a good thing about it, from the practical standpoint, I don't have to work any specified hours. I'm assigned a certain number of families to keep in touch with and help, and I'm supposed to see each family once a week—at least for a few minutes just to keep in touch with them, longer if they need any help I can give—but I can do it afternoons, evenings, Saturdays, any time I want."

"Sounds like a good deal," I said. "All right, now the Chojnackis."

"They were one of the first families I was assigned to, and they've been on my list ever since. There's just Mrs. Chojnacki left now; there were three Chojnackis three years ago. Her husband, Stanley—probably originally Stanislaus, since he was born in Poland—was a drunkard. Not the vicious or cruel type, just weak. But he couldn't hold a job and couldn't keep from spending any money he did get on drinking. They almost never had enough to eat despite the fact that Anna—that's Mrs. Chojnacki's first name and I call her that by now—worked as much as her health would let her, more than she should have, for that matter. Stanley died two years ago. Of pneumonia.

"Anna has done a little better since then than before. Her health has been a little better—although she's far from being a well woman—and she's been able to work more hours at the laundry. She and Jimmy had enough to eat, if not anything over. Probably she'd have been taken off my list except for her troubles with Jimmy. Do you know about that?"

"I know he had a record for stealing and picking pockets."

Nina nodded. "And it was almost as though he just couldn't *help* stealing whenever he had a chance. He was a good kid in every other way, not mean or belligerent. Good to his mother— except for the hurt it caused her to have him in and out of reform school and—and being what he was. It wasn't so much that he needed money, although there was that, too; Anna wasn't able to give him any pocket money."

"Did he try working?"

"Lots of times, but he just couldn't hold a job for long. He had a kind of fierce independence that made it hard for him to take orders or to take any reprimand he didn't think he deserved. And whether he was working or not—this is why I'm sure it wasn't just a matter of money—he'd steal. And every time he'd lose a job for stealing from his employer it was harder for him to get another job next time."

"Doesn't sound like a very nice kid," I said.

"That's the funny thing about it, Sam. He was a nice kid, in spite of the way that makes him sound. And a smart one, too. He got excellent grades in school—I checked his record at elementary school when I started working with the Chojnackis, and of course I had access to his records at South Side High while he was a freshman there and he was doing wonderfully well—scholastically— right up to the time he was expelled. For being caught rifling clothes in the locker room of the gym.

"And he really wanted an education. He spent most of his evenings reading, and not reading just junk. I've seen lots of the books he brought home from the public library—history, biography, literature. And grammar and composition. Sam, he spoke flawless English, better than mine, and he came from a home where only Polish or very broken English was spoken. He wanted to write."

"I'll be damned," I said. "Listen, do you happen to know whether he went to Whitewater alone Saturday morning, or whether he was with someone?"

"No. Why does that matter?"

"I'm not sure that it does. Do you know who his friends were?"

"I—I'm afraid I don't know that either."

"You don't happen to know whether he knew a boy named Westphal?"

"*Obie* Westphal?"

"Yes."

"Why—they must have known one another by sight; they were in the same class at South Side. But they wouldn't have been friends."

"Why not? I know they're from different social strata, but if Jimmy was as literate as you say, that might not have mattered."

"But—they wouldn't have had any interest in common, Sam. None at all. Obie gets good grades in school, but he isn't *interested* in studying or reading as Jimmy was. And Obie's wonderful in athletics and Jimmy hated anything like athletics. Probably because he was small and not very strong, not able to compete in anything that took strength. And—oh, they were as different in every other way as their backgrounds were different. No, they might have known one another slightly—I don't know about that—but they certainly wouldn't have been friends. There wouldn't have been any one common interest to bridge all the differences. Why do you ask about Obie?"

"Jimmie had Obie Westphals wallet in his pocket when he was killed. He must have lifted it shortly before."

"*Sam!*" Nina looked frightened. "That isn't going to be in the paper, is it?"

"No. Not in the *Herald*, anyway. We knew that before we went to press the first day and didn't run it then so there's no reason why we should now. And the same goes for the *Journal*, I guess. I read how they handled it Sunday—the story broke too late for their Saturday morning paper—and they didn't mention the wallet. They must have known."

"Thank God for that. Mrs. Chojnacki mustn't ever find that out. It would almost kill her."

"Why? I mean, she knew Jimmy stole. So why would one more time matter?"

"Because—well, Anna is deeply religious, Sam. And it happens that Jimmy hadn't been in any trouble—hadn't stolen anything, as far as she knew—for two months or so before he died. And her one big consolation in what happened, the thing that keeps her from going to pieces completely, is that she can think he'd reformed, that he 'died good' she put it, that's the idea she clings to. And if she ever learns he died just after stealing again, with the stolen property right on him—"

"I can see that," I said. "Not that I'm religious myself, but I can see how that would be important to someone who is. Okay, Nina, she won't learn from me. And if the police didn't tell her that right away, when she was notified about the accident, I don't think they ever will."

"Oh, I hope not. That's the thing that keeps her going, the consolation of believing he died a good boy. And too, he'll have a nice funeral; that means a lot to people like Anna. The amusement park is paying for it."

"They are?"

"It must be the park because Anna told me someone is paying for it and doesn't want his name known. I told her it must be the park management—or possibly the concessionaire who runs the roller coaster—and the reason they're doing it anonymously is that it might seem like they admitted responsibility if they did it openly. It wouldn't matter—I mean, Anna realizes they're *not* responsible and she wouldn't sue. But they couldn't be sure of that."

I considered telling her who was really paying for the funeral and then decided not to. I'd promised Haley I wouldn't tell and there wasn't any good reason for breaking that promise to tell Nina. In fact, it might be better if she and Mrs. Chojnacki kept on thinking what they thought now.

"What time is it, Sam?"

I looked at my watch. "A few minutes after twelve. Afternoon. It's legal to have a drink now; want another one?"

"Thanks, Sam. I don't think I'd better. Are you hungry enough to have some lunch?"

We moved to the coffee shop for lunch and then Nina said she'd better get back and finish her remaining calls.

She double-parked beside the Buick when I pointed it out to her. I opened the door on my side but I didn't get out yet.

I asked, "Where are you living, Nina?"

"I have an apartment near the school."

"Are you in the phone book?"

She looked at me for a long moment. "You're still married, aren't you, Sam?"

"I'm married, yes. But I still want to know."

"But it's no good for us to see one another again if—"

I didn't help her.

"Well—you can *look* in the phone book and sec, can't you?"

I grinned at her and got out of the car. "Might do that sometime. Bye, Nina."

I had to close the door quickly because the car was starting.

I watched it around the corner and wondered if I'd ever call her. Not whether I wanted to, but whether I would.

Back in the Buick I sat behind the wheel a minute or two and then I drove the few blocks to Whitewater Beach. That was one of the places I'd intended to go; I might as well now while I was so near.

There weren't many adults there, but the midway was full of kids. As I walked back toward the Blue Streak I passed the fence over which Jimmy must have climbed, and over which I myself had climbed Saturday afternoon. There was an addition to it now, three strands of barbed wire atop it, spaced four or five inches apart. They weren't taking chances, anymore, of kids getting across that fence into the area beyond.

A girl was in the ticket office of the roller coaster, but she hadn't opened the window yet; she was counting out change and bills and putting them into the compartmented change drawer.

Up on the starting platform the same big beefy man in the straw hat was going over the seats of one of the two cars with a feather duster.

He turned as he heard me coming. "You again. What this time?"

I grinned at him. "Nothing much this time. Think I'll take a ride today. Press privilege, or do I buy a ticket?"

He grunted. "Buy a ticket. We'll be open in five, ten minutes. Soon as I run each car around once."

"You're opening later today."

"Weekday. Two o'clock weekdays. Ten o'clock Saturdays, Sundays, holidays. Look, what's the big idea? You trying to *make* something of that accident?"

I shook my head. "Thinking of writing a story about roller coasters."

"Oh." He thought that over a minute. "Well, put in it how safe they are. That Saturday business was the first accident *mine* ever had, and the only ones I've heard of on others have been where people do something crazy like standing up in the car or leaning over the edge of it. We're safer than railroads. A hell of a lot safer than automobiles."

"I'll put that in," I said. "Did you find a fountain pen around here Saturday afternoon?"

He shook his head. "Nope. Lose one?"

"I had it not long before I talked to you and missed it just after I left the park. Say, I'll bet I know where I dropped it. I was watching the workmen fix up the track back where the car went off and was bending over looking at it. I'll bet that's when it fell out of my pocket. I'll go back and look there."

I stepped down off the side of the platform. He said, "Hey," and I turned. He said, "I'm not going to run the cars while you're back there, so don't take long."

"Don't be silly," I told him. "I'm not going to be *on* the tracks. I'm not crazy. And it may take me awhile to look around in that high grass. Go ahead and start when you're ready."

I walked on back along the tracks, past the high scaffolding of the first big hill, the up slope and the down slope. When I got to the place where the tracks came down to ground level I stopped and, a few feet back from the tracks, bent down and pretended, in case anyone was watching, to be looking for something in the high grass.

A minute or two passed and then I heard it, the clicking ratchet sound I'd heard in my dreams, the sound of a car being pulled up the incline toward the top. It was *loud*, just as loud as it had been in my dreams Sunday morning. Nobody could possibly have failed to hear it, nobody who wasn't deaf or nearly so. And Nina would have mentioned deafness, if there'll been any, when she was telling me about Jimmy; physical handicaps of any sort would surely be mentioned by a social worker describing a case.

The car was coming over the top now and the clicking stopped, but instead there was a gathering roar of sound that made me take a step back although where I'd been standing was a safe distance, four feet away. The sound crescendoed and maybe it was imagination but the very ground under my feet seemed to shake as it went past and shot up the hill beyond.

I was shaking a little myself whether the ground under me had or not.

And I knew now, for sure, what I'd suspected—*one* of the things I'd suspected—all along. The death of Jimmy Chojnacki hadn't been an accident.

I couldn't picture it that way at all.

But I could picture two boys standing back here together, hearing that ratchet and knowing a car was coming, standing deliberately close to the track for the thrill of it, but still a safe distance back. And just as the car starts down the hill I could see one of the boys, the bigger and huskier of the two, taking a quick look back toward the midway to be sure nobody was watching through the one narrow space through which it was possible for them to be seen and then, just as the car roared to the bottom of the hill, giving the smaller boy a push that sent him sprawling face down and arms out in front of him, flat across the tracks.

That I could picture, and it haunted me.

I'd wanted it to go away but it hadn't. It had grown instead until it had driven me back to town from Lake Laflamme to try to prove that I was wrong—or right. Until now it had just been a hunch—oh, a hunch based on bits of conscious and unconscious knowledge, as all hunches are—but now it was more than that. I knew, or at least I thought that I knew.

I heard the clicking of the ratchet again. The other car was starting around now. I didn't want to stay there and see and hear it go by so I went back to the platform along the scaffolding of the hill.

"Find your pen?"

I shook my head.

"Well, look, if that is where you lost it, maybe the painter found it back there when he went back to put on the second coat. And he might have turned it in to lost-and-found. Might as well ask there."

"I will," I said. "Thanks. That would be where the main office is, back of the bandstand?"

"Yeah. Say, if you're really going to write a piece on roller coasters—and give us a break in it—forget what I said about buying a ticket. Ride all you want to. Here—get in this car now."

"Thanks, but I'll come back later when you've started drawing business. I want to have other people riding too so I can watch their reactions."

"See you later then."

3

The Lost and Found Department was a window in the side of the wooden building that housed the office of the amusement park, not a window with glass in it but with a wooden door that opened inward. The window was closed but there was a bell button beside it and lettered over the button as an instruction, "Ring Bell."

I rang bell.

A few seconds later the window opened and a young man with red hair and freckles looked at me through it.

I flashed the press card. "Were you on duty at the window here Saturday?"

"Up to five o'clock, yeah. Someone else was on in the evening."

"I want to ask you about a billfold that was turned in with identification showing that it belonged to a Henry O. Westphal. Do you remember it?"

"I remember *about* it. It wasn't turned in, exactly."

"What happened?"

"Well, somewhere around noon—I don't remember the exact time but it was before I went for lunch at half past twelve, Gilman came around. Gilman's the cop who's on duty here days. He wanted to know if a kid named Westphal had inquired here about a wallet and I told him no. He said, 'He probably will as soon as he misses it and when he does tell him to look me up; I've got it for him. I'll be over near the Blue Streak for a while.' So I asked him why he didn't just leave the wallet here for the kid, and he told me he had something to tell the kid along with giving him the wallet.

"So about ten or fifteen minutes after I'm back from lunch —I just hang out a sign 'Window Closed, Back at 1:30' while I'm out—the bell rings and it's the kid asking about his wallet and I send him to Gilman, and that's all I know about it."

"Thanks," I said. "Do you know if Gilman's around now?"

"He'd be on duty, yeah, but I don't know just where he'd be. Somewhere around the park."

A blue uniform is easy to spot and I spotted one walking down the midway a few minutes later. I caught up to it and found that it contained the policeman I'd seen, and had shown my press pass to, when he'd been guarding the fence over which I'd climbed to watch the workmen finish the track repair Saturday.

"Officer Gilman?" I asked him.

"Yeah. You're the reporter that was around Saturday, ain't you?"

I admitted it. I told him what I wanted to know.

He told me, "Somewhere around twelve Lieutenant Grange comes here from the funeral parlor and gives me the wallet. He says it was on the kid that was killed that morning but that it wasn't his wallet, see? The dead kid was a pickpocket and he must have lifted it. So the right owner, Henry O. Westphal was the name in the wallet, would miss it and come around asking at the office probably. And he explained what had happened about the mistaken identification and about the Westphal kid's parents being notified and—do you know about that part of it?"

I told him that I did.

"Well, he wanted me to explain things, what had happened, to the kid and tell him to go home and wait for his ma and pa there, because they'd want to see him and reassure themselves kind of after a false alarm like that.

"So I kept the wallet and left word with Red over at the Lost and Found Department to send the kid to me if he asked there. So Red sent the kid over and I gave him the wallet and the message. That's all there was to it."

"Did he say anything about how he'd lost the wallet, whether he knew it had been stolen and not just lost, anything like that?"

"No. What difference does that make?"

"None, I guess. Did you happen to look in the wallet to see how much money was in it?"

"No, but the Lieutenant told me. He said there was fifteen bucks in the wallet and I took his word for it. He says I should ask the boy how much was in when he lost it, just to check. So I did and he said fifteen bucks all right."

"I wonder why he didn't miss it sooner," I said. "It must have been stolen before ten and he didn't miss it till after one-thirty."

"Wondered a little about that myself and we were talking so I asked him. He said he'd left the park not much after ten and had driven downtown, that he hadn't tried to spend any money except change until he tried to pay for his lunch. He drove right back to the park but the window was closed so he had to kill time and go back after half past one. Well, that's all there was to it, except he said he'd go home right away and I guess he did."

On my way out of the park I stopped at a phone booth and used the directory to look up the Westphals, address, which I'd forgotten since Saturday morning. It wasn't too far, about two miles. It would be in the Oak Hill district, a good residential neighborhood despite the fact that it's bounded on one side by the freight yards.

I didn't call the phone number, although I made a note of it in case I wanted to call it sometime. Right now I wanted a look at Obie Westphal if I could get one without having him see me or know that I was looking at him. I didn't want to talk to him yet.

I drove there, past the house. It was a nice-looking place, newly painted and with a big, well-kept yard surrounded by a white picket fence. It was a big house, too, at least ten rooms; if only Mr. and Mrs. Westphal and Obie lived there, they had plenty of space.

I U-turned in the next block and came back; I parked on the opposite side of the street facing the house and two doors down so I could sit there and watch through the windshield. All the houses in the block were set back about the same distance from the street so from where I parked I could see the front and one side of the house and more than half of the yard.

I sat there and nothing happened; no one left or entered the house. Someone was there, though, either Mrs. Westphal or a maid or housekeeper; once I saw a dust mop shaken from an upstairs window. I looked at my watch after a while and it was four o'clock. The bus was leaving now that would have taken me back to Lake Laflamme, and I wasn't on it. I wondered if I'd get back there at all.

At half past five Mr. Westphal came home in the blue Chrysler sedan I'd seen him driving Saturday afternoon.

He left it at the curb in front of the house and went inside.

At half past six lights went on inside the house and half an hour later they went off again and Mr. and Mrs. Westphal came out of the house together; they got in the car and drove away.

I drove past the house slowly, making sure there wasn't a light on anywhere. I'd wasted about four hour; obviously Obie wasn't home and hadn't been home.

So I kept on going, but I didn't try to follow the Westphal car. I was almost starving by then so I headed for the nearest business street and found myself a restaurant I got my order in and then went to the phone booth.

It was about time I quit thinking about only one aspect of what I suspected and took a look at it whole.

I dialed the number of the *Journal* and asked for Don Thaley. Don is a closer friend of mine than anyone on the *Herald*; I could trust him farther than any of my fellow reporters. Besides, the city room of the *Herald* would be closed now, but the *Journal* is a morning paper and Don would be working now and since he wasn't a leg man he'd probably be in.

He was.

"Don? This is Sam Evans. How's everything?"

"Fine. Hey, I thought you were on vacation and supposed to be out of town."

"I am. On vacation, I mean. But something came up that brought me back to town, something personal."

"Do I know her?"

"Quiet; please. Don, I want you to get me some dope from your morgue and then forget I asked you for it. For reasons of my own I don't want to go to the *Herald* for this."

"Sure, Sam. What is it?"

"I want the dope on the four—I think it's four—fatal accidents that happened at South Side High in the last few years. Names, dates, and anything else. One was a boy who fell out of the tower window, one was a boy who slipped and hit his head on something, I forget what, and there were two drownings in the pool. One of them was a teacher."

"Good Lord, what do you want all that for?"

"I'm checking up on what's probably a wild idea. And I don't want to talk about it until and unless I get something. But if you'll dig that dope for me it gives a drink at Murphy's, first chance we get to meet there."

"Okay, no questions asked. But, Sam, I don't know offhand how I could get it for you right away. There must be a story on each of those cases in our morgue but they'd be separate, each under the name of the victim of the accident, and not cross-indexed under South Side High. I remember a couple of the accidents, wrote the stories myself from dope I got over the telephone, but that was a year or so ago; I don't remember the names now."

"Is there anyone there who might remember them?"

"Hmmm. I doubt it, not any one person anyway. If I canvass the office I might get all or most of the names."

"No, don't do that. I'll get it somewhere. Thanks anyway."

"Your best bet would be someone who works at the school, a teacher maybe, or anyone who's worked there the last several years. They might remember the names and if you can give me the names I can dig the rest for you. Don't you know anyone who works there?"

"Sure," I said. "I should have thought of that."

Not that I hadn't. I'd thought of calling Nina, of course, but I guess I'd been afraid to.

I went back to the counter and ate. Then I went back to the phone booth, looked up Nina's number and called her. She was home.

"This is Sam, Nina. Are you doing anything?"

"Why no, but—Sam, hadn't we better drop this? It was nice seeing you again today. But you're married."

"Okay," I said. "Maybe you're right, Nina. But there's something I want to ask you. How many fatal accidents have there been at South Side High in the last few years?"

"Three—no, four. Why?"

"Do you remember the names of all of the persons who were killed?"

"I think so. The teacher was Constance Bonner. The boy who fell from the tower window was named Green— Greenough, I think, but I can't remember his first name. The Negro boy who was killed in the locker room was William Reed. And the girl who was drowned—no, I can't think of her name, Sam. That was two years ago and she was a freshman then; she'd just signed in and I didn't have many records on her so I don't remember. Is it important, Sam?"

"It is to me. Do you know where I could find out?"

"Why, I guess I can find out for you by looking it up in my diary. I keep a sort of journal, day-by-day stuff. I suppose it's a silly thing to do but—Well, if I hunt back I can find the entries I made when each of those accidents happened. But it'll take a little while to find them."

"Can you take time now to do that? And I'll call you back in half an hour, an hour, whenever you say. How long do you think it'll take you to find them?"

"I don't know. I might hit the right entries right away or it might take me—Oh, come on around, Sam, since you really—I mean, I thought you—"

I grinned at the mouthpiece of the telephone. "Okay, Nina. And we might as well have a drink while I'm there. What shall I bring a bottle of?"

"Anything you want."

"That sounds bad. As though you drink anything and everything. How'd you go for Manhattans again?"

"Fine. And I happen to have a bottle of vermouth and some maraschino cherries; you can bring just the whisky."

"The vital ingredient. Okay, be seeing you."

I'd forgotten to ask her address so I had to look up the listing in the phone book again. It was on South Howell Street, a number that would be a few blocks west of South Side High.

I knew Nina would be curious as to why I wanted the information and I wasn't ready to talk to anybody yet about what I suspected, so I got a story ready on the way over.

The address was an apartment building, nice-looking but not swanky. I found Nina's name and pushed the button beside it, then caught the door as the lock clicked.

Nina opened the door to my knock. She wasn't wearing her glasses, and she was beautiful. Dark brown hair neatly but not precisely waved; it looked soft and touchable. Oval face with skin like a schoolgirl's, even to a few faint freckles on the nose; full lips, smiling, parted just enough to show the edges of perfect teeth, parted just enough to be perfect for kissing. A quilted silk housecoat molded the curves of her body.

She closed the door behind me. "I haven't looked it up yet, Sam. I'd just finished eating when you called and I wanted to do the dishes and straighten up the place."

"No hurry. Let's make a drink first." I handed her the bottle I'd bought. "You know where things are, so I'll let you make the first one."

"All right, but you can help by breaking out a tray of ice

cubes. I guess you can find them."

I guessed that I could, since the refrigerator was in plain sight in the alcove of the room that formed a kitchenette. It was a one-room apartment but a largish room, nicely furnished. Wall-to-wall carpeting in beige that matched the upholstery of the chair and sofa, matching walnut in the wooden pieces, walls papered in unfigured tan. A room in shades of brown, an attractive, peaceful room.

We made drinks and sat down with them, I on the sofa and she on the matching chair, a safe six feet distant.

"Nina," I said, "I'm really curious why you haven't married. You said it was a long story—but unless it's something you don't want to tell me—"

"It's not *really* a long story, unless I wanted to go into detail about every man I've known. I've had chances to marry, several times. But none of them—well, none of them happened to be anyone I thought I'd be satisfied to spend a life-time with. Probably I was too fussy—and will end up an old maid because of it."

"I doubt it. But don't tell me that you haven't—" I didn't quite know how to put it, but she spared me from trying.

"Had any affairs? A few, Sam. I haven't been promiscuous, but I haven't been completely celibate all the time. I'm human. But any time it's happened it's been more than—than—"

"A romp in the hay?"

She laughed. "Yes, more than a romp in the hay. Maybe that's what's wrong with most men; they think sex is only that."

"Maybe that's what's wrong with most women," I said; "they think sex must necessarily be more than that. Not that it can't be. But even hay is nice stuff."

She laughed again. "Let's not fight a skirmish in the war between the sexes. Sam, you make us another drink—now that the ingredients and paraphernalia are out on the sink where you can find them—while I see what I can find about those accidents in my journals. But—why are you interested in them?"

I said, "I'm writing an article, something I hope to sell to a magazine, and I want to finish it this week while I'm on vacation. You've heard of accident prones, haven't you?"

"People who keep having accidents? Of course. The current theory, I think, is that subconsciously they want to die; they have a death wish that their conscious mind isn't aware of."

"Right. Well, my article is going to try to prove—partly seriously, partly facetiously—that the current theory is wrong because there are buildings as well as people that are accident prone. And a building hasn't got a subconscious mind."

"Buildings? Are you out of your mind, Sam?"

"Maybe out of my subconscious one. But it happens to be a fact, Nina; there are buildings that have more accidents happen in them than the law of averages allows. And not because they're badly designed or dangerous in themselves. It's just that they're prone to have accidents happen in them."

"Sam, that's crazy."

"Maybe it is—and that's why I'm writing it as though I'm writing tongue in cheek, whether I am or not. But I've got a lot of data on buildings that have had considerably more than their share of accidents. And I want to add South Side High to my roster."

"But—four accidents in three years. That's not so awfully many."

"Isn't it? *Four fatal* accidents? There are three other high schools in town, all about the same size as South. Each of those three is over twenty years old and two of them never had a fatal accident. The other had *one*, about five years ago, and that happened on the football field; kid had his neck broken in scrimmage. South Side's the newest of the four, about fifteen years old, and it's had four fatal accidents, and all of them within the last three years."

"But it didn't have any before. Doesn't that prove—?"

"It proves, if anything, that it became accident prone three years ago. Accident prones among people aren't born that way;

they become accident prone at some time in their lives."

"Sam, that's such a weird idea that it really might make a good article—for a Sunday supplement anyway. All right, make those drinks and I'll get my journals."

I made the drinks and when I came back with them she was sitting with three largish volumes, the size of ledgers, on her lap; one of them open. I could see that it was handwritten, in the small neat handwriting that I now remembered from our high school days. Each of those three books, presumably one each year for the last three years, must have contained a hundred thousand words or so if it was filled.

She closed the opened one as she took the drink I handed her. "I've found two of them already, Sam, the first two; they both happened three years ago. The boy who fell out of the tower window was the first one."

"Tell me about it."

"I was right about the name, Wilbur Greenough. He was a freshman." She shivered a little. "I remember that one well because it was the first serious accident I'd ever seen, the first dead body I'd ever seen—except at a funeral, of course."

"You mean you actually saw it happen?"

"No, but I heard it, and I saw him right afterwards. He fell from one of the front tower windows and landed on the front steps. I was working at my desk—the school offices are still in the same place, on the first floor front—and I heard a noise outside that sounded like—well, a hard thud. Then I heard a girl scream and I ran to the open window and looked out, and he was lying there on the steps. And it was awful—his head had hit and cracked open and there was blood and—"

I saw that wasn't doing her any good, so I said, "Skip that part if you want, Nina. Was there any investigation made?"

"Yes, of course. But it didn't bring out much. Nobody saw him fall—until he landed, that is. It was during second lunch period, near the end of the period; he'd already eaten. He must have gone up into the tower and either leaned too far out of the window looking down or else climbed out on the ledge. There's a six-inch ledge along the row of three windows. And all three of the windows were open; he might have climbed out of one and tried walking along the edge to come in at another window. They found out that other boys had done that."

"Were any other students up there in the tower room with him?"

"Apparently not; at least they never found out that there were any other boys up there at the time. Since then the door to the tower has been kept locked, unless it's actually in use. And that isn't often. The Drama Club uses it for rehearsals and the school band practices up there; that's about all. It's unlocked only when either of those groups is scheduled to use it.

"That was in late September, not long after school had started. And the next accident was in January, the Negro boy who fell in the locker room. His name was William Reed. I didn't put any details about it into my journal, but I guess there wasn't much to put down. Nobody knows just how he fell because he was alone in the locker room at the time, as far as they could find out, but he'd hit his head on the sharp corner of a bench. He wasn't found for several hours."

"Several *hours?* Good Lord, how could he lie there that long?"

"It was the last period and he was about the last, or one of the last ones getting dressed; he'd taken a shower after gym—probably didn't have a tub or shower at home and took a long one. And his locker was in the last row back; even if there were a few boys left dressing in other rows they wouldn't have passed him on their way out. The janitor found him when he got around to sweeping in the locker room."

"Investigation again?"

"*All* the accidents were investigated. But since nobody saw the accident happen, there wasn't much they could find out. There was a recommendation made that the benches be replaced with ones with rounded edges and I think it was done;

I'm not sure."

"And the next one, the freshman girl who drowned, was two years ago? Will it be hard for you to find that one?"

"No, because I'm pretty sure it happened right after school started and that gives me about the right date, so I may find it quickly."

She'd put her drink down on the coffee table and was leafing through another of the books. After a few minutes she said, "Here it is. Oh yes, her name was Bessie Zimmerman. I didn't put down much about it because I didn't even know her, but I remember that it happened during a swimming period in the morning."

I said, "When we went there, girls and boys didn't use the pool together; a swimming period was for one group or the other. Is that still true?"

"Yes. It was a girls' class. There were a lot of girls in the pool and she must have got a cramp and gone under right away and nobody saw her."

I could rule that one out, I thought, but to keep up my pretense I'd have to show it as much interest as the others.

I asked, "How long was she under? It couldn't have been more than a minute or two before somebody found her, could it?"

"It probably wasn't, but they couldn't resuscitate her; they tried for a long time. People seem to differ a lot in how they respond to resuscitation; some have been brought back after they've been under water a relatively long time. And with others a minute or two under water is too long."

"And that leaves the teacher who drowned. You said her name was Bonner?"

"Constance Bonner. That was only four or five months ago, February or March or thereabouts. In this other book, the current one. Do you think I'm silly to keep a journal like this?"

"No, but isn't it a lot of work?"

"Not as much as you'd think. Half an hour or so several

times a week. I don't make entries every day, just when some-thing happens worth recording. Pleasant things as well as un-pleasant ones. I started doing it five years ago."

"Too bad," I said. "That means I'm not in it. Unless you put in having lunch with me today."

Her head was bent over the book in her lap. "I haven't yet, but maybe I will. I can't seem to find about Constance Bonner."

"Sure that you made an entry?"

"Yes, almost a page." She looked up. "Sam, that's the only one that might not have been an accident. And if it wasn't, it wouldn't fit your article."

"You mean she might have been killed deliberately?"

"No, of course not. But there was a strong suspicion that she committed suicide. The circumstances—wait till I find it; I might as well wait to tell you. It's here somewhere."

Pages turned some more. "Here it is. It was in January, earlier than I thought. Wait till I read it."

"Why not read out loud?"

She looked up again. "I'd rather not, Sam. It's just—well, some of the things in these books are so personal that I've never let anyone read a line of it or read any of it to anyone. This particular entry wouldn't matter but—well, it's a matter of prin-ciple."

"Okay, I can understand that. Read it to yourself then. Want to kill the rest of that drink so I can make us another?"

"All right. Or are you trying to get me drunk?"

"Deponent refuses to answer," I said.

I heard her close the book while I was making the drinks; out of the corner of my eye I saw her take the three books to a desk in the far corner of the room and lock them into the bottom drawer. She slipped the key in a housecoat pocket and came over to join me at the sink.

"Now that I've read it again, Sam, I think that it was suicide. But there wasn't any proof that it was—just circum-stances—so the police put it down as accidental, whether they really thought so or not. I mean, they decided she could have fallen in the pool. She couldn't have gone in to swim because she couldn't swim a stroke, and besides she had all her clothes on. But she could have fallen in, except that she had no reason to be there beside the pool."

"It was outside school hours, wasn't it?"

"Yes, it was in the evening. There was an evening meeting of the Drama Club and Miss Bonner was the faculty adviser of the club so naturally she was at the meeting. It was from seven till nine. When the meeting broke up she told the kids she wasn't leaving right away, that she was behind in her work and might as well put in an hour or two in her classroom while she was there, grading papers—it was just after mid-year exams. So when they left, she went to her room—"

"Had she acted normally during the meeting?"

"There were conflicting stories on that from the kids, I remember. Some of them thought she had, others thought she acted strangely. They all agreed that she was pretty quiet and didn't say much, though. Anyway, she walked to the front door with the club members and let them out and locked the door again. She must have gone to her own classroom for at least a while because she turned on the light there although there wasn't anything to indicate that she'd graded any papers.

"Well, about three o'clock in the morning a squad car went by on its regular rounds and the policemen in it saw a light on in the basement of the school and they decided to investigate; sometimes, they knew, teachers worked evenings there, but never until three in the morning. They carried a key to the school, for emergencies, and they let themselves in. They found the light was in a classroom and that a woman's hat and coat were on the desk there, as though she might still be in the building, so they looked around. They kept opening doors and when they opened the one to the room with the pool in it they saw the lights were on in there and they went in. They found her body in the pool."

"That's entirely an inside room," I said. "The lights wouldn't have shown outside. Was Miss Bonner's classroom a basement room?"

"Yes. And not far from the pool. Oh, it could have been an accident; she could have gone in there for some reason and fallen in accidentally, and without being able to swim she'd have drowned all right. But why, unless she wanted to commit suicide, would she have gone in there at all?"

"I don't know," I said. "Did they find that she had any reason to kill herself?"

"Well, no specific reason. But her parents—she lived at home with them—said she'd been acting strangely for a few weeks. Happy at times and very unhappy, moping, at other times. Almost—they didn't put it this way—almost manic-depressive. But she wasn't in any trouble that they knew of. I think the police would have called it suicide if they could have found any reason at all for her to have killed herself."

I said, "It sounds like suicide to me, Nina. A person's reasons for killing himself wouldn't necessarily show on the surface. Especially if it was true that she was mentally unbalanced. And the symptoms you said her parents described do sound like manic-depressive all right. How well did you know her?"

"Just to speak to. Last year was her first year at South Side, and it just didn't happen that we got acquainted. She was even younger than I by a year or two, about twenty-four, I think. She taught English."

That one, too, I thought I could forget about. The circumstances just didn't fit, and suicide really seemed like the probable answer. Only two out of the four were left and maybe I was crazy in thinking what I'd been thinking, even about those two.

All right, I thought; I'll quit thinking for tonight.

4

I made us another drink. I was feeling mine a little, but I wanted to feel them.

We talked about not much for a while. And then I actually got as far as the door, with my hat on, and Nina with her hand on the knob to open it for me. But I put one arm lightly around her and kissed her. And then both my arms were around her and both hers around me, her hands pressing my head forward, my lips against hers hungrily, so hard that it almost hurt.

After a minute or two I whispered, "I don't want to go, Nina."

"I don't want you to. I know it's wrong, but—"

My lips stopped hers. It seemed right, very right. And I knew now that I'd known all along, since Nina had surprise-ingly opened the door of Mrs. Chojnacki's flat, that this was going to happen.

It happened very wonderfully, and it still seemed right.

TUESDAY

1

I WAS alone in bed when I awakened. There wasn't a clock in sight and I remembered that Nina was one of those people, she'd told me, who don't need alarm clocks; they make up their minds to awaken at a given hour and always do. My wrist watch told me it was twenty minutes after eight.

I sat up on the edge of the bed and reached for my clothes on the chair beside it. There was a note for me lying on my clothes where I couldn't have missed it.

Sam: You're still sleeping so soundly that I won't wake you. Get yourself breakfast here if you wish—there'll be coffee left in the pot that you'll only have to heat and you'll find bacon and eggs in the refrigerator—but please be quiet about it. And be quiet when you leave. If you want to phone me during school hours the number is Grand 6400.

Nina

I dressed and left quietly without getting myself breakfast. I didn't know anything about Nina's neighbors, but I didn't want to take a chance of being heard in her apartment at a time when they might know she had already left it. I had breakfast at a restaurant and then drove home. I showered, shaved and put on clean clothes. Then I called Grand 6400. Nina's voice answered.

"Sam, Nina," I said. "Can you talk freely?"

"Yes, sir. He's not in right now. Shall I have him call you back?"

"I'm at home, West 3208. In the phone book, if you didn't write that down. But call as soon as you can—I'll wait here, but I'll just be waiting for your call."

"Yes, sir, I'll have him call you as soon as he comes in. I don't think it will be very long."

It was about ten minutes.

"Sam, I *could* have talked to you, but there were people in the office and I didn't want to have to be careful what I said. I thought I'd rather wait till I could get to the phone booth."

"Give me *some* credit, Nina. You didn't have to explain. Thanks for letting me sleep this morning. I needed it. I feel fine."

"Do you feel the same way you felt last night?"

"Well—at the moment, not exactly. But give me time—until this evening, maybe. You weren't planning anything? For to-night, I mean."

"Not until now."

"Good girl."

"No, I'm not. Would you like me if I was a good girl?"

"Of course not. But listen, darling, I may not be able to see you until late in the evening. There's somebody I've got to see first—and it isn't another woman."

"All right."

"What time will you get home?"

"Before five o'clock, I think. I'm taking off early today, half past one, so I can go to the Chojnacki funeral. After that, if there's time, I'll call on one or two other cases on my list but I'll still be home fairly early."

I said, "I'd forgotten about the funeral. Do you think it will be all right for me to drop in for it?"

"Why—I don't know why you'd want to, but I don't see any reason why you shouldn't."

"Probably see you there, then. Bye, darling."

2

Chief of Police Steiner was in his office when I got to police headquarters and I had to wait less than half an hour to get in to see him. I handed him a fifty-cent cigar I'd bought on the way there. He peeled off the cellophane and sniffed it appreciatively so I struck while the appreciation held.

"Like you to do me a favor, Chief."

"Always glad to help the *Herald*, Sam." He should be; the *Herald* and Colonel Ackerman had got his job for him. I might have let it go at that, but it would be too easy for him to happen to learn that I was on vacation this week.

I said, "It's for me, not the paper; I'm on my own time. I'm writing a magazine article on accidents—various screwy ways people can get themselves killed. How are chances of my browsing through the file on accidents."

"I guess there's no reason why not. We've got only the non-traffic accidents here, though. If you want the traffic ones—"

"I don't," I said. "Traffic accidents are pretty much all alike, and I'm looking for unusual ones, or ones with screwy angles. Like one I read about recently—forget where it happened but it wasn't here. Painter fell off a platform roped down from the eaves of a building, fell three stories and wasn't hurt a bit except it knocked the wind out of him. Got up and stood there getting his breath back and an unopened can of paint that he'd had on the platform and had knocked over when he fell rolled off the platform three stories above him, hit him on the head and killed him."

Steiner grinned. "Don't recall reading about that one, but I guess we've had a few funny ones here too. Might remember some if I tried, but if you're going through the files anyway, you'll come across 'em."

"How's our accident rate compared to other cities?"

"Oh, about in line. If you want statistics on types of accidents and comparison with other cities, look up Carey over in the mayor's office. Year or so ago he did a statistical analysis for the mayor, who wanted to know how we stood compared to other cities. He was mostly interested in traffic accidents, but he covered all kinds while he was at it."

I didn't see how that would help me but I said thanks, I might do that. Chief Steiner buzzed for his secretary and told him to lead me to the file cabinets on accidents, non-traffic, and turn me loose there.

There was a discouraging number of four-drawer file cabinets. Five of them, all filled with folders on non-traffic accidents. But they didn't look quite so discouraging when the secretary—a tall young man in horn-rimmed glasses—told me they held accident folders for twenty years back, which meant I'd have to go through only a fraction of them.

"There's one drawer for each year," he explained. "The accidents—these are only fatal accidents, of course—are arranged chronologically. But in front of each drawer there's a sheet that's made up at the end of each year, an alphabetical list of names of victims and the date of each, so you can find any given one without having to go through the whole drawer. That is, if you know the name of the victim and the year the accident happened in."

I told him that was swell. I took off my coat and hung it over a chair and dived in. If the secretary had stuck around to watch me get started I'd have had to carry out my pretext by working chronologically backwards, but he didn't so I started out by looking up, since I knew the year and the names of the victims, the four accidents at South Side High.

Except for addresses, exact dates and times of day, and some irrelevant details, I didn't learn anything beyond what Nina had already told me. I didn't find any mention of the name

I was looking for. Not even as a witness.

It was after noon by the time I finished studying those four file folders and I didn't have time, if I was going to have lunch and make the Chojnacki funeral, to start looking through the other files. I talked to the tall secretary again on my way out, explaining that I hadn't finished and would be back later or some other day.

3

It was cool and comfortable in Haley's funeral parlor; air-conditioning kept out the heat and the stained-glass windows of the chapel tinted and mellowed the sunlight that came through diem.

I sat in a back corner, as inconspicuously as possible. The coffin that held what the roller coaster had left of Jimmy Chojnacki was on a flower-banked bier up at the front.

There were about twenty people there and Nina was the only one I knew. But I could guess that the woman in black next to whom Nina sat and to whom she was whispering must be Anna Chojnacki.

The organ was playing softly now. From outside, far away but getting nearer and louder, came the drone of a plane going overhead. Its sound made me think of the horsefly that had flown around the *Herald* editorial room last Saturday morning and I remembered Harry Rowland's saying, "My God, I thought you were praying."

The minister was praying now and the organ had stopped. He was a tall thin man with a face like a horse, but with a good voice. I had his name and the name of his church on the back of an envelope in my pocket. Haley had told me when I came, thinking that I was covering the funeral for the paper; not to disillusion him, I'd written them down.

"For Jesus said, I am the resurrection and the life, in me shall . . ."

Out of the corner of my eye I saw a man standing now in the doorway of the chapel, a big man with dark hair turning gray. The man who was paying for this funeral, Armin Westphal. I'd wondered if he was going to come; it was one of my reasons for being here. And he'd made it, if a little late.

When the prayer was finished he came in quietly and took the seat nearest the doorway.

The organ played again and a fat Italian-looking woman with the face of a Madonna sang. Her voice was beautiful. The organist was good, too. He wove little patterns of notes around the melody, as harpsichord music used to be written to fill in for the lack of sustained notes.

"In midst of life, we are in death . . ."

I could tell from Anna Chojnacki's shoulders that she was weeping silently.

I didn't hear the sermon. I was thinking my own thoughts. Obie Westphal's father had come to the funeral of Jimmy Chojnacki. Another thing, meaningless in itself as were all the other things. Why shouldn't he, in a sudden impulse of generosity caused by relief that his son was still alive when he'd thought him dead, offer to pay for the funeral of the boy who'd really died and whose mother was too poor to pay for it? And why, since he was paying, shouldn't he come?

But I'd seen Armin Westphal's face last Saturday afternoon as he'd left here, and I wondered now if this was the only such funeral he'd paid for.

When the service was over Westphal slipped out quietly. I gave him time to get away before I left. In case I wanted to talk to him later on some pretext I didn't want him to recognize me as having been at the funeral too.

I wanted more than ever now to have a look at Obie Westphal, in the flesh and not a photograph.

I drove out to the Westphal house. This time I parked beyond it so I wouldn't be in the same place, but I moved my rear vision mirror so I could see all of the front of the house.

I sat there and watched it and nothing happened except that about five o'clock Mr. Westphal came home in the blue Chrysler. This time he put it in the garage instead of leaving it out front. Lights went on inside the house at half past six, and by seven I was beginning to wonder if I was again wasting my time.

There was only one way to find out. I drove to a nearby drugstore and phoned the Westphals. A woman's voice answered and I asked, "Is Obie there?"

"No, he's been visiting a friend in Springfield since Sunday. He'll be back tomorrow at two o'clock. Who shall I tell him called?"

"You needn't bother," I said. "It's nothing important and he wouldn't know my name anyway. I'll call again after he's back."

I hung up and swore at myself for having wasted time both yesterday and today.

I called Nina's number. "This is Sam, darling. Just finished the business I had to do. Have you eaten yet?"

"I was just getting ready to eat. I waited as long as I could and just now gave up hearing from you in time."

"Good, then you can wait a little longer and you'll have a real appetite. Want to grab a cab and meet me somewhere?"

"Let's eat here, Sam, I just took a bath and I'm in my housecoat; I don't feel like getting dressed and going out. I've got some canned chop suey I can open for us. How does that sound?"

"Horrible," I said. "I'm feeling carnivorous. If I pick up a couple of thick steaks will you fry them for us?"

"Will I? That sounds wonderful. I guess I'm feeling carnivorous too. Hurry, Sam."

1

I WOKE first. Nina was cuddled against my back and I pulled away, turned and raised myself on one elbow to look at her. Even asleep she was beautiful. Her face was as sweetly innocent as a sleeping baby's. Her hair looked even better a little tousled. She lay with one hand under her chin, her forearm between her breasts, hiding one of them but accentuating the other. I leaned over and kissed it gently.

When I raised up her eyes were open, looking at me.

"Love me, Sam?"

"I don't know," I said honestly. "I was just wondering. I know I want you.'" I lay down again and pulled her tightly against me.

"You shouldn't love me," she said. "You mustn't."

"Why not?"

"I'm a wicked woman."

"Prove it."

She nibbled gently at my ear. I said, "That's not very wicked."

"What do you want me to do? *This?*"

2

Again I went home to clean up and change. At ten o'clock, which I figured was late enough, I drove to Radnik Street and parked in front of the tenement in which Mrs. Chojnacki lived. I sat in the car a minute or two thinking up what approach I should use in talking to her. I could, of course, get her to talk freely by introducing myself as a friend of Nina's, but I didn't want to do that; she'd tell Nina I'd been there and then I'd have to explain to Nina and that wouldn't be easy without telling her the whole story. And I wasn't telling anyone that, as long as I had so little to back it up.

So I had to work out a lie, and I decided against using even my right name lest, in talking to Nina later, Jimmy's mother might mention it.

I went up the stairs and knocked on the door and this time Nina didn't open it. I'd seen Mrs. Chojnacki at the funeral service but not closely. She was tall and thin, almost gaunt, and with huge tragic eyes.

I said, "My name is Herbert Johnson, Mrs. Chojnacki. I'm an attorney." She looked a little blank. "A lawyer. I represent the person who paid for your son's funeral. He would like to know—"

"You come in."

I went in. The room and the furniture were shabby, but clean and neat.

"You sit down, Mr. Johnson. You like cup coffee maybe?"

I started to decline, then realized that drinking coffee would keep me there long enough to work the conversation any way I wanted it to go, and to do it casually. So I said yes, I'd like coffee. She went into the kitchen and came back in a few minutes.

"Is making. You from man who runs ride at the park?"

"I'm sorry," I told her, "my client wants to remain anony—he doesn't want anybody to know who he is. What we want to know is whether the service Mr. Haley gave you was satisfactory. Before we pay the bill, in other words, we want to be sure everything was all right."

"Yes, *very* nice funeral. I saw you there."

I nodded. "My employer wasn't able to come, so I came instead."

"Thank you. Thank you much."

"My employer said to tell you that paying for the funeral isn't much, but he's glad he was able to do that for you."

"You thank him for me. Was very kind."

I said, "I can't tell you how sorry I am about Jimmy, Mrs. Chojnacki. Personally, I mean. I've heard a lot about him. He must have been a fine boy."

"Good boy, yes. Sometimes he was bad but— He died good. I thank God for that."

"He went to South Side High School, didn't he?"

"For one year, yes. Then—"

I spoke quickly to save her embarrassment. "I know a boy who goes there; he must have been in Jimmy's class. Obie Westphal, Henry O. Westphal his right name is. Did your Jimmy know him, do you happen to know?"

"He never say name. I don't know. I don't knew all his friends, so could be he knew that boy you say."

"Who was Jimmy's closest friend?"

"Pete Brenner. All the time with Pete Brenner. Other friends, sometimes, mostly Pete."

"Is Pete Brenner going to South Side now?"

"No, he quit after two years, to work. In fruit market down block. Wait, I get coffee now."

I waited, and filled in the time looking around to find a picture that might be Jimmy Chojnacki. I couldn't find one. So when Mrs. Chojnacki came back with coffee for both of us, I got her talking about her son. She talked readily, seemed to want to talk about him. What wasn't irrelevant, though, was stuff I'd already learned from Nina. But I let myself seem to get more and more interested until when I asked if she had a photograph of him I could see, the question seemed natural.

"Yes, *good* picture. Last year man came selling coupons for picture, only dollar. But cost six dollars more after. You want to see, Mr. Johnson?"

I wanted to see. She went into the bedroom and came back with a four-by-six portrait photo in a cardboard folder and handed it to me.

Jimmy Chojnacki had been a good-looking boy. His face was a bit weak, but not vicious. And he had those deep-set, dreamy eyes some Polish kids have. And behind the dreaminess a sort of Gypsy wildness. Looking at that picture it no longer seemed quite so strange that he'd been both a pickpocket and an embryonic writer. A dreamer and a thief. Well, François Villon had combined those qualities and had done a good job of it. Maybe Jimmy Chojnacki would have, too. If he'd had a chance.

I admired the picture and said I thought my employer would like to see it or a copy of it, that he'd never seen Jimmy and would be interested. Would she mind if I borrowed the picture just long enough for me to let a photographer copy it? Or did she have the negative that she could lend me instead?

I got a break; she had extra copies of the picture and I could have one; she was glad to send one to the man who paid for Jimmy's funeral. She'd been high-pressured, I gathered, into taking half a dozen prints besides the one covered by her coupon and still had two of them left besides the one in my hand so I could have that one to take with me. I put it in my pocket and thanked her.

I managed to find out one thing more by leading the conversation around to Whitewater Beach and how often Jimmy had gone there. He went there often, almost every Saturday. And last Saturday, as far as she knew, he'd gone there alone.

I drove downtown. Now that I had a picture of the Chojnacki boy I needed a picture of Obie. And there was a good one in the *Herald* morgue.

The morgue is on the second floor, the editorial offices on the third. If I used the back stairs I probably wouldn't see anyone I knew except old Hackenschmidt, who ran the morgue, and he probably wouldn't know I was on vacation this week. He didn't, and I got the picture without question, and I didn't see anyone to whom I had to explain what I was doing there when I was supposed to be fishing at Laflamme.

I drove south again and put my car in the parking lot at Whitewater Beach. It was almost noon then; most of the concessions would be open, even on a weekday.

I walked slowly down the midway. Most of the smaller concessions were open, the ones that would probably have been open as early as ten last Saturday. None of them was doing much business as yet. The few that had people in front of them at the moment I skipped and went back to after I'd talked to the concessionaires at places beyond. I showed each of them the two photographs, one of Jimmy and one of Obie. All I wanted to know was whether they remembered seeing the two boys together or either of them separately. When I got an affirmative answer I tried to pin it down as to when.

But I didn't get any affirmative answer concerning seeing the two boys together. A lot of them remembered seeing Jimmy around. No special times, just around in general. Which wasn't surprising, since I already knew he'd hung around the park a lot. The girl on duty at the lemonade stand said he'd bought drinks there quite a few times, she thought. But she didn't remember when the last time was, except that she didn't recall seeing him for a week or two. And Obie's picture drew a complete blank from her. He'd looked vaguely familiar to a few others. Only one person—a ring game concessionaire—definitely recognized him, and it turned out that he didn't remember seeing him at the park; he was a football fan who followed high school football and had seen Obie play. He was only a few years out of high school and had played football himself. He wanted to talk football but I didn't want to. I moved on. The first time up the midway I had to skip the lunch stand that was almost across the areaway that led back to the first dip of the Blue Streak; it was too busy.

On my way back, picking up the few I'd missed the first time, I took the Blue Streak for a stopover because my beefy friend in the sailor straw had just got there. He wasn't operating yet, but he was doing some paper work in the ticket booth. I rapped on the glass and he raised the window.

"Hi," I said. "Recognize either of these kids?"

He looked at the pictures I put on the ledge in front of him and then shook his head.

"You saw one of them all right," I told him.

He looked puzzled for a second. "You mean one of 'em's the kid who—"

"I thought you were the first one there. Didn't you see him?"

"Jesus, did I see him? Face down across the tracks I saw him. And I didn't roll him over to look at his face either. Why should I?" He looked down again at the pictures. "But if it's one of these, it'd have to be the dark-haired one, not the blond kid. Say, are you still harping on that accident? I thought you was writing an article on roller coasters."

"I am. But there's one angle on the accident I'm still investigating. Probably doesn't mean anything."

"On the level, you a reporter? Or a cop?"

"A reporter." I grinned at him. "Which means I could be either one. I mean, if I was a cop I could say I was a reporter. But if I was a reporter I couldn't claim to be a cop—not without going to jail for it."

I left him puzzling that out and went on down the mid-way. The lunch stand still had customers. But it occurred to me that I was getting hungry myself so I stopped and ordered a hamburger sandwich. When the grizzled man who ran the counter brought it to me a few minutes later I had the two pictures lying on the counter facing him. "Recognize either of these kids?" I asked him.

He bent over to look at the pictures. "Umm—that dark-haired kid I've seen around. And the blond one too, but not so often."

"Ever see them together?"

"Don't think so."

"Remember when you last saw the blond one?"

"Hell, no. I see thousands of people a day. How'd I remember— Hey, wait a minute."

He rescued two hamburgers off the grill and put them into buns and served them. Then he came back.

"Look," he said. "I might remember at that. But why should I? I might be getting the kid in trouble. You a cop?"

I said, "I'm a lawyer. And you might be getting the kid *out* of trouble. He's in it already, and he needs an alibi for—for a certain time. He says he was here at the park then and I'm trying to find somebody who can prove he was."

"When's the time?"

"Wouldn't mean much if I told you first, would it?"

"It was Saturday morning, early."

"How early? Before ten o'clock?"

"Damn if I know. I got here around past nine, maybe a little later, but I was busy for a while getting things ready. He was my first customer that day. It could have been before ten."

"How do you remember for sure it was last Saturday?"

"That was the day the kid was killed on the Blue Streak. Jeez, I heard it—heard wood splintering and the noise the car made when it ran off—and ran over there."

"Was that before or after the blond kid bought something here?"

"After. But it couldn't have been more'n a few minutes after."

"But he wasn't still eating at the counter?"

"No. I'm sure because I took a look to be sure there weren't any customers, or any coming. Then I pulled the bills out of the register—took a chance on the change—and ran over to see what the crash had been."

"Did you see the blond, kid over there?"

"Not that I remember. There were six or seven people around by the time I got there, but I don't remember him being one of them."

"You're sure he was alone while he was at the counter here?"

"Sure. He bought a coke, that's all, and stood there to drink it. The bottle was on the counter."

"Did you see him leave? Which way he walked?"

"Nope, I was back getting things ready for the day's business. I didn't stand there *watching* him drink the coke and go away. All I know is he wasn't there any more by the time I heard the crash."

And that was all I was going to learn from him, so I followed through with my pretense of wanting an alibi witness by taking down his name and home address. And I'd finished my hamburger by then and wandered off. I tried the couple of remaining concessions I hadn't got yet and then went to the parking lot and got in my car.

I hadn't really expected to, but I'd got something after all. Not much, but something. Obie had been right near the scene of the accident and just before it had happened. If only I could have found someone who'd seen him and Jimmy *together* just before the accident . . .

What do you mean, accident? I asked myself.

And not murder either, exactly. Murder means there's a motive. And Obie had no motive for killing Jimmy Chojnacki. Certainly and above all, he didn't know that his billfold was in Jimmy's pocket.

But does a tiger need a motive? Oh, it has one often: hunger.

But not always even that. A rogue tiger will kill for the pure savage joy of killing.

3

I had a date with a tiger.

Not to talk to, not yet, but damn it I wanted a look at him. And I was pretty sure I could see him at the railroad station at two o'clock. Mrs. Westphal had said he'd be back at "two o'clock" from Springfield and there was a two o'clock train that came through there. If he'd been coming back by car she'd have said "early in the afternoon" rather than such a specific hour. Private automobiles don't follow timetables.

It was now half past twelve; I didn't want to eat lunch yet, though, because the hamburger had killed my appetite. And it was too soon to start tor the railroad station.

Maybe, while I Was so near, I could look up the Pete Brenner whom Mrs. Chojnacki had mentioned as Jimmy's best friend. She'd said he worked at the fruit market "down the block"; there wouldn't be more than one or two fruit markets on Radnik Street in or near the 2900 block. And it would kill time for me.

I drove to Radnik and along it slowly. There was a fruit market near Paducah, a block and a half from where Mrs. Chojnacki lived. I found a place to park and went inside.

It was fairly busy. There were more customers than clerks so no clerk accosted me, and none of them was a kid that could have been Pete Brenner. I walked on to an open doorway at the back and looked through. A boy of about seventeen was working at a big table back there, bunching carrots. The color of his hair just matched the carrots he was handling. I went through the doorway and walked up to him.

"You're Pete Brenner?" I asked him.

He turned around and his eyes gave me a dusting-over. They weren't shifty eyes, but they were hard and suspicious. They took all of me in before he said "Yeah."

He was going to be tough to handle. He wasn't going to swallow any of the stories I'd been handing around so glibly the last few days. He wasn't going to answer any questions beyond that first one without having a reason to answer them.

There was only one reason I could give him, besides the truth and I wasn't going to give him that. I took the reason out of my billfold. "Want to earn a fin by answering a few questions?"

"Who are you?"

I grinned at him. "If I'm answering the questions it'll cost you a fin instead of me."

"What are the questions?"

"They're about Jimmy Chojnacki. And he's dead so you can't do him any harm by answering them."

He looked up over my shoulder at what must have been a clock on the wall behind me. He said, "I'm takin' off for lunch in four minutes. Wait outside. Boss don't like me to gab in here while I'm workin'."

"Okay, Pete," I said. I went through the fruit store again and waited just outside the door.

In a few minutes he came out. He said, "I got only a half hour. Can we talk while I eat?"

"If it's near here."

"Across the street. That hamburger place."

I thought I could eat another hamburger myself by now. Added to the one I'd eaten at the park it would hold me until dinner time. "Swell," I said.

We sat at the counter, down at the far end. I took out the five-dollar bill and put it down between us as soon as the counterman had taken our orders and had gone front to the grill. Pete Brenner glanced at it but didn't make any move to pick it up.

He said, "Listen, you can't buy me for five bucks. Besides that, I want to know who you are and what this is all about. If it's okay, then I'll answer your questions—if I like 'em."

No, there wasn't going to be any use handing him a story I couldn't prove. He was a tough little redhead, and he knew it.

I put my press pass on the counter. I said, "I'm a reporter. There's my name and my paper, the *Herald*. I think I've got an angle on Jimmy's accident. Maybe it's screwy but if it isn't, it's going to be a big story. And it can't hurt Jimmy. If I get the story I won't quote you unless you want me to, so it can't hurt you."

"What's the angle?"

"That's my business. I'd be a sucker to tell you. You could take it to a reporter on the other paper in town and peddle it to him."

"Let's see if I like the questions."

"You were Jimmy Chojnacki's closest friend?"

"I guess I was."

"When did you last see him?"

"The evening before he was killed, up to about midnight. Him and me bummed around awhile, shot some pool. He was goin' home when he left me."

"Did he say anything about what he was going to do the next day, Saturday?"

"Yeah, he said he'd probably go over to the park, White-water."

"Alone?"

"I guess so. I usta go with him sometimes but since I got this fruit market job I can't get off Saturdays. That's the busiest day they got there."

"You're sure he wasn't going to meet anyone there?"

"Hell no, I'm not sure. But if he was he didn't say so to me."

The counterman was bringing our sandwiches. "Which one of you wanted the French fries with?"

"Mine's the plain one," I said.

He reached for the five on the counter. "Take 'em both out

of this?"

"Sure."

He brought the change and left. I pocketed it and put down another five-dollar bill.

Pete looked at it. "That's all you wanted to know?"

I nodded, and he stuck the bill into his pocket. "You didn't get much for it," he said.

"Guess I didn't" I said. I hadn't, but then I hadn't expected much. And I hadn't yet asked the final question; I'd waited deliberately until after he'd taken the money so I could ask it casually. I was pretty sure he'd answer anyway, and it wouldn't be one of the paid-for answers.

I waited some more, until we'd almost finished our sandwiches and until a few remarks about how damn hot the weather had been had intervened. Then I asked, "Do you know a boy named Obie Westphal?"

"Sure. That is I know him by sight; I don't really *know* him. He was in my class at high. I mean, the class I was in until I quit a year ago."

"Do you know if Jimmy knew him?"

"Just about like I did, I guess."

"He never mentioned him?"

"Not unless we happened to be talking about football. We both went to a couple of South Side games last fall so naturally we talked about 'em. But Jimmy didn't really *know* Obie, or maybe just enough to say hi."

He picked up the last of his French fries and then turned to look at me before he put it in his mouth. "What's Obie got to do with this?"

"Nothing," I said. "I went to South Side myself and still see a football game now and then. I was trying to remember whether Obie would be playing this coming season or whether he graduated last June."

"Oh. Well, he's got a year to go. He started as a freshman the year Jimmy and me started, so he was a junior last year."

His eyes turned hard and suspicious again. "How'd you know we went to South Side? I didn't say that till after you asked about Obie?"

"You're not the first person I talked to. How'd you think I knew you were a friend of Jimmy's, and found you?"

"All right, how did you?"

"That'll cost *you* five dollars."

He laughed. "You win. Thanks for the fin, and the lunch."

I left him in front of the restaurant and walked to my car. I'd have to drive fairly fast now to make the railroad station by two o'clock.

4

I made it, and I needn't have hurried. The bulletin board showed that the train was going to be twenty minutes late. The station was crowded, and it was hot as hell. I couldn't find a vacant seat, so I leaned against a post that gave me a good view of the door he'd come through.

I watched the door and waited.

I knew him the minute he came through it. He looked a bit older than he looked on the picture in my pocket and quite a bit bigger than I'd guessed him to be. Quite a bit bigger than I am. At least six feet tall and a hundred and eighty, maybe ninety pounds. He was a young giant with shoulders made to order for football. He had short blond hair and didn't wear a hat. He was good-looking as hell. Just about every girl who saw him would be nuts about him.

He carried a light suitcase—at least it seemed light the way he carried it, but from the look of his shoulders he might have carried it that way even if it had been loaded with bricks. He put it down just inside the door and stood looking around. Then he grinned; he yelled "Hi, guys!" He picked up the suitcase and started toward two other young men—or high school kids, whichever you want to call them—about his age. Both of them wore striped T shirts; one of them carried what looked like a clarinet case.

They stood talking a minute and then all three drifted over to the soft drink counter. They had cokes and Obie paid for them. He drank two himself, rapidly, as though the train ride had made him thirsty. Then the three of them headed for the door labeled Men and went through it.

I found a vacant seat on a bench from which I could watch the door without being conspicuous. I watched it for what seemed quite a while, and when I looked at my watch I saw that it had been quite a while. I remembered then that the men's room of the railroad station had a door on the other side that led through a cigar store to the street.

I went into the men's room and they weren't there. I went on into the cigar store and they weren't there, either; not that I'd expected them to be. I thought, what a hell of a shadow I'd make.

The proprietor was picking his teeth behind the cigar counter. I bought a cigar and asked, "Three high school kids come through here from the station a few minutes ago? One of 'em a big blond kid?"

"Yeah," he said. He took the toothpick out of his mouth. "They got in that car that's been parked out front, the one I been laughing at."

"What about it?

"Stripped-down jalopy with a wolf's head on the radiator cap and painted on the side, *Don't laugh; your daughter may be inside.*"

"The blond kid drive it?"

"Nope, the one with the squealer."

"Squealer?"

"The clary, the licorice stick." He grinned. "I talk the language. I got two kids in high."

"God help you," I said. "Have a cigar."

I gave him back the cigar I'd just bought from him and went out, leaving him staring at me.

I got in my own car half a block down the street and sat there trying to think until I realized how hot I was and that I could think just as well with the car moving, no matter where.

That is, if I could think at all. Just then, I could only wonder if I was stark raving mad to have thought *what* I'd thought about Obie Westphal. Now that I'd actually seen him it didn't really seem possible. Tigers drink blood, not cokes. And one may smile and be a villain, but can a homicidal maniac grin as Obie had grinned at his friends? I didn't know.

I was driving toward South Side High School, I realized, and only a few blocks away now. And then I was in front of it and I swung the Buick in to the curb and cut the engine. I sat there looking at my alma mater, at the big beautiful building set well back from the street. A proud building and a building to be proud of, with a proud straight tower that went three stories higher than the rest of the building. And it would have been from one of those three windows in the middle floor of the tower, five stories above the concrete steps, that the freshman named Wilbur Greenough had fallen—or had been pushed. The year Obie had entered high school.

But did that mean anything? Do two and two make twenty-two?

I suddenly realized that I was parked in plain sight of the windows of the school office and that if Nina should look out she might see and recognize the car and wonder why I was parking there.

I started the engine again and drove away. I headed for the Westphal house. I wanted to think things out and if I parked where I could watch the house again—this time knowing at least that Obie was in town—I'd have plenty of chance to think while I did my watching.

I parked again where I'd parked the first time I'd been

there; it was the better of the two places to park by day because my car was under a big oak that shaded it.

A man in work clothes, a handyman or a part-time gardener no doubt, was mowing the lawn behind the white picket fence. He stopped often to take off his hat and wipe sweat off his face and forehead with a big blue bandanna. The whirring of the lawnmower was a familiar, homey sound.

Let's start, I thought, with Jimmy Chojnacki. Why was I sure that Jimmy's death hadn't been an accident?

Lots of little things. Mainly the sound of the ratchet on the first uphill of the roller coaster. It's a sound that's too loud to be overlooked and it's unmistakable for what it is. From the bottom of the hill beyond that first upgrade no one could possibly nor hear it and not know that a car was coming. Only someone deliberately trying to commit suicide would choose that time to cross the tracks.

Well, people do commit suicide. Why couldn't Jimmy have lain down across the tracks and waited for the car to kill him?

Because people don't commit suicide suddenly and irrelevantly in the middle of another act. I suppose a pickpocket may decide to kill himself, as anyone else might, but it wouldn't be in the middle of an act of crime, a freshly lifted billfold in his pocket. Even if, after stealing Obie's wallet, Jimmy had decided to kill himself, automatic reflexes would have seen him complete the act of theft by taking the money out of the wallet and getting rid of the leather. I happened to know a pickpocket once during my days as a police reporter. I'd talked over his profession with him—he was proud of his skill and liked to talk about it—he told me that a pickpocket's first and obsessive thought, once he's lifted a wallet, is to get the incriminating evidence of the wallet itself off his person as quickly as possible. And there are plenty of ways of getting rid of one unobserved, even in a crowd; he'd told, me some of the most common methods. And if Jimmy had been back there by the roller coaster tracks alone, he could have got rid of it easily. Even if he'd thrown it away without bothering to take the money out of it, he wouldn't have killed himself with it in his pocket. He'd surely have thought of his mother, if for no other reason, and he couldn't have known that the police would not tell her that he had died with stolen property in his pocket.

Nor is suicide itself, I believe, ever a sudden and unpremeditated thing. It's an idea that takes build-up, working up one's courage to the irrevocable act. And while a man—or an adolescent boy—is building up his courage to match his despair he most certainly would not take time out to pick a pocket on his way to death.

No, suicide was out completely, much, much less likely than accident.

There was even, come to think of it, one way in which it could have been an accident.

Jimmy could have seen Obie drinking his coke at the stand. Possibly Obie had paid for it with a bill out of his wallet and Jimmy had seen the wallet and the pocket into which Obie had returned it. Jimmy could have walked behind Obie, lifted the wallet, headed quickly for the low fence that led back to privacy. Obie could, have turned and seen Jimmy walking away rapidly —he'd have been too smart to run—and, remembering why Jimmy had been expelled from school, could have touched his wallet pocket and found the wallet gone. He could have given chase and Jimmy, running for his freedom, might in that case have taken the chance of trying to beat the descending car across the tracks, tripped and fallen . . .

That's a way it *could* have happened as an accident. But if so, why would Obie have ducked instead of staying and explaining what had happened?

And why had Obie's father not looked happy to learn that his son was still alive, and why had he offered to pay for the funeral of the boy who'd died in Obie's stead?

It could be reconstructed another way and those things would be explained.

Obie had turned and had seen Jimmy heading for the fence, but did not, as yet, miss his wallet. He had waved and said "Hi" and Jimmy would, of course, have stopped. Obie, his coke finished, had strolled over and asked Jimmy where he'd been going back there. Jimmy, frightened because he had Obie's wallet, would have . . .

I tried to put myself in Jimmy's place. What would I have said? "Just going to take a look around back there." And Obie, "What's back there?"

I'd have figured, if I'd been Jimmy, that the wallet, now that Obie'd seen me, was too hot to keep. But back there I could drop it, money and all, the first chance I had. And when Obie missed it I'd help him hunt for it and find it for him if he didn't find it himself. The money would still be in it and although Obie might suspect what had really happened there wouldn't be any proof that it hadn't simply fallen out of his pocket. He wouldn't do anything about it.

Back by the tracks, the wallet still in Jimmy's pocket. Burning him, but he'd have to wait for a moment when Obie was walking ahead before he would dare take it out and drop it.

The clicking of the ratchet. The roller coaster car coming up the hill. Neither of them would have to explain to the other what that sound was. Obie saying "Let's stand here and watch it come down past us." Side by side, possibly three feet back from the tracks. The car coming over the top of the hill—empty, no witnesses. Obie taking a quick look back to be sure nobody happens to be standing on the midway, looking back toward them, in the one small area that afforded a view back over the fence. Nobody. They are completely unobserved. His hand going up behind Jimmy Chojnacki's back and, just as the car roars toward the bottom of the hill . . .

Then, quickly, over the outer fence only a few yards beyond the tracks. Out of sight he could have been, almost before the crash had quit echoing. Thinking, once he was clear, that there was nothing at all to connect him with Jimmy Chojnacki—until, later, he discovered that his wallet was gone and maybe guessed what had happened to it. But having to go back anyway to inquire at the Lost and Found Department. Learning that the wallet had caused an erroneous preliminary identification, that his parents were coming back.

And did Obie know that his father would guess the truth?

A car drove past mine and swung in to the curb in front of the Westphal house, brakes squealing with the suddenness of the stop. Well, technically it was a car. It had four wheels and a body. But there weren't any fenders over the wheels and there wasn't a top over the body, not even a folded-back one. There was a moth-eaten wolf's head where the radiator cap should have been and there was lettering on the side of the body; it had gone past too fast for me to read and the angle was wrong now, but the cigar-store proprietor had already told me what the lettering was.

There were seven in it now, all of high school age, four boys and three girls. The boy who'd carried the clarinet case was behind the wheel, and a girl and Obie in the front seat with his; the other four, two and two, were in the back seat. Obie got out, waved and said something I couldn't hear, and went through the gate and up to the house. He was still carrying his suitcase so apparently they'd been riding around —and getting recruits— since I'd seen three of them at the station. The jalopy started off so fast that I think the back wheels spun before they gripped the pavement.

I remembered that detectives in stories always carefully time the observed movements of a suspect, so I looked at my watch. It was twenty-seven minutes after four o'clock, if that matters.

I could hear the slam of the screen door as he went inside.

I went back to my thinking. I'd thought of the four fatal accidents at South Side High within three years the moment I'd begun to suspect that there was something not kosher about Jimmy Chojnacki's death. Maybe just the fact that both Jimmy and Obie had gone to South Side made me think of them. I had to admit that they didn't look very conclusive now. One of them was definitely eliminated; he could hardly have killed the girl who'd drowned in the girls' swimming class. And the drowning of the teacher seemed pretty unlikely. It didn't fit the pattern of the others. But there was one thing I wanted to know: Had Obie been a member of the Drama Club? Was he one of the group Miss Bonner had let out of the building after the meeting that night, so he could have known she was going to be there alone that night? If he had been, then I still couldn't rule out Constance Bonner as at least a possibility. I'd have to remember, next time I was with Nina, to lead the conversation around to Obie so I could ask whether she happened to know if he belonged to the Drama Club. No, I couldn't ask it just that way; I'd have to ask if she knew what school activities if any Obie went in for besides athletics. That would be a natural enough question.

Or where could I look at a last year's Year Book of the high school? It would have a group photograph of the Drama Club and I could see whether Obie was on it.

A few minutes before five o'clock Mr. Westphal came home in the Chrysler. Again he put it away in the garage.

At six o'clock it occurred to me that since Obie was still home he was obviously going to stay there at least through dinner, even if he was going out somewhere in the evening. And that now would be a good time for me to dash away for something to eat and I'd have time to get back before he left if he was going to leave. I drove to a restaurant and had a quick meal. I got back not much after six-thirty, and felt pretty sure he'd hardly have left sooner than that. He hadn't; he obligingly proved it at seven o'clock by coming out on the porch for a few minutes, apparently for a little fresh air. He didn't glance toward my car; it was getting fairly dark by then, though, and I doubt if he could have seen that anyone was sitting in the car even if he had looked. I was sure it was Obie and not his father only because he strolled to the end of the porch and back and I saw him briefly silhouetted twice against a lighted window.

After he went back in I began to feel that I was wasting my time. He probably wouldn't go anywhere, his first night back home after his trip to Springfield. And if he did and I followed him, he'd probably go only to a movie or a friend's house.

Well, what did I expect him to do? Go hunting?

5

At nine o'clock he went hunting.

He came out and stood on the porch a minute. I thought maybe it was for another breath of fresh air and I was going to call it a night if he went back in.

But he came on down the steps and out the gate in the white picket fence. He turned west and started walking, not fast, not slow. He passed my car, bur on his own side of the street; he didn't look my way. It was plenty dark by then and he couldn't possibly have seen that anyone was in the car if he had looked.

I waited until he'd gone almost a block before I got out of the car and started to walk after him. I kept on my side of the street and kept my distance. The streets were almost deserted and I didn't dare get closer. There were trees and I couldn't see him often, but I'd get an occasional glimpse.

We weren't heading toward any bright-light district. We weren't heading anywhere that I knew of unless it could be the freight yards, the jungles.

When he turned at the next corner I knew that's where we were going. We were on a street now, after I'd made the turn too, where there weren't any trees to give me cover, but I took a chance and closed up the distance a little anyway. I was less than half a block behind him when he started across the first tracks.

But it didn't do any good; I lost him completely the minute he got in among the cars. It's a fairly big jungle; dozens of tracks wide and almost a mile long. A hundred people could lose themselves in it.

I wandered around for half an hour and then gave up. I didn't even see any hoboes; there were probably some around but they'd Se asleep in empty boxcars by now probably.

I went back the way we'd come and got in my car and sat there. A little after half past ten Obie came walking back. He went inside the house and a couple of minutes later I saw a light go on in an upstairs front room and saw Obie's silhouette against the shade; he was going to bed.

I drove to the nearest tavern and had myself a drink. While the bartender was pouring me a second one I went to the phone booth at the back. I dialed a number and got an answer.

"This is Sam, Nina. May I come around?"

"Why—I thought you weren't coming tonight, Sam. I'm in bed."

"Wonderful," I said. "I'll be with you in twenty minutes."

THURSDAY

1

PEOPLE should never talk at breakfast. Not about anything serious, anyway. At breakfast one is too sensible, one sees things too clearly on the practical side.

Nina and I got up at the same time and she'd insisted on making breakfast for both of us.

She started it. "Sam, if you don't mind my asking, what were you doing yesterday evening? I know it's none of my business but—"

It wasn't, but I could hardly tell her that. I should have had a lie ready but I didn't have, and I couldn't think of one on such short notice.

"Working," I said.

"But isn't this your vacation?"

"Sure. This was research for something I'm free-lancing. It wouldn't interest you."

"How do you know it wouldn't? Of course, if you want to be mysterious about it—"

"Nina," I said, "you're talking just like a wife."

I know I couldn't have found a worse thing to say if I'd worked on it. I looked up at her to see how she'd taken it, and she hadn't. She was glaring at me.

"I'm sorry," I said. "I shouldn't have said that. I didn't mean it. And I didn't mean to sound mysterious; I just didn't want to sound boring. I'm still working on that article about buildings being accident-prone. Yesterday afternoon I spent at police headquarters going through their accident records and statistics. Yesterday evening I spent at the *Journal*, hunting up things in the morgue."

"The *Journal*? Why not your own paper?"

"It's an afternoon paper. The *Journal's* a morning one. There's a skeleton force on evenings in some departments, at the *Herald*, but the morgue isn't open. And I've got friends at the *Journal* who fixed it for me to use their morgue." I grinned at her. "From what happened afterward, at least you can't suspect me of spending the evening consorting with another woman."

It should have made her smile but it didn't. She said, "It wouldn't have been any business of mine if you had, Sam. This is just—just an affair between us. I haven't any claim on you."

Why must women always bring up things like that? It was perfectly true, of course. Particularly from Nina's point of view because she hadn't known there was a possibility of it's being anything more. I'd told her that Millie was out of town for a week or so, nothing beyond that. I didn't think it was fair to tell Nina that there was a possibility of Millie and me breaking up our marriage. I hadn't seduced Nina by holding out a possibility of marrying her. Time enough to tell her about that if and when it happened and if, by then, I was sure I wanted to marry her. I thought I was sure, but—well, there's a big difference between wanting like hell to sleep with a woman and wanting to marry her.

But how the hell could I answer what she'd just said.

I tried. "Nina, what we're having is something wonderful.

And it's not just physical; you know that. I don't know whether there's love involved—partly because I'm not sure what love is—but there's at least affection. Affection and enjoyment—isn't that enough to go on, for a while anyway?"

But this seemed to be her morning for soul-probing. "Sam, do you think I'm a p-pushover? You must think so."

I could laugh at that. "No man's ego, darling, will ever let him think a woman is a pushover for other men just because he can have her."

No, no man's ego ever lets him think that, but he always wonders a little.

I could see from her face, though, that the answer didn't completely satisfy her so I did what I should have done several minutes ago. I walked around the breakfast table, put my arms around her, bent down and kissed her. That's the only answer that makes sense to such questions as she'd been asking. Women always twist the meaning of words but they can't twist the meaning of a kiss—and they understand it better, anyway.

We finished breakfast in peace.

And I had sense enough to walk to the door with her—again she wanted me to wait a few minutes after she'd left so we wouldn't be seen leaving together—and put my arms around her and kiss her again.

But after the kiss she said, "Sam—" And I said, "Yes, darling?"

"I don't think you'd better come around—or even phone—tonight."

"Why not?"

"Well—if for no other reason, I need sleep. At least one good *long* night's sleep. I want to get to bed by nine o'clock—and to sleep. I'm a working girl. Sam."

"All right," I said. "Eliminate the 'if for no other reason' and it's a deal."

"Fine. I'll need sleep, Sam. I guess that's why I'm irritable. I guess there isn't any other reason."

I kissed her again and this time she kissed back as though she meant it.

2

I went back to the salt mines. I hadn't mined any salt the other time I'd been there but then I'd taken time to look only at the file folders on the four fatal accidents at the high school. This time I wanted to do some random and miscellaneous browsing through as many of the other files as I could cover in a day.

But first I wanted to eliminate a possibility. Before I went to the file cabinets I stopped by the desk of the male clerk to whom I'd talked day before yesterday.

"Heard there was an accident in the jungles last night. Have you had a report on it yet?"

"The jungles? Oh, you mean the freight yards. No, there wasn't any last night."

"Sure you'd have the report by now?"

"Oh, yes. It would have been on my desk this morning. There were reports on four accidents last night, one of them a fatality, but they were all auto accidents."

"I thought they weren't handled in this department."

"They aren't. Traffic department, upstairs, handles them. But we get a duplicate of the preliminary report on any accident that involves car damage or bodily injury. Chief Steiner likes to look them all over, just in case."

I said, "I don't get it. In case of what?"

"In case one of them might correlate with something else we're working on. Say there's a robbery somewhere at two o'clock in the morning, two men involved. And it turns out there was a traffic accident, two men in a speeding car, several miles away and twenty minutes later. Might or might not be the same two men, but it'd be worth checking. It takes only a minute or two a day for him to give the traffic accident reports a quick look and once in a while it pays off. Ever hear of Tony Colletti?"

"Sure, the bank robber. He was caught here a few years ago."

"Because the Chief read accident reports. We'd had a tip that Colletti was in this neck of the woods and one morning there was a report on a minor accident involving a guy named Anthony Cole. Antonio Colletti—Anthony Cole. And an out-of-state license and driver's license. Where'd you hear there was an accident in the freight yards last night?"

"Just an overheard conversation in a tavern," I said. "I must have heard wrong about when it happened. But I'd like to check through past accidents that may have happened there. Do you have a cross index to them, by any chance, or will I just have to come across them in the files?"

"If they're accidents involving moving vehicles—which includes freight engines or freight cars if they're moving at the time—you'll find them upstairs in traffic. It's a funny technicality maybe but we've got to draw the line between traffic and non-traffic accidents somewhere and that's the line."

"You mean if a hobo falls off a stationary boxcar it's a non-traffic accident, but if he falls off one while it's moving—even being shunted around a freight yard, it's a traffic accident?"

"Sounds screwy but that's the way it is. Of course most railroad accidents are outside freight yards and really are traffic accidents."

"Thanks," I said. "Think before I start on these files I'll mosey upstairs and see if they have a separate file on freight-yard accidents. I've got a hunch I'll find some I can use. Will I have to get permission from somebody to look at the files up there?"

"Don't see why. The Chief said to let you look through the accident files and those are accident files too. But ask them to phone down and check with me—my name's Springer—if they give you any trouble."

They didn't give me any trouble.

Better yet, railroad accidents were filed separately and there weren't too many of them so it wasn't too difficult to run through and pick out those which had happened in the freight yards. In five years—which was as far back as I checked— there'd been twelve fatal accidents there.

And seven of the twelve I could easily eliminate. There'd been witnesses to them or else they were accidents of such a kind that they couldn't possibly have been deliberately engineered. Another one—a hobo who had died as a result of having both his legs cut off by the wheels of a freight car—I eliminated after I'd read it through to the end and had discovered he'd lived for two days and had regained consciousness. If he'd been pushed, he'd have mentioned it.

But there were four others, all within two years. And any or all—or none—of them could have been what I was looking for.

A hobo had fallen between the cars of a moving train just heading out of the yards and gathering speed. Another had died the same way except that the fall had been between two of a string of cars that were being shunted from one side track to another. In both cases the bodies had been found an hour or two later, badly mangled, but it was possible to reconstruct what had happened by checking car movements and blood on car wheels.

A brakeman, or what was left of him, had been found on the tracks after an entire string of freight cars and the engine pushing it had passed over him. He'd just gone off duty and was on his way back to the office to punch out. Presumably he'd tried to cut across the tracks in front of them and had been run down. But they hadn't been going fast; he must have stumbled and fallen in front of them. Or he could have been pushed or knocked down in front of them.

The fourth accident was to a hobo again. This time there

was a witness, in a way, the engineer of the engine that had run over him. He'd been looking out his window and just as the front of the engine, which was going forward and not pushing or pulling any cars, had come level with the end of a string of stationary empties the hobo had run or jumped from behind them right in front of the engine; almost as though he'd done it deliberately, the engineer had said.

Or as though someone standing behind him at the end of the string of stationary cars had given him a sudden push?

All four of those accidents had happened after dark, one as early as eight o'clock in the evening, one as late as two in the morning.

Any one of them could have been an accident. All four of them could have been accidents. So could all of the deaths at the high school, the death at the amusement park. So, I felt sure now, could other deaths in other places. Where else had Obie hunted?

3

I went back downstairs to the non-traffic accident files.

Working backwards chronologically I started going through them. A quick glance at each was enough for most of them. If there were no witnesses I looked to see how the accident happened and if there were witnesses I looked for one name among them. Not expecting to find that name, really, but on the off chance that once Obie might have made a kill and not been able to get away fast enough to keep from being corralled as a witness, probably the only witness. I was looking for a case in which, say, a man had fallen to his death from the roof of a building and maybe other witnesses had seen him land but only one had seen him fall—a boy who'd been on the roof with him, a boy named Henry or Obie Westphal, who'd seen the victim walk to the edge to look down and then lose his balance.

By noon I'd looked at hundreds of files and had gone back almost three years and hadn't found anything. After a while I'd quit looking to see how accidents had happened unless there were names of witnesses to them. There were too many that had happened to people who were alone or presumed to be alone and which could have resulted from a sudden strategic push if someone had been there to give it and then run. I wasn't going to let myself get psychopathic about this thing—unless I already was—and start suspecting Obie in every apparently accidental death that could conceivably have been a kill instead. He couldn't have killed *all* of them.

Chief Steiner's secretary wasn't at his desk when I went out to eat lunch but he was there when I came back.

"Finding any good cases for your article?" he asked me.

"A few," I said. "But it's tough going; most accidents are pretty routine. I'll have to dig back more years than I thought to find enough screwy ones."

"Uh-huh. Say, an uncle of mine died in a screwy type of accident once. Maybe you can use it. Fell and killed himself because of termites in his wooden leg."

"You're kidding me."

"I'm not. He'd used a wooden leg for several years after an amputation, then got a new aluminum one, put the old one out in a shed. Couple of years later something went wrong with the new leg and he went out and got the old one to use till he could get the new one fixed. Put it on and it broke under him half an hour later and pitched him down a flight of stairs. Termites had eaten most of the inside of it away."

"That I'll *have* to use."

"Better look it up and be sure I'm right on the details. You'll find it in the drawer for—let's see, it was around twelve or thirteen years ago. Nineteen forty-one or nine-teen forty. His name was Andrew Wilson; look it up in the yearly alphabetical list for one of those two years, the list at the front of the drawer."

"I'll do that. Thanks a lot."

I went back to the files and spent a couple of hours going back another couple of years. No luck.

It had been a wasted day thus far except for what I'd found in the traffic accident files upstairs, those four accidents within two years at the freight yards. All of them, in the light of what I knew and suspected, looking pretty fishy to me. Of course I'd probably not have given them a second thought if it hadn't been that Obie had gone there the evening I'd followed him.

Still, nothing to get my teeth into. No proof of Obie's connection with any supposedly accidental death except that of Jimmy Chojnacki, and there the only direct proof was the presence of Obie's wallet in Jimmy's pocket when he died. And the lunch counter man's story that placed Obie at his stand just before the accident and gone at the time the accident happened.

I'd hate to try to convince anyone else on evidence like that.

I started away from the files and then turned back. I'd better carry out my pretext by looking up the report on the death of the secretary's uncle; he might ask me something about it when I passed his desk on the way out.

I pulled open the 1939 drawer and took out the alphabetical list. Half a dozen W's on it, but no Wilson. But it was in the alphabetical list in the 1940 drawer; Andrew Wilson, and the date. I looked up the report and read it; the secretary hadn't been kidding me. Termites in a wooden leg. Maybe, I thought, I really should write that article on screwy accidents. Andrew Wilson would make a damned good lead for it.

I started out again, got almost to the door, and stopped as though I'd walked into something solid. Hadn't one of those names under W in the first drawer I'd looked in, the 1939 drawer, been *Westphal?*

Well, what if it had, I asked myself. My God, in 1939 Obie would have been four years old. And besides, those alphabetical lists for each year were lists of the names of *victims* of fatal accidents, not witnesses or others involved It must be just a coincidence. Westphal is not too uncommon a name.

I went back to the drawer and looked at the list again.

Westphal, Elizabeth, April 16.

I fumbled a little finding the file; I went past it in the chronological sequence and had to go back. Then I had it in my hand, a thin manila file folder with only three sheets of paper in it. I flipped it open and glanced at the top sheet, a copy of the death certificate signed by Dr. Lawrence J. Wygand. I knew him.

Elizabeth Westphal, age 5 yrs., daughter of Mr. and Mrs. Armin Westphal, 314 S. Rampart St. . . .

I closed the folder and the file drawer; I took the folder over to the window and sat down on the sill. I stared at the folder, almost afraid to open it.

This, I thought, might be the key I was looking for. But could it? In 1939 Obie would have been four years old.

But he hadn't been an only child. Grace Smith had been wrong about that. He'd had a sister a year older than himself. She had died—accidentally.

I took a deep breath and opened the folder.

The death certificate was a photostat of the original. Cause of death; severing of spinal cord between the first and second lumbar vertebrae. Other indications; severe contusions and lacerations of back, left forearm and right calf. Time of death; approximately 3:10 P.M. Time of physician's examination: 3:15 P. M.

The next two pages consisted of a typed report of a routine investigation of the accident, signed by a Lieutenant John Carpenter.

The five-year-old girl and her four-year-old brother—called Henry in the report—had been playing in the back yard of the Westphal house on Rampart Street and had both climbed into a tree near the back fence. They had never been told not to climb it for it was a tree they could not ordinarily have got into; its lowest branches were well out of reach and the trunk too big around for them to climb. But Mr. Westphal had been pruning the tree and had left a stepladder leaning against the trunk. By means of the stepladder it had been easy for the children to climb into the tree and both Mr. and Mrs. Westphal were inside the house and were unaware that the children had done so.

Mr. Westphal had been upstairs and had happened to look out a back window to see what the children were doing and had seen them in the tree. Just as he was about to throw open the window to call to them to be careful and stay where they were until he could come to help them safely down, Elizabeth fell out of the tree. She landed on her back across the fence and from there on into the alley behind the yard. She had screamed while she was falling.

Mr. Westphal had rushed down the stairs. Mrs. Westphal was in the living room, running the vacuum cleaner; the sound of it had kept her from hearing the scream from the back yard. Mr. Westphal had yelled at her to phone Dr. Wygand to rush around fast. He had run on out into the alley and found Elizabeth unconscious, probably already dead. He had carried her into the house and put her on a sofa. He and Mrs. Westphal were still trying to find a heartbeat or a sign of life when the doctor arrived and pronounced her dead. Neither of the West-phals had looked at a clock nor had Dr. Wygand when he received the emergency call but the time of the accident was established within a minute or so because the doctor had looked at his watch when he made the death pronouncement. It was then 3:15 P. M. Dr. Wygand also lived on Rampart Street, less than a block away, and it had taken him only two or three minutes to get there; allowing a minute for the phone call and another minute or two after his arrival before he had glanced at his watch, the accident had happened about five minutes before. The doctor had stated that, in all probability, death had been instantaneous.

The fence across which the girl had fallen was a board fence five feet high; the limb of the tree from which she had fallen was about twenty feet from the ground, about fifteen feet from the top of the fence.

The boy, Henry, had said that his sister had climbed the tree first and he had followed her. He had been astraddle of the limb just behind her; she had tried to hold onto the limb with her legs only and had reached both hands above her head to try to catch the limb above but had lost her balance in doing so. He had tried to grab at her and had managed to touch her but not to hold on.

He had got down from the tree safely and under his own power while Mr. Westphal had been coming down the stairs and running to Elizabeth in the alley.

Mr. Westphal had been unable to verify his son's story of exact details of how the girl had fallen. He had seen the children through a partial screen of branches and leaves so he had not had a clear view of what had happened. But the boy had seemed quite intelligent for his age and there was no reason to doubt his version of how his sister had happened to fall, the lieutenant who wrote the report stated. He added, gratuitously, that it was probably well the boy had not succeeded in grabbing his sister; otherwise they would both have fallen.

That was all.

I put back the folder and closed the file drawer.

I left, and luckily the secretary wasn't at his desk when I passed it, so I didn't have to stop and talk about termites to him.

There's a bar almost directly across the street from police headquarters and I headed there and ordered myself a beer; I wanted a chance to think.

I had something, but I didn't know what I had. Can a four-year-old boy commit murder?

Or could it be that Obie hadn't pushed his sister but their father had *thought* he had? Suddenly a new possibility occurred to me: What if Armin Westphal, and not Obie, was psychotic? What if Obie had never killed anyone but Armin Westphal had the delusion that his son was a killer, a delusion that dated from the death of his daughter? Wouldn't that account for his paying for the funeral of Johnny Chojnacki? If Westphal was psychotic—

4

Suddenly I wanted to know all I could learn about Armin Westphal. Maybe Doc Wygand could tell me something. I went to the phone booth at the back of the tavern and phoned him.

"Sam Evans, Doc," I said. "Going to be home about half an hour from now and free to talk awhile?"

He chuckled. "Free and getting bored. Come on out, Sam. Don't know if you knew, but I retired three months ago. Almost beginning to wish I hadn't."

"Be right out," I said.

I finished my beer on my way past the bar, then I went out and got in the Buick and drove to Rampart Street. The telephone directory had told me he still lived in the same place. He'd been a close friend of my parents and I'd liked him a lot too, although I hadn't seen him often since their deaths.

He was dressed in disreputable old clothes and working in his garden when I got there. He took off canvas gloves to shake hands and said it was good to see me again. "Nothing wrong, is there, Sam? I mean, I hope you didn't want to see me professsionally, did you? If so, we'll just forget that I retired and—"

"No, Doc, I'm feeling fine. Just want to ask some questions about a case you had once."

He sighed. "Almost hoping you had something wrong with you. Shall we go inside to talk or would you rather go over there?" He gestured toward some garden furniture in the shade of a big oak tree. I chose the shade of the tree and we went over and made ourselves comfortable.

"Still working for the *Herald*, Sam?"

"Yes, but I'm on vacation this week. So what I want to ask you about is something I'm interested in personally. It—well, it could lead to a newspaper story if it breaks, but I'll promise not to quote you or use your name if that happens."

"Ummm, but don't forget that a physician can't reveal— Well, go ahead and ask your questions. I'll have to decide whether I can answer them or not. "What's the case?"

"A girl named Elizabeth Westphal who fell out of a tree, right in this block, a neighbor of yours."

"Yes, I remember. Armin Westphal's kid, must have been at least ten years ago. What do you want to know about her?"

"Not the medical details. Everything but that. Family background in particular, what you know about other members of the family, in particular."

"Good, then I won't have to watch what I say at all. I knew the Westphals when they lived here—haven't seen Armin very often since—but none of them were ever patients of mine. Except that time when the little girl was killed, and she was dead when I got there so there's no medical confidence involved there; I can even talk about that."

"All right," I said, "let's start with that, then. One question in particular. Did you get the impression that Armin Westphal may have thought his son deliberately pushed his sister out of that tree?"

Doc had been leaning back comfortably. He sat up straight now and stared at me. But he thought for seconds before he answered.

"No," he said. "Good God, why would he have thought that?"

"He saw it happen. Not too good a view because there were leaves and branches in the way, so he might have thought he saw Obie—Henry—push his sister off the limb and yet not have been sure enough of what he saw to say so—even if he *would* have said so about his own son."

Doc leaned back again in his chair. "It's just barely possible, Sam, now that I think back. Armin did react to his daughter's death in a way that was a little different from and in addition to normal grief. But I interpreted it otherwise—and I still think I was right. I thought he blamed himself and was building a guilt complex."

"Why would he have blamed himself?"

"Two reasons. The first one, minor, his carelessness in leaving that ladder against the tree. If he hadn't left it there the kids wouldn't have been climbing in the tree; they couldn't have. That's silly, of course. But the other reason isn't. There's a chance, a pretty damn small one, that he *did* kill his daughter by picking her up and carrying her into the house. You don't do that to someone with a broken back."

"How small a chance, mathematically?

"I thought it was a pretty fair chance at first. I'm afraid I almost lost my temper with him for his stupidity in moving her before I got there. But then I went out into the yard and looked over the scene of the accident and learned how it happened and I realized that it was almost impossible for her to have been alive when he reached her."

"Why?"

"Because she'd fallen on her back on top of the fence and then had another fall of five feet to the ground. The top of the fence had broken her back; the nature of the injury showed that clearly. A broken back, though, isn't necessarily a fatal injury; lots of people live with broken backs. But when the broken vertebra or vertebrae cut or too seriously injure the spinal cord that runs through the vertebrae, death is pretty damn quick. Now Elizabeth's back was so badly broken—imagine falling fifteen feet and taking all of the impact diagonally across your back on the narrow top of a fence—that the chances are a thousand to one she was killed there and then. But with a back that badly broken she'd sustained an additional five-foot fall into a concrete alley. If the top of the fence hadn't killed her there was another one chance in a thousand that the impact of the second fall, with her back already badly broken, wouldn't have killed her. There's your mathematical answer, incidentally; figure the permutation of two thousand-to-one chances and you get a one-in-a-million chance."

"Did you tell Westphal that?"

"By that time my temper was gone and I went even a little farther than that to reassure him. Why give a man who's already on the road to being neurotic something to build a guilt complex around, on a million-to-one chance that he had been guilty? I told him there was no doubt whatsoever—which, for practical purposes there wasn't—that Elizabeth had been dead by the time he moved her."

"You say he was on the road to being a neurotic. Just what do you mean, Doc?"

His shaggy white eyebrows lifted. "Didn't you know he's an alcoholic? I thought you knew something about him."

"Not much. I didn't know what you just told me. Listen, why not start from scratch, from whenever you knew him first, and give me the works?"

"All right, but I'm dry. Wait till I get us some cold lemonade; there's some ready in the refrigerator. Or would you rather have beer? There's some beer cold too."

I told him I'd just had a beer and would rather stick to that.

He got us each a can of beer and made himself comfortable again. He said, "Let, see, I've lived here twenty years. Armin built the house at three-fourteen about five years after I bought this one. I got to know him slightly while he was building it."

"Did he own his store then?"

"No, he was a traveling salesman for a hosiery company. Did very well at it, made good money. You wouldn't think to look at him that he'd be a good salesman but he must be—or at least must have been. He was already, in addition to building his own house, planning on going in business for himself.

"I didn't get to know his family until they moved in after

the house was ready. Amy—that's his wife—and the two children, Elizabeth and Henry, one year apart. Let's see, they'd have been three and two years old then, or about that. I noticed you called the boy Obie a few minutes ago; he didn't get that nickname until around the time he started high school. You know it comes from his middle name, Obadiah?"

I nodded.

"Well, my wife and I got to know them fairly well after they moved in. They weren't really close friends but we played bridge with them once in a while. Never had 'em as patients, though. They already had a family doctor and besides I believe Armin thought I was a little fusty and old-fashioned.

"Armin was quite a heavy drinker even then. Maybe not quite an alcoholic yet, but close to it. That means there was some hidden conflict in him somewhere, but I didn't get to know him well enough even to make a guess what it was. But it was later, after Elizabeth's death, that his drinking definitely took on the pattern of alcoholism. There are different types of alcoholics, you know; Armin's the periodic type. Doesn't touch the stuff for months at a time, sometimes as long as eight or nine months, although six would be nearer average, and then he's off on a drinking bout and won't come home for a week or two, once that I know of as long as three weeks. Refuses to be cured, won't go to a san unless it's just for a brief rest cure to get his health back after an unusually bad bout."

"You're sure he's still that way?"

"Yes. His last one was only four or five months ago. I haven't seen him that recently, but I happened to hear about it from a mutual acquaintance."

"What do you know about Mrs. Westphal?"

"Amy's a fine woman. Not overweight mentally but, as far as shows on the outside, a good wife and mother. Well, maybe too good a mother, the kind that dotes too much on children and spoils them. And Henry got a double dose of it after he became an only child, but I guess he came through okay. I've heard he's quite a football hero in high school. Well, if his mother's spoiling him didn't turn his head, that probably won't either."

"When did you see him last?"

"Quite a few years ago. He was in the fourth or fifth grade of elementary school then. Matter of fact, I saw him only a few times after they moved away from Rampart Street."

"And when was that? And, if you know, why?"

"It would have been in—ummm—nineteen forty-three. As to why, I'd say it was a combination of reasons. It wasn't just because their daughter had been killed there—they wouldn't have stayed four more years if that was the only reason—but they didn't like the place so well after that. And in nineteen forty-three there was the war boom and the housing shortage; Armin was able to sell for just about double what the place had cost him to build six years before, during the depression. He used that profit to set himself up in business, to start his store downtown. And I understand he's done well with it."

"Tell me one thing, Doc. After Elizabeth's death, did you notice any change in Westphal's attitude toward the boy?"

He looked at me sharply. "Are we back to the idea that Armin may have thought Henry pushed his sister out of the tree deliberately?"

"Let's say I'm still trying it for size."

"All right, I guess the best answer I can give you is that I probably wouldn't have noticed any difference, unless it showed damned plainly. For one thing, I wasn't looking for it. For another I didn't see much of the two together. If we played cards with the Westphals, it was generally at our place because, being in active practice, I wanted to be available for phone calls. And they had a maid who lived there, so there wasn't any worry about baby sitters on their end.

"But come to think of it, I don't remember Armin talking much about Henry after that, if at all. And he probably *was* different with the boy because he was different with everyone.

That's when he started to get moody and—well, definitely neurotic."

"Did he ever play with the boy, take him places?"

"Why—not that I remember specifically, after that accident."

"But he did before that?"

"Yes, he'd take Henry for walks, play with him in the yard, things like that. You know, Sam, maybe you've got something at that. The more I think of it the more I think maybe his attitude toward Henry did change then. I mean, even more than he started changing in general. Mind telling me what this is all about? Not that I insist on it if you'd rather not."

"I'd really rather not, Doc, if you'll forgive me. Someday maybe, but not right now."

"Sure. How's Millie these days?"

"Fine," I said, and let it go at that. I didn't want to talk about Millie. So I asked him some questions that got him talking about his garden. It was five o'clock when, with the story that I had to go home to dress for a dinner engagement, I managed to get away and to forestall being pressed to stay and eat with him.

A fine guy, Doc; my parents had shown good judgment in choosing their friends. I wonder, now that it's all over, if I'll ever tell him the truth. I don't think so. It can't do any good, and there's no reason to.

5

Because I wanted to be alone to think things out again, I went home. I couldn't have picked a lonesomer place for it. And I'd been stupid to come home before eating because there wasn't anything to eat here and I'd have to go out soon again anyway. I wasn't hungry yet but I'd get that way sooner or later and I didn't want to interrupt myself once I started, so I walked the two blocks to the neighborhood delicatessen and bought rolls and sandwich meat and some pickles. Nothing to drink. I was going to figure things out cold sober.

Back home I found the walk had given me enough appetite to make and eat a couple of sandwiches so I got that over with. Then I got an old card table from the basement and set it up in front of the most comfortable chair in the living room to put my feet on. I think best with my feet up.

I sat down and put my feet up.

There were two main possibilities and I had to think each of them through and decide which one was probably right.

One, maybe Obie *wasn't* a killer. I'd been sure he was until this afternoon, but what I'd just learned opened up a completely new line of thought.

Armin Westphal was at least neurotic, any alcoholic is. But maybe he was farther off the beam than that. Starting with the death of his five-year-old daughter, he could have built up a systematized delusion that his son was a murderer—without any basis in reality except something he *thought* he saw thirteen years ago.

Or he could even have seen Obie push his sister without having witnessed a deliberate killing. Murder by a four-year-old would be something damned unusual, but lying by a four-year-old isn't; Obie's story of how his sister happened to fall might quite easily have been pure invention to avoid punishment. He'd said, for instance, that she'd climbed the tree first. A natural thing for him to say when it turned out that climbing the tree had been wrong. And the rest of the story could have been a protective lie too. Maybe they'd been scuffling in fun. Or even *not* in fun; suppose Obie had climbed the tree alone first and then, as a joke, dropped something on his sister's head. She'd climbed up quickly to slap him and—

Yes, there were dozens of ways in which the scene in the tree could have so happened that Westphal could have I thought he saw Obie push his sister out. Or he could have genuinely seen Obie push her accidentally. And he could have known that Obie's story of what had happened up there was a lie and assumed it to be a deadly lie instead of a protective fib.

Now add that to his own guilt feelings for having left the ladder by the tree and for having been so stupid in his excitement that he'd picked up Elizabeth and carried her when, after seeing how she'd landed on the fence, a broken back was a virtual certainty. Suppose that, despite the doctor's reassurance after his initial bawling out, Westphal still felt responsible for his daughter's death. The human mind, even one that isn't neurotic, can take devious ways to duck or shift responsibility. Such as, in Westphal's case, shifting the blame to his son, becoming more and more convinced that his son was a murderer.

Watching him from that moment on, suspicion growing into certainty and certainty growing into obsession. Seeing confirmation of his obsession in a thousand words and actions completely normal to childhood. *The toy pistol. "Bang, bang, you're dead."* The cowboy stage. Cops and robbers.

Children *are* killers—in their fantasies. Killing is as natural to them as breathing, and as free of malice. Swords and six-guns and Buck Rogers blasters and the staccato chatter of the machine gun. What boy, from five to ten, doesn't kill thousands, sometimes thousands in a single day, in his mental world where every bullet hits and every shot is fatal? With every *bang* another redskin bites the dust, another cop, another robber, another enemy soldier, another Martian. The collective killings in our nurseries could depopulate the world in a single day, the universe within a week. It's the catharsis that lets childhood rid itself of the bloodlust that is our heritage from mankind's past when bloodlust was necessary to survival.

But God help an obsessed man who'd watch his son playing for confirmation of his obsession that the boy with a psychopathic killer who had killed once and might kill again.

Bang, bang, bang.

And real death? Well, it doesn't take much to feed an obsession. Any accidental death that happened for miles around and which, even remotely, barely possibly could have been caused by a boy of whatever age Obie was at the time would have been looked on by Westphal with dark suspicion. Where there was reasonable possibility—like the accidents at high school—that Obie could have been guilty, Westphal's obsession would make him certain.

As he'd been certain that Obie had lulled Jimmy Chojnacki and without knowing, or at least before learning, any of the details of the accident except that there'd been an erroneous preliminary identification because Obie's wallet had been in the pocket of the dead boy.

Well, I'd come to believe the same thing myself, hadn't I? But not until I'd learned at least *some* of the details, and not until I'd watched Westphal's face as he'd entered the funeral parlor thinking his son was dead, watched it again when he'd left knowing that his son was alive and waiting for him at home, even then not until I'd gone in and talked to Haley, my curiosity aroused by Westphal's unnatural behavior, and had learned that Westphal had volunteered to pay for a pickpocket's funeral.

My main reason for suspecting Obie had been his father's reactions. And what I'd learned today had given me a possible, maybe a probable explanation that left Obie innocent; I'd been led astray by the delusions of a paranoiac.

Yes, but what about the story of the lunch-stand man that placed Obie so near the place at so near the time of the death?

I'd already thought of—and discarded as improbable— another explanation of how Jimmy could have died. It seemed less improbable now. *Obie missing bis wallet, turning and seeing Jimmy heading back over the fence giving chase. Jimmy trying to beat the cars across the track because he was trying to escape.*

And with what I knew now I could make a guess as to the rest of it, Obie's reason for making himself scarce before the body was found, for not waiting and telling how it had really happened. Obie must know of his father's suspicions of him. He'd have known that his father, if no one else, would never believe his story, without proof except his own word, that jimmy's death had been accidental. He'd have run away without thinking twice. Later, of course, he'd have remembered that Jimmy had still had his wallet; he'd realize that to avoid suspicion it would be necessary for him to go to the Lost and Found Department and ask for it. But he'd waited a few hours, for things to cool down, before he'd gone there. Never guessing, of course, that since Jimmy had carried no identification of his own a mistake in identification would cause his, Obie's, parents to be notified that their son was dead.

That explanation made sense now.

And what did I have besides that? The coincidence of four deaths within three years at the high school? But I'd already learned that one of those four, the drowning of a girl in a girls' swimming period, couldn't possibly have been caused by Obie. And that the other drowning, the teacher Constance Bonner, seemed quite probably a suicide and anyway didn't really fit the pattern of the type of killing I'd pictured Obie doing.

Four accidents within two years in the freight yards? All four of them could have fitted the pattern, yes, but why should I think Obie caused them just because he'd gone there the one evening I'd followed him. There'd been no accident there that particular night. And there were at least a dozen reasons, legitimate ones, for his having walked there. A randomly chosen objective for a pleasant stroll on a warm summer night. A destination, such as a friend's house, beyond the yards, and a short cut through them. A human and unmurderous interest in hoboes. An adventurous interest in railroads and a predilection for hopping and riding moving freight cars.

So what did I have left? Nothing that couldn't be explained away by mild coincidence.

And yet—

I wasn't sitting with my feet up any more now. I'd got my start thinking that way, but now I was pacing. I'd pushed the card table aside and I had the whole length of the living room to pace in. It's a good room for pacing, narrow but longish.

And yet, I thought, *I've got a much better case against Obie than l had before. If he is a killer, I can see why.*

The other side of the coin my friend the doctor had handed me.

In what dark way might a boy react to his father's belief that he was a murderer?

Let's start it that way from the crisis point, the death of Elizabeth Westphal. No, I still wouldn't follow Westphal there, no matter what he might have seen in the tree. A four-year-old boy as a deliberate murderer, that I wouldn't buy. But I could see a boy warped into becoming one, over the course of the years of his formative period, by his father's unwavering belief.

Let's say he had pushed his sister. In play, in a scuffle, maybe in defense because she was trying to push him. In whatever manner, for whatever reason, but not to kill her. In his story of what had happened, he lied a little bit, naturally. He daren't admit that he had pushed her; he was trying to save her, but couldn't.

But then he learns that his father had seen that push. His father thinks he is a murderer. His father keeps on thinking so, more and more strongly as the years go by. The years, let us say, from four to thirteen. Nine years of being thought a murderer, nine years of being matched, of feeling and being made to feel that he is unnatural, a freak, a thing to be feared and hated.

And likely, for that very reason, he *didn't* indulge in the normal killings-in-fantasy of childhood. Certainly not at any time when his father was around watching him. His father's brooding, watching, somber gaze—under that, would he ever dare point a finger and say *bang*, even at the most imaginary Indian, let alone at a living playmate? Would his father ever have bought him a toy gun, a cap pistol, a rubber knife, any of the pseudo-lethal things normal to boyhood?

If he ever said or even thought *"Bang, bang, you're dead"* it would have been in secret and with a feeling of deep guilt because death and killing were real to him; he had already killed, in reality, and thereby he was denied the catharsis of the imaginary mowing down of enemies.

He had killed his sister. Oh yes, he would have come, by the age of eleven or twelve or thirteen, to believe that. How accurately does anyone remember the details of and the motives behind any act he committed at the age of four, years later?

A month or two after the incident, he would still have remembered that the push had been in fun, in play. Even then, he wouldn't have been sure. And eight or nine years later? By then the true memory would have been supplanted by a false one, so firmly imbedded that any other version would have been sheer fantasy.

And how he must have come to fear and hate his father! But probably the fear and hate would be buried deep, buried under layers of guilt and awful knowledge of his own viciousness and abnormality.

Henry the murderer, Henry the unspeakable.

Obie the hero, Obie the athlete, the lionized, the admired.

Henry the murderer, Obie the hero.

Schizophrenia.

All right, all right, I told myself, I'm guessing of course. I haven't got enough, I don't know enough to do these parlor tricks with psychoanalysis. I'm guessing.

Well, what's wrong with guessing, as long as I don't wear a groove in the carpet while I'm doing it?

Of course there'd been a balance to Armin Westphal. What had Doc told me about Obie's mother?

Amy's a fine woman. Not overweight mentally . . . a good wife and mother. Well, maybe too good a mother, the kind that dotes too much on children and spoils them. And Henry got a double dose of it after he became an only child . . .

Certainly not overweight mentally if she failed to recognize the symptoms of her husband's mental illness, to feel the weight of his obsession, however devious he was in concealing it from her.

She must, of course, have felt at least inadequacy in his attitude toward his son, but there was so simple and natural an answer to that. Love the boy twice as much herself, spoil him, be wonderful to him in every possible way to make up to him the apparent lack of love his father showed for him. Of course, Armin didn't *really* feel that way, and although sometimes Henry seemed almost—well, almost *afraid* of his father and was so quiet when his father was around, that was just his way. And although Armin's way of showing it was strange, he must love his son deep down and deeply else why would he *watch* the boy so much and so intently. Why would he ask him so many questions? Mostly when she wasn't around, but that was natural; men didn't want women around when they did their serious talking. She had a wonderful son—so big and handsome for his age, so smart in school, so admired by everyone. And she had a wonderful husband, if only he could get over that awful drinking, and if only he didn't act so strangely sometimes. But then he worked so hard, for all of them.

She must have spoiled the boy terribly after he became her only child. And like as not Oedipus had reared his head somewhere in those years, although God knows Obie wouldn't have needed jealousy of his mother to make him hate his father, if I had the picture right.

Meanwhile growing up, gaining wisdom and stature. From the size of him now, he might have been as strong as a man at thirteen. Able, maybe, to lick his own father—and certainly able to now at seventeen—but afraid to. That's the one thing he'd always be afraid to do.

I'd guess thirteen to be the age at which Obie made his first kill. In his own mind, convinced by then that he had killed his sister, believing that for nine years, it would have been his second. Why did I pick thirteen? I don't know; it could have been sooner than that, much sooner. Not more than a year later, though, if the two boys who had died at South Side during his freshman year had been his victims.

The first kill, especially, must have been unplanned. Maybe all of them were—although his visit to the freight yards looked as though he hunted opportunities.

He'd have been in some dangerous place, say on a roof, with one other person. No one else around, no one watching. The other person—friend or stranger, it wouldn't matter— standing near the edge, Obie behind him. And it would come to him: *Why, just a push and I could kill him easily, just as I killed my sister.*

Suddenly the blood had pounded in his temples, and he had pushed. He had killed.

Whom had he killed? His father, of course. The one being he wanted to kill and feared to kill, he killed in effigy. And killed in effigy again and again, any time a foolproof opportunity came or could be contrived.

Did he know that, I wondered; did he know whom he killed? Or did his subconscious mind hide that dark fact from his conscious one? Did he know only the sudden savage delight each killing gave him, without recognizing the source of that wild ecstasy?

All right, Sam, I told myself, you've got two perfectly good solutions and which one do you like best?

One, Obie's killings are the delusion of a paranoiac father.

Two, Obie's killings are the result of his father's obsesssion.

Pay your money and take your choice.

Either fitted.

And I wanted to kick furniture through the windows because I didn't know which. I wanted to kick myself because I couldn't simply accept the first one, which was just as possible as the second. Because if I could accept that I'd merely been fooled by Westphal into momentary sharing of his delusion, then I was through with this thing and it would be off my mind.

I wouldn't have to do a damned thing about it except forget it. It would mean Westphal was insane, but that wasn't any business of mine. Not if it hadn't made a killer out of his son. Not if all those deaths at the school and in the jungles had really been accidents, and if Jimmy Chojnacki had really fallen across the tracks because he'd been running away from a pursuer.

But how the hell could I decide? The only one of those deaths that was fresh was that of the Chojnacki boy and I'd dug into that as hard and as far as I knew how to dig. All of the others were months or years ago and how could I possibly connect Obie with any of them now?

Wait, I told myself, you've been wondering how to prove that Obie caused those deaths, or some of them, and maybe that's impossible, but why not try it from the other end? Maybe I could prove that Obie hadn't caused them.

It would be difficult if not impossible, now, to find proof that Obie had been elsewhere at the times of the freight-yard accidents. But I might be able to prove that he couldn't have caused any of the three accidents still under suspicion at the school.

There was an even chance, for instance, that I could prove he hadn't pushed the Greenough boy out of the tower window. Nina had told me it had happened during second lunch period. The school day at South Side is divided into eight three-quarter-hour periods. Schedules are so arranged that approximately half of the students have their lunch time during the fifth period, from 12:00 noon to 12:45 P.M. and the other half during the sixth period, from 12:45 to 1:30 P.M. Otherwise the school cafeteria couldn't handle them. But suppose Obie's schedule for his freshman year gave him first lunch period and a class at the time the Greenough boy had fallen?

And if, that same year, Obie had not had a final period gym class, it would become highly unlikely that he had killed the

Negro boy in the locker room. Not impossible; he could have gone to the locker room in the gym after some other last-period class so it wouldn't give him a complete alibi, but it would lessen probability. Or he might have been absent from school completely on one of those days. Attendance records would show.

As for the teacher Constance Bonner, well, that was probably a suicide anyway. But I could almost completely rule out Obie if I could learn from his record that he didn't belong to the Drama Club during his junior year. Only the members of that group, whom she had let out of the building when the meeting was over, would have known that Miss Bonner had stayed there to grade papers.

Nina could find those things out for me from the school records. I hated to ask her to because I couldn't without telling her at least part of the truth about what I was after and without admitting that I'd been lying about my reason for asking the questions I'd already asked her about the accidents. She'd place those dates and times and know that I was trying to connect Obie Westphal with those three deaths. And she'd remember that I'd already asked her casually whether Obie and Jimmy Chojnacki had been friends.

But I didn't see any way I could find out those things except through Nina.

I looked at my watch and it was nine o'clock. She'd said she was going to bed early to get a long night's sleep, but surely she'd hardly have turned in this early.

I phoned her. It even came to me, as I heard the number ringing, that maybe she'd be feeling differently by now and want me to come around to stay the night. After all, after three nights in a row I wouldn't keep us up *very* late tonight.

"Hello."

"This is Sam, Nina. Still annoyed with me?"

"I wasn't annoyed with you, Sam. It's just—I was being sensible for once."

"Still feeling sensible, darling?"

She laughed a little. "No, I'm not. I was hoping you'd call. I was afraid you were annoyed with me for being so silly this morning. I want you to come around, dear. But—"

"Oh, no," I said.

"Oh, yes, I'm afraid. It started today, Sam two days early. So I'm going to be a good girl and get to bed early whether I want to or not."

"But you don't have to turn in *this* early do you, Nina? There's something I want you to do for me. Well, there were two things but now we can rule out one of them. Can I, though, drop over for just a little while? A half hour, maybe? I'm calling from home and I can be there in twenty minutes."

"Please don't, Sam. I'm really dead tired; I'd just turned in when the phone rang. Another three minutes and I'd have been too sound asleep to have heard it. Whatever it is you want me to do, I'm afraid I couldn't. I'm half asleep now."

"It's nothing for you to do tonight. I just wanted to explain it to you so you could do it tomorrow."

"Can't you tell me over the phone?"

"It's— I'm afraid it's too complicated for that."

"Then can't it wait a day, Sam? Please?"

"All right," I said. "Go to bed and pound your pretty ear. Good night."

"Good night, darling."

"Will I see you tomorrow night?"

"If you wish, after what I just told you."

"Don't be a goof," I said. "If you think my wanting to see you is for one reason only, I'm glad of a chance to prove other-wise. And how's about my taking you out to dinner for a change? Will you be ready at—say, half past six?"

"But—aren't you worried about someone seeing us to-gether?"

"Of course not. But if you are—and I suppose that, working for the school board, it wouldn't do you any good to be seen with a married man—we can drive out to some place in the country where there wouldn't be a chance in a thousand of either of us seeing someone who knows him."

"I think it's better that way. Yes, I'd love to, Sam. I'll be ready at six-thirty. And thanks for skipping tonight; I'll be sound asleep in minutes. 'Night, darling."

"Good night, Nina."

"Love me—just a little bit?"

"What other possible motive could I have for feeding you tomorrow evening?"

She laughed, and we said good night again and hung up.

I wasn't sleepy and I decided I wanted a drink before I turned in, maybe several drinks. I wanted to quit thinking, too. I'd have to wait a day now to have Nina get me the dope from the school files that might help me make up my mind about Obie, and maybe it would be a good thing for me to forget it for a day. Damn it, this was my vacation.

And besides, I wanted to talk to someone. About anything except the family Westphal.

I drove to the Press Bar across the street from the *Herald*. It was Thursday night now; I wouldn't have any trouble explaining to the boys why I was in town. I could simply say that five days on the lake had been enough and that I'd come back a little early.

Ordinarily there'd have been anywhere from two to ten people I knew in the Press Bar at nine-thirty on a week night. Tonight, because I wanted company, there wasn't one. Even the bartender must have been a new one; he was a stranger to me.

I drank a few beers, though, and got into a conversation with the man next to me at the bar, but it was a one-sided conversation because he wanted to talk baseball and I know nothing about baseball and care less. But beer and baseball combined to make me sleepy so when I went home and to bed somewhere around eleven o'clock I went to sleep the moment I put my head on the pillow.

FRIDAY

1

IN my dream I was standing at the end of a swimming pool. The pool was filled not with water but with ink, black ink. Somehow I knew, although of course I couldn't see through the ink, that I was standing at the deep end, just a foot or so from the edge. And in my dream I couldn't swim, although actually I can. Someone or something was standing behind me. I wanted to turn but couldn't. Then there came a whisper from behind me, "Turn now," and I turned. A few feet away stood a creature with the body of a man or boy—a big, strong, young boy in slacks and a white T shirt—and the head of a wolf. The wolf's head whispered, "Don't laugh; your daughter may be inside." Then the wolf's head changed to the head of a tiger and it said, "Turn again, Dick Whittington," and I turned obediently to face the deep end of the dark pool. There was a push in the middle of my back and I started falling into the pool, and woke suddenly before I got there.

I was wide awake and I lay there thinking about that dream and wondering what it could mean. I don't mean that I think dreams have meaning in the Gypsy Dream Book sense nor yet do I follow the Freudians in believing in sex symbolism back of every dream. The only thing in that dream which, to my mind, could have been a sex symbol was the wolf's head and my mind had picked that up from the radiator ornament on the jalopy Obie's friend had driven. Where, of course, it was a deliberate, if adolescent, sex symbol. And the "Don't laugh; your daughter may be inside," phrase was a natural association with the wolf's head; it had been lettered on the same jalopy.

Most of the other things were easy to place, too, although I didn't see how Dick Whittington got in there unless as a random association with the phrase "Turn again"; there's an English nursery rhyme something like "Turn again, Whittington, thrice Lord Mayor of London."

But the body under the wolf's head had been Obie's and the change to a tiger's head was easily explicable; I'd thought of Obie metaphorically as a tiger more than once. The inkwell, that was obvious enough for a newspaperman. True, printer's ink is not a liquid; it's the consistency of thick paste and wouldn't work very well in a swimming pool, but dreams aren't so literal as to insist on a point like that.

And the pool itself and not being able to swim and the push—my mind had picked those things from the death of Constance Bonner, the teacher who had probably committed suicide. The deep end—well, if Obie *had* killed her by pushing her into the pool he'd certainly have chosen the deep end for the purpose. Or maybe my subconscious was telling me that I was going off the deep end in regard to the whole thing. And maybe, I thought, my subconscious was all too damned right if that's what it was trying to tell me in the dream.

Meanwhile my body, now that I was awake, was telling me something else. It was telling me that I'd drunk quite a bit of beer and that I'd better go to the bathroom before I went back to sleep.

I got up and went to the bathroom and came back, and I couldn't sleep. I kept thinking about Nina, for one thing, wishing I was with her tonight—even under the circumstances. And wondering whether I loved her; whether I'd want to marry her if Millie and I broke up. And whether I wanted Millie and me to break up, or whether basically I was still in love with Millie and the affair with Nina was just an affair, wonderful right now, but nothing important or permanent.

But damn it, I didn't *want* to decide that now; I didn't even want to think about it. I wanted to stall, to see what was going to happen, to let the decision come to me instead of my hunting for it. And I should wait until Millie came back and find out what she had decided. If she wanted to try playing house again, I should, an all fairness, be able to give it a try; it wouldn't be a fair try if I'd already decided that I loved Nina more. And if I decided now that I definitely didn't love Nina then, in fairness to her, I should break things off now before she got too emotionally involved, if she wasn't already, and was hurt. And I didn't want to break things off.

I thought, damn a society that insists on monogamy.

My thoughts went round in circles. Like the horsefly under the ceiling of the editorial room last Saturday. Less than a week ago. It seemed a lot longer than that. But when I'd watched that horsefly I'd never heard of Obie Westphal or Jimmy Chojnacki, and I hadn't seen Nina for so long that I'd almost forgotten about her. Certainly I had no thought of having an affair with her this week. I'd been looking forward to a week of fishing and hunting and poker playing at Lake Laflamme.

Millie still thought that's where I was. Instead, Millie, I'm here, sleeping alone in the bed in which we've had so much happiness. And thinking of you, but of another woman too. Wishing I was with her tonight. But not that she was here, in this bed we've shared, with me. Funny what strange scruples and sentimentalities people have. As though it matters where something happens.

And you, Millie, have you tried an extramarital experiment this week of limbo?

I tried to picture Millie with someone else and then wished I hadn't tried; the very thought hurt. Damn the double standard, damn everything, damn not being able to sleep. Damn not being able to sleep.

The luminous dial of the clock beside the bed had told me it was two o'clock when I'd wakened from that dream. It told me now that the time was three-ten. I'd been awake an hour and ten minutes, after only three hours' sleep, and I was getting wider and wider awake every minute.

Was Nina by any chance awake now, wondering, worrying? Was Millie?

Three-sixteen. Millie had mild insomnia occasionally. She had something in capsules that a doctor had prescribed for it. Dormison. Had she taken the bottle of capsules with her or was it still where it usually stood, on the top shelf of the medicine cabinet? I got up and lighted a cigarette and then headed for the bathroom again. The Dormison wasn't there. Millie had taken the bottle with her.

Maybe, I thought, I should hit myself in the head with a hammer. Or a blackjack, except that I didn't have a blackjack. Warm milk might help but there wasn't any milk. Or more beer, but there wasn't any beer in the house, or anything else to drink. Or anything to— Yes, there was something to eat. There was still some sandwich meat and two rolls left downstairs from what I'd bought at the delicatessen. Thank God for small favors.

I went downstairs. Made a sandwich. Ate it. Felt wider awake than ever. Damn Millie for taking all of the sleeping capsules with her; she might have left a few. But then she didn't know I'd be home this week and besides I'd never had insomnia.

Until now. Like the stock gag of the nightclub emcee who says other emcees always have stories to tell about things that happen to them on the way to the club, but nothing has ever happened to him on his way to the club. Pause. Until tonight.

And maybe, just maybe, Nina was awake too right now. Why wasn't I a telepath so I could know? In her bed, with my arms around her, my body to hers, I could maybe go to sleep and she could maybe go to sleep. But she probably was asleep. Everybody on my side of the world was asleep except me. On the other side of the world it was day and all the Chinamen were awake but I was the only person awake on my side. And I was alone and lonesome and wide awake.

I went back upstairs because I'd left my cigarettes there. I lighted one and sat on the edge of the bed to smoke it. When I finished it, I'd try once more to go back to sleep. Three-fifty now. I'd been awake almost two hours after three hours' sleep on the night on which I was going to catch up with my sleeping. Well, I still could if I ever got back to sleep again; there wasn't any reason why I couldn't sleep as late as I wanted to.

That was a bright spot. Look for the bright spots.

What bright spots? I'd probably never sleep again. No sleep to knit the raveled sleeve of care, and how damn raveled can a sleeve get?

I finished the cigarette and turned out the light. And lay there wide awake with my mind making like a horsefly. Circling from Millie to Nina and back and again, and I didn't want to think about them because I might come to a decision and I didn't want to.

But I did want to decide about Obie, and why couldn't I think about him? I guess because I'd thought myself out the evening before. I'd lined up two possibilities, the only two I could see, and I'd carried each of them as far as I could with the data I had. Farther, in fact; I'd been doing a lot of guessing too. If I thought about Obie now I'd just be going over the same territory again, my mind again making like a horsefly, the same horsefly in a different room.

No use even trying to decide between those two alternatives on Obie until I had more data. I'd have more data when Nina had checked—

Suddenly I swore to myself, realizing something I hadn't realized before. Tomorrow—today rather—was Friday, the last school day of the week. If Nina didn't get me that information from the school records tomorrow, she wouldn't be able to get it until Monday, three days from now and my vacation over.

Three days lost, and the only days I'd have completely free before going back to work and maybe Millie being home to boot, for a long time. The three days I had left in which to put in full time following my hunch. Or my delusion.

I could get up early—or get up now and stay awake; I might as well—and have breakfast with Nina, explain to her then.

But it was such a complicated, touchy thing to explain. Having to admit to her that I'd been lying to her on other fronts, too; the reason for my interest in the accidents at the school, my questions about the Chojnacki family.

At *breakfast?* Look what had happened at breakfast this morning or yesterday morning, Thursday morning. I was sleeping, or not sleeping, alone tonight because of it.

No, I didn't want to explain to Nina over breakfast why I wanted to know if Obie Westphal's class schedules gave him alibis for murders. In fact, I didn't want to have to explain that, and admit the lies I'd told already, to Nina at all.

Why couldn't I get that information myself? Right now?

There wasn't a night watchman at the high school building; Nina's story of how the body of Constance Bonner had been discovered by a squad-car patrol proved that. And they'd investigated only because there was a light on. I knew where the file cabinets of students' records were—or at least where they'd been when I attended school there—and it wasn't in line with any window. I had a little pencil flashlight that I could use without a chance of it being seen from the outside. True, I'd have to break or jimmy a window to get in but there surely wouldn't be any burglar alarm system. And I knew the layout.

Was I kidding myself? Did I have the guts to commit a burglary, even a relatively safe and easy one? A breaking-and-entering, really, since I wouldn't be stealing anything.

I looked at the clock. Ten minutes after four. An hour and a half, maybe, until dawn. And I could dress in ten minutes, be there in another twenty. For three precious days.

I still didn't know if I was kidding myself. But I got out of bed and dressed, fast. I was in my car, driving, in less than ten minutes and what with the emptiness of the streets at that hour I made the trip in only fifteen minutes, and without speeding.

I drove past, making sure the building was completely dark, and parked a block and a half away. I checked that I had the things I'd picked up on my way out of the house; the pencil flashlight, a handful of rags in case I had to break glass, a small crowbar. The crowbar was going to be a problem to carry. I solved the problem, though. One end was curved so I dropped it down inside my trousers with the curved end hooked over my belt. With my suit coat buttoned, it wouldn't show. But it banged uncomfortably against my right leg just above the knee when I walked.

I walked back to the school without having seen a person or a car. I took a good look around, and a good listen to make sure no car was coming, before I cut back across the grass and got behind the trees and shrubbery on the west side of the building. That would be the best side because the cover was better and because, too, the windows were better situated. The bottom of the lowest row of windows on that side was just flush with the ground and the windows couldn't be seen at all from the street. If I'd got that far without being seen, I was doing all right.

I stood there a few minutes, waiting to be sure that I was still doing all right, and to let my eyes get used to the darkness. Or the not-quite-darkness; there was just a touch of gray to the sky already.

When I could see fairly well, I started moving. I decided to pick a window in about the middle of the building because there I'd be farthest from any residence where some light sleeper or insomniac might hear glass breaking if I had to break glass.

But I didn't get all the way to the middle of the building

and I didn't have to break glass. God loved me. Someone had been careless; there was a window open, wide open.

I lowered myself through it and waited another few minutes—I don't know why—and then, shielding the pencil flashlight with my hand, I found my way across a classroom and into the corridor. I knew my way. Around one turn and up the middle stairs and right across from it were the offices.

The file cabinets were still in the same place. At a distance and angle from the windows and around a corner from them so I could use my flashlight, with reasonable care, without a chance of its being seen from the street. I didn't know how they were arranged but I saw one drawer labeled *1953*. And since it was now only the summer of 1952 I thought the date must mean the class of 1953, which would be Obie's class. I opened it and I was right. The folders in each bore a name, arranged alphabetically. And among the W's I found a folder labeled *Westphal, Henry O.* I took it back into the far corner, still safer from the windows, and opened it on the floor. I had his schedules for the three years he'd attended the school, his grades and his credits, his attendance record and a few other things that weren't important from my point of view. I got the information I wanted except that there wasn't in the file any record of extracurricular activities such as membership in school clubs. Then I remembered that would be covered in the school annuals and that there was—or had been—a neat chronological row of them in the bookcase on the opposite side of the room. I put Obie's file back in the cabinet and closed the drawer.

And then went to where the bookcase was. Or used to be. It had been moved to another wall but I found it and I found the 1952 volume of the school annual. I found the pages, two of them, devoted to the Drama Club and studied them. I put the volume back in the bookcase left the way I had come.

The sky was definitely gray now.

I was a block away from the school when the squad car passed me, being driven slowly. Two men in it. The one on my side, not the driver, looked me over as it went; but I must have looked all right, even for a five o'clock in the morning pedestrian, for the car kept on going.

But half a block farther on it pulled in to the curb in front of the car I'd left parked there. My ancient Buick. I had to keep on walking; I'd been seen and if I turned around and started the other way they'd have been stupid not to pick me up for questioning. So I kept on going toward the Buick, and the crowbar that I hadn't had to use banged against my leg at every step.

One of the two policemen was still in the squad air parked just ahead. The other had his foot on my front bumper and was writing out a ticket. He looked up from his writing as I came close. "Your car?"

I nodded.

He said, "The whole Goddam block to park in, nothing else near, and you park in front of a fireplug. Been drinking, pal?"

I looked and I *had* parked in front of a fireplug. It was so ridiculous that I wanted to laugh and, for the moment, I quit being scared. I said, "No, I haven't been drinking. But my parking there sure must look as though I had been. My God, I deserve a ticket for that one."

I should have argued; I should have realized that it makes a cop suspicious if you don't argue with him.

He looked at me. "Where you been, this time of night?"

The other cop was getting out of the car now, coming to join the first one. The crowbar hanging down my right trouser leg felt as though it weighed a ton and must be noticeable a mile away. But my mind was still working.

I said, "Visiting a friend," and had the rest of my story planned.

"We passed you walking almost a block back. Where does your friend live? How come you didn't park in front of his house?"

I took a deep breath and let it out as though I was trying to decide whether to tell him something or not. Then I said, "I parked over a block away on purpose, Officer. And for the same reason that I'm leaving at this hour, before her neighbors might be awake and see me."

"Let's see your license."

I reached for it thankfully. If they were going to pat me over for a gun—and find that damned crowbar—they'd have done it before they let me reach into a pocket for my wallet. I was okay now; I could show them I was a solid citizen and not a burglar. That crowbar would have been something to explain. I handed them my wallet, opened out, instead of slipping the driver's license out of it; that way they could see the license under the celluloid window on one side and my press pass under the window on the other.

The cop who'd just got out of the car looked over the other's shoulder. He said, "Reporter. What the hell, Hank, he'll just square a ticket if you give him one. Come on."

"Not this time," I said. "Think I want to tell Joe Steiner I parked in front of a fireplug in an empty block at night? And have him kid me about it for the next year? This one I'll pay, if you give me a ticket."

The first cop put his foot on the bumper again, ready to write. He said, "Okay, if you want one."

The second one said, "Ahh, nuts. Give the guy a break. He had hot pants when he parked there. His mind wasn't on fireplugs."

The first cop took his foot off the bumper and put the pad in his pocket. He said, "Okay, okay. Next time *look*, though."

I said, "Thanks, boys. How's about telling me your names? So if they ever pop up in a story I'll at least see that they're spelled right."

They told me their names and how to spell them and we talked a few minutes. Then they got in the squad car and drove off.

I got behind the wheel of the Buick, turned on the lights and started the engine, and then decided to sit there and jitter a minute before I started driving. I got the crowbar out and reached over and put it on the floor in the back seat. I never wanted to see a crowbar again in my life.

And how damned lucky it was that I hadn't had to use it to break in! If I'd had to jimmy a window there'd be a burglary report made tomorrow by the high school. And since this was their beat those squad cops would get the report and, solid citizen though they now thought me, they'd remember the hour of my return to my car and want to ask me some more questions. Oh, I could have bluffed it through, even with Chief Steiner, by sticking to my story and refusing to divulge the name of my mythical friend to give myself an alibi. But it wouldn't have helped my standing with the police department. As things had worked out, though, I felt sure that I'd left everything at the school just as I'd found it and that there wouldn't be any report of a burglary.

I drove home because there wasn't any other place to go. I wanted a drink badly, several drinks. But there wasn't anything to drink at home and where can you get a drink or a bottle at five o'clock? Of course I could commit another burglary, a liquor store this time. But not right now, thanks. Some other time, not right now.

It was getting light by the time I got home.

Well, I'd found out what I wanted to know, and without having to confide in Nina so she'd get the information for me. The file on Obie plus the annual for the last year had given me the three facts I wanted. And I wished now that they had been otherwise. If I could have given Obie an alibi for, say, two out of the three deaths that he might have caused at the school, I might have been able to write off the whole thing and forget it. But things hadn't been that simple for me.

In his freshman year Obie had had a fifth-period algebra class; that meant his lunch period was the second one. He could have pushed Wilbur Greenough from the tower window. He had been in the same gym class as the Negro boy who'd been killed in the gym locker room.

And he'd belonged to the Drama Club. In fact, he must have been a very active member of it because the two pages of the school annual of last year given to the Drama Club had shown scenes from and listed the cast of the three plays the Drama Club had put on. Obie had played the lead in one and a supporting role in each of the others. There was every chance that Obie had attended the meeting that preceded the death of Constance Bonner and had known that she was alone in the school building after it.

I'd noticed too that one of the three plays had been Shakespeare's *Othello* and that Obie had played the role of Iago. Iago, murderer. Iago, almost the only villain in literature who knew he was a villain and gloried secretly in his villainy and his cleverness in concealing it. Had Obie *chosen* that role?

I'd glanced back in the faculty section of the annual too and had looked at the picture of Constance Bonner. With a light tasteful black border around it and the date of her death. Just "Died, January 24, 1952"; whether accident, suicide or murder not specified.

So Obie could have killed all three of them.

All right, Sam Evans, what now? Where do you go from here?

2

Five-thirty in the morning is a hell of a time for it to be unless you're sleepy or unless you've got something to do. I'd never felt wider awake in my life and there wasn't any use in my going back to bed.

There wasn't any use in my doing anything else either. Particularly there wasn't any use in my trying to think any more about anything. Nor in trying to read to pass the time; I did try that and found I couldn't concentrate for two consecutive sentences.

I wandered around like a lost soul for a while and then decided I might as well be doing something useful so I straightened up the house. Washed the few dishes and glasses I'd used, made the bed, did a little dusting in places where dust showed. Daylight by the time I'd finished all that. I remembered the coal bin in the basement that had broken last winter and which I had to fix sometime before we ordered more coal in the fall. And that sometime had might as well be now. I started to change into old clothes for the job and then decided what the hell, why get even old clothes full of coal dust? I went down to the basement wearing only a pair of shoes, the ideal costume for carpentering a coal bin. It was a lot bigger job than I'd thought; I didn't finish until almost ten o'clock. I took off the worst of the dirt at the faucet in the basement and then went upstairs to the bathroom and shaved while I drew a full tub of hot water.

I got in and it felt good. I made myself comfortable with my head on the end of the tub and the next thing I knew the water was cold and twelve o'clock whistles were blowing. I dried myself and dressed. I could have gone to bed instead and slept a few more hours except that I was ravenously hungry and there was nothing in the house.

I went to a good restaurant and ate a big meal. When I came out it was a bright afternoon and I had a bright idea. There's a small privately-owned lake only twelve miles from town on Highway 71 where the fishing is fairly good and where you can rent a boat, a rod, full fishing equipment. Why didn't I get away from everything I'd been thinking about and worrying about and have myself at least half a day's fishing? Afternoon isn't the best time, of course, but I still might catch a few and if I didn't it wouldn't matter too much.

I got in the Buick and headed out of town west on 71. I was just a mile or so past the city limits when I began to be convinced that I was being followed. By a jalopy.

I hadn't been looking for a tail, nothing had been farther

from my mind. But I'd happened to notice this jalopy—it wasn't the topless one with the wolf's head on the radiator; this one was a hard-topped coupe, vintage of about 1930—while we were still back in town. I'd noticed it because I'd come perilously close to running a red light, and I'd looked in my rear vision mirror to see if a police car or motorcycle was coming after me. None was, but I saw that the car behind me was running the light too, taking more of a chance than I had. And it had stayed with me, dropping hack to a little greater distance when we were out of town traffic, but passing cars when I passed them and yet not passing me, holding his distance behind me and not closing up, when I slowed down quite a bit to see what he'd do.

He was good at it. I'd probably never have noticed him if it hadn't been for what had happened at the stop light.

It scared me a little. Obie? Apparently he didn't have a car of his own, but he could have borrowed one from a friend—and the jalopy following me was the kind of car a high school kid would be likely to have. But why would Obie be following *me*? I thought back and couldn't figure any way in which he could have learned that I was interested in him. I hadn't asked many people questions about him and none of the people I'd even mentioned his name to had been close to him or likely to tell him about it

Dr. Wygand? I'd come nearer to talking frankly to him than to anyone else but it was ridiculous to think he'd have called Obie or even Armin Westphal to say I'd been asking questions. Doc is a right guy. The only person I'd talked to about Obie who could have felt close to him was Grace Smith, his classmate, but that had been while she and I and everyone else had thought Obie had been killed by the roller coaster and my questions had been the legitimate questions of a reporter at work. No, that was out.

But who else would be following me in a jalopy? Police or private detectives don't use conspicuously ancient wrecks like that one for tailing.

All I could tell at the distance it kept behind me was that there was only one person, the driver, in it.

Did I have nerve enough to force the issue and find out who he was? I decided that I did but that I'd rather do it in a town, where there'd be other people around, than out here on the open road. Barnesville, a town with a wide main street, good for making U-turns, was only a mile or two ahead and I'd do it there. I drove at an even speed and the jalopy kept an even distance behind me. It dropped back a little when we entered the town.

I made my play when we were a little way into Barnesville but not yet to the business section. I went to one side of the street and drove along slowly and pretended to be watching street numbers. I made a point of not looking back but the jalopy didn't pass me.

I stopped in front of a house and got out. I managed to glance back without seeming to do it deliberately as I closed the door of the car. The jalopy was parking about half a block behind me. Still too far for me to see the driver or read the license plate.

I did what I thought was a nice bit of acting, a double take on the house number, as though I'd read it wrong the first time. I made a pass at going back to my car and then pretended to decide that there was no use moving it and that I'd walk back to the right number. I started walking briskly back toward the jalopy, pretending to watch the house numbers to my left but able, since it was in the general direction I was walking, to keep a watch on the jalopy too. I figured that by the time he could do anything I'd be close enough to get a look at him and to read the license plate.

But maybe my acting hadn't been so hot or maybe he was smarter than I'd given him credit for being. Apparently he'd kept his engine running and I hadn't taken more than a dozen steps before he shoved his car into gear and got the hell out of there. He U-turned right from the curb and headed back the way we'd come.

He must have had a good lead on me by the time I got back to my car and got it started; I hadn't been smart enough to leave the engine running. And a stream of traffic materialized and kept me from U-turning for another minute or two—and that was too long. I drove back to town as fast as I dared but I never caught him. Maybe he'd played safe by turning off just outside Barnesville somewhere. Or maybe the jalopy was a hot rod and he'd simply walked away from me.

Well, there was one thing I could do, anyway. Find out whether Obie was home. I parked and went into a drugstore, used the phone booth to call the Westphal residence. A female voice answered and I asked if Obie was there.

"Just a moment, please."

I wanted to be sure; she might think he was somewhere around when he wasn't. But a minute later Obie's voice said, "Hello." I recognized the voice; I'd heard him talking to his friends in the railroad station a couple of days ago. But he'd never heard my voice and I didn't want him to. Nor the click of a phone being hung up on him. I just waited until he'd said "Hello" a few more times and then replaced the receiver on his end.

It hadn't been Obie in the jalopy that had followed me. His home was on another side of town, a good five miles from here. And the jalopy couldn't possibly have done ten miles while I'd chased it five, not unless it had averaged over a hundred and twenty miles an hour for ten miles, five miles of which was on city streets. And that was ridiculous.

I drove back out on Highway 71 and spent the afternoon fishing at the private lake but I didn't enjoy it very much. I kept wondering and worrying about that jalopy. I tried to tell myself I might have been mistaken about it and that its U-turn and getaway just when I was walking back to it had been coincidence. But I knew damned well it hadn't been.

I caught three pike but when I stopped home to dress for

dinner with Nina I gave them to a neighbor. If I'd taken them with me to Nina's she might have insisted on cooking them for us and I'd decided definitely that I wanted to take her out this evening and didn't want any argument about it.

No car, jalopy or other, followed me between home and Nina's. I made sure of that because if whoever had followed me before wanted to pick me up again he'd have been waiting somewhere near my house to do it.

3

I got there a few minutes early but, miraculously, Nina was ready. She was beautiful in a white silk dinner dress that fitted her like a coat of paint and set off her slightly olive skin and dark hair and eyes.

I kissed her and it was as though I hadn't kissed her for weeks and had been missing her every minute. Her lips were hungry against mine and she clung to me. Then she put her head back but kept her arms around me and looked at me, her eyes a little misty.

"I'm so glad you came tonight, Sam."

"I am too, darling."

"There isn't much more time, is there?"

I knew what she meant and I wanted suddenly to tell her there was all the time in the world and that I loved her to pieces. But I didn't know for sure whether that was true or not and so I couldn't say it.

"I don't know," I had to say. "All I know is that right now I love you."

She smiled. "Thanks for that, anyway. And I'm sorry—I didn't mean to sound so serious. It's been wonderful."

"It's still wonderful," I told her. "Don't make it sound like a valedictory." But I was thinking: This is Friday evening. Millie will probably be home the day after tomorrow. And what will happen then?

I knew one thing that wouldn't happen. I wouldn't live with Millie and keep on seeing Nina, clandestinely. There'd have to be a clean break one way or the other.

Nina stepped back from me. "Let's have one drink here before we leave. Like a Martini?"

"I'd love a Martini."

"As much as you love me?" Her tone was light.

"At least as much."

"Good. You break out the ice cubes while I get the rest of the things."

The Martinis were excellent. We sat together on the sofa to drink them and my arm went about her as naturally as though it belonged there, which it did. And you need only one hand to drink a cocktail; not always even that if there's a coffee table in front of you to put it down on.

After we'd finished our drinks I drove us out to the Club Caesar. It's small and pretty expensive, I'd heard. But I could stand the expense for one evening and the expensiveness had one advantage; there was little likelihood that anyone I knew would be there. And no one was.

We each had another cocktail and then a good dinner, a damn good dinner. T-bone steaks, if it matters. It did matter then because I was starving by the time the steaks came.

After dinner we danced, and not to a blaring orchestra but to music made by one man on one piano. A good man, a good piano, and good music. Music that you could talk against easily when you wanted to sit at your table and talk, as we did about half of the time. I've often wondered why the less you pay at a place the more music you get, in volume.

We talked about her jobs, the school one and the social service one, about my job, about old times—our classes at high school and our teachers—and Nina could tell me which ones of them were still teaching there—and it was as though Nina and I hadn't until then really got around to talking much. And somehow we seemed closer to one another than we'd ever been before—even in bed.

After a while Nina said, "Let's go back to my place, Sam. We can have a nightcap there."

I looked at my watch. "It's early, only eleven. And tomorrow. Saturday. No school."

"I've got to get up early just the same. My other job— I've got a nine o'clock appointment."

"All right," I said. "If you won't kick me out too soon after we get to your place. You had a good night's sleep last night. Or did you?"

"Ten hours, yes. Did you get to bed early?"

"Eleven o'clock." I didn't add that I'd slept only about three hours then and another hour or so in the bathtub it around noon.

"Good. Oh—what was it you wanted to talk to me about last night, Sam? Sorry I didn't feel up to letting you come around, by the way."

"Nothing important," I said. Then I remembered I'd said last night that it *was* important. "Something I wanted you to find out for me from the school files. But I got the information myself." And then I realized what I'd said and added quickly, "Today, from the newspaper files." Damn, that had been a silly thing to say. I thought that I'd covered all my tracks at the high school last night, but if I hadn't, if Nina knew that the offices there had been entered last night, I was giving myself away.

But apparently everything was all right. She asked, "Something in connection with your article on accidents?" And I nodded and she let it go at that and I didn't have to think up any further evasions.

I called for the check and it wasn't as stiff as I'd expected.

Driving back, I watched closely for headlights that might be following me, but there weren't any. Once in town I took a route that used little frequented streets and for blocks at a time there wasn't any other car in sight.

We made Martinis again. We were getting to be a good team at it. Fast and efficient, each of us having his allotted part in the operation. It just couldn't be, I thought, that this was the last or almost the last time we'd make them together.

And again we sat on the sofa with my arm around her and I felt at peace and unworried. Which worried me. It's one thing when a married man feels excited about a woman other than his wife; he can get over that. But when he feels at peace with her, it's serious.

And suddenly I wanted to level with Nina. Not about our personal relationships, not about that until I was sure and it would be wrong for me to be sure until after I'd seen Millie again. I mean about what I'd really been investigating, or trying to investigate, this week. About Obie, and what I thought he was. It was something I'd have to talk over with someone, sometime, if only to see how it sounded when put in words. And would she laugh at me or take it seriously?

"Nina, how well do you know Obie Westphal? What do you think of him?"

She pulled away far enough so she could turn and look at me and there was surprise in her face. "Sam, why on earth are you interested in Obie Westphal? You asked me questions about him earlier this week."

I thought, not yet; tell her in a minute but first get an unbiased opinion, what she thinks of him now before I tell her anything. Or maybe evasion had become a habit by now, too strong to break suddenly. I said, "I told you why I was interested, then. I spent last Saturday morning working on him, writing an obituary, a sob story, before it was known that the boy who was killed was Jimmy Chojnacki and not Obie. I read about him, what there was in our files, and I talked about him to one of his classmates who had a crush on him, and I wrote about him. I got interested in him, say, like you get interested in a character in a book." I took a sip of the drink in my free hand

and pulled Nina back against me with the other. "Only with a
character in a book all you can ever learn about him is what's in
the book. But Obie's not only real, he's still alive after I wrote an
obit on him. So why would it be strange that I'm interested in
him."

Why, I wondered, had I gone that far, been that elaborate.
Now, if I leveled with her, it was going to be tougher to explain
and I'd have to admit that I'd lied to her just now as well as
earlier in the week.

Nina put her head on my shoulder. "Well, I don't know him
personally except just to speak to. But he's so popular, so prominent at the school that the teachers talk about him a lot, almost
as much as the students. Of course being a football hero is
enough, in a school. But being so personally attractive and such
a brilliant student besides being an athletic hero—well, it makes
him pretty unusual."

"Just how brilliant a student is he? Leads his class?"

"I think he easily could if he wanted to. His average is in
the top ten per cent, and that's without studying very hard. He
can't put in much time on studying with all the other activities
and athletics he goes in for. And he admits he doesn't study
much."

I said, "A high school boy doesn't admit that, he brags
about it. But here's what I'm really digging for. He's too good to
be true; there's got to be a flaw, a fault somewhere, or I just
can't believe him. Nobody's perfect, and one boy can't have just
everything. I think he's queer."

"You think—*what?*"

"All right, it's a guess. But there's something to base it on
anyway. Grace Smith—that's the classmate of his I talked to
Saturday morning while we thought he was dead, and she was
all broken up about it, incidentally—said he not only didn't have
a steady girl, but usually went stag to parties. And—" I started to
say that the time I'd seen him in the wolf's-head jalopy the two
other boys had had girls and Obie hadn't, but I changed it.

"—I've heard the same thing from other places. It isn't normal, is it, for a boy with a whole school full of girls mad over him not to take advantage of some of it. Especially one as well developed and mature for his age as Obie. If he isn't queer, then he's sexually retarded."

"But at seventeen, Sam, you hadn't—At least you told me I was the first, and that was in our senior year and we were both eighteen then."

"True, and I wasn't kidding you. But dammit I *went* with girls, dated 'em, long before then. Generally I was going steady with someone, and I never stagged a party in my life."

Nina's shoulder, against mine, was shaking. I turned and looked at her; she was giggling. "What's funny about that?" I wanted to know. "You know it's perfectly true."

"I wasn't laughing about that, Sam, not about what you said about yourself . But—Sam, if I tell you something that's a secret, will you promise never to— You're not planning to *write* anything about Obie, are you?"

"Nope."

"And you won't tell this to anyone? Word of honor?"

"Cross my heart and hope to die."

"I was laughing at how *wrong* you were about Obie. A little over a year ago, near the end of his sophomore year, he got into a little trouble for seducing a maid they had working for them at the house, the Westphal home.

And he'd have been only sixteen then; he beat your record by two years. That's what I was giggling about. Your thinking he was queer."

"So I was wrong. I've been *wrong* before. Who was he in trouble with? And how did the school get in on it if it's something that happened at home?"

"I didn't mean trouble really, except with his parents. The girl didn't go to the police or anything like that—and anyway she probably seduced him; she was older. But Mama Westphal was so worried about it that she came to the principal of the school for advice."

"Old Emerson? Must have shocked the bejesus out of him. What did he tell her?"

"It wasn't Mr. Emerson. Probably luckily for everybody concerned. He's still principal there, Sam, but he was out for a few months right about then, in the hospital for an operation— gall bladder trouble; he was quite ill for a while. The school board sent us a younger man, Ralph Sherbourne, to take over during those months. Mama Westphal talked to him about it and he was modem and sensible enough to tell her it was nothing to worry about. That while he didn't condone it, there was nothing abnormal about a boy of sixteen having his first affair with an older woman."

I thought of Constance Bonner. I asked, "How much older?"

"I believe she was twenty-five or thereabouts. And there was a question whether she seduced Obie or he seduced her, and it wasn't anything serious anyway."

I said, "And Obie at sixteen was probably a couple of years ahead of his age in physical development. Right now at seventeen he could probably pass for twenty, somebody told me. But go on, if there's any more you know about it. I'm interested."

"There isn't much more. Ralph calmed down Mama Westphal and told her he'd have a heart-to-heart talk with Obie. And he did and Obie was sorry about it and promised to behave himself."

"Did you ever see the girl, the maid? Or a picture of her?"

"Of course not. Where would I see her? Why do you ask that, Sam?"

"Wondering something. Oedipus. The girl was probably the same physical type as Obie's mother."

"Maybe. I suppose it could be that. I've never seen Obie's mother either. I wasn't there, the day she came in. But if Obie takes after her, she must be good-looking. Have you ever seen Obie, Sam?"

"No," I said. "Just a picture of him in football costume that was in the file on him at the *Herald*, along with the sports stories we'd run on him. And you can't tell much from a picture of somebody in football clothes and helmet."

"I've got a copy of last year's school annual," Nina said. "There are several pictures of him in it. Want to see them?"

I'd seen them last night at the school, or at least the ones in the Drama Club section, but I couldn't very well say so now. So I said yes, I'd like to see them.

She had only to lean forward to get the annual. It was on the bottom shelf of the coffee table in front of us, with some magazines and other books.

"Our drinks are all," I said. "Let's make another before we look at that. He's probably in it a dozen times and it'll take a little while to leaf through it."

"All right, but this one had better be our last. I'm feeling them."

"Good. Glad they're not being wasted. I'm feeling mine too."

We made us each another drink.

Then I watched while Nina leafed through the book, stopping whenever there was a group photograph that included Obie—and he was in quite a few of them. He stood out in every group, too; you couldn't miss him. I saw again the three group pictures of Drama Club casts that included Obie.

I asked Nina, "Is he as good at acting as at everything else?"

"Good for an amateur. I saw all of those plays, as it happens."

The last picture of Obie in the book was the best one I'd seen yet, an eighth-page portrait shot among the pictures of class officers.

Nina closed the book and put it back under the coffee table.

"Nina," I said, "how many people know what you told me about Mrs. Westphal's asking for advice about Obie's affair with that girl? Is it general knowledge among the teachers there?"

"Why—no, Sam." She moved away from me a little. "Aside

from Ralph Sherbourne, I'm the only one at the school who knew about it. He told me later. And you'll guess why he happened to talk about it to me, so I might as well tell you. Do I have to add anything to that, spell it out for you?"

I pulled her back against me again, both arms around her this time. I said, "Of course not. It's none of my business, Nina."

She snuggled against me. "I told you I'd had affairs, a few of them. And Ralph was one of those few. And he was single and wanted me to marry him. Maybe I should have, but—well, he's a nice guy but I just didn't love him enough to sign a life contract. Damn it, Sam, maybe the only men I can really love are ones I can't have. Do you still want to kiss me, Sam?"

I answered without words. After a while she pulled away gently just enough to free her lips for talking. "Sam, I shouldn't, but I'll have one more drink if you will. I guess I slept too much last night; I just can't get tired."

We made the drinks and this time I sat in the easy chair and pulled her down into my lap.

After a while I said, "Darling, must I go home tonight? It's so damned lonesome there and I hate it. I didn't sleep much last night in spite of going to bed early. Can I sleep with you, even if I have to behave myself?"

She turned her head so I could see her smile. "Will you wear a pair of my pajamas?"

"I will not. But you can. And I'll sleep in my shorts. That's two layers of insulation."

"All right, Sam, yes, I want you to stay."

Later, in bed, I held her tightly.

"Do you think I'm a wanton woman Sam?"

"Of course not."

"But I feel like one. Right now. And I'm not very sick, darling; it was mostly a false alarm. Do you want me, Sam?"

God how I'd been wanting her.

Later, I remember saying, "Nina darling, I love you, I love you." Or words to that effect.

SATURDAY

I WOKE too early again. Not from a dream this time; if I'd been dreaming I didn't remember. Faint gray at the windows, probably about half past five, Daylight Saving Time, maybe six. Nina had set her mental alarm clock for eight, saying that would give her time for her nine o'clock appointment and that I could sleep longer if I wished and leave as late as I wanted to.

But here again after only a few hours of sleep I was wide awake and knew that I wasn't going back to sleep no matter how hard I tried. And Nina is a light sleeper; I couldn't get up without waking her too. Besides, if I did get up, what could I do?

I lay there and stared at the barely visible ceiling. No horse-fly circling there. Just my thoughts again. Why hadn't I told Nina the truth last night? Just force of habit, maybe; I'd been lying so much this last week that the truth didn't come naturally any more, not in explaining my reason for asking questions about Obie. Well, it didn't matter; Nina had talked plenty about him, maybe even more freely than she would have if I'd told her my suspicions and she'd thought them ridiculous. As she no doubt would have. Apparently Obie was damned attractive even to women Nina's age. In fact—

Whoa, I told myself, don't get a wild suspicion like *that*.

Not about Nina.

But there was the Suspicion sitting on the foot of the bed grinning at me, a nasty grin.

"Go away," I told it.

"How about the way she giggled when you wondered whether Obie was queer or not?"

I glared at the Suspicion. "Why shouldn't she giggle? She knew it wasn't true!"

"Right, my naive friend. She knew it wasn't true. But would the matter have seemed so *funny* to her if she had that knowledge third hand? And Nina isn't the giggly type. In fact, you never heard her giggle before—not since high school days anyway. But if *she'd* had an affair with him and he was a pretty virile guy, as he probably is, maybe twice or three times as much so as *you* are, then your suddenly suggesting he might be homosexual would have been *really* funny to her, so much so that a giggle just had to pop out and she couldn't stop it."

"But she explained how she knew! Do you think she could make up a circumstantial story like that on a second's notice?"

"I doubt if she made it up. Probably there was such a substitute principal and he did have an affair with Nina—maybe he even really wanted to marry her, although that could have been embroidery. And probably the servant girl business and Mrs. Westphal's trip to the school really did happen. Don't you see why that makes it all the more likely?"

"No, I don't."

"Because you don't want to see. Ordinarily Nina would never have thought of having an affair with a seventeen-year-old. But after knowing that he'd already had an affair—at least one affair—with a woman approximately her age, she'd look at Obie with new eyes, wouldn't she? And she admits she found him damned attractive—and there'd have been curiosity too, wondering what he'd be like in bed. Curiosity gets women into more affairs than passion does."

I said, "You're crazy. But at least the Constance Bonner

business makes sense now. *She* must have been having an affair with Obie. And that's why she made an excuse to stay at the school after the Drama Club meeting. He came back for a clandestine date with her. Since she was living with her parents that was about the only place—"

"Nina isn't living with parents. She's got this—"

"Shut up. I'm thinking about Constance Bonner. This accounts for that part about her having been acting strangely, being depressed. If she'd become seriously entangled emotionally with someone she couldn't possibly marry . . . But Obie killed her. He didn't kill Nina. Doesn't that prove—"

"You know it doesn't. He doesn't have to kill every woman he makes. Just if a perfect opportunity pops up, maybe, like a woman who can't swim standing at the edge of the deep end of a swimming pool where a push will kill her. Or maybe he had a sane motive for killing Constance and led her to the pool deliberately. Maybe he was through with her and she wouldn't let go and she was threatening him with something."

"What does it matter? Anyway, you've just trying to change the subject. We were wondering about Nina and Obie, remember?"

"I still say you're crazy. Nina isn't that kind of a girl."

"How long did it take you to make her? Met her Monday noon and slept here Monday night. And don't give me that stuff about having been sweethearts in school. That was a long time ago."

"Nuts. And anyway, you're building an awful lot on one giggle."

"You know there's more than that, now that you think about it. The way she talked about him, described him. The fact that she has that school annual with all the pictures of him— and knew where they were. She hasn't got school annuals for other years since you and she were students there, has she? Just that one, and it's got a lot of pictures of Obie in it. Don't you think she might have bought it for that reason?"

"There could be other reasons," I said.

"Name one. And that annual is only two months or so off the presses, by the way. Her affair with Obie could have been quite recent. How do you like *that* thought? Obie may have been in this bed with her within a month or so. Maybe they just broke' it off before you met her—and you got her on the rebound. From *Obie*. Isn't that nice to think about?"

"Get out. Get away from me."

"You know I never will, until you know for sure one way or the other. I'll be with you all my life."

"But I won't believe you."

"Of course you won't, but you'll always wonder. And you'll keep remembering other little things. She called Mrs. Westphal *Mama* Westphal, a kind of humorous deprecation, although she never met her. Where'd she pick that up, huh? She saw all of the plays of the Drama Club that Obie played in last year. Adults seldom go to high school plays unless they have relatives in the cast—or something."

"But she *works* there."

"Yeah, yeah. Plenty of chance to come in contact with him. And remember our figuring out this Oedipus stuff? That means Obie would pick women of the same general physical type as his mother, ones who remind him of her in some way. And Nina's the size and build for that, same color hair, same shaped face. Same general type as the Bonner woman, too, as far as you could tell from a portrait photograph. Never thought of that till just now, did you? And you'll keep thinking of other little things and—"

I said, "Get out."

The Suspicion laughed at me.

I turned my head and looked at Nina.

The Suspicion said, "Go ahead and wake her up, make love to her. And if she happens to close her eyes while it's going on, as she usually does, you'll wonder whether she's pretending that it's Obie again instead of only you. Some fun, huh?"

I swore. I said, "You *won't* get me to do what you want me to do. Those journals of Nina's—"

"It would be a lousy trick to look in them, sure. Even if you just skimmed, looking for one thing, and tried not to read or remember anything else. But you're going to do it."

"Are you sure of that?"

"Sure I'm sure. Because now that you've got me it'll be an even dirtier trick if you don't. Because that's the only way you can ever get rid of me and you know it. Do you love Nina?"

"I—don't—know."

"Last night you thought you did. You told her you did. But you never can love her again unless you find out I'm wrong. And is it fair to Nina for you to change toward her because of a nasty Suspicion like me, when you can get rid of me forever by skimming through one or two of those diaries?"

"But what if I can't find—?"

"Don't worry, you'll find it if it's there. If there's anything at all about Obie there'll be plenty about him and it won't be hard to find even if she disguises the name. And you can love her in spite of anything else you might find there. You don't care how many *normal* affairs she'd had in the last year or so. And you can skip this last week and not read anything she may have written about *you.*"

"All right, damn you."

"Just play possum now. It must be almost time for—"

Nina woke and got out of bed. I played possum all right; as long as I did so that Suspicion sitting on the end of the bed would be invisible to Nina. If I talked to her she might see it, or at least guess that something was wrong.

So I kept my eyes closed and didn't move except to breathe while I heard her shower and dress, make herself breakfast and make a scratching noise with a pen that I guessed meant she was leaving a note for me.

After the door closed I looked at the clock and decided I'd stay as I was another ten minutes so I could still pretend to be asleep if she came back for a purse or a coat or a handkerchief. But she didn't. I got up and read the note first:

Dearest: I'll not work long today. My nine o'clock appointment will take me at least an hour but maybe I'll make that my only call of the day and come home right after. If I make another call or two they'll be short; I'll be back between half past ten and eleven o'clock. If you're up sooner than that, why not make yourself some breakfast here and wait for me? I can make us a picnic lunch and we can go somewhere out in the country and have a wonderful quiet Saturday afternoon together. And I won't hold you to what you said last night, but I'd love to hear you say it again. Or was it the Martinis talking? If it was, I'll forgive you.

                                        Nina

Yes, it made me feel ashamed of myself, that note. But I still had to do what I was going to do. And it wasn't quite nine o'clock now so I had an hour and a half to do it in. An hour, to give myself a big factor of safety.

I dressed quickly.

The lock on the desk drawer in which Nina kept her journals looked as though it would open with a hairpin but it would be easier and better if I could find where Nina kept the key to it. I tried to remember where she'd taken the key from and where she'd put it afterwards, the night she'd opened that drawer to get me data on the accidents at the school. No, I'd been making drinks and hadn't seen her get the key or open the drawer, but afterwards she locked the drawer again and put the key in the pocket of her housecoat. A quilted silk one.

I found the housecoat among her clothes in the closet, but of course the key wasn't in its pocket. That would have been a temporary repository until she could put it in its usual place while I wasn't watching.

I tried the unlocked drawers of the desk itself first; it wasn't there. But my second guess, the dresser, was right. It was under the paper lining the bottom of the drawer. A minute later I was on the sofa with the current volume of Nina's journal.

I leafed through the blank pages quickly until I found the most recent entry, dated *July 17, 9:15 P.M.* That would be Thursday evening, two days ago, just after I'd phoned Nina. There was about a page of it beginning: *"S. just called and wanted to come over. Wanted him to, but I'm too awfully tired, too much in need of a full night's sleep and if he comes over I know what will happen. I'll turn in as soon as I finish this . . .*

I managed to stop there, remembering that I'd resolved not to invade Nina's privacy any more than I absolutely had to and that what she might have written about me wasn't any of my business.

I leafed back a full week to the pre-Sam period, reading only the dates of the three entries, two short and one several pages long, she'd made during that week. I managed not to read them but couldn't help noticing that my initial occurred frequently in the long entry, which was dated Tuesday afternoon, the day after the night I'd first slept here. I'd have given a lot to read that entry but my conscience wouldn't let me.

I skimmed rapidly over entries, mostly shortish ones, for a month's time, averaging two or three entries a week, and mostly things about her social service work. Names were either written out in full or abbreviated for convenience rather than disguise; I saw *Anna Choj.* several times. Apparently Nina used initials only for entries concerning matters clandestine. Knowing that let me leaf more quickly through the next few weeks, back into May.

An entry dated *May 20* stopped me because it didn't seem to contain any names or even initials. I started skimming it and then found myself reading carefully.

So it's been a week now and I guess I'm over the worst of it. But I'm glad that it happened; it was the most wonderful experience, the most wonderful month, of my life. Yes, right or wrong, I'm glad it happened. And of course I knew that it couldn't last. Too, it was such a terrible risk; if it were even suspected. I'd have lost my job, both my jobs. And probably have had to move away to another city and start over again; it would have been terrible. And yet, oh God, I just couldn't help myself . . .

There was a cold feeling in the pit of my stomach. I didn't finish it. I jerked back a dozen pages at once. *May 7, 4 A. M.*

Again O. came first after midnight; he left a few minutes ago. I love him, I love him, and I mustn't let myself love him. I must keep this just a physical affair to me as I know it is to him. But how can I? He is superb; he is everything a woman dreams of.

I heard the door opening and turned; Nina stood there smiling. Whatever was in my face as I looked at her she didn't notice at first. "Sam darling, Mr. Wolfram was called away suddenly just as we started to talk and I thought since that was off I'd come right home and we could—"

Then she must have seen my face, really seen it, for the first time. Then the book I was still holding open and the open drawer of the desk.

She did it the way that was best for both of us; I'll give her that. She turned white with anger. She came around and jerked the book out of my hand and threw it; then she slapped my face again and again with force that rocked my head and hurt me almost as much as I was already hurt inside in another way. And monotonously in a low voice she was calling me things and using words that I'd never heard a woman use before.

And there wasn't anything I could say or wanted to say

even if she'd have given me the opportunity. And then, I don't know exactly how I got there and it doesn't matter, I was outside the closed door, in the hallway. I still hadn't spoken.

I walked downstairs and around the corner to my car.

2

Home felt different. It felt like home, empty as it was, something I had come *back* to instead of fleeing from. Just the familiarity of it threw things into better perspective. A lot of things.

I could see my affair now with Nina for what it had been— an affair and nothing more. A very pleasant affair while it had lasted. And I could have wished it to end differently, but at least that ending had been final, for both of us.

I found that I didn't hate her, either; I felt sorry for her. But just the same I never wanted to see her again, however casually. Even if she ever wanted to see me again—and she wouldn't— and even if this was the end of the road between Millie and me, I could never again want to kiss her or touch her.

And I'd never forget that giggle and what had prompted it.

What now, though, about Obie? Not about his amours; they were very definitely no concern of mine. But about the murders, the killings. I hadn't anything besides my hunch and my suspicions, of course, not a shred of concrete evidence. But with those suspicions so strong and with every fact I'd been able to learn seeming to corroborate them, did I have the moral *right* to drop the matter now and forget it?

No, I didn't. But there was a simple answer that would free me. When I'd started this it had been a hunch built on a few flimsy indications. Maybe they were still flimsy but now I had a lot of indications. Enough to go to Chief of Police Joe Steiner with. I could tell him everything—well, almost everything—that

I'd learned.

And then it would be up to him and I'd be out from under. Even if he laughed at me, I'd be out from under. And maybe he wouldn't laugh. I could put the case, now, so it would sound strong enough to make him want to dig a little even if only to prove to me that I was wrong.

But not today. I still felt too lousy about Nina to want to do anything about it today. And my mind felt a bit foggy, too, and I wanted it clear when I talked to Steiner, so I wouldn't miss any points.

I killed some time doing housework again and when it got near noon I decided that, since I'd be eating some meals here from now on even if Millie didn't return right away, I might as well restock the larder and have food on hand. I made a shopping trip to the nearest supermarket.

Getting myself a lunch and eating it and washing the dishes from it lasted me until two o'clock and at two o'clock the phone rang. It was Harvey Whelan. "You all right, Sam?"

"In the pink," I told him.

"Uh—whatever it was you went back to town for, it's all okay? You got it under control?"

"Absolutely."

"Good. We got back a little sooner than we'd planned, too. Last night. Got tired of playing cards two-handed. And we're going to have a Saturday afternoon poker game, two-bit limit, seven-handed if you come; we got four others already."

"Swell. I'll be there. How soon?"

"Come on as soon as you can. Five of us are starting now. We called you twice about an hour ago, Sam, but you weren't in."

"Out shopping. Okay, be there in half an hour."

The game didn't break up till almost midnight and I cashed out forty-two bucks to the good.

SUNDAY

1

T H E alarm clock wakened me and it was still the middle of the night, still completely dark, only when I reached out and pushed the button that should have stopped it, it didn't stop. It kept on ringing. Not steadily; it stopped a few seconds every once in a while and then started again. And in the few seconds of silence I could tell that the alarm clock in my hand, an electric one, wasn't even humming, wasn't running at all. The luminous hands stood at five minutes past three. And it wasn't the telephone; the telephone sounded different. The doorbell. Someone was ringing my doorbell at five minutes after three only maybe it wasn't five minutes after three because the clock wasn't running. But anyway it was the middle of the night and somebody was ringing the doorbell. I got my feet out of bed onto the floor and by that time I was thinking a little bit, but not much. I was thinking, as I started groping my way across the room toward the light switch, that Millie had come home on a train that got her back in the middle of the night, and then I remembered that Millie has her own key and wouldn't ring the doorbell. So it had to be a telegram, a telegram in the middle of the night, and a telegram in the middle of the night is bad news always, at least until you read it, somebody dead, and the only person I'd be sent a telegram about in the middle of the night was Millie and Millie must be dead or anyway hurt, an auto accident, sudden sickness, and the bell downstairs ringing, ringing, ringing and I couldn't find the light switch. And then my fingers found the switch and clicked it and nothing happened, nothing at all, no light came on and the doorbell kept ringing, ringing, still ringing as I groped my way across from the useless light switch to the hallway door and through the door to the blacker blackness of the hallway, a blackness almost tangible engulfing me, holding me back, and I had to hurry, hurry, hurry before the telegram went away and I wouldn't know what had happened to Millie. Hurry, hurry, running my hand along the hallway wall to guide me to the head of the stairs. The doorbell stopped ringing, started again. Hurry. (All of this taking time to tell but only seconds to happen.) Hurry, hurry; the doorbell not ringing any more, the telegram going away because the man would think by now, surely by now, that I wasn't home. My right hand groping for the knob at the top of the banister, my left hand still guiding along the wall, walking faster than I dared. It was my left hand that saved me, my left hand touching the light switch at the head of the stairs. I still wasn't thinking coherently but I did realize that I could go down those stairs faster if there was a light. I stopped and flicked the switch. It clicked uselessly, as had the one in the bedroom. But the fact that I'd stopped, or at least slowed down, to click it saved me from going head first down the long straight flight of stairs to the first floor. For I was leaning slightly backward when I put my foot forward for the first step of the stairs. My bare toes kicked into something that was between me and the step. Kicked hard, because I was still in a hurry to get down there, darkness or not.

The thing I kicked went over the edge and bounced noisily down the steps. At that, I almost lost my balance and went after it, but my right hand found the ball of the newel post and pushed me back; I fell, but I fell backward and not forward headfirst down the stairs. I think I let out a yelp of pain too, for my big toe felt as though it had broken from kicking whatever object it had kicked.

Whatever I'd kicked bounced several times on the stairs and hit bottom with a thud that seemed to shake the house. The doorbell broke off in mid-ring.

And in the sudden stillness I could hear footsteps run lightly across the porch, down the walk. And a scraping sound that I couldn't quite identify, and then silence.

If I'd run immediately into the front bedroom and looked out the window, I'd probably have seen him. But I didn't; just at that moment I was still too confused to do anything. If I had any thought at all it was the thought that the man with the telegram was going away before I could catch him. Only after seconds, after I'd got to my feet again and was standing at the head of the stairs ready to try again, did it come to me that there was anything strange about what had just happened, that telegraph deliverers don't *run* away if they decide no one is home and a telegram would be delivered to me at night only if it couldn't be telephoned and that *I* hadn't left any heavy object right at the head of the stairway.

In any case, whoever had rung the doorbell was gone; I'd missed him. And now the first and most important thing was *light*.

I hobbled back into the bedroom, taking my time now, found my trousers over the back of the chair and got matches out of the side pocket. I struck one, and there was light. I wasn't blind, at any rate.

I parlayed another match into an old flashlight that I remembered on the shelf in the closet. The batteries were weak but it was still usable.

I flashed it ahead of me and had dim light to guide me along the hallway and down the stairs.

A few feet from the bottom of them lay my portable typewriter, half in and half out of a broken carrying case. It had been, when I'd seen it last, only a couple of yards from where it now lay, just inside the front door and in its case. In messing around the house this morning, yesterday morning, I'd remembered that it was overdue for cleaning and oiling and had put it in its case and stood the case near the front door so I'd remember Monday to take it to town with me when I went back to work. Well, now the frame was probably sprung and it wouldn't need cleaning and oiling.

But how had it got to the top of the stairs? During the last few hours of that poker game we'd done a little drinking but not too much; I'd been too nearly sober when I'd got home to have carried that typewriter up the stairs and left it standing crosswise at the edge of that top step.

I looked out through the glass panel of the front door and saw nothing but the porch, the yard, the sidewalk, the street, all dimly illuminated by faint yellow light from a street lamp half a block away. And I was still thinking in terms of telegrams; I opened the door and looked to see if there was a card hung on the outer knob, one of those cards that tells you a messenger has tried to deliver a telegram in your absence.

I looked down to be sure nothing had been pushed under the door and I stepped out on the porch and made sure nothing had been put into the mailbox.

Silence and an empty street.

No car had driven away after I'd heard those lightly running footsteps; I was sure of that. But what had that scraping noise been? And then, as I realized what that sound *might* have been, I began for the first time to get scared.

A bicycle left lying across the curb could have made that sound when it was picked up, the scrape of a pedal against cement.

I stepped back into the dark house and closed the door and then opened it again to see if the night latch was on. It was; the door was locked from the outside.

I remembered that the lights upstairs were on a different circuit from the downstairs ones and I flicked the hallway light switch by the front door. The light went on.

I went into the living room and turned on the lights there. I was awake by now, damned wide awake and damned scared. I stared at the telephone, wondering if I should phone the police.

And got a better idea. Obie, if it had been Obie, had left here not much over five minutes ago. On a bicycle it would take him at least ten minutes, maybe fifteen, to get home. Another five to get undressed and back to bed. If I phoned the Westphal home and woke up his parents and told them to look for Obie in his room— Well, he'd have some tall explaining to do. Then, too, unless they lied for him, and I doubted if both of them would, I'd have more than a guess to take to the police.

I'd forgotten the Westphal phone number but it took me only a minute to look it up and place the call. I heard the buzz that meant the phone was ringing and I waited, thinking out just what I was going to say.

But no one answered. After a while the operator's voice sing-songed, "They do not answer. Shall I keep on ringing?" and I told her yes, that it was important.

But another few minutes convinced me that I'd been outsmarted. Obie would have thought of that possibility and he could easily have muffled the bell of the telephone so it couldn't have been heard upstairs, could even have wedged something between the bell and the clapper so it wouldn't ring at all. The sound of ringing that you hear while a number you call is being rung isn't really the sound of the other instrument ringing; it's a sound that originates in the switchboard circuit. It synchronizes with the ringing of the other phone but you hear it just the same even if the other phone's bell has been silenced.

And this wasn't Obie's first dead-of-night venture while his parents slept. There was proof of at least one other in Nina's diary. He'd have figured out long ago some way of being sure that no phone call would wake his parents while he was gone and lead to possible discovery of his absence from his room.

Reluctantly I put the phone back in its cradle.

The police? Too late now. If he wasn't home already, he'd be there and safely in bed, the phone unmuffled, by the time I argued them into sending a squad car to wake up respectable citizens in their own home in the middle of the night.

I was shivering, sitting there; the night had turned cool and I'd been sleeping in only shorts. I went upstairs with the dim flashlight and put on slippers and a bathrobe.

2

Down into the basement to fix the upstairs lights. It would be a blown fuse, of course. It was and I replaced it with a new one. He wouldn't have come down here; he could have done his fuse blowing upstairs when he carried my typewriter up there; all he had to do was screw a bulb out of an upstairs hallway socket and short circuit the socket with a pocket screwdriver or something similar.

I went to the kitchen and started coffee in the percolator. Then upstairs to dress. No use trying to go back to sleep now.

And besides I was afraid to. What if he came back to try again? No, I didn't think he would, tonight. Some other time. Some other way.

A steering knuckle loosened on my car? Or what? Whatever it would be it would be something that would look like an accident, would leave no positive proof that it hadn't been. Obie killed only that way. He could easily have strangled me in my bed tonight or he could have beaten in my brains with a hammer or cut my throat with a carving knife from the kitchen. And he was enough bigger and stronger than I that I couldn't have stopped him from doing any of those things even if I'd awakened in time.

Back in the kitchen I poured myself coffee, and my hand was shaking and some coffee slopped over into the saucer. But why not? This was the first time anybody had ever tried to kill me.

And I'd never be safe again while Obie was free.

But how had he known?

I shoved that thought aside because I thought of something of immediate importance, something I had to do right away, even ahead of calling the police. In fact, calling the police could wait until I'd had time to think on it a few angles so I could present them—or rather Joe Steiner personally—with a story that made sense down the line by including a way in which Obie could have known I was investigating him.

Millie. Millie came first. I had to phone her at her sister's in Rockford and tell her to stay there, not to return, until I phoned her again that everything was all right. This was Sunday and she might be taking an early morning train unless I called her right away.

The call went through quickly. Millie must have wakened and come to the phone when her sister did; she came on the line right away when I asked for her.

"Millie, when are you planning to come back?"

"Today, Sam. Nine o'clock train. It'll get me there at three twenty-two. Will you meet me? I was going to phone and ask you to, if you were back from Laflamme."

It was all right then; if Millie was asking me to meet her, then things were going to be all right between us. Besides, I could tell from her voice.

I said, "Millie, don't come. You'll have to trust me and take my word for it, but I want you to stay there until I tell you it's all right to come back. It's something I can't explain over the phone."

"I don't understand, Sam. Don't you want me to—"

"Millie, I want you to come back more than anything on

earth. I love you to hell and back," I said. And I did, too; I'd found that out only an hour before when I'd first thought the ringing of the bell meant a telegram and that a telegram meant Millie was sick or hurt. "It's nothing that concerns *us*. But it's awfully important that you stay away a little while, maybe just another day or two. And I'll tell you the whole story when I send for you. Won't you trust me until then?"

"Of course I trust you. But—are you in any danger?"

She'd come back despite me if I said yes. I said, "No, not in any danger. Trouble yes, but not any danger. And it's something I've got to straighten out before you come back. Love me, Millie?"

"Yes, I learned that, being away from you. I guess our separating for a week was a wonderful idea. But can't you give me even an idea what this is all about?"

"Honestly I can't, over the phone. But I'll promise you this; if it's going to be more than a few days I'll come there to tell you what it's about, the whole story."

"All right, Sam. Goodbye, dear."

"Goodbye, beloved."

For a moment, after I cradled the phone, I thought of going there, to Rockford, today. I wanted to see Millie, to tell her everything—except one thing that I'd never tell her, of course. And that one thing no longer meant anything or mattered; it had never happened.

But I must wait till after I'd talked to Joe Steiner; his reaction to what I was going to tell him was a damned important factor in deciding howl was going to stay alive. If he took me seriously and started digging, he'd get the truth. And if Obie was a killer he'd get Obie and have him in an institution for the criminally insane before you could say Oedipus complex.

And even if Joe Steiner laughed at me and told me I was crazy, I'd be better off for having told him. I'd see to it somehow, even if I had to go to him and talk to him, that Obie knew I'd told everything I knew and suspected to the police, and that if anything happened to me from now on the police would take a dim view of its being an accident. Also I'd tell Obie that I was through, done, finished, investigating no more, that I'd been investigating him, yes, but that now I'd protected myself and done my duty as a citizen by taking my findings to the police and I was bailing out.

And I *was* bailing out. I had to, if it was ever going to be safe to let Millie come home. I'd done enough, too much, on my own; from now on it was up to Joe Steiner and I should have gone to him in the first place, no matter how nebulous my suspicions had been then. Why hadn't I? That sudden violent affair with Nina, maybe, had kept me mixed up, had kept me from thinking clearly.

Sunday morning, a good time to see him, too. Six o'clock now so I'd better wait at lease a couple of hours, then I'd phone him and find out what time during the day I could have a talk with him.

At least a couple of hours to wait and that gave me time to think out, or try to think out, answers to the two loose ends my story would have otherwise.

First, who had followed me in a jalopy that afternoon, at a time when Obie had been home? I simply couldn't believe that Obie had an accomplice. Oh, I know that such things happen. Leopold and Loeb. Morey, Pell and Royal, the three Michigan teenagers who'd murdered the nurse; I'd recently read the series of articles about them in the *Saturday Evening Post*. Maybe, come to think of it, that was why the concept of a high school boy as a psychopathic murderer hadn't seemed too incredible to me. I hoped Chief Steiner had read those articles; if not I'd refer him to them. And there were other cases, not many but a few, in which psycho kills hadn't been solo jobs. Psychopaths, like birds of a feather, sometimes flock together; if one of them is homicidal he can lead the other or others down the bloody path of murder.

But Obie as a member, even as a leader, of a team? I just

couldn't swallow it. He *had* to be a lone killer or the whole picture I'd formed didn't make sense.

I could weasel out of that one easily enough by failing to mention it to Steiner; I had a more coherent story for him without it. But that wouldn't be fair, and besides he might be able to fit it into the picture even though I couldn't. It had to fit in somewhere; it just couldn't be an irrelevant coincidence that someone had trailed me by mistake or for some reason not connected with what I'd been doing.

The other problem was just as puzzling. Why had Obie tried to kill me last night?

I didn't see how he could possibly know that I was investigating him. Doc Wygand? No, I'd have bet every cent I owned against a last week's newspaper that Doc wouldn't have told anyone that I'd asked questions about the Westphals. Doc isn't that kind of a guy. And no one else I'd talked to could remotely have guessed the nature of my interest in Obie. Except possibly—

Nina? It didn't make sense that Nina would have called or seen Obie yesterday after the parting scene between us. It didn't make sense, but it could have been. Women do funny things. Maybe for reasons of her own Nina had wanted Obie to know that I knew about the affair between them. Maybe just for an excuse to talk to him again, maybe to try to get him back for a while, even for a one-night encore. But she couldn't have told him I suspected him of murder, because she didn't know that herself.

Wait! She could have told him without knowing herself, if there'd been conversation about me. She could have mentioned my interest in him, the questions I'd asked about him, and then mentioned that I'd asked even more questions about the fatal accidents at the school. Those two things would have added up all right, to Obie. He'd have known the real reason for my interest.

Suddenly I got a picture that sickened me a little to think

about. Nina phoning Obie, telling him there was something important to tell him that she couldn't say over the phone. Would he come to see her tonight so she could tell him? Obie sneaking out of his own house after his parents were asleep and spending a few hours with Nina—and why not, once more, even though the affair had ended? Learning, because they would have talked too, that I'd asked a lot of questions both about him and about the accidents. Learning too by a carefully worded question or two that my wife was out of town and that I'd be alone in the house tonight. Getting my address out of Nina's phone book, probably when she went into the bathroom. Stopping to see me on his way home.

That was the way it added up, the only way I could figure how Obie would know that I was onto him, and I hated it. I hated the thought that he had probably come here from Nina's bed. The bed I'd slept in the night before—and in which I'd told Nina that I loved her, less than thirty hours ago.

I didn't *want* to hate Nina. I tried desperately not to. I told myself that if Obie had come back to Nina when she'd called him, it meant that she had been the one who had broken off the affair originally, a month or so ago, and that her calling him back had been reaction, an act of defiance against me because I'd read her diary and learned about it. And as soon as she regained her senses she'd stop the affair again, for the reasons she'd stopped it in the first place. Thinking that made me feel a little better. Not much.

I poured myself another cup of coffee and it was the last of the pot; it would be my sixth cup since I'd made the coffee. And this time I made myself some breakfast to go with it and another pot of coffee. Daylight out now, and in an hour or so I could make my call to Steiner.

But damn oh damn, what was I going to tell him, without bringing Nina's name into it, about how Obie could have learned that I was investigating him? For a minute it had me stumped; then I felt better when I realized the question would probably never occur to him if I told him that I'd asked questions of a lot of people who knew Obie. It would seem natural that the news would get back to Obie if only I didn't stress how careful I'd been to avoid just that.

At nine o'clock on the head I phoned Steiner.

3

A woman's voice—Mrs. Steiner's, I guessed—said, "I'm sorry. He isn't home."

"Do you know where I can reach him?"

"I'm afraid you can't today. He went on a fishing trip for the weekend."

Damn. "Do you know when he'll be back?"

"They're driving back early tomorrow morning. He's going right to the office. He'll try to be there by nine o'clock, his usual time."

Twenty-four hours to wait! I said, "This is very important. Do you happen to know *where* he's fishing? I'll drive out there, even on the off chance of finding him."

"He mentioned the river, but I don't know just where. They were going to rent a boat."

That made it hopeless. You can fish the river anywhere, either side of town for forty or fifty miles, and especially if he was out in a boat, I wouldn't find him in a week. I thanked her.

"Pardon me, but if it's police business his office is open, of course. Captain Kuehn is in charge on Sundays."

I thanked her again and hung up. There was no more use telling my story to Kuehn than in writing it in a letter to Santa Claus. Kuehn is skeptical and sarcastic, and to top it off he doesn't like me. His mind would be closed even before I started to talk. Of course if I died accidentally a week or two later, he'd remember and do something about it then, but that would be a little late to do me any good.

All right, then, I'd wait till Steiner got back, but I wasn't going to wait in this house, a sitting duck if Obie decided to try again right away. I'd spend today and tonight at a hotel downtown. Tomorrow morning I'd phone the *Herald* and tell them I'd be an hour or two late and I'd be at Steiner's office waiting for him when he showed up.

I went over the house again straightening things and closing and locking windows—there'd been two downstairs windows open so I hadn't had to wonder how Obie got in—and then I threw a few things into a bag and took off.

Before I took my car out of the garage or even turned on the ignition I raised the hood and looked things over carefully, especially what I could see of the steering mechanism. I couldn't spot anything wrong or any signs of tampering. Apparently Obie hadn't thought of that one yet. Or maybe, since he didn't have a car of his own, he wouldn't be enough of a mechanic to know how to do a job like that. Just the same I didn't do any speeding on my way downtown.

I got myself a room at one of the smaller hotels where I didn't know anybody and wouldn't have to do any explaining, and put my car in the parking lot next door to it. I got some magazines in the lobby and killed the day reading and with a double feature movie. I didn't run into anybody I knew.

After an early dinner, around six o'clock, it occurred to me that possibly—contingent on what Joe Steiner did after he'd heard what I had to tell him—might be advisable for me to stay at the hotel for several days instead of only tonight. I'd been thinking of a one-night stay when I'd tossed a few things into a bag and I'd need a few things more. And this evening, right now, would be the safest time for me to go home to get them.

I got the Buick out of the parking lot and drove home.

Almost home, anyway. As I turned the corner into my block I saw a car parked facing the way I was heading, across the street from my house and a few doors away from it.

And the car was a jalopy, a black coupe, vintage of about 1930. The jalopy that had followed me out of town Friday afternoon.

If I'd had time to think I might have been afraid. But there wasn't any time; if I was going to pull in and park behind it instead of going past, I had to swing the wheel right away. I swung the wheel and pulled in to the curb behind the jalopy and only a few feet away.

4

The back window of the jalopy was small and not too clean; I still couldn't see who was behind the wheel. He must have been able to see back, though, well enough to recognize either me or the Buick. I heard the whir of his starter the moment I pulled to a stop behind him. But before he could get the engine going I was out of my car and alongside him.

Hard eyes looked at me from under carrot-colored hair. Pete Brenner, the Dead End kid best friend of Jimmy Chojnacki.

"Hello, Pete," I said.

He didn't answer. He tried to stare me down.

"Why did you follow me the other day, Pete? Why were you waiting here tonight?" I kept my voice calm. I just wanted to know; I didn't want to start trouble.

"You ought to know. Jimmy Chojnacki."

"What about Jimmy?"

"I got thinking after you and me talked. That accident didn't sound like one. I think maybe he was bumped off."

I said, "I think maybe you're a smart kid, Pete. I think Jimmy was bumped off too. Would you like to know who did it?"

"Are you kidding? He was my best friend."

I leaned a hand against the top of the car. "Good," I said.

"Then we can get together on this. But when you got that idea, why didn't you just come to me? Instead of following me."

"Why should I trust you? I didn't know what your angle in it was."

"My angle? Hell, I showed you my press pass. I'm a reporter."

"But you're on vacation this week. I mean last week. You were on vacation the day you talked to me. I know that 'cause I *did* go down there to talk to you, after I got thinking about Jimmy, see? And then I got wondering about you too. What your angle was, if you wasn't working. And slipping me that fin—for nothing. That didn't add up either."

Yes, that had been a mistake, I saw now. I should have leveled with Pete Brenner and I'd have got more out of him—if he had anything to give me—than for any amount of money. Well, I had a chance to correct that now.

I said, "I see how it must have looked funny to you, Pete. But I was onto something big and I wanted to play it close to my vest. That's why I gave you the five, rather than explain."

"But what's this about vacation?"

"I gambled my vacation on getting a big story, that's all. Come on in the house with me. We can talk better there."

"We can talk all right here." I'd answered his questions but he was still suspicious.

"Sure," I said, "but we can talk better there. I think Jimmy was murdered. I think I know who killed him. But I'm not going to tell you standing here."

"All right." He got out of the car and followed me to the house, up on the porch.

I bent over and put the key in the lock. Something hard pressed into the small of my back. He said, "Stand still. I just want to see if you're heeled before I go in there with you."

I stood still and let him reach around me and feel for a shoulder holster, pat pockets. Then I turned the key and went in, snapped on the hall light. I looked around carefully for any sign that I'd had a visitor again before I said, "Let's go out in the kitchen. I'm going to have a can of beer. Want one?"

"Sure."

When we were sitting at the table with a can of beer apiece, I said, "Now listen, Pete, there's no reason why I shouldn't tell you this—for practice, if for no other reason. Tomorrow morning I'm going to be telling it to the police, straight to Chief Steiner. But I want two promises out of you before I start talking. One, you'll keep this under your hat, talk about it to nobody. Okay?"

"Okay."

"The other, if I sell my idea to you, you won't try to do anything about it on your own. No private revenge, strictly up to the cops."

"Okay."

"It better be. Are you really carrying a gun?"

"Nah, that was a pipe I stuck in your back."

"All right, here we go. I think Obie Westphal killed Jimmy."

He started to laugh and I waited till he finished. When he quit laughing he stared at me. "What in hell gives you a screwy idea like that?"

I told him, starting right at the beginning, the whole story. Except that I left Oedipus in the closet and, of course, I left Nina out of it. But I took the accidents at the school one at a time, and told him about the freight yards and—well, the whole works. Even and especially what had happened last night.

"Jesus," he said when I finally stopped talking.

He believed me.

He said, "Jesus, I wish you'd told me this Wednesday. It was me that damn near got you killed last night. I talked to Obie about you yesterday afternoon, trying to find out what he knew about you."

That was good hearing, although I couldn't tell him so. It made me feel a lot better to know that Nina hadn't told Obie.

I said, "That wasn't your fault, Pete. Forget it. But now that you know the score, can you add anything? Was there anything you didn't tell me Wednesday that you can tell me now?"

He shook his head slowly. "No, damn it. But here's what happened with me. After you asked me them questions, I got thinking about what happened to Jimmy, and I began to think maybe he had been bumped off. I didn't have as much as you to go on; I didn't know about Obie's old man paying for the funeral or about Obie's leather being in Jimmy's pocket when he got killed. But I thought like you did about the racket that car makes going up the first hill on the roller coaster, and that Jimmy couldn't of not known the car was coming, see?"

I nodded.

"I did a lot of thinking that evening. Next morning I went in and quit my job—not just account of that, I'd been meaning to; it was a lousy job and I can get a better one. I wanted to talk to you and find out what your angle was, so I went down to the *Herald*. I know a copyboy works there. Billy Newman. So I ask him where to find you and he tells me you're on vacation, outa town fishing. That ain't the way I had it from you so I got curious about you. I made up my mind to watch you for a while and see what you were up to. Went out to your house early that evening. Your lights were on so I knew you weren't outa town like your paper thought."

"You followed me that evening?"

"Yeah, to the Press Bar somewhere around nine, came home about eleven, and went to bed. Anyway your lights went off and I went home. Didn't tell me much. I went back and tried again noon the next day. Tailed you downtown to a restaurant—I caught a sandwich across the street from it while you was eating—and then you started outa town on Seventy-one and I stuck with you. That's when you spotted me. Friday, that was.

"Well, after that I knew you'd know my car so I had to give that up. I did some more thinking and remembered you'd asked a question or two about Obie Westphal. So yesterday afternoon I looked him up and asked him if he knew you. He didn't and wanted to know what it was all about, so I told him about you asking questions about Jimmy Chojnacki and then about him, and that's how he got onto you."

"But what were you doing out front this evening?" I asked him. "You weren't going to try tailing me again in the same car, were you?"

"Nah, I'd decided to talk to you account I wasn't getting to first base. Waiting for you to get home. But when you pulled in behind me like that it scared me for a minute; that's why I'da scrammed if I coulda got the heap started quick enough. Say—"

"What, Pete?"

"You say the one night you tailed Obie he took a walk to the jungles. What time was it?"

"He left the house around nine, came back about half past ten."

"Maybe he'll go again tonight. And with two of us we maybe wouldn't lose him."

"Nix," I said. "I'm through. Tomorrow the police, and no more making like Nick Carter. Besides, don't you think he'll be *watching* for a tail tonight?"

"Sure, but he won't see one. We use my jalopy; he's never seen it. We park a long way off, just close enough to see his front gate. If he takes off for a stroll and heads toward the jungles we don't follow him, see? We take a different route and get there first. We'll be waiting back in the dark and pick him up after he comes in. And by that time he'll have watched for a tail all the way there and be sure he ain't got one so it'll be easy."

"Get thee behind me. No, Pete."

"Maybe you shouldn't, if he's ever seen you. Think he has?"

I thought back and said I didn't think so. He'd learned of my existence for the first time yesterday afternoon. I'd been playing poker at Harv Whelan's then and hadn't got home until midnight. Even if Obie had been watching the house and had seen me come home he would have seen me only at a distance and in the dark; I'd driven right into the garage and closed the doors from the inside. It had been plenty dark back there. I couldn't have been more than a shadow as I crossed from the side door of the garage to the back door of the house. And this morning I'd gone to the hotel early and had stayed downtown all day till an hour ago.

I said, "But he knows you, Pete."

"Don't worry about me. I can keep out of sight in a jungle." He stood up. "Well, I'm gonna try it anyway. If the cops pick him up after you talk to 'em tomorrow, this is my last chance not to miss out on all the fun."

"He probably won't go out tonight anyway."

Pete grinned. "Then what's to lose? I'll try it an hour or two anyway. So long."

I knew I couldn't stop him and I didn't want to let the fool kid go alone. I said, "Wait. Okay, I'll go along. We give up at ten o'clock." I looked at my watch. It was half past seven. "But give me ten minutes first. I came home to get a few things and I might as well while I'm here. Then we'll take both cars until we're a few blocks from Obie's; I'll leave mine there and get in yours. That way I won't have to come back here and you won't have to drive me downtown afterwards."

We did it that way. Pete parked the jalopy almost a full block away but at a point from which we could see the front fence and gate of the Westphal place. Far enough away that if he came out and walked toward us instead of toward the freight yards we'd have plenty of time to U-turn and get away. Or get down out of sight until he'd passed; the car itself wouldn't mean anything to him.

I hoped to hell that Obie would stay home and that nothing would happen.

At a quarter of nine Obie came through the gate and started walking the other way, toward the jungles.

We had plenty of time—it would take him twenty to twenty-five minutes to walk it and we could do it in five minutes in the car, even by a roundabout route so we wouldn't have to pass him—so Pete waited almost five minutes before starting the car. By then he'd be another block or two away and there wouldn't be a ghost of a chance of his hearing us take off.

Pete drove fast but skillfully. Half a block from the freight yards he turned the car into an alley and from the alley swung off onto the loading zone for a warehouse. We walked quickly back to the street and into the yards. In plenty of time; Obie wasn't yet in sight.

Not many strings of cars on this side of the yards tonight but two, on the fourth and fifth tracks over, were parallel and it was dark between them. The moon was bright but low in the sky; it was easy to see in the open but plenty dark in the shadows.

Looking through between two cars a few minutes later we saw him coming. He was walking into the yards at the same angle we'd taken. Pete said, "He's coming the way we did. He'll walk through here between these strings. Let's go down the line and find us an empty to duck in till he's past. Then we can follow him."

It sounded like good advice. We walked fast between the cars and the first empty was four cars down on our right. Pete climbed in. He said, "Come on. He'll be showing in a minute."

He was showing now, just walking around the end of the last car and starting toward us. Maybe I suddenly went a little crazy. I didn't get in after Pete. I whispered to him, "Get back out of sight and stay there. I want to talk to him. Stay right around the corner of the door so you can listen."

He whispered back, "Okay, pal," and then I couldn't see him anymore.

If Obie could see me there in the shadows four cars away, it would be dimly. I had a little time to get ready. I whipped off my necktie and stuck it in my pocket. I turned the rim of my hat down all the way around and the collar of my coat up. I bent down and got a double handful of dust and rubbed it over the toes of my shoes. Then I brushed the worst of the dust off my hands and ran them over my face; luckily I hadn't shaved that morning and with dirt on top of a light beard it would look like several days' growth. Luckily too I'd been wearing this same suit most of the week without having it pressed, and it was a neutral color that didn't show whether it was clean or dirty. Even in the moonlight I could pass for a hobo.

I fumbled out a cigarette and stuck it in my mouth, then took a few steps to meet Obie as he came close. "Got a match, kid?" I asked him.

"Sure." He took a book of them from his pocket and lighted one for me and held it out in cupped hands. I held the tip of my cigarette to the flame.

His face, momentarily brightly lighted, grinned at me cheerfully. A schoolboy grin. So natural a grin that I couldn't help wondering if I was wrong down the line, if a series of coincidences had led me—

"Swell night, isn't it?" he said.

I nodded and just said, "Yeah," because my mind was doing handsprings trying to get back to believing what it had believed before. This kid couldn't be a killer. There was a catch somewhere.

"Just get in town?" he asked me.

I nodded. "How's work here?"

"All right, I guess. I'm still in school myself. What kind of work do you do?"

"Printer," I said. "Linotype operator. Say, do you—"

To the south of us a locomotive hooted and released steam and the clank of couplers drowned out what I'd started to say. The string of cars behind me was moving, and the car Pete Brenner was in was rolling away from us.

We both stepped back as the cars started to move. It put Obie's face in the moonlight. His eyes were boyishly eager. He said, "Let's hop 'em. I love to ride cars around the yards."

He ran lightly and grabbed the rungs of a car going by us. I hesitated; I almost didn't. If he'd urged me to do it, if he'd even looked around to see whether I was coming, I wouldn't have.

But he was climbing on up the rungs to the top of the car. The train wasn't going fast yet; it was easy for me to run and swing up after him. He was sitting on the catwalk when I got to the top. He was lighting himself a cigarette, again cupping his hands around the match.

He said, "Love to ride cars. Got to quit pretty soon though when school starts again. With studying and football I don't get time to come here. Ever play football?"

"No. Haven't the build for it," I said. Over the noise of the train and the rush of wind we had to talk loudly. I flipped my cigarette, a fiery arc into the night, and shifted to sit down more comfortably by the brake wheel. It was nice and cool up there. I didn't blame Obie for liking to do this.

I started to turn around to say something that would get him to talking again. My hand, resting lightly on the brake wheel, saved me from dying in the next second.

The push that sent me off the end of the freight car, into the space between it and the car ahead, was so sudden and so strong that it would have knocked me off the car even if I'd been ready and braced for it. But my left hand tightened convulsively on the iron brake wheel and I dangled there between the moving cars, only the narrow coupling between me and the roadbed.

And Obie was bending over reaching for my fingers to pry them loose from the wheel. Bending down that way put his face in shadow; I still don't know whether, in the act of murder, it was the smiling face of a schoolboy or the mask of a fiend. It's probably as well I didn't see and don't know; I might be having nightmares about it either way. I don't know which way would have seemed the worse.

In that second of hanging on, of thinking I had only another second or two to live, there was one part of my mind that remained calm enough to cuss me out for the utter fool I'd been. I'd *known*, and yet without even thinking what I was doing I'd put myself in this spot. I'd been so sure he wouldn't recognize me as Sam Evans that I'd forgotten completely the fact that under these circumstances I was in just as deadly danger whether he knew me or not.

His hands were on my hand now, prying fingers loose. I tried frantically to get my other hand up to the wheel but I couldn't, with so precarious a grip, swing my body to make my right hand reach that high.

Then, above and past Obie's head, I saw something swinging down. Even over the noise of the train I heard a thudding sound and then Obie was falling forward toward me. My right hand managed to grab the edge of the catwalk to supplement my failing grip on the wheel and it pulled me in closer to the end of the car. Even so, his body scraped against my back as he went over.

Then a hand grabbed my wrist to help me and it was Pete Brenner, bending over the end of the car. Still in his right hand was the pipe he'd had in his pocket. I should have known it wasn't a pipe for smoking. It was an eight-inch length of lead pipe.

He suddenly realized that he was still holding the pipe and that he didn't need it any more. He tossed it off the side of the car and used both hands to help me back up.

I looked down then. Obie was doubled over across the coupling between the cars but his body was starting to slide off. He went off head first; I saw his head hit the rail and then the car was over him.

A minute later the clank of couplings told us the train was slowing down, probably to reverse but we didn't wait for a ride back. We got off and took the quickest way out of the yards, and back along streets to where Pete had left his car.

We didn't talk much but Pete explained what had happened. When the car he was in had started moving, he'd stuck his head out of the door and had seen me following Obie up the rungs to the front end of the car that was three cars behind him.

He'd jumped out of the door and caught the same set of rungs as it went by. He'd been holding onto them just below the top of the car, listening to us talk. Then when I'd yelled—I hadn't known that I had but it didn't surprise me—when Obie had pushed me, he'd come over the edge and slugged Obie while Obie was trying to pry my fingers loose from the wheel.

He drove me to my car and we parted there. I drove home and fast. I made a phone call to the airport and then phoned Millie. I told her everything was all right now and that not only could she come back but I desperately wanted her, needed her, to come back tonight, that if her brother-in-law would drive her to the airport right away she'd just make a plane that would get her home before midnight, and that I'd meet that plane. And she said that would be wonderful.

MONDAY

1

AT nine-fifteen Harry Rowland went by my desk on his way out. He said, "Ed wants to see you, Sam." I got up and went into Ed's office.

He said, "How was the vacation, Joe?"

"Fine," I told him.

"I'll give you an easy one to start on. Funny thing, too. Remember the last day before your vacation we thought a kid named Westphal was the one killed at Whitewater and you were going to do a story on him?"

"I remember," I said.

"The Westphal kid was killed last night. Hopping cars in the freight yards, fell between 'em. Wheel went right over his head—but there's no doubt about identification this time."

"How much you want on it?"

"Don't spare the horses. His father's an advertiser, and Rowland says the kid was quite a high school celebrity in his own right. Rowland'll cover the details on the news end; you just write up the kid like you were going to do before."

"Sure," I said.

"Take your time and make it good."

I went back to my desk and fished in the back of the top drawer. It was still there, the story I'd written nine days ago. It began: *"Today under the wheels of a White-water Beach roller coaster—"* I took a thick soft copy pencil and obliterated that. I made it read. *"Last night under the wheels of a freight car at the C. D. & 1. yards—"*

I read it through, all six pages, and didn't change another word. But I shouldn't turn it in for at least an hour, so I sat there staring at nothing. Until, up near the ceiling somewhere a fly started making a hell of a commotion . . .

Bruin Asylum

Make Your Reservations Today!

The Witching Night
C. S. Cody – Booking Now

A Garden Lost in Time
Jonathan Aycliffe – Booking Now

I Am Your Brother
G. S. Marlowe – Booking Now

Dr. Mabuse
Norbert Jacques – Booking Now

Walpole's Fantastic Tales, Volume I
Hugh Walpole – Booking Now

The Magician & Other Strange Stories
W. Somerset Maugham – Booking Now

The Bat Woman
Cromwell Gibbons – Booking now

The Undying Monster
Jessie Douglas Kerruish – Booking now

BRUIN CRIMEWORKS

-DEATH AND TAXES
-TO CATCH A THIEF
-THE LONG ESCAPE
-CARAMBOLA

Fredric Brown

-KNOCK THREE-ONE-TWO
-MISS DARKNESS

New **Fredric Brown**
   Double Novels:
-Vol. I: THE FAR CRY &
THE SCREAMING MIMI
-Vol. II: NIGHT OF THE
JABBERWOCK &
THE DEEP END

James Hadley Chase

-NO ORCHIDS FOR MISS BLANDISH
-FLESH OF THE ORCHID

Elliott Chaze

-BLACK WINGS HAS MY ANGEL

Paul Bailey

-DELIVER ME FROM EVA

Bruno Fischer

-HOUSE OF FLESH

Edward Anderson
-FEELS LIKE RAIN

C. St. John Sprigg
-PASS THE BODY
- THE CORPSE WITH THE
SUNBURNED FACE

Visit the scene of the crime